Hourglass

Hourglass

Book One:
The Turning

JO KEMP

Copyright © 2021 Jo Kemp

The moral right of the author has been asserted.

Apart from any fair dealing for the purposes of research or private study, or criticism or review, as permitted under the Copyright, Designs and Patents Act 1988, this publication may only be reproduced, stored or transmitted, in any form or by any means, with the prior permission in writing of the publishers, or in the case of reprographic reproduction in accordance with the terms of licences issued by the Copyright Licensing Agency. Enquiries concerning reproduction outside those terms should be sent to the publishers.

Matador
9 Priory Business Park,
Wistow Road, Kibworth Beauchamp,
Leicestershire. LE8 0RX
Tel: 0116 279 2299
Email: books@troubador.co.uk
Web: www.troubador.co.uk/matador
Twitter: @matadorbooks

ISBN 978 1800462 977

British Library Cataloguing in Publication Data.
A catalogue record for this book is available from the British Library.

Printed and bound in Great Britain by 4edge Limited
Typeset in 12pt Adobe Garamond Pro by Troubador Publishing Ltd, Leicester, UK

Matador is an imprint of Troubador Publishing Ltd

For my son Luke

'The Universe is full of magical things patiently waiting for our wits to grow sharper.'

Eden Phillpotts (1862–1960)

In April 2019, NASA released breath-taking images of the Southern Crab Nebula in honour of Hubble's twenty-ninth birthday. Using the powerful Hubble Telescope, it revealed a hitherto unknown 'hourglass-shaped' star system.

The object was first reported in the late 1960s but was assumed to be an ordinary star. However, in 1989, astronomers used the European Southern Observatory's La Silla Observatory in Chile to photograph a roughly crab-shaped extended nebula, formed by symmetrical bubbles.

Ref: (Google search: Southern Crab Nebula images)

There *has* to be a connection. The Hourglass – the shape of infinity – is a fabulous journey through the improbable made probable. Migrants from other galaxies and dimensions have always lived amongst us and travel is not confined to physical laws.

Prologue:

The Vision

It was weird. It was like watching a film – but it wasn't, because he was actually there, albeit passively. He knew he was there because he could smell the hot air and feel the dust in his mouth. There was the dryness too, a total absence of water. And a stillness.

Because time adheres to its own laws, everything unfolded in deliberate slow motion. Also, such was the clarity of image, details like the legs on a fly or the denim weave of the ragged shorts the young boy was wearing – stained with oil and grease – were so vivid and so magnified, one felt compelled to marvel and to want to reach out and touch them.

It was the same story over and over: the hot Puerto Rican sun beats down on a local boy playing with a football. He's barefooted – isolated – in some derelict parking lot. Carefully, he positions the ball and selects his target. He then kicks the ball which arcs, exactly as intended, and smashes through a grimy third-floor window. It doesn't matter; nothing there matters. It wasn't his football.

But something has changed. The sun dips behind a rogue cloud and the colours, once so sharp and vivid, take on a muted, indigo hue and the shadows become a peculiar shade of blue. The dirt floor – the sand – changes from gold to ochre and then burnt orange. In fact, everything looks burnt. Inside the building, a shaft of sunlight has caused a pile of abandoned oilcloths to smoulder. The draught of air, created by the football smashing through the window, ignites the fire, which, as it takes hold, draws in more and more air.

The boy watches with his mind's eye as a long way away, the dry brown leaves of a palm tree hang limply; then, almost imperceivable at first, the leaves twitch. It's nothing, just a breeze, but the breeze takes hold and the leaves awaken. They get drawn into a rhythm swaying this way and that until throughout the entire plantation, whole avenues of palms have united, stepping up the momentum until they too are raging. Or are they cheering? So great becomes the wind that sweeps across the landscape, all things in its path are devastated. When it reaches the sea, the elements of water and air combine, causing the sea to froth and boil and deafen. As it rises and swirls, it creates a colossal vortex – a vast and unpredictable column of water – which teeters and balances up through the clouds as if a clown juggling plates.

It has thirstily consumed everything in its path. The water is cold and enveloping. Its power is immense. The boy is strong and tries to fight being drawn in but it's futile. He's sucked into it – he has no choice – and he doesn't want to be there but then he sees from some elevated position that there's more than one. There are now dozens and horror – a terror – grips him. It's not where he is or what's happening to him; it's the weight of the terrible knowledge implanted in his head and he tastes seawater and then nothing, only an unquenchable thirst and a rasping dryness.

Raif had become accustomed to this psychic intrusion which would come upon him when he least expected, much like a headache. He'd first experienced it about four or five years ago – certainly before Uncle Frank's funeral and still had no idea as to its meaning – if indeed it had any meaning – but rather than dwell on it, he accepted the inevitability of its intrusion and took comfort in the normality of his surroundings, usually the familiarity of his bedroom. Here his eclectic collection of novelty clocks all whirred or ticked or struck or chimed soothingly with the symmetry interrupted only by the sound of a distant bus or vehicle passing.

He assumed, quite naturally, that this experience – this strange visitational vision – was privy only to him and he had no inkling that another being, who would prove to be pivotal in his life, shared this same curious premonition.

1

1996

It was the most peculiar sound. Almost indiscernible, it was akin to a peripheral vision where you can see something but at the same time, you can't if you try to look at it squarely. This was a buzz, or was it a hum? To some, it would be a high-pitched whine and where it came from would be anyone's guess as you stared into the infinity of the warm night sky with nothing beneath other than the endless rolling hills of the English countryside.

Yet it was there in the quiet of dusk and it was getting louder. Now it carried an overtone of urgency – impatience even – as the industry of the maker was either running late or eager to get to his or her destination.

Dina was in her garden finishing up having spent the day waging war on the weeds which grew quicker (and taller) than anything she could cultivate. Her house, thatched and sunken, lay deep in the countryside, accessible only by a track not even the postman would risk. It was overgrown and ram-shackled in a way that was homely and stuffed with artefacts and curios, the most favourite being her two longcase clocks, of which only one appeared to be working. Dina was a true believer – a devotee – of sentience. She believed in the sound principles of animism proclaiming that all objects, places, creatures, plants, rocks, rivers and so forth (even weather systems) possessed a distinct spiritual essence and, in their own way, were as alive as she was. Her clocks, therefore, were no exception and this supportive faith resulted in her living amongst the things she loved without the constant need for human company.

However, occasional visitors were more than welcome, and Dina very quickly picked up on the sound which now resonated all around her. In birdlike fashion, for indeed she was birdlike in both manner and stature, she blinked a bright eye suspiciously and cocked an ear as the first gaze of moonlight fell on the silver and turquoise rings that bedecked both her restless hands.

"That sounds like Motto." She smiled knowingly and, pulling a favourite cashmere close to her shoulders, she went inside to put the kettle on.

She paused to acknowledge her oldest longcase clock – Mr Cuff of Shepton Mallet – and smiled as she always did, at his crotchety ways and unhurried pace. A rotation of painted scenes directly above his dulled face recorded the passing of the day and she was amused by the depiction of the cheery moon with its gay, rosebud lips as she thought how delightful it was to see a moon so obviously confused as to its gender.

She was mildly curious as to what the actual time might be and consulted her other longcase clock, Mr Bath. He hailed from Cirencester, not that this carried any significance, but he could be relied upon to tolerate no nonsense. He rang out dutifully informing her that in his world it was exactly ten o'clock and since dusk was approaching, Dina took it to mean ten o'clock at night – give or take an hour or two – as opposed to perhaps ten in the morning.

Motto didn't materialise but Dina nevertheless took her cup of tea outside into the remains of what might have once been a conservatory and lowered herself onto the rickety bentwood sofa where she leaned comfortably against a large floral cushion stained with watermarks. She observed the night-sky canopy, so magnificent in its hugeness, and identified – those that she could – the twelve planets she'd visited on her psychic travels. Silently, she recited the list as if a litany. Mercury, Venus, Earth, Mars, Ceres, Jupiter, Saturn, Uranus, Neptune, Pluto, Charon and the new-comer 2003 UB313 of which even she knew very little about.

During her long uncharted life, she'd travelled greatly and had wandered – as she liked to put it – many an astral plain, but of late there hadn't been the need. Her role within the dictates of the Collective, the Collective being a sacred body ordained to serve the Hourglass, was that of Keeper – Keeper of the Hourglass. Privately, she thought this was an unduly grand title since to date very little had been required of her in this capacity other than to reassure, at regular intervals, there was nothing to report. It was a position bestowed upon her since birth and due to the longevity of her association, her affinity with the Hourglass was regarded as unique. However, this passive responsibility was all about to change and by looking at the alignment of the stars and calculating the encryptions catalogued in her sacred Almanac, she knew that at long last the time of the Turning was fast approaching.

Impatient to be doing something, Dina got to her feet and paced back and forth. She caught a glimpse of herself in the ornate small round mirror hanging next to the inner door. The mirror wasn't there for the purposes of vanity; it was there merely because she liked the way it captured the sun at sunset. However, she paused and gazed into it hoping to see either reflection of the past or a mirror to the future.

She saw neither – just herself. She had a good bone structure with high cheekbones and haughty good posture. Her skin, although lined, still held a bloom, and it was a kind face. A wise face. It was a face that had seen many joys and tragedies and had broken many hearts – and was still breaking hearts, she confirmed secretly. She scanned her face for courage and found it was still there. She looked and wondered if she was still up for the task, and as she tied her thick, now greying hair up into an untidy mound, she decided she was. In fact, she couldn't wait.

But preparations would need to be made. She knew the approximate location of the Hourglass because this had been instilled in her by the Collective since childhood but that was a long, long time ago. She wasn't unduly concerned about needing to be specific since she knew roughly where it was, and anyway, she had sufficient faith to know it would be the Hourglass itself which would guide and reveal itself to her, not the other way around. She was just wondering what preparations she should make when she saw, as plain as day and not travelling too fast, a shooting star. It arced across the sky, leaving a beautiful shimmering trail. Dina held the moment, transfixed. "Is this part of it?" she wondered. "… A prelude to the Turning ceremony?"

It was a fair enough question to ask seeing as she'd never turned the Hourglass before, let alone having even seen it in the flesh, so before jumping to conclusions she listened to her instincts – that small voice inside her – and decided it wasn't.

"Far too… theatrical." She snorted dismissively, and even though she knew it to be foolish for a woman of her age and wisdom, the child within her couldn't resist. "But I could still make a wish," she added mischievously.

"I wish… I wish…

"I wish Motto would hurry up and get here before his tea goes cold!" She laughed and, shaking her head, went off inside to find some biscuits.

She returned with a fresh pot of tea and a plate of digestives. She resumed sitting in her chair and listened again for the whereabouts of the high-pitched whine, which, predictably, was getting closer as it climbed over the horizon. Sure enough, a spot of light appeared in the distance and was moving rapidly in her direction, so pulling an old patch-worked quilt up over her knees, she continued her vigil and waited.

Young Raif Braithwaite, a boy aged nine-and-a-bit, with his tenth birthday falling on the approaching summer solstice, had never heard of Dina living in a condemned cottage buried in undergrowth not far from the south coast of England. He'd only been down that way once, to one of the big seaside resorts to see an aunt whose husband had died suddenly. Raif was just five years old at the time and recalled how he didn't much like Aunty Mary – he didn't like her cloud of sweet perfume or the way she kept patting his head. However, on the plus side, she had given him a prized clock.

"It was one of Frank's," she'd said mistily as she gazed at Uncle Frank's newly enlarged photograph on the mantelpiece. "He'll have no need for a clock where he's gone."

Raif recalled how she'd constantly checked the room for displays of sympathy and he never could decide if the sighs were sighs of relief or sadness, especially when his mum told him later that throughout the marriage Frank had frequently been *away…*

"Oh, thank you very much!" he responded politely and meant every word of it as he dutifully looked up at the photograph. "It's a wonderful clock and it'll take pride of place in my collection."

"Frank was most specific," the aunt said with eyes looking heavenwards. "He'd said before he died – well, obviously before he died – he said young Raif must have this clock. So, there you are. Not my taste, I have to say, but it takes all sorts… Enjoy."

As Aunty Mary reached for the clock, Raif continued to look at the photograph of Uncle Frank. He looked nice – sort of smiling – then Raif had the shock of his life when he was sure – *he was absolutely sure* – that Uncle Frank winked at him! He jumped back and checked the room to see if anyone else had seen this. They hadn't but he nevertheless hastily put down his paper plate – worried he might drop it – being careful not to spill the wet, coleslaw vol-au-vent down his new, bright blue pullover. He didn't want the embarrassment of dropping his plate on the swirly carpet either. Still feeling shocked by this very real experience and with his hands now free, he accepted the clock graciously. It was quite heavy for a five-year-old, so willing adults quickly came to his aid and the clock was placed on the table where it remained silently if not a little incongruously until it was time to go. Raif kept looking back up at the photograph but Uncle Frank didn't wink again.

It was a long drive back to Strawberry Bridge, just west of Halifax, and Raif, sitting in the back of the family's old *but very reliable* Ford Escort, had time to study the clock next to him on the leatherette seat. It was raining heavily and as Raif watched the rivulets streaming down the window, he puzzled as to why Uncle Frank would have wanted him to have it because he could never actually recall having met Uncle Frank. Still, the clock was now his and he decided that Uncle Frank must have heard about his collection and wanted it to go to a good home. Who knows?

Raif later found out it was a French Empire mantel clock, circa 1830. It was in reasonably good condition and Raif was convinced it was made of solid gold. It looked gold – gilt bronze gold – with a white enamel face and roman numbers. The maker, a rather grand Frenchman called Lenormand a Meaux, had signed his name taking up two lines, but the figure, the classical warrior brandishing his sword, who looked to be no more than ten years old himself, was what Raif liked best about it. He looked brave and defiant and, if anything, a bit cheeky. He stood in a classical sword fighting pose and Raif knew, he could see it in his shining gilt face, that apart from looking a bit dandified, this boy meant business. A frieze on the base of the clock told a story of some kind of shipwreck and a tempest and winged creatures, and a goddess emerging from either the waves or the clouds (Raif couldn't decide which) confirmed to Raif that this barefoot boy in his helmet, cloak and armoured loincloth was a true fighter. But for what cause? Searching for clues, Raif studied the back-to-back birds embossed on the base on which the clock stood. One was definitely a dove and the other was some kind of raven or crow, and they clearly didn't like each other.

The rain came down harder now. Raif closed his eyes then instantly regretted doing so as the vision came to him again, only this time it all happened faster as flashes rather than a narrative. Raif knew it so well: the boy, the football, the wind, the water…

In a form of shorthand with the images jostling to get through, Raif allowed it to pass then opened his eyes. The sky had since darkened, and his dad had put the headlights on. Mum was asleep, her head nodded forwards onto her ample chest. Raif leaned forwards between the seats and gently put his hand on her shoulder to steady her. Despite the windscreen wipers being on high speed, it was becoming impossible to see anything. The noise of the torrential rain hammered on the windscreen, on the roof, on the bonnet as the whole world outside reached a deafening crescendo. Suddenly the water hit them like a brick wall, shattering the windows, releasing them into a noisy black abyss. Either they'd come off the road and driven headlong into a river or they'd been hit by some kind of tsunami. Frantically, Raif thrashed around and reached out for his mum and dad but there was nothing, only black water which dragged him down deeper and deeper. What could he do? What could anyone do? There were no reference points to give placement or direction. It was what Raif always imagined it must be like to be in a black hole only this could only be a black hole filled with water…

Which way up? Which way out?

Paralysed with fear, he was sure he was on the point of drowning when from out of nowhere a bright light shone and it was enough for him to exhale his last reserves of breath and, with a tremendous effort, follow the thin trail of bubbles which he believed, logically, would lead him to the surface.

He was right. Raif broke the surface and gasped. At first, all he could think of was taking in huge gulps of air – air he noted was hot and smelled of flowers. Disorientated, he looked around and found himself alone and washed up on the banks of a small oasis. A couple of token palm trees formed the backdrop together with some other shrub-like plants he didn't recognise, although the large pink flowers they bore reminded him very much of rhododendron. Where on earth was he? Where was Mum – and Dad – what was this place? Was he dead? Was everyone dead? It was all too much. Raif pulled his knees to his chest and rocked and remained like this until he felt brave enough to peep through the crook in his elbow.

The oasis was surrounded by a vast empty desert. Sand and sand dunes stretched as far as the eye could see and above, a clear blue cloudless sky. No longer fearing any immediate danger, he got to his feet and began walking towards the oasis but found that the longer he walked and the faster he walked, he seemed to get no closer.

"Thou art doing it wrong!" Someone laughed behind him.

Raif turned and was amazed to see the boy warrior. "I know you," said Raif, shielding his eyes. "You're the boy on my clock." But he hadn't got his clock, and where was this place? "Am I dead?" he asked, as it seemed the most logical explanation considering the course of events.

"No, thou art merely borrowed," replied the young warrior. "Here, catcheth this."

And from out of the sand he picked up a ball and threw it to him. Raif caught it but before throwing it back he looked and saw it was made of glass, and inside, he could clearly see his clock on the back seat of their Ford Escort. Despite the sound being very faint he could hear the radio was on, playing *Sounds of the Sixties*. Dad was still driving, and Mum was still asleep.

As if finding himself in a desert next to an oasis wasn't weird enough, talking to the golden boy warrior from his clock was even weirder.

"I brought thee forth," said the boy warrior. "Thou needest to know, thou needest to be made ready."

"Made ready? Made ready for what? You talk funny," he added.

"Ath too dost thou," retorted the boy soldier.

Both boys regarded each other and, having registered their differences, accepted there was no need to pursue this line of conversation further. Raif turned to more pressing matters. "Why am I here and not there?" he asked, still looking into the glass ball.

"Because they all cometh here first."

"Why? I mean, who does?"

"What dost thou want – who or why?"

"Both," said Raif. "Or neither. I just want to know why I'm here, and anyway, where's here?" Raif waited for the boy warrior to speak. He needed answers, he needed to know to make some kind of sense of all this.

"Thou art here because thou art the Chosen One. Thou art here to be made ready…" said the boy warrior eventually.

"Made ready for what and how did I get here, wherever this here is?"

Obviously enjoying himself, the boy warrior drew strange circular pictures in the sand before replying. Raif found this infuriating but said nothing.

"Art thou aware that we standeth now in another dimension?"

"No?"

"Art thou aware that that journey will takest thee to turn the Hourglass?"

"No. What Hourglass?"

Again, the boy warrior sighed but Raif had now cottoned on to it being better to wait and keep silent as too many questions were confusing – like it took a while for the words to catch up and register.

"I will tellest thee only to make ready," said the boy warrior at last. "To learn and accept that life is but an illusion. Thine eye seeth what thy hand toucheth not. Thou hast to believeth and keepeth faith. Dost thou believe thou art really here?"

Raif thought about this. In this funny language, the boy warrior was making no sense, but he decided the best way to find out whether or not this whole fiasco was or wasn't real would be to pinch himself. If it hurt, it was real.

It hurt.

While he did this, he kept his eyes fixed on the boy warrior. He shut his eyes for a moment then opened them again. The boy warrior was still there and so was the vast desert behind him.

"Yes," said Raif truthfully. "I'm really here."

"Hast thou ever sat astride a tortoise?" asked the boy warrior, seemingly changing the subject.

"A tortoise? What's a tortoise got to do with all this?" he replied now getting even more confused and perhaps a little upset.

"Would thou likest to ride upon one?" said the boy soldier interrupting his thoughts.

In truth, Raif thought he would. He'd love to ride one but that surely wasn't about to happen.

"Then rideth this one!" The boy warrior grinned.

And the boy warrior stood aside as the biggest tortoise Raif had ever seen lumbered out from behind a skinny palm tree.

This in itself was an impossibility but Raif clung on to what the boy warrior had said about believing and walked steadily towards the fabulous creature.

The tortoise's shell was smooth and shiny and Raif marvelled at the colours contained within. Gently, not wanting to alarm the creature, he put his feet into the wrinkled folds of ancient leathery skin and hauled himself up.

"I'll raceth thee!" called the boy warrior laughing. "And I'll giveth thee a league start!"

The tortoise started walking at a slow, stately pace, whereas the boy warrior seemed to be running as fast as his legs would carry him but never catching up.

"I toldest thee!" he called, stopping to catch his breath with both hands resting on his knees. "Trust and believeth. Thou art the new Foundling and before thou art tenfold, someone will cometh for thee. Forgeteth not what thou hast learned here…"

And then he was gone. Raif slid off the tortoise's back into the soft, warm sand.

"Thanks for the ride," he said, turning back to address the tortoise but incredibly, she too had gone.

Once again, Raif found himself alone. He sat in the warm sand and felt small. In fact, he'd never felt so small as he gazed at the empty landscape around him and wondered what it meant to be the Foundling. Strangely, he didn't feel frightened. He felt empowered but didn't know why. But where was he? How would he get home? Would he ever get home?

Just as these thoughts were beginning to take hold, creating as they did so a deep-seated fear – a sense of dread and foreboding – which was beginning to rise dangerously to the surface, another anomaly beset him. The sand beneath him began moving. Not very fast at first but soon it started to gain momentum. Raif scrambled to his feet and backed away from the oasis. Further and further he scrambled until he turned and stumbled, falling against the drag of the sand, and found he was running just as fast as he could. He turned for a moment and watched as the oasis was swallowed up, and he hoped desperately that both the boy warrior and the tortoise would be safe. The sand kept on shifting until Raif too felt the warm clutches around his ankles and he knew. He knew he had nowhere to run to.

Everything appeared to take place in slow motion. He knew it would be pointless to fight – to struggle – so instead, he gave in to the sand. Sure, he was frightened, terrified more like, but he kept hold of what the boy warrior had said, 'believe and have faith' and something about the eye not seeing what the hand was touching. Or the other way around. It didn't change anything, but it helped and Raif found he no longer felt afraid. He just felt curious.

Soon he was outside himself, looking down. Somehow, he knew it was him even though he was older and was now wearing a red pullover and jeans as opposed to shorts. He got smaller as he got further and further away until he was just a tiny red speck in a vast ocean of sand. But there was more. A blinding blue light enveloped him and propelled him upwards into a void where he could see that this vast ocean of sand was contained within an hourglass, and he could just make out the tiny red speck as it flooded from the top half of the sphere into the bottom part. Then it started to shake more and more violently with a discordant sound of interference getting louder until it roared in his ears.

A popular song from the sixties suddenly cut through with such clarity it made Raif jump. He blinked and looked around.

"Martha and the Vandellas, 1965," said his dad knowingly, tapping the steering wheel in time to the music as he continued to sing along with the song. Mum had woken up and had resumed crocheting yet another vast beige tablecloth.

"We'll soon be home, love," she soothed in her soft Yorkshire accent. "Did you have a nice nap?"

It was fully dark by now and the rain had stopped.

"You missed a right cloudburst," continued his dad, wiping the misted-up windscreen with his sleeve, and with his kind blue eyes, he smiled at Raif via his rear-view mirror, dodging the floral cardboard air freshener which dangled between them. He carried on humming. And his mother smiled and carried on crocheting.

"By the way," added his dad as if he'd suddenly remembered, and he fished in his pocket, "Aunty Mary forgot to give you this. She said she couldn't open it, but I'll have a look when we get home. She said Frank wanted you to have it along with the clock. He said you'd understand when you're older."

He passed Raif a small, oval silver box. He tried to open it but couldn't since there were no catches or markings, but it felt nice; it felt comfortable in his hand. "Thank you, and thank you, Aunty Mary," he said, curious as to why he'd been bequeathed such an unlikely heirloom.

"What do you make of this?" he whispered, showing it to the boy warrior on his clock. And whether or not it was just a bump in the road as they turned into the drive or something more mysterious, he was sure he heard a clock strike. It was just the once.

"What's a Foundling?" he asked his parents.

2

Raif never forgot that strange car journey in the torrential rain as they drove back in their old Ford Escort from Uncle Frank's funeral. That was five years ago now and he still had the gold/gilt mantel clock which took pride of place in his bedroom amongst all the other clocks he'd acquired since he'd started his collection. Although forever silent, the boy warrior had become Raif's friend and confidant. Never really having had many friends of his own – apart from Benny when he wasn't glued to a computer game – Raif had become accustomed to his own company. It wasn't out of choice, it was more out of circumstance since he'd spent great chunks of his childhood dogged by illness with long, drawn-out intervals of convalescence. It meant friendships were always transient since unfairly he always seemed to be the one who'd remain long after new-found friends were discharged.

He'd watch the plain utility clock which, more often than not, was positioned usefully above the main ward door. He'd lie there watching, counting the hours and minutes before visiting time when sometimes – but possibly not – his mum or his dad would appear wreathed in smiles and small news. He'd wait too and cope with the mounting sadness that within ten, twenty, thirty minutes or so, his latest new-found friend would be collected and bundled off home with fond goodbyes and promises that geography would either forget or never permit.

The boy warrior was different. They shared a secret – the secret of the desert – and now Raif knew not to overwhelm him with too many questions. It was enough for him to know that the boy warrior would always be there, happy to listen and to tell Raif – in his head – all about his incredible adventures. Raif would examine the frieze on the base of the clock and imagine over and over what it could mean. Why did the dove and the raven fight? What was the cause of such a tempest?

Such a preoccupation with time in a boy with such a vivid imagination led to Raif collecting clocks almost to the point of obsession. He knew he was different. He had a photographic memory for a start, so for every clock he came across or acquired, he could recite the full history of the clock, its acquisition and its own particular idiosyncrasy. Some whirred and struck, others chimed. Some were fast, racing ahead while others dawdled as if they had all the time in the world which, in their own reality, they did.

Most of Raif's clocks had been gifted, rescued or acquired in some way or another. This was his rule since apart from him not being able to afford to buy clocks – not on his pocket money – he truly believed in the power of destiny. "If I'm supposed to have a certain clock then nine times out of ten, I'll get it." What amazed him was how easy it was for him to *will* something to happen and how *willing* people were to part with the clocks that had failed them in some way or other. "Who knows what *the right time* is anyway?" he'd ponder as he walked up the hill towards his house with some latest prize under his arm.

As a consequence, Raif had an extremely large collection. Clocks that reminded his dad of his school days – and the fear of being late. Clocks from tea rooms where older ladies took afternoon tea. Clocks from offices where people watched the minutes drag by. Factories where workers clocked on and off. Clocks that woke you up for school and clocks that said it was time to sleep. Clocks that made you laugh, made you think, made you admire, or wonder or feel safe. Silly clocks, novelty clocks, commemorative clocks. More clocks, too, still stacked in the corner, patiently awaiting the privilege of wall space.

The only type of clock Raif didn't yet possess was a longcase clock – a *grandfather clock* – but he knew of one in Mr Khan's Furniture Emporium, just off the High Street.

Mr Khan's Furniture Emporium was a storehouse of antiquity and curiosity where the bizarre was as commonplace as the glass-eyed taxidermy which glinted in the recesses.

Raif often went to Mr Khan's Emporium. He just liked being there and although the store was often quite full of people talking in whispers, you rarely saw Mr Khan himself. Raif wondered how Mr Khan managed to stay in business but his dad had said something about 'other irons in the fire' and that he thought it unlikely for the big clock to ever get sold. This pleased Raif and he decided he'd call in there after shopping with his mum.

Soon it would be his tenth birthday, and it just so happened it was on the same day as his mum's birthday. Dad always joked about there being one less date to remember but Raif just liked sharing the day with her. She liked roses; in fact, she loved roses, and whenever anyone wanted or needed to buy her a present, she always said the same thing, "Surprise me why don't you with a lovely rose."

It'd surprise her if she got chocolates instead, thought Raif and chuckled.

He was very pleased that their shared birthday was on 21 June. Not only was it the summer solstice, which meant there were lots of weird celebrations going on – his friend Benny told him about the hippies who went up on the moor and took all their clothes off – it was also The Longest Day. "What a cool day to have a birthday on," Benny had remarked rather enviously.

Having left his mum at the supermarket, Raif set out on his own and saw exactly the right rose to buy the minute he walked into the shop. It was within his price range and it was in a pot. It had a long stem, held upright by a bamboo stick, and had a whole mass of lovely red blooms.

"My word! You've grown!" remarked Felicity, who ran the shop single-handedly. Raif smiled awkwardly; he hated comments such as this, especially when he knew they weren't true. He knew for a fact that he hadn't grown one inch since his last birthday. He knew for a fact that, uncannily, he looked exactly the same, with his curly, mousy brown hair, his terrible thinness and startlingly white alabaster complexion. The only thing she might have noticed, but didn't, was that he no longer had asthma. Before he would have wheezed and struggled, needing to sit down after climbing the hill, but now he could climb anything. He could climb mountains.

"Yes," he agreed because it was easier, and handed her the rose which he'd already identified as a mini Meillandina Standard Rose, knowing his mother would be extremely pleased with it.

With the rose wrapped in pretty paper with a cellophane bonnet, it was quite easy to carry. Nevertheless, Raif put it down just inside the door at Mr Khan's Furniture Emporium, making a mental note not to forget it on the way out. He stepped inside jauntily, but as soon as he did, he knew something was different.

For a start, it was quite dark, much darker than usual and whereas previously there'd always been some kind of strange music playing faintly in the background, now it was eerily silent and deserted. Mr Khan was nowhere to be seen – but that wasn't unusual – although there was a still-warm cup of tea on the cluttered bureau which doubled as a desk.

"Hello?" he called warily.

It was as if Raif had spoken with a thousand megatons of sound. It was as if the mere vibration of his voice was enough to cause an avalanche or earthquake. The room shook with such velocity that Raif was sure – he was absolutely sure – that the entire building would collapse around him. Instinctively, on hearing such a noise, Raif cowered into a ball and covered his head with his hands and didn't dare to look up until the noise stopped. What on earth had happened?

Transfixed to the spot, there was nothing he could do. He looked around and could only assume there must have been some kind of explosion but that being the case, why wasn't he covered in dust and debris? How odd.

There were no cracks in the walls other than those that had always been there. He looked up expecting to see a gaping hole in the ceiling, but instead, a thick striped awning supported by scaffold poles covered, presumably, whatever damage may lay behind it.

I don't remember seeing that before, he thought and deduced it must have been there, although how could he have missed it?

There was no rubble or fallen plasterboard as one might have expected with a blast so loud but there was definitely a circle of disruption where chairs had fallen over, and even quite substantial tables had been upended. Bric-a-brac had been scattered to the edge of what seemed to be an invisible circumference where it gathered like leaves blown in autumn. He was relieved to see that despite their involuntary manoeuvres, nothing appeared to actually be broken, but what of the gargantuan grandfather clock?

Raif looked over through the archway to the back room and there, in a shaft of light, stood the clock. Unmoved and untouched.

Relieved that the clock appeared undamaged and momentarily forgetting about what had just happened, Raif felt drawn to examine the great clock more closely. He wanted to look inside and marvel at its chains, pendulum and workings, so picking his way through the bric-a-brac, up-righting anything that had fallen over, he approached the clock with an element of caution.

As he approached, the grand old clock loomed larger. In fact, the closer he got the bigger the clock became. Raif looked up at it in wonderment. The panelled door had become the size of an average house door and he had to climb on a chair – a rather rickety Queen Anne chair – to reach up far enough to turn the catch to enable him to look inside.

The door swung open with surprising ease and rather than being presented with a lot of cobwebs and dormant workings, he gasped at seeing such a hive of bright mechanical activity. Although it was quite dark inside he looked up and could see well-oiled chains and pulleys turning on cogs and wheels and a giant brass pendulum which glinted as it caught the light as it swung back and forth, back and forth, in a steady rhythmical manner.

"Greetings, Clock Boy! What maketh thou of this, then?"

Raif jumped so much at suddenly hearing a human voice he almost fell off his chair. He swung around and couldn't believe his eyes! There was the boy warrior, gold from head to foot, lounging in a chair making a paper aeroplane out of the manuscripts scattered on the floor.

"It's you!" exclaimed Raif. "The boy warrior off my clock!"

"Boy warrior? I likest that!" He beamed. "But pray, my name is Spiritas and thou must callest me thus. It pleaseth me greatly to be in your good company again. Raif... the boy Foundling... I salutest thee." And making a grand gesture of it, he performed his deepest, most theatrical bow.

Raif felt embarrassed. He thought such a display was silly but to meet up with... with Spiritas... again was quite something and, naturally, he had a million questions to ask – least of all, the cause of the apparent explosion.

"Did you do this?" he asked and gestured at the upturned furniture.

"I hurried forth..." explained Spiritas somewhat sheepishly. "'Twas not my purpose to alarm thee but Tempus Fugit thou knowest."

"Tempus what?" asked Raif.

"'Tis of no matter," replied Spiritas who seemed eager to change the subject as he was far more interested in the inner workings of the large grandfather clock.

"It got bigger," volunteered Raif.

"As so it must," replied Spiritas, obviously happy that everything was going to plan. "It needeth to be such if thou art to walk inside it when *she* cometh to take thee. Thou wilt know. Thou knoweth too that the Collective sendeth thee thy blessing."

"Who are the Collective?"

"Thy guidance. Mighty and revered."

"And who's *she*?"

"Anakee."

"Anakee who?"

"It matters not for now. As I imparted to thee in the desert... thou art the Foundling and the time for the Turning is all but upon thee."

"The Turning?"

Raif couldn't keep up. What was a Foundling, who was the Collective – who's Anakee when she's at home – what did he mean – the Turning – what about the big bang and where did Spiritas appear from? He couldn't altogether follow the Olde English speech that Spiritas insisted on using and what would be the point anyway when all his answers were in riddles.

"I'll just go with the flow," he conceded and suddenly felt very tired.

Spiritas appeared to pick up on Raif's fatigue as he stopped what he was doing and closed the clock's door.

"All will cometh clear to thee in the fullness of time. Thou must keep the faith and believeth in what thou cannot believeth in. Study the wisdom of Zeno's Paradoxes, keep within thee an open mind. This is only the start and thy life will never be the same… Go forth and fulfillest thou thy destiny."

Both boys fell silent. Something had passed between them that bonded them as friends, but they had neither the words nor the history to express this. Awkwardly, Spiritas finished the paper plane he'd been making and held it in his outstretched hand. He brightened and smiled warmly. "Giveth this to Gideon when thou knowest him. Tell him Spiritas giveth it."

And with that, he walked into the invisible ring. He turned just the once and raised his hand in farewell just as the ring imploded. Then he was gone.

Raif experienced his all too familiar sense of loss. Like being left behind when the other children had gone. Like remaining on the platform when everyone else had boarded the train. Like watching the car drive off leaving him staring out from the bedroom window. Leaving him behind. Alone.

He looked at the small paper plane, folded it carefully and put it in his pocket. He felt even more confused. Who would *fetch* him? Where would *she* take him? And what about Mr Khan's wrecked Emporium…?

Dolefully, Raif looked around. The grandfather clock, so large and foreboding, had returned to its normal size and he could hear faint sitar music coming from the front of the shop. He picked the scattered papers up off the floor and replaced the Queen Anne chair. Feeling a little guilty, he looked again at the small paper plane before slipping it back into his pocket. He felt taking it wouldn't really matter considering the carnage in the shop. No one saw him because the Emporium was deserted, but that being the case, why did that shadow move? And that ostrich standing in the corner – did its eye blink or was it just a trick of the light?

Walking back into the main body of the Emporium, Raif could see there was no longer any upheaval to speak of. Had he imagined it or had time jumped around and played tricks on him? The Emporium was deserted save for Mr Khan wrestling with a corner of the large striped awning, suspended between a couple of scaffold poles, obscuring the ceiling above.

"Ahh… just the person." He beamed cheerfully on seeing Raif. "Please could you hold this for a moment while I turn on the lights. It is a big moment…"

Raif grasped the corner of the large, striped sheet and made sure he kept it taut.

"I will only be one moment."

While he waited, Raif looked around at the room and everything seemed perfectly normal. Mr Khan must have tidied up and made a very good job of it. He looked up too and while he hoped nothing would fall, he was curious to know what was behind the striped awning.

He quietly hummed the song his dad liked so much while he thought about Spiritas and decided there and then that whatever happened, he'd do what he said he would and *go with the flow*. He liked that expression; he'd heard it on Radio 2.

Mr Khan returned and once again took charge as he flicked on the lights and tugged the long blue rope to release the blue striped awning.

"Now the big moment! The great unveiling!"

With a flourish, Mr Khan snatched away the striped awning.

It was breath-taking. Blue mosaics, crystals and shards of blue glass of every hue danced light across the new domed ceiling. It was as beautiful as it was spectacular.

"It is Byzantine inspired but of my own design." Mr Khan beamed proudly. "It was a special commission to bring this place the good karma of blue light."

"It's beautiful," complimented Raif and he really meant it. "It's an honour to be present at the opening ceremony. Thank you so much, I will truly never forget this day…

"Thank you…" he repeated.

Mr Khan just beamed even more widely. "Always follow the blue light," he advised, "and keep the faith."

And with that, he took Raif's hands and pressed them between his own. It was a strange sensation, which provoked in Raif an overwhelming feeling of wonderment. He fleetingly saw the universe in all its magnificence then one by one, as the stars faded and the lights went out, this feeling was overtaken by a longing to be home surrounded by the things that were familiar to him.

He had a lot to think about – a lot to process – like the invisible circle, seeing Spiritas again and who was this Anakee? The paper plane smuggled in his pocket…

Outside it was raining. In fact, it was pouring down, but he hardly noticed or cared. All he wanted to do was run.

"Wait! You forgot this!" called Mr Khan waving the rose he'd left on the doorstep.

3

Dina listened. The humming sound had gone now, so had she been mistaken? Surely not. She'd seen the shooting star – she'd even wished on it – so it had to mean Motto was in the vicinity or soon would be.

She continued to listen but now the sound had been replaced by something Dina found equally pleasing: silence. Not a bird, nor a distant dog barking. No traffic sound or some distant delivery broke the silence. Not even the sound of the wind. It was a silence loaded with an omnipotent presence and it made Dina feel peaceful.

It was, therefore, no small wonder that she almost jumped out of her skin when Motto coughed politely behind her.

Rather than dance down from the heavens before alighting on something which took his fancy – which is what Dina had expected – Motto appeared in full human form as a tall, rather skinny man of indeterminate age who was light on his feet.

"I heard you coming." She smiled as she recovered and poured the tea. It always amused her that Motto's chosen *modus operandi* was that of a large bumblebee, only this time he'd arrived in human persona.

He wore a black shirt and trousers with yellow braces; the only things that perhaps made him reminiscent of being a bumblebee were his yellow and black striped socks, a ridiculous furry body warmer and a skull cap. He also wore perfectly rounded light-reactive sunglasses to conceal his curious multifaceted eyes.

Dina passed him a china teacup covered in rosebuds. Once piping hot, it had almost gone cold now, but no matter as she reached for the honey jar on the shelf behind him. He yawned and flopped himself dandily into the cushioned chair beside her.

"May I?" he asked as he delved into the jar. She watched as, using only his delicate fingers, unselfconsciously, he ladled the honey into his mouth. He then polished off the biscuits and looked around to see if more might be forthcoming.

Dina produced another jar of honey and watched as he skilfully devoured it. Motto worked for the Collective and spent half his time – if not more – in the guise of a bumblebee, and as bumblebees have an exceptionally fast metabolism rate it meant that he needed to consume a great many calories, preferably honey. This wasn't helped by the enormous distances he was required to travel, often at short notice, with his various *sorties* not necessarily confined to one dimension. To use an old-fashioned term, his principal function was that of an enchanter as well as a fulfiller of dreams delivering shooting star wishes. In order to have mobility, with his personal safety rating high on his list of priorities, he'd been given – and had chosen – the ability to morph into a bumblebee, recognising that in doing so the only principal downside would be a constant need and craving for sugar.

"You see, no one ever kills bumblebees," he'd maintain

stoically. "Also it's a wonderful way to travel incognito and I make it widely known to predators that I carry enough venom to knock out an entire army."

Dina knew that Motto loved his vocation and would take every opportunity to talk about it, and like old friends, she always welcomed his conversation.

"As you know..." he began, stretching out and languishing on the chair, "... shooting star wishes are hugely open to interpretation. Shall I go on?"

Dina found a third jar of honey and more digestives then settled in her chair knowing he'd be expanding on this. She'd heard much of it before, but she liked his stories and the sound of his rich honeyed voice. She hadn't heard a '*human*' voice for quite some time.

Motto took off his glasses and polished them vigorously using a corner of the water-marked cushion, providing while he did so the opportunity to see the complexity of his multifaceted eyes.

He replaced his glasses and continued. "It's interesting that with wishes the degree of ambiguity afforded borders on the political and as a consequence – by and large – the obligation to grant a wish is fairly easily fulfilled. For example, if the wish is for wealth – this foolishly being the most commonplace – the following day or week, the wisher would find money down (say) the back of the sofa or in a crack in the pavement. Health is the same. The recipient happens to not get that cold that's going around, or trips on the stair but doesn't break anything.

All these and their many variants are easily handled. The recipient experiences a feel-good factor while still asleep and the respective wish is fulfilled a day or two later, mostly by the recipient's own hand. Usually, they don't remember it anyway but they're happy if they do."

"Tell me the story about the yellow bicycle," encouraged Dina. She knew he'd want to rest awhile to let his calorie cargo settle and she loved the story anyway.

"Ahh… the yellow bicycle." Motto smiled and slipped his shoes off. It was one of his favourites, and now sated by the honey and biscuits Dina had plied him with, he was ready to again recall his *pièce de résistance*.

"A boy once wished for a yellow bicycle and was wide awake when I arrived. The first bit was easy because before the sight of me could register – imagine a man-sized bumblebee with these eyes appearing at the end of your bed – I had the sandman dust ready. One short puff was enough. He was out like a light."

"So how did you get around the bicycle being yellow?" asked Dina. "It sounds most specific."

"Very cleverly," Motto confided. "I managed to present the wish in such a way that the word 'yellow' was associated with sunshine evoking a feeling of happiness. Therefore, the bicycle (which the boy was getting for his birthday anyway) didn't actually have to be yellow because the boy's perception of the bicycle was yellow, and this applied to every bicycle the boy ever owned regardless of what the actual colour was. Such was his fondness of the colour yellow, and bicycles in particular, that the boy went on to win the Tour de France in later life."

"How wonderful," said Dina as she pictured the now-adult boy crossing the finishing line. A flash of canary yellow.

They talked some more about times past until Motto heaved his shoes on again and got to his feet. "Now I must be on my way," he said. "You made a wish and that wish has been granted. Here I am, and it was a lovely cup of tea, but I have to confess, I was on my way over here anyway on Collective business."

"Oh," said Dina and faltered. The Collective only communicated with her by letter and for them to send Motto could only mean it was something quite important.

Motto handed her a small buff envelope and her heart sank. She hoped he wouldn't see the concern which passed like a shadow across her face.

"I hope it's good news," he said helpfully. "And you know you can call me if ever you need me… Promise. Promise you will?"

She nodded and gave him a big hug then turned away as he donned his head torch, morphed into a bumblebee and headed off into the night sky across the moonlit patchwork of fields.

Dina cleared the cups, plates and biscuit crumbs off the tea tray and wiped it down carefully. She sat down with the tray balanced on her knee and opened the letter with a sense of trepidation. It was as she thought. If it was something really important – but when did she ever get a letter from the Collective that wasn't really important – it would arrive in this form. Carefully, she opened the envelope and tipped the tiny spiders within onto the tray then removed the blank piece of paper and spread it out.

"Now then, what have you got to say?" she asked as she breathed on the spiders gently.

After recognition of Dina had registered – the letter could *only* be read by the intended recipient – the spiders ran and chased around then settled randomly on the blank piece of paper. One by one, they found their place, and out of the chaos, legible order was formed as the spiders joined and linked into spidery writing, moving down and re-forming two lines at a time. The letter said…

> My dearest Dina,
>
> I will keep this brief. We've had news that Darke has escaped Carcerem and is plotting to prevent the Hourglass from being turned on/around the imminent Summer Solstice. You are aware of the potentially catastrophic consequences if he succeeds. We are concerned too that this solstice coincides with a (full) Blood Moon meaning anything could happen (remember '67. Who could forget how close we all came?).
>
> We are aware that as Keeper you'll be retrieving the Hourglass shortly. At least we have a new Foundling – the boy named Raif – who will be delivered to you. Still mourning Canatu, but aren't we all?
>
> Peace and love,
> Pythia

Dina's heart thudded; this was worrying news about Darke. She was, of course, aware of the pending summer solstice coinciding not only with the anticipated date of the Turning but also with the full blood moon and could only hope that the Hourglass would endeavour to steer clear of these dates and their subsequent unpredictable influences…

Or was that all part of it?

Somewhat nervously, Dina had to concede that having never turned the Hourglass before – and in fairness, no one in 3,141 years had done so either – there was no one who could be called upon as an authority as to the correct procedure. She had her books – her Almanac – and she'd studied the *Prophecies* since she could first read but there were no specific instructions to speak of. All she knew was that a Foundling had to do the actual Turning and it would be handy too if Gideon the elusive Finder could make himself available.

"Oh dear," she sighed, and a great wave of sadness enveloped her when once again she recalled the tragic untimely death of Canatu, such a bright and bonny child. Canatu the Foundling. Canatu whose life had been prematurely terminated...

"What hope for the future?" she pondered as she thought about this new Foundling who'd suddenly come to the fore. *What was his name... Raif? But we know very little about him.*

But Dina had more immediate problems. First, she had to *find* the Hourglass or at least be in a position to enable the Hourglass to find her. She knew where it was – more or less – hence her having lived on the south coast for more decades than she'd care to admit. She knew that if and when it came to it the Hourglass would seek her out; 'it will come forth out of the wilderness and seek thy presence' were the reassuring words from the *Prophecies*, but they weren't much to go on, especially in light of the catastrophic goings-on which began in the year 1775.

Originally, the Hourglass was sealed in a small sepulchre within the grounds of a sacred temple located on the highest point on the south coast of England. Pilgrims came from far and wide to pay homage but in 1775, and then again in 1828, two unexplained landslides occurred. The temple remained unscathed until 1838 then (the following year) 1839 (The year of the Great Landslide) created what became known as *The Undercliff* or – more accurately – *The Great Chasm*. In fact, at this point, Dina had to reach for the works of one of her favourite authors, the great novelist and collector John Fowles. He knew the area well so who better to reacquaint her with a true picture. She read the passage out loud...

> *... the Undercliff is in short, a triumphant denial of contemporary reality, an apparent sub-tropical paradise, a Robinson Crusoe landscape that seems at a glance the ruthless developer's dream. Not a roof to be seen,*

not a road, not a sign of man. It looks almost as the world might have been if mankind had not evolved, so pure, so unspoiled, so untouched it is scarcely credible, so unaccustomed that on occasion its solitudes may feel faintly eerie.

The fact that it might have once been a cheerful place gave her hope but she knew that was his perception, not hers. Something had happened. Something happened that had nothing to do with the neglect and abandonment caused by the landslides as it was some time after this realignment that local folklore quoted possession, devilry and enchantment. Strange creatures were glimpsed, noises were heard ripping through the night sky. Noises that were not of this world. Sometimes a dense fog would form and linger stubbornly, unwilling to move even though the sun rose high and hot in the sky. It became a place where no man ventured and of those few who did, not all returned.

Dina was now faced with having to venture in there. She always knew that one day she'd have to make this journey but now, as it loomed as a very tangible reality, she felt unprepared. The fall – the great landslip of 1839 – all but destroyed the temple, leaving the derelict remains isolated and inaccessible on a small but high, vertically sided island known locally as Chapel Rock. Rumour and speculation surrounded the cause of the landfall. Many scholars within the Collective believed it was an attempt to extradite the Hourglass by forces unknown, whereas others believed it was the Hourglass itself that had engineered such an impenetrable defence.

Dina sighed as she conceded yet another problem. A problem she'd always kept at the back of her mind but had never found a satisfactory solution to. How would she get

Canatu – or now, the boy Raif – over to Chapel Rock? She'd privately hoped that Pythia would have intervened in some celestial way – or that Gideon would have swash-buckled a way through – but both these solutions were now looking highly unlikely. She'd not heard anything from Gideon and Pythia had given no inclination of assistance in her recent communiqué.

What troubled her throughout all these machinations were the possible implications – the potentially catastrophic consequences – should she fail to keep the Hourglass safe. She felt in that one single moment that the whole future of the world hung in the balance, resting precariously on her shoulders. She knew enough about the Hourglass to know that if it were to ever fall into the wrong hands order would disintegrate and the consequences of chaos would take root. She knew too that if this happened, she would be partly or wholly responsible.

On the positive side, at least a Foundling to replace Canatu had come forth, but this was nevertheless dwarfed by her profound sense of unease. Her hackles were up but she knew there was nothing more she could do other than fulfil her role as Keeper, but what filled her with the premonitions of a new dread was the news that Darke had escaped...

With a heavy heart, Dina conceded the day and went inside. She paused as she passed Mr Cuff and looked up at him as if for guidance. Mr Cuff said nothing and just stood there, stoic, silent and immovable until the strangest thing happened. He gurgled into life and struck a single note. Not only that, but the painted scenes which rotated above his clock face also began to slowly rotate, only they didn't go clockwise as they should have done, they rotated in an anti-clockwise direction. Dina watched, transfixed. Firstly, the moon with his rosebud lips lost his cheery smile and frowned before dipping behind the clouds. She continued watching as the clouds parted as the image slowly came to a halt to reveal a scene depicting a deep, dark chasm. The Great Chasm. It was depicted as a great gash in the landscape around which the sea boiled and retched. Around which no birds or animals ventured. A landscape the sun couldn't reach where one could all but taste the chill in the air. It was a sad place. A forlorn place. It wanted to join in but couldn't.

But what was this? A single ray of sunshine pierced the black clouds. It led her eye towards rocks laid out like stepping stones, although some were barely visible beneath the surf. She gazed at the vertical cliff face and wondered: were those shadows footholds perhaps, or merely abandoned nesting sites?

Dina had seen Mr Cuff in many moods and had shared many a tantrum with him but much as she was familiar with his painted scenes of hill and dale and of sun and moon, she'd never seen this landscape before. She had no immediate idea as to how to interpret what Mr Cuff might be telling her until later that night it struck her. She sat bolt upright in bed and announced loudly, "I do believe I've been shown a way through the Great Chasm!"

One would have thought that Pythia – Pythia the Mahdi, the immortal High Priestess from the outer reaches of the galaxy from the Hourglass Nebula itself – would have chosen anyone other than Gideon to not only be the designated Finder but also the principal *protector* of the boy Raif. The boy identified to be the Founder. The child who was necessary to play a crucial role in the Turning, thereby continuing the highly satisfactory balance between order and chaos throughout the known galaxy.

But Pythia in her infinite wisdom had chosen *exactly* the

right person for the very qualities he displayed to annoy her. His timekeeping was abysmal; he was totally unpredictable – chaotic even – although she didn't like the use of this word. He was a rogue, a rebel, and he didn't want the job. Whereas Gideon had been happy, and one could say privileged, to take care of the previous Founder Canatu, her death had affected him deeply since he'd felt largely responsible despite Pythia pointing out that *everyone* felt largely responsible and, in this respect, he was blameless. However, she knew he didn't feel blameless. As far as he was concerned, he'd failed; he'd failed himself, he'd failed Pythia, he'd failed the Collective as a whole – he'd failed the whole world as a whole – and most tragically of all, he'd failed Canatu whom he'd loved as a father, Canatu having no father of her own. As a consequence, he had no wish to be involved, preferring instead to resume his nomadic lifestyle, his *no strings attached* bohemia and freedom. He had his own wounds to lick.

But Pythia wouldn't hear of it and despite his protests and objections – none of which held water – she knew only he would have the courage, the strength and the cunning to protect Raif and ensure the Hourglass was turned, particularly in light of the news that Darke had escaped. He had the motivation, he just hadn't realised it. He hadn't realised that his supposed failure could – if he chose to use it – be his greatest asset. Revenge. There is no greater motivation than revenge and Pythia was quick to point this out.

But dealing with Gideon wasn't going to be easy. His hot-headedness and unpredictability made it hard to keep track of him and this would be hampered further by him having – amongst other things – access to the five principal means of intergalactic travel. Although Pythia had the power to remove this privilege, she was reluctant to do so particularly as Darke was out there somewhere.

To give Gideon time, and to show him that she wasn't *entirely* dependent on his co-operation, she'd permitted Anakee to go and fetch the boy and bring him to them. It was a wise move since there'd been no sign of Gideon at their pre-arranged meeting place.

She found him, eventually, alone in a room devoid of furniture other than the utility chair he was sitting on and the small sparse table in front of him. There were no windows and nothing on the walls. The lighting was fluorescent and inaccessible. She wasn't sure if he'd been there for days or only minutes but knew he'd be unconcerned anyway. He'd be content to wait for however long in his cell-like room, knowing that at some point she'd show up. He wouldn't be concerned since he'd no doubt have a substantial backlog of things in his head to catch up on – probably his thoughts on Stephen Hawking's latest thesis (always a favourite) and possibly a few paragraphs from *Zeno's Paradoxes* as a little light relief. His contemplation was broken by the sound of voices.

"Yes, yes and thank you. I'm well aware of that…"

A woman's voice, feminine yet authoritative, drifted up the corridor. Not moving his eyes from the focal point he'd chosen on the wall opposite – the evidence of some previous disagreement – he heard the key turn, the door open and close again.

"What are you doing here?" she demanded in an unnecessarily loud stage whisper. "You were supposed to come and meet me?"

She noted the CCTV on the wall. She gave it a certain look and the light went out. "Well?"

Gideon turned his attention away from his chosen focal point and smiled weakly. "Did you know Parmenides's doctrine proclaimed that '*all is one*' and that contrary to the evidence of one's senses, the belief in plurality and change is mistaken, and in particular, that motion is nothing but an illusion?" he enquired in a kind, educated voice which belied his appearance.

"Not off-hand," replied Pythia, knowing from experience it wouldn't be a good idea to get drawn into a philosophical discussion with Gideon, not unless one had no qualms about losing any argument.

"Didn't think so," he replied. "Neither did that policeman."

It transpired that in a failed attempt to get to Pythia's meeting on time – her time – he'd jumped two sets of lights as he'd weaved what he now understood was the wrong way through a one-way system, hence finding himself detained in police custody.

Pythia had neither the time, the energy nor the inclination to listen to any kind of defence about how he'd got there, and she knew it would be pointless anyway since by the look of him they were already arguing. She was dressed appropriately to look like a neutral middle-grade solicitor, rather than a High Priestess, whereas Gideon had taken quite a different tack, probably, in hindsight, just to irritate her. Although he couldn't be described as handsome with his shock of unkempt hair, his bear-like frame and what might have once been a fine nose long since broken and never fixed, he had charisma nevertheless but still chose to look ridiculous in oversized camouflage trousers held up by a wide leather belt. He wore army boots with the laces missing and a World War II flying jacket, sadly full of bullet holes. His shirt betrayed signs of effort since, although frayed, it appeared clean and he'd finished off the whole *ensemble* with an incongruous flat cap and no socks. It was little wonder they'd locked him up.

Not allowing him to see he'd riled her, Pythia was short and to the point. "I've sent Anakee to bring the boy Foundling to you. You will then take the boy to Dina who will lead you to the Hourglass. Do I make myself clear?"

Gideon turned and looked at her. His sharp blue eyes, one a slightly different shade to the other, shot through her causing her to momentarily catch her breath as a history charged between them. They had no need for words. They never did.

She turned to leave, anxious to be gone from this memory but as she did so she paused. "Take care…" she said softly, "… and by the way, did you know that Darke has escaped?"

She closed the door behind her leaving Gideon alone again. He sat there motionless for a few moments and resumed contemplating his focal point. After a while, he stood up abruptly, picked up the chair he'd been sitting on and hurled it violently at the mark on the wall.

With Pythia having secured his release, Gideon was reunited with his battered dark green pick-up truck parked rather haphazardly, directly outside the station on double yellow lines. Somehow, no one seemed to have noticed or penalised the effrontery. He rummaged through the open-topped back noisily as he searched amongst the crumpled boxes, ropes, spare batteries, tools, chains and winches to find what he was looking for, to finally unearth it buried under an oiled jacket, next to his muddied boots which were under two sheets of plywood wedged fast with a broom handle next to a baited fishing rod behind half a bag of plaster which had long since gone off.

"Driving music!" he exclaimed holding up a CD and, now with renewed purpose in his life, he blew the dust off it and leapt into the driving seat.

He sang tunelessly as he turned on the ignition, loaded the CD player, pressed play and slammed the truck into gear to drive off at high speed more or less in the direction of the south-west.

It was dusk when Gideon drove through the golden expanse of wheat fields. He was thinking about Anakee and whether Pythia was right in allowing her to fetch the Foundling. Part of him felt guilty, he should have gone, but another part of him said – in a louder voice – that Anakee *needed* to be a part of this to find closure.

"Damn!" he exclaimed. "That's exactly what Pythia's done to me!"

And for the first time in a long time, he felt better. He felt he could do something to go at least part way to putting things right, but what of Anakee? She was a quiet girl – intense would best describe her – who always seemed preoccupied with things going on in her head like she was constantly wrestling with some three-dimensional cryptic crosswords. He knew very little about her background other than that both she and her younger sister Canatu had had a rough time as kids. Anakee, always highly protective of her sister, had been deeply affected by Canatu's untimely death and he feared how she would react when she too learned that Darke had escaped. Or maybe she knew already? It was all wretched and these were the thoughts that were going around and around in his head as he drove even faster into the darkening sky. The golden wheat fields flashed past like ghosts in a vast expansive desert as the flies and moths splattered his windscreen, occasionally flying in through his open window and annoying him.

One such insect – a rather large bumblebee – was Motto.

"Gotcha!" Gideon grinned, relieved to have a distraction to lift his mood as he trapped the insect in a discarded plastic cup and held it fast against the windscreen.

"I really wish you wouldn't do that!" exclaimed Motto, bursting through the plastic to become his full-sized human manifestation. "You know I cannot tolerate confined spaces and I would've much preferred to remain as I was for a little while longer. It would've saved me having to sit here and endure your endless conversation!"

Gideon laughed, pleased to see his old friend. "So, what's going on?" he asked.

4

Raif was up in his bedroom feeling rather disgruntled. When he'd got home after his experience in Mr Khan's Furniture Emporium, the rose he'd bought for his mum looked fine but now it was decidedly worse for wear. The blooms had withered, and some had even turned black. What he couldn't understand was that when he'd got back it was perfectly alright but then this happened.

It wasn't his fault; he didn't do anything wrong.

He was just pulling on his trainers to go and take the rose back to the shop when there was a tap-tapping on the door. He was puzzled. No one ever came to his bedroom and if they did, they'd just barge in or his mum would shout up the stairs to him first.

Maybe he hadn't heard her?

Raif opened the door to find a girl, probably in her late teens, wearing black from head to toe staring quizzically at him with the most penetrating green eyes Raif had ever seen. She was only slight – not much taller than he was – and wafer-thin. Her hair, which was as black and as glossy as the clothes she was wearing, was pulled back off her face, emphasising high cheekbones and a pale, mask-like flawless complexion.

"Hello, Raif. I'm Anakee." She smiled then noticed the blackened rose he was still holding. "Is that for me? Because if it is, that's *not* a good sign…"

"Err… no… it's for my mum… well, it was but look at it…"

He paused realising he was having a conversation with someone he'd never met before. "Sorry… but do I know you?" he asked.

"Not yet, but you will. You've been expecting me."

Not waiting to be invited in, Anakee marched into his room and made straight for the display of clocks. She picked out the gilt clock which took pride of place and patted the golden head of the boy warrior. "Hello, Spiritas," she said pointedly and planted a deliberate kiss on his head.

"You know him?" exclaimed Raif.

"Yes, of course. He was sent to prepare you."

To begin with, Raif was speechless. Words could not express what a relief it was to be talking to someone who actually knew Spiritas to be real. That he wasn't just some invisible friend he'd made up.

"He told me I was the Foundling and that someone – she – and I suppose that's you, would come and take me to turn the Hourglass whatever that is and that…"

He tumbled over his words until his voice trailed off when he realised how ridiculous and far-fetched he must have sounded. However, Anakee appeared to think quite the opposite and listened with great intensity.

"So, what did Spiritas tell you?" she asked.

Raif thought for a moment. "He showed me you could run before you could walk. That things aren't necessarily what they seem. There is no such thing as a coincidence since all things happen for a reason. He told me to have faith and to believe. He told me to trust my instincts rather than trust my eyes. That I have a destiny to fulfil. That life is but an illusion. That time is transient and..."

"Is everything alright, love?" called Raif's mum up the stairs. "I heard voices?"

Raif froze, not knowing what to say and hastily pushed the blackened rose under his bed in case she too came into the room.

"It's just a friend..." he called.

"Anakee," mouthed Anakee in a stage whisper.

"She's called Anakee... she's come about a clock."

Anakee nodded conspiratorially and Raif felt pleased at coming up with a good response, especially when Anakee smiled at him and he felt a warmth between them.

"How did you come by the clock?" she asked, examining the gilt clock, showing particular interest in the frieze that ran along the base.

"My uncle Frank... well Aunty Mary really... because Uncle Frank had died, and I was at his funeral. He'd said I was to have it."

"And Spiritas... how did you meet him?"

"On the way home from Bournemouth. We ran into a terrible storm on the motorway and somehow I ended up in the desert next to an oasis and I rode a giant tortoise... you think I'm making this up, don't you?"

"On the contrary," replied Anakee. "Anything else...?"

"The desert started sinking and I was in an Hourglass. I became a tiny speck in a vast universe.

"And I have visions!" he blurted out suddenly as if there was an opportunity here to exorcise them. "I... I thought all that was one of them!"

"I'm not surprised," said Anakee gently. "I'm not surprised by anything to do with the Hourglass... Tell me, how much do you know about it?"

Raif sat down on his bed heavily and stared at the floor. "I don't know really. It's all in dribs and drabs but I know it's important and I've got to turn it. Apparently, I'm a Foundling... is that the same as being adopted?"

Anakee smiled and sat down next to him. "No, not quite but I think it'd help if I just explained a few things to you seeing as Spiritas is rather good at leaving big holes... isn't that right!" She laughed in the direction of the clock where Spiritas stood. Unmoved.

"It's very simple really," she continued, turning her attention back to Raif. "Give or take a few miscalculations on our part, the last time the Hourglass was turned was 3,141 years ago. The *Prophecies* decree that a Foundling – a boy or a girl, aged ten years old – will come to the fore to turn the Hourglass when the time arrives. My little sister Canatu was the Foundling. She was the same age as you but tragically she died – five years ago now – so in the time left, we had to find a replacement and you popped up, hopefully, to save the day..."

"Why a ten-year-old?" asked Raif.

"It's the age decreed by the *Prophecies*. It's when a child is old enough to have the knowledge yet still be young enough to be representative of purity and innocence. The *Prophecies* are most specific. You see, he or she isn't chosen or elected. He or she is *found* much like in Buddhism when a new Dalai Lama is found."

"How do you know a child is a Foundling and not just any other child? Do they look different?"

Raif was worried that he always felt he was different to other children. He didn't know if this was due partly to the long spells he'd spent convalescing, or his peculiar interest in time... maybe it was. Or maybe he just didn't fit in.

"No," Anakee reassured him, "the Foundling doesn't look any different because we're all hugely different to each other anyway with different interests, different personalities and different backgrounds. What happens is a member of the Collective is *shown* a child then it's up to him or her to *recognise* this and inform the other members. It's a psychic thing."

"How did you find me?"

"Uncle Frank... well of course he was no ordinary Uncle Frank. He was a member of the Collective and quite a character. When we lost Canatu he predicted uncertain times ahead and insisted we identified another Foundling immediately in case... in case anything went wrong..."

"I'm so sorry," said Raif putting his arm around her, "you must miss your sister terribly."

"It's okay, it's not your fault. It's no one's fault... it's just how it is."

She smiled bravely and composed herself before continuing. "He wasn't your real Uncle Frank. Apparently, he found you when you were two years old, abandoned in an immigration holding camp with no record as to your actual parents. He placed you in the care of Ian and Vera – your adoptive mum and dad – and I for one had no knowledge of you until Gideon – the Finder – brought you to our attention."

"I know I was adopted," said Raif, thinking back. "But I don't remember ever meeting Uncle Frank. At the funeral, he looked nice in his photograph; they had a big one of him propped up on the mantelpiece. He winked at me – honest."

Anakee nodded knowingly. Little did he know that this must have been the moment he was *shown*. Little did he know from that moment on his entire life would change.

"All things happen for a reason," concluded Anakee wisely, "and I'm of a mind you're more special than we'd realised. Now I think it's time we got going."

"I'm just going out for a bit..." Raif called out to his mum in the kitchen as he closed the front door. He could hear the familiar sounds of the radio and took comfort in the fact that everything seemed very and extremely normal.

"Where to now?" he asked Anakee once they were outside.

"We'll go and meet up with Gideon. He's crazy but you'll like him. He's the Finder, he's the one who'll be looking out for you, but first, Mr Khan's Furniture Emporium. By the way, did Uncle Frank give you anything other than the clock?"

"Only this, I always carry it." And Raif took the slender oval silver box from out of his pocket. Anakee examined it and shrugged her shoulders. "Means nothing to me but show it to Gideon."

"Oh... and Spiritas gave me this." From amongst the boiled sweets, elastic bands, biscuit crumbs and a few coins, Raif produced the rather crumpled paper plane.

"Interesting..." said Anakee and shook her head. "What is it about boys and pockets...?"

They set off at a brisk pace in the direction of Mr Khan's Furniture Emporium. Raif didn't look back and asked no more questions. As they walked, Anakee took the opportunity to explain a little more about the Hourglass.

"Apparently, it's all based on Pi – and I don't mean a custard pie!" she joked, eager to keep the mood light-hearted. "This means it hasn't been turned for 3,141 years or so, but that time is nearly up, so it needs turning again."

"Why does it need turning?" asked Raif.

"To continue maintaining the correct balance between order and chaos. Well... that's what it says in the *Prophecies*."

"What about your sister?"

"I don't want to talk about that right now," replied Anakee, trying to keep her voice level. "It's enough for you to know that her life was taken, and the culprit banished to a remote prison – a planet on the edge of the galaxy known as Carcerem – from which there is no escape. He – or it – is probably dead by now and good riddance."

"Yeah… good riddance," echoed Raif and Anakee smiled. She could see that Raif didn't really know what he was talking about but wanted to be supportive, nevertheless. "So…" she continued, eager to change the subject. "All we've got to worry about now is a blood moon coming full on the summer solstice just as you turn ten years old."

"Why? Does that matter?"

"Maybe not but put it this way… The last time we had the summer solstice and a full moon on the same night was in 1967 when the world went topsy-turvy. We're not saying it'll happen again but back then it became known as *The Summer of Love*. A social phenomenon when over 100,000 people converged on San Francisco. It was a defining moment in the planet's history when peace and love came head to head with their opposites – or, to put it another way, order came head to head with chaos. It became a bona fide movement causing ordinary everyday citizens from all over the world to hold hands, band together and question everything about themselves and their responsibility towards humanity and the environment. Good job too because without that happening – and the world acting on it – this planet would have died long since."

"My dad sings a song about San Francisco. He likes the sixties," offered Raif quietly.

"He sounds like a good bloke, your dad," she said and picked up the pace.

5

M<small>R</small> K<small>HAN'S</small> F<small>URNITURE</small> E<small>MPORIUM</small> <small>LOOKED ALL TOO</small> familiar to Raif and he found this reassuring. The fabulous blue ceiling mural looked just as splendid – perhaps even more so – as it sparkled in the sunlight.

"I was here for the unveiling," he whispered to Anakee with a note of pride in his voice. "This is where I met Spiritas again... I don't know how he got here and he made a bit of a mess but somehow it all got cleared up and Mr Khan... he didn't even notice!"

Anakee groaned. "Tesseractic travel. Spiritas is useless. He really should read the manuals."

"Tessa what?" asked Raif, sounding puzzled.

"Tesseractic travel... How he got here... I'll explain later."

There was no sign of Mr Khan, although he must have been there, in the back office perhaps, because the door was open. Raif looked around and called once or twice but he didn't materialise so Raif decided he must be happy to leave them to it.

Meanwhile, Anakee went over to examine the large grandfather clock standing in the far corner. She looked quite small next to it and Raif – having been through all this before with Spiritas – wasn't in the least bit surprised. Neither was he surprised when he crossed the room to join her and found he'd become the same size as she was.

"Spiritas told me to not necessarily believe all I see." He grinned. "So I won't!"

"And all things are relative," reminded Anakee.

As before, the door into the workings of the clock had become the size of an average house door and, also as before, Raif climbed onto the same Queen Anne chair to reach the handle, some four or five feet off the ground. He helped Anakee up and they both peered inside.

"Good," she said as they both clambered in. "They've left a light on."

There was plenty of room to stand up and Raif thought it was wonderful. Clock heaven! They were standing inside what appeared to be a large chamber festooned with chains, ropes and pulleys. Two colossal cylindrical iron weights hung side by side in a slow race to the bottom and to aid them on their way, a gigantic pendulum swung back and forth, back and forth, and one had to be vigilant and keep clear of their path. Every time the pendulum completed its arc, a strong definitive tick resonated from somewhere up in the darkness.

"Where do we go now?" asked Raif in a respectful whisper.

"Have you heard of *Ruralactic* journeys?" she asked without whispering.

"No...?"

"I thought not... Well, it usually starts in a hedge or something like that, but this is okay – it's wood so it's more or less the same thing. Come on, we don't want to be here when the clock strikes the hour or it's goodbye eardrums!"

And taking his hand she led him through the darkness to the top of a dimly lit spiral staircase.

The spiral staircase, which was rickety, to say the least, soon gave way to a more level and less steep passageway with a dirt floor and walls of roots, rocks and soil. It was a sort of tunnel with glow-worms stationed at intervals, lighting their way. Raif had never seen a glow-worm before, although he'd heard about them at school, and was concerned at them being underground.

"Don't worry," said Anakee, sensing his concern. "We won't be long – then they can all go home. Look out for the other creatures instead! Mind you don't step on them!"

Raif was amazed. He was amazed by the number of beetles, spiders, mice, snakes, rats, centipedes, woodlice, voles, weasels, moles, and a host of other small creatures besides, who were hurrying this way and that taking absolutely no notice of them. It was like he and Anakee were invisible.

"Is this real?" he asked.

"How real or unreal do you want it to be?" replied Anakee. "And anyway, does it matter?"

"I... I suppose not..."

But he stayed close to Anakee nevertheless and as the reality – or the non-reality – of where they were and what was happening took hold, he began to feel afraid. He could cope with it when he assumed it was some kind of exaggerated dream and he wasn't far from familiar surroundings like the car or his bedroom or at Mr Khan's Furniture Emporium... but this was different. He'd actually said goodbye to his mum and now he was in a place with *no* reference points. It was alien to him, it was underground. It was strange and outside his comfort zone. He understood dreams, or visions as he sometimes called them, but this was no vision. He could smell the damp, could feel the darkness and had no control over the increasing feeling of panic rising within him.

"Not long now," said Anakee, aware that Raif had turned an even whiter shade of pale. "Are you okay?"

"Yes," he lied, on the brink of wanting to turn back but to stop himself he needed some distraction. He wanted Anakee to talk. He just wanted her to talk about anything.

"What's that word you used… tessa reactic?" he asked. "You said that's how Spiritas got to Mr Khan's."

"Tesseractic," she corrected. "Well, that's a big question but very simply it's a means of travel between dimensions. If you imagine the world – your world – is akin to… let me see now… a layer of filo pastry… do you know what that is?"

"Yes, my mum uses it. She says she should make it from scratch but it's easier to buy it readymade. It's very nice…"

"I'm sure it is. Anyway, just like the layers and layers which make up filo pastry, this world – this dimension – is duplicated with an infinite number of other dimensions. Some are the same, more or less, and are known as the Parallel Universes – then there are others which are completely different. It's as if we're a page in a circular book, there's no beginning and no end. Just infinity. The Hourglass by virtue of its shape and purpose understands this and is representative of this infinity. Apart from a very few, travel between dimensions is banned by the Collective because who knows where we'd end up if entire populations were constantly jumping from place to place. It's really risky too and the teachings – or should I say the learning of how to do it – can take the wisdom of many lifetimes… Does that answer your question?"

"So Spiritas uses it to travel between these dimensions?"

"Yes. Spiritas is closely allied to the Collective like he's a pet or mascot and as such, he's got a special pass. He's allowed to use it – but sparingly! Trouble is, he's not very good at it, hence the big bangs and the mess!"

Listening to Anakee and picturing not only his own world but the vastness of the galaxy with its infinite number of other dimensions, planets and other universes made Raif feel his fear was insignificant by comparison and he accepted, there and then, that there was a huge… colossalness – a word he'd just invented – that he'd never fully understand. All that mattered to him right now was playing a part in keeping the right balance. Like a clock, it was all to do with balance. He understood this and didn't feel quite so afraid.

6

With a pale, pustulated thumb festering around a carefully manicured nail, Darke terminated the call he'd just received. His workforce, collectively known as the Contractors, ran into many thousands and came from all walks of previous life and planets. Most were primarily deaf-mutes from birth but if any were suitable on arrival and not yet deaf and mute, a simple operation corrected this. Only a few retained full audio functionality; they were referred to as The Elite. The call was from one such operative.

"So, they have a new Foundling," he rasped, stroking the silk-skinned boa constrictor coiled within its glass prison. His tightening grip around the creature's throat registered his mounting excitement. Pleased as he was, he still breathed the words with some difficulty since despite the apparatus installed within his chest cavity, breathing this mix of oxygen wasn't easy.

Where had this new Foundling come from? With all his contacts, his wealth and his *influence*, how come it had taken until now to learn of his existence? He'd not heard a hint nor a whisper since that business with Canatu until now.

In his immaculately tailored dark-charcoal suit, coordinated with a handmade shirt and contrasting silk tie – expertly knotted in a full Windsor – Darke adjusted his platinum cufflinks and crossed the room. The only sound was the click-click of his highly polished shoes on the white marble floor.

He stood in front of a vast, plate glass wall and stared into the depths of the millions upon millions of gallons of clear, fresh water retained behind it and glimpsed – just for one tiny infinitesimal moment – the absurd possibility of his ambition failing. It couldn't, and by way of triumph, he banged his fist hard on the plate glass which absorbed the blow soundlessly. He'd built his kingdom – his sanctuary – and the aquifers were all but full. All that was left to do was to implement his strategy. The Foundling – this new Foundling, a boy called Raif – was now out in the open and vulnerable to being tracked and captured. He'd failed when he was convicted for the murder of Canatu and was imprisoned but his genius had enabled him to escape. That same genius would not allow him to fail again.

Darke walked towards the oval-shaped door, which opened automatically and turned left down a long tubular corridor. The obscure lighting was functional and heartless. He stopped at the lift where the doors opened soundlessly and pressed the button to the sixth floor.

Six athletic men from mixed races were engaged in a noisy and vigorous game of basketball, spurred on by their coach who blew his whistle the moment Darke entered the gym. To a man – each player identical in grey tracksuit bottoms and white tee shirt – they stopped what they were doing and respectfully looked straight ahead, fully to attention. With a small wave of his hand, Darke granted them to continue their game while the coach joined Darke by the door.

The coach was an older man, origin unknown, and although Mongolian traits were evident in his appearance there was an element of his DNA not of this planet. He didn't speak, he merely stood next to Darke as both continued to watch the play in progress.

"I need two men to track and bring me a boy. Who would you recommend?"

The coach didn't respond until two of the players had separated off.

"Those two... Horlik... Horlik and Amstron." He pointed.

Back in his sanctuary – his inner sanctum – Darke prostrated himself naked on a glass table beneath a thin white gauze. He closed his eyes and surrendered to his mind as a gentle blue light penetrated his body.

Darke knew about the Hourglass. He knew about the *Prophecies* but was a scholar, a disciple – a fanatic even – of the *Alternate Prophecies* which predicted – through chapter and verse – a very different hostile and defeated world where the balance had tilted.

The Foundling would lead him to the Hourglass, and he would snatch both. In doing so, this simple act – this simple act of denial – would put in motion a course of events that would devastate the centuries of control and the predictability of order. For his own ends, he would unleash chaos and fulfil the predictions of the *Alternate Prophecies*.

His vision of this planet – so dependent on life-sustaining water – loomed large in his mind as too did his vast reserves of clean water now strategically stockpiled in secret aquifers throughout the key continents. It wouldn't happen overnight, but it would happen soon. Global warming and climate change already threatened and was accelerating. Soon, as the balance tipped, the world would be plunged into darkness as it exponentially descended into the apocalypse.

Word would travel. Fake news. Alarming news. The lemmings would run. He would hold one of the keys to survival – water. While wars raged above him, he would lie in wait ready to tap into his vast underground reserves. His currency. Only he could influence destiny because he would hold Power Absolute.

He felt no sadness or remorse. No prick of conscience at the havoc he'd wreak. For too long the Collective had encouraged the weak and allowed the sloth of mankind to dominate. He would purge the planet and start again. He arose and donned a full blue robe fastened high at the neck and approached a pedestal on which rested an ancient copy of the *Prophecies*. He selected Genesis 6 and referred to Noah and The Great Flood…

> … *I will wipe mankind whom I have created from the face of the earth – men and animals and creatures that move along the ground and birds of the air – for I am grieved that I have made them…*

In an act of sacrilege, he then placed a copy of the *Alternate Prophecies* on top of it and referred to a corresponding chapter.

> … *and the world will be seized and held to ransom by a great drought.*

Darke closed the book and read no further. In his madness, it was enough for him to think he shared an affinity with Noah and he was amused that his grand design, although similar in principle, was, in practice, entirely the opposite.

7

After having been woken by her epiphany — her realisation that Mr Cuff had, most definitely, shown her a pathway through the Great Chasm — Dina chose to pace the moonlight then sprawl under a large hand-knitted blanket, which she certainly hadn't knitted herself, in a cushioned armchair with her feet up on a battered camel saddle that had served for many years as a footstool. The whole visitation from Motto had also left her a little unnerved and she wondered, quite seriously, if she was really up to the job. She rummaged around on the table for one of her many pairs of glasses and selected a pair that were the least broken. She wanted to read Pythia's letter again to see if she'd missed anything. To see if there was anything to read between the lines.

Carefully, she emptied the envelope onto the tray and the spiders seemed none too pleased at being disturbed considering the hour. However, a few co-operated and re-formed, somewhat reluctantly, to become a postscript that was short and to the point.

> P.S. I've sent Anakee rather than Gideon to collect the boy initially so she may come along too. She

> doesn't know about Darke yet so keep an eye on her, would you?
> x

Satisfied there was nothing cryptic or hidden in the message, Dina set about cleaning windows. She didn't usually clean windows before dawn. In fact, it would be true to say she never cleaned windows – not hers and definitely not anyone else's – but that's what she'd decided to do and she was making a fairly good job of it.

She needed to give herself time to think and this particular task demanded just the right balance of mindless concentration to enable her to contemplate the prospect, and the all-important practicalities, of going into the Great Chasm. She examined too, while at her task, whether it would be better to find and bring the Hourglass here or to leave it where it was. After all, it had successfully remained aloof for the past 3,000-odd years so surely it could wait a little longer until Gideon and the boy Raif arrived, then couldn't they all go together? Gideon was good at mountaineering, or so he'd once boasted, meaning she could just traipse along with Raif, do the Turning, then they could all go home again.

"Mohammed and the Mountain." She thought laterally. "If only it were that simple." She knew instinctively it'd be a bad idea but what bugged her was she didn't know why.

"A little bird tells me you're going forth into the Great Chasm," said a mournful voice from within the olive tree which leaned up against the house. Dina looked around and singled out the eyes – the extremely large eyes – belonging to one of Pythia's envoys, a prominent and doleful barn owl.

"Yes, that's right," replied Dina, not finding it in the least bit unusual to be having this conversation. In fact, she was extremely pleased that Pythia had seen fit to send him along.

"I was just debating whether or not it would be better to…" she continued before being cut short.

"I know exactly what you're debating, so please… please… don't bore me with reiteration. Of course, you cannot take the boy! The Foundling… what's his name? Raif, that's right. Raif. Good grief, we've lost one already and what do you think his chances of survival would be in the Great Chasm…? Well…?

"I'll tell you. Zero. And if not zero, what's that expression? Don't tell me. Err… now then… yes… The proverbial *not a cat in hell's chance*. It'd be… Madness… Pure folly."

Dina gave the barn owl a moment to compose himself following his outburst. He'd certainly made his point and whatever he advised she knew it wouldn't do to argue. In fact, she was rather relieved for him – on behalf of Pythia, of course – to make the decision for her.

"Far better you go alone and employ stealth. There are forces within there that would sniff him out – and snuff him out – in no time. Your chances aren't that great, I have to say, but they'll be a damn sight better if you haven't got a child in tow and as for Gideon…!"

Barn owl ruffled his feathers to demonstrate his disapproval at the very idea of Gideon lambasting his way through the undergrowth. Dina waited for him to settle down again. "I was only weighing up the options," she said in her defence. "But be assured, and let Pythia know, I'll do as you advise, particularly in light of this conversation."

If she had doubts before, she viewed her prospects now with an even greater sense of foreboding. Not only was it likely she'd fall to her death, but the barn owl had also just confirmed the whole place was alive with very hostile devils and devilry.

"Oh… And I'm aware that Darke has escaped," she added gloomily as if she hadn't already got enough on her plate.

"That isn't good… that isn't good at all but you'll just have to be vigilant. Remember, there's a lot depending on you, but it's your destiny so let's play down the negatives, shall we? Go via the eastern holloway. I'll meet you there to point you in the right direction."

"Thank you," said Dina and she meant it. She was relieved that at least the decision had been made. Barn owl didn't mean to be gruff – it was just his way – and she knew that underneath it all he was desperately concerned for her safety.

"I'll set off early tomorrow morning," she reassured him. "We'll worry about all that tomorrow and when the time comes but, in the meantime, how about joining me for breakfast… Could you manage a little apple crumble?"

"I thought you'd never ask!" replied the barn owl happily and he swivelled his large eyes towards the kitchen.

Having made up her mind, or, rather, having had her mind made up for her, Dina felt much better and once again more in control. She'd leave – as she'd said – the following morning, and now charged with a new and urgent purpose she busied herself in tidying up and making ready. As she did so, she brought Chapter Three of the *Prophecies* to mind.

> *Four opposing extremes exist. Good being the opposite of Evil and Chaos being the opposite of Lawfulness. With the Collective being at the centre of this crossroad, a careful balance can be maintained. Where there is Order, there is continuity and harmony. Undermining the Collective by preventing the Hourglass being turned would disrupt this balance and, by whatever means, Evil would gain a powerful foothold. Chaos would ensue.*

The Prophecies
In the Beginning. Chapter 3 vs 8–12

She knew this often-recited passage well. It had been instilled in her since she first learned she'd become the Keeper. What bothered her now was not only the perils that lay ahead, it was that Darke was out there too and there's no greater fear than the fear of the unknown. But there was no time to dwell on this and certainly no time to be in a quandary as to whether or not she'd make it through the Great Chasm. Quite simply, there was no other choice, but who knew what allies and accomplices Darke may have enlisted? How many eyes watched from the shadows?

Dina selected a rather dog-eared ordnance survey map from the hall drawer and took it into the kitchen where she un-concertinaed it, shook it out and smoothed it on the table. As her eyes weren't as good as they used to be, she took up the large, green-rimmed magnifying glass which lived more or less permanently in the fruit bowl. Somewhat frighteningly yet with great purpose, she raised it to her eye.

Her elegant fingers traced and cross-referenced the coordinates she needed. On paper, it seemed relatively straightforward and, fortuitously, not too far away, but she knew the terrain around the Great Chasm was both treacherous and unstable with sudden rockslides and pools of green sand forming where they hadn't been before.

The Great Chasm was identified but not detailed. It ran along and adjacent to the shoreline for several miles, and because of further sudden landslides, it had become more or less impenetrable. Even access by sea was thwarted by rip tides, dangerous rocks and its sheer instability. An entire mythology had grown up and multiplied around it. Tales of strange beasts, wolves and the undead. She didn't doubt for one moment that it was all highly dangerous but what *was* known to Dina – yet little known to anyone else other than members and allies of the Collective – was the existence of local holloways, also known as greenways, stoweys, trods, rudways, dykes, sarns, and, perhaps more applicable in Dina's mind, fearways, dangerways, coffinpaths, corpseways, and ghostways.

These holloways, by any given name, existed as magical but dangerous secret pathways. They were shortcuts. Often devoid of sunlight, weathered and hewn from the unscrupulous habits of lost generations, they ran as deep ravines or creases in the landscape; shady, hidden and treacherous. They were a very useful means of travel. Choose the right one and one could arrive at a given destination almost as soon as one had set off. It was called – by those in the know – '*Ruralactic*'. It was a land-based means of travel and if one could imagine the world as (say) a ball of honeycomb, one could understand the physiology and therefore the usefulness of these highly convenient pathways. Only those with an experienced eye could find and use them, and needless to say, Dina used them a lot.

Although appearing placid and unremarkable on the outside – often being presented as a hedge of beech or privet – once probed any given holloway would reveal the entrance as being jealously guarded by fierce nettles and briars. Once inside, unrelated trees put aside their differences and conferred to knit tightly together, their branches tangled and poised ready to thwart and expel unwelcome visitors. Opportune tree roots and ivy contorted too to trip and outwit as they strangled themselves into grotesque visions of alchemy while hart's tongue, shining cranesbill, hemlock, stinkhorn, broomrape and toadflax seeped their silent poisons.

Dina knew of the eastern holloway barn owl referred to and, with a bit of luck, it would lead her deep into the heart of the Great Chasm. She had no idea what she might be confronted with when she got there and indeed, with all the landslides and so much rain, it may prove she'd have no alternative other than to turn back. But Dina wasn't the sort to turn back and to speculate served no useful purpose.

But now to more practical matters. It would be a robust walk, to begin with, and she'd call in at the Co-op *en route* to pick up a few essentials. She thought she'd pick up a few apples for the barn owl too – better to keep on his right side – so, happy with her plan and her OS map, she busied herself with the preparations. She cleaned her walking boots, lined up some socks, shook out her beret, chose a small cotton bag she could sling over her shoulder and then decided what might – and what might not – be useful for her journey, bearing in mind she didn't want to carry too much weight. She settled on a small handy pack of tissues, a box of matches, a small, lined notepad with a pencil fitted down the spine, a penknife from out of the kitchen drawer and a hip flask of sloe gin. She later forfeited the hip flask due to its weight and knew a torch would've been a good idea but couldn't find any batteries so she made do with a couple of candles. Her shower-proof jacket hung ready by the door and she knew there was money in the pocket.

Satisfied there was nothing else to do other than to get a good night's sleep, she looked out across the countryside from her tiny window and watched as the clouds parted to reveal a waxing moon chasing headlong across the sky.

8

The morning saw torrential rain. The sort of rain that fell straight and indiscriminately to bounce off stone and tin alike while creating rivulets and gullies on surfaces more yielding. This didn't please Dina but neither did it put her off. She wound her clocks, said her farewells and wondered when, and, if she'd be back. Of course, she would. She'd be back in no time with a story to tell and the Hourglass tucked safely underneath her arm. It would be wonderful to see Gideon again – she hadn't seen him since just after Canatu had died and she hoped he'd be in better shape. Maybe, when this was all over, they'd have time to talk, and what of this boy Raif?

The eastern holloway was located just behind the Co-op. She didn't arrive until mid-morning because of the rain impeding her progress but now it had stopped and the whole world was steaming. Invisible to all, other than those in the know, the entrance could be found in the laurel hedge that was through the car park, past the disabled parking (at the end near the front entrance) and to the right of the trolley park – not that many people bothered to take their trolley back.

It was disguised amongst the glossy leaves and Dina noted that the hedge was in need of some attention. Rather self-consciously, she walked nonchalantly alongside it – up and down, up and down – feeling and brushing it with her hand as she did so. Fortunately, the rain had deterred shoppers, so she was largely unobserved.

"There you are!" she whispered with a note of triumph as she came across it. For Dina, the entrance was unmistakable, so making a mental note of just how far along the hedge she'd have to go, she darted into the shop.

Happily, there was no one in the Co-op she knew other than Mrs Weatherby's daughter on the checkout, who was a sullen girl called Alice who – in Dina's view – had both a weight and an attitude problem and who, for some reason, was always highly suspicious of Dina. She had a mass of tattoos down both plump arms which depicted aspects of the occult and it was possibly Dina's recognition and disapproval of these symbols that may have alerted the girl's cautionary mistrust.

Dina had decided she only needed a couple of apples since she couldn't remember what else she'd come in for, but on going through the checkout, she discovered she'd been mistaken about there being money in her pocket.

Alice smirked and shifted noisily in her orange plastic chair while she pressed the buzzer to call the manager, Dina having requested an IOU. Both parties waited as the manager failed to materialise and Dina began to feel increasingly exposed and more than a little hostile towards the large girl in the orange chair. Alice – on the other hand – appeared to be enjoying Dina's humiliation and her ownership of the *impasse*. The obvious and easiest thing to do would have been to leave without the apples but in Dina's mind she'd promised – the apples were programmed in, so to speak – so there was only one thing she could do. She locked eyes with Alice and Alice, her face still wreathed in contempt, locked eyes with Dina just as Dina grabbed the apples and made a run for it.

Once outside, Dina didn't have long, but she had time enough to resume her contact with the laurel hedge before the manager appeared and shouted to her across the car park. He started running towards her and it was at precisely that moment her hand felt the yielding underbelly entrance to the holloway, and quickly and seamlessly, she slipped inside.

The holloway didn't bar her way. On the contrary, each recognised the other as kindred spirits as the strangled ivy, nettles and brambles momentarily parted, then joined forces with the latticework of branches to close their ranks conspiratorially behind her. From the other side, she heard a muffled question being exclaimed profanely but it quickly faded to nothing to leave an oppressive eerie silence. The holloway led away magically in front of her down a slight gradient through the mud, ruts and reeds.

"And so… it begins," she breathed and was glad she had her boots on.

Even though the torrential downpour had left its mark, Dina was making good progress and, lured into a false sense of security, she contemplated that the Great Chasm may not be as bad as she'd first thought since far from being sinister, it was all rather pleasant. The sun sneaked in and created dappled shadows on the grassy banks and made the puddles sparkle.

"Don't be fooled," piped up the barn owl wisely. "Don't ever be fooled by what you see, because what you see may conceal what you'd rather not see." The barn owl was perched on the overhanging branch of an oak tree and his proximity enabled him to share the same eye level as Dina. She was curious as to why she hadn't spotted him earlier.

"I've brought you some apples," she said, taking them out of her pocket and placing them within his reach on a ledge nearby. Dina refused to let his warnings douse her good spirits although it was rather unnerving to be so close and so one to one with his enormous unblinking eyes.

"Thank you, that was thoughtful of you," he replied and swivelled his head a full ninety degrees to observe them.

"Actually, your eyes aren't that enormous," she observed. "What's enormous are the large circles around them."

"Quite right, it's all to do with perception."

"It's always all to do with perception." Dina sighed a little impatiently. "But right now, I just need to know the way forward unless, that is, you're coming with me?"

"Not possible," he replied and swivelled his head to add gravitas to his wisdom. "It's your destiny, not mine. All I can tell you is to keep going forward and if you come to a crossroad, always choose right."

"Do you mean right as opposed to left or right as opposed to wrong?" she asked, and the barn owl merely rolled his eyes heavenwards.

"That's for you to decide," he replied, and Dina felt none the wiser.

She turned and looked down the holloway at the roots and the shadows. The canopy of green suddenly looked oppressive, suffocating and hostile. What little light there was dimmed, and a chill wind lifted and rattled the leaves. There was a presence in here and she didn't like it.

"So I keep on going that way?" she said with trepidation.

"Keep going forward," replied the barn owl and he redirected his gaze to join her staring gloomily into the abyss.

9

Raif, on the other hand, was having a far easier time of it having decided to stop questioning everything in favour of doing what Spiritas had advised, which was to keep an open mind. Besides, what alternative did he have? He could have refused to take part, but he was a nearly-ten-year-old boy with an enquiring mind, so how could he have resisted the appeal of such an adventure?

With this new mindset, rather than being afraid, Raif had really quite enjoyed making his way down the spiral steps within the longcase clock and he'd felt strangely at home inside its workings. He found it comforting rather than scary – like being in a small church – and the groans and ticks he could hear only made him feel more at ease.

He also liked sauntering along and chattering to Anakee in what she had described was a hollow tree root – a holloway is what he thought she'd called it – and he'd even joked about it being a trunk route…

Anakee seemed to not understand his play on words but Raif thought it was funny and wondered if the day would ever come when he'd be able to relay this silliness. Perhaps to his dad...? He continued to think along these lines for a while longer before coming to a fork in the road.

"Which one do we take?" asked Anakee.

Raif answered without hesitation. "The right one of course!" He laughed and ran ahead of her.

Anakee was taken by surprise by the immediacy of his answer. "Why so sure?" she asked when she'd caught up with him.

"Right or wrong, we want to go the right way... don't we?"

"What if you had multiple choices? Say twelve doors. Counting clockwise, which one would you choose then?"

Raif stopped and thought for a moment. "Well, considering where we are and what we're up to, I'd say door number eight."

"Why?"

"Because the Hourglass is shaped like an eight, so there's no other choice. Also, I know lots about astrology and the eight-pointed star is the star of Ishtar which is the star of Venus. Seeing as what's happening is something to do with peace and love, eight has to be the right number."

Anakee appeared to be quite taken by his logic. "You have hidden depths," she said. "Come on, let's see where it takes us."

Raif followed Anakee into the darkness. "What if I'd chosen a different number?" he asked.

"It would have taken us Nowhere," she replied. Raif wasn't sure if she was talking in riddles or if there actually was a place called '*Nowhere*'. After all, anything was possible here in this place but he decided not to pursue it – at least not at the moment.

"I wish I had a sister..." he said instead.

"Well, I can be your sister," she beamed, "and you can be my brother."

10

Having been asleep for some time, Motto woke up just as Gideon pulled into the empty car park of an unremarkable rural inn situated off-road along a perilous track mined with deterring pot holes. It was difficult to see it from the road since it was within a couple of hectares of dense woodland, mainly oak and ash. An old sign swung from what looked horribly like gallows announcing it as 'The Rune Inn' and it depicted a faded, peeling picture of what looked like an Elizabethan poacher high tailing it off into the woodland. The signage above the door was too weathered to be legible but it wouldn't have mattered anyway since the wording was just a jumble of stick men and hieroglyphics. Without applying the handbrake, Gideon abandoned his truck in its usual parking place and made towards the back door of the inn. He glanced over his shoulder once to check his shepherd's hut was still where he'd left it at the edge of the meadow and, as far as he could tell, it wasn't on fire.

Gideon had chosen to live in a shepherd's hut since it was ideal for his purpose. He could tow it anywhere, he didn't have to endure neighbours and he greatly enjoyed the freedom.

"Let's see what's been going on," he said with raised eyebrows as he pulled the door open for Motto and followed his friend inside.

There were the usual huddles of muted conversation and loners contemplating the middle distance. Again, like the inn itself, the entire ambience was unremarkable. Gideon ordered a local ale for himself and a large jar of honey from the top shelf for Motto. The pretty and silent barmaid nodded to the sounds in her headphones and didn't view the order as being anything out of the ordinary. No gratuitous words were spoken, and no money changed hands.

They found a table and Motto took stock of their surroundings and on closer inspection – without making it too obvious – he realised that, without exception, everyone in the inn harboured some peculiarity. A webbed hand here… A tentacled arm there… Too many feet under the table. It made him feel rather at home.

"So, we await the arrival of the Foundling," he said conversationally but keeping his voice down until a large gentleman dressed entirely in tweed approached them.

"Mind if I join you?" the tweeded gentleman asked and without waiting for an answer lowered himself heavily into a vacant chair. He took out a green checked handkerchief and mopped his brow. His red face glistened hotly and he appeared unable to speak for quite a few moments but on catching his breath his rheumy blue eyes twinkled.

"How the devil are you!" he exploded in friendship, leaping up and lunging forwards, engaging Gideon in a violent bear hug. Motto, a little startled by the camaraderie, pulled back.

Gideon laughed, delighted to see his old friend. "I didn't recognise you in all that tweed. Whatever possessed you?"

"Needs must, old boy. Now, who's this?"

"Henry, this is Motto; Motto, this is Henry!"

"Charmed I'm sure," replied Motto, not looking in the least bit *charmed*, and he drew back while the two men – the two old friends – continued to reacquaint themselves.

The last time Henry – Henry Mullet Broadbent – had met up with Pythia was quite recently, upon the moors just west of Halifax, hence his choice of tweed. She'd wanted to be sure that Anakee had made contact with the Foundling and that all was well. Henry was there to be her eyes and ears.

"You'll like the boy Raif. He's got a smart head on his shoulders without being cocky. Oh yes… and he loves clocks. By all accounts, he's got hundreds of them."

Motto listened in. Like Gideon, he hadn't known of the boy's existence until fairly recently, such was the secrecy that surrounded him, and now there was great excitement within the Collective that not only was a Foundling waiting in the wings, but the long-awaited Turning was imminent.

"Yes, Anakee is bringing the boy to me, then it's up to Dina. You've met Dina, haven't you?"

Henry Broadbent's eyes went sort of misty. "Indeed I have," he replied, his voice full of longing laced with innuendo.

"Well, that's another story for another time," interrupted Motto quickly. "Let's stick to the here and now, shall we?"

Henry shuffled uncomfortably in his chair. Whether this was due to amorous thoughts of Dina or the itchiness of his tweed, Henry couldn't decide as he scraped his chair closer. "Look, old boy, would you mind if I relaxed for a moment or two? It's dashed hard keeping up this persona for any given length of time."

"No, of course not," said Motto, "go ahead."

Henry ferreted for his handkerchief and, taking a big breath, blew his nose as hard as he could. There was a sort of popping noise and Henry Mullet Broadbent transposed into something not dissimilar to a large, mottled walrus.

"Ah, that's better," he said losing the plumb in his voice as he repositioned his bulk in the chair. "It's the tweed, you see – it absorbs ten times its own weight in water and it's itchy."

Motto gasped at the sheer surprise at seeing Henry as his true self.

"Your turn now!" Gideon laughed.

Without hesitation, Motto assumed his own *modus operandi*, that of a large, man-sized bumblebee, while Henry looked on – impressed.

"Okay, now we're all relaxed, can we talk about Darke?" continued Gideon, and at the mention of the name, the room fell silent and all heads turned. Motto looked around at the sea of faces – many different faces originating from many different dimensions and many different planets too.

"By the way," he asked Gideon, "where exactly are we?"

"At the centre of the universe," said Gideon and winked. "Think of it like any village pub. Surely you've been here before?"

"Of course but it... it looks different?" replied Motto in truth. "And in fairness, there's more than one crossroad between dimensions... I just wasn't sure which one this was."

"Can we get on?" asked Broadbent. He lifted his heavy jowled face and shook his head which caused the ripples of fat to undulate and be set in motion. "Darke is a problem. His very existence is a threat to our future, so we must pool our resources and share what we know," he conceded. "Gideon, you are the Finder and we charge you now that as soon as the Turning has successfully taken place, you must find and eliminate him."

11

Still mulling over her conversation with Barn owl, Dina had said her farewells and was now alone as she looked, with no small amount of trepidation, into the gloomy depths of the holloway. What on earth was she doing here and even if she did manage to get through and retrieve the Hourglass, why did it have to be so *difficult?* She shivered involuntarily when she realised she was actually experiencing fear. Pure unadulterated fear. It coursed through her veins like a bad adrenaline rush and it was a feeling she hadn't experienced in a very long time. Her skin prickled. It wasn't the fear of being there, it was her instincts telling her she was being watched by something terribly evil and she was the prey. Every step that led her deeper into the undergrowth, every twig snap, rustle and bird rush made her jump and startle.

"Face your fear, examine your fear, let your fear approach you and face it. Hold fast and your fear will pass through you..."

She recited this mantra from the *Book of Dune* as she had done before in times of crisis and sure enough her fear passed through to be replaced by more positive energy. She forced herself to think about the wonderful times she'd had in the holloways – the bluebells and the birds singing. Dappled sunlight filtering through spring green leaves and the sound of tinkling streams and laughter.

Such thoughts help to speed her on her way but the path, such as it was, became crowded and obscured by overgrown brambles and nettles. She wasn't sure at which point the holloway ended as she entered the Great Chasm but it was now unmistakable. The pathway gave way to uncharted territory where there were no paths to choose from. Curious trellises embroidered with lichen hung from branches and she knew that to trip or fall could prove fatal in this excommunicated place. Its solitude and isolation felt eerie and the air, once clean and charged with ozone, now took on a more sulphurous taste. The light was deserting her too, creating a clinging chill in the air that got into her bones and into her psyche. One could so easily get pixy-led, unaccountably confused as the shadows leaned one way then another, pausing only fleetingly to allow the closing of the day to illuminate the silent green slime pools that lay in waiting, eager to seduce.

Small cliffs, sheer and craggy, cleverly concealed their feigned fragility as the steep grey strata competed and dissolved to create neurotic unstable unions of mutual dependency where, as one collapsed, the others, as if heartbroken, became fatally affected.

Undeterred, Dina followed her instincts and kept moving forwards and to give herself courage, and to combat the awful silence, she recited – rather aptly, she thought – a few lines from *Henry V*…

> *Once more unto the breach, dear friends, once more;*
> *Or close the wall up with our English dead. In peace*
> *there's nothing so becomes a man as modest stillness and*
> *humility: But when the blast of war blows in our ears,*

then imitate the action of the tiger; Stiffen the sinews, summon up the blood...

She couldn't remember any more but soldiered on, making it up as she went along, finding appropriate snatches on the way. However, despite her camaraderie, her passage became more and more difficult as if the whole place had developed a grudge against her. She was scratched and clawed at, tripped and bruised, and it seemed that as soon as she took one step forwards, she paid the price by going two steps back. And what had started to worry her – as if she hadn't got enough to worry about already – was that soon, at some point, it would be nightfall.

Normally, Dina would consider pending nightfall a blessing, but she hadn't really considered how dark it would become in this hostile place as she watched the dark storm clouds gather to chase off the moon.

Darkness fell like a great black boulder – suddenly and finally without warning. With equal theatre, thunder cracked an almighty bolt and the ground was seared by a shard of brilliant lightning illuminating its victim in a macabre and terrifying way. Her hair became charged with the static around her. Her eyes were reduced to startled pin pricks. Whatever was happening was not of this world and with the adrenaline pumping *fight or flight... fight or flight...* Dina chose the latter and ran.

Fighting and clawing her way through the undergrowth – not knowing if she was running towards danger or away from it – it was if the storm was tracking her, baying at her heels, trying to catch her as lightning struck, left and right, forcing her on ever faster, ever more recklessly, until unwittingly, she reached the edge of the precipice.

She didn't see it. There was nothing to see. She was blinded by lightning and the torrential rain in equal measures, as slashing branches whipped her as if in punishment. It was little wonder she went headlong. The initial impact was loud and painful but the dull thuds that followed were less so until it all became strangely beautiful. Beautiful to be free of the noise and chaos. Beautiful to feel the air clean and sweet again. Beautiful to feel so… untroubled.

She knew as she soared into nothing more than the sound of the wind that the abandon would be short-lived but she nevertheless felt as if she had all the time in the world to reflect on her life. The good things and the bad. The loves and losses, the mistakes and triumphs, and the decision, which was that if she could do it all over again, would she? Would she have done anything differently?

She didn't have the opportunity to answer this question as she struck whatever it was that was coming up to meet her. Branches and rocks repeatedly laid claim, sending searing pains through her now broken rag-doll body until, mercifully, everything became still and silent.

It's been a good life, thought Dina philosophically as the soothing darkness folded over her. *It's just a pity that…*

But she didn't get to finish the sentence.

12

As he clambered out of the side of a decayed oak tree, anyone could have mistaken Raif for just a young lad out playing and enjoying himself. His hands were a bit muddied, his jeans were scuffed, and his red V-necked jumper had earned a few snags here and there.

The same couldn't be said for Anakee. She stepped into the sunlight elegantly and effortlessly. Her sleek black tunic with its simple neckline, elbow-length sleeves and wide trousers looked fresh and newly worn. Her *ensemble* was Indian in feel but at the same time, not so. Her dark hair was tied back from her enquiring oval face and her aura was one of calm and detachment.

The roof of The Rune was just visible above a canopy of trees, and in the foreground across a patch of scrubland that may once have been a lawn, Gideon was gathering firewood. He looked up and saw Raif, who stood his ground as he wondered who this great bear of a man could be. Should he hide? Should he be afraid of him? He turned to Anakee for guidance.

"It's okay… it's Gideon."

Still not sure as to what he should do, he turned and looked at the tree they'd just climbed out of. To Raif, all trees looked more or less the same and as there were several others that were also decayed or crumbled, he thought it might be a good idea to mark their tree in case they needed to get back. Hopefully, without being noticed, he picked up a small pebble and pressed it into the bark.

Just as he did so, a large shadow fell across him.

"You should never look back…" advised Gideon, who had come up behind him and now towered over him. Raif was startled for a moment but Gideon smiled and extended his hand. "The Finder meets the new Foundling."

Anakee quickly put a protective arm around Raif's shoulders.

"This is Raif," she said, taking over.

"And I'm Gideon."

"Hel-lo!" called Motto, who, in recognisable man form, bounded over to join them and shook both Raif's hands vigorously. "We're both – we're all – so very extremely pleased to meet you. It's a pleasure – an honour – it really is very, very good to have you here."

Squinting, because the sun was behind him, Raif looked up at Gideon. He was a tall man anyway and something about the attitude of his stature made him seem even taller. Gideon held the boy's gaze and it was then Raif noticed that one of Gideon's eyes was just a slightly different shade of blue to the other.

"We're going to get along just fine," Gideon reassured him and extended his hand for the second time.

Raif hesitated for a moment then extended his hand too and shook it. It was a large, firm, reassuring handshake, which made Raif feel safe. Their hands remained locked together for a few moments – longer than one would have done normally – while each studied the other and, like an enchantment, a communication flowed between them.

"Are you interested in clocks?" asked Raif as a smile spread across his face.

Gideon led the way towards the shepherd's hut with its painted green timbers and aluminium chimney stack emitting curls of fragrant-smelling wood smoke. It had four wheels – one on each corner – and Raif couldn't wait to clamber up the steps.

"Do you tow it?" he asked Gideon, examining the coupling, the wheels and the undercarriage.

"I most certainly do, all over the universe. Shall we go inside?"

The first surprise – but by now Raif was getting used to surprises – was that the hut was considerably bigger on the inside. It had an open wood burner at the far end and the whole place could only be described as a shambles; a sprawling brocade-covered armchair dominated a supporting cast of lesser chairs, all of which had seen better days, the carpet was a minefield of rucks and patches, and the walls – painted a shade of primrose yellow – were festooned with weird pictures of galaxies, ancestry, folklore and the mysterious consequences of alchemy.

The place was cluttered with books and, much to Raif's delight, clocks. Clocks of every description to equal his own collection, only each and every one of them displayed a different time.

"Why is that?" he asked Gideon. He knew the time in London would be different to the time in New York and so on, but there couldn't be that many different timelines in the world.

"The universe is a big place," answered Gideon, who grinned and tapped his nose.

Raif was in his element examining the clocks, the books and the alchemy which littered every surface. Motto chatted to Anakee and Gideon did his best to answer the barrage of questions, mostly questions to do with time and space, that Raif threw at him. He wanted to know *everything* but Gideon had to admit that for a boy his age, he seemed to know a great deal already.

"I like reading," he said. "When you're lying in bed for months at a time and you're not allowed out, it's the best way to climb out of yourself. You can be anyone and anywhere you want to be."

Much as Gideon wanted to talk to Raif and learn as much as he could about the boy, he was also desperate to talk to Anakee. He hadn't seen her since Canatu died and they both shared the same pain and tragedy of her loss.

"It's good to see you," he said quietly. "It was such a bad time... and I just need to say how sorry I am. I was so fond of her. She was a remarkable child and her death was a travesty that I'll never really come to terms with."

"Nor me," said Anakee. "But anyway, thank you – thank you Pythia – for understanding it was important for me to be a part of this... Look at him... Raif's a great kid."

They talked for a while and began the journey that would help them both heal, while Motto got creative in what could have been termed the kitchen, and Raif pulled out more books to examine.

"Errr... not that one!" said Gideon jumping to his feet. It was an ancient copy of the *Alternate Prophecies* he was leafing through and it was perhaps unwise for someone as young as Raif to view the contents.

"No... please... let me!" said Raif insistently. "I know about this!"

Gideon looked at the passage he'd turned to at random and at the primitive illustrations which accompanied it.

"It's about the waterspouts," exclaimed Raif in amazement. "It's like what I've had in this dream over and over... the water disappears! Look, it says so here!"

"You have visions?" said Gideon slowly and he looked at the boy in almost disbelief. "And are you telling me you can *read* this?" The text was written in some ancient language that even Gideon had trouble translating.

"Yes?" said Raif, not seeing the problem. "Not all of it but mostly. It just happens in my head..."

Gideon took the book and closed it. Of all the omens and strange events surrounding this turning of the Hourglass, this latest revelation had to be the most curious.

"How much do you know about the Hourglass?" he asked.

"Not much... other than it's an early type of timepiece... Shall I tell you?"

"Yes, please do."

"Okay... as the shape of an hourglass is essentially two circles joined together, the combined fluidity represents infinity. It's a constant figure of eight with the number eight being critical in balancing both the material and spiritual aspects of experience.

"I think you'll find it's all to do with Pi, which is why the Hourglass, as Anakee explained, has to be turned every 3,141.5926 years – to be exact, that is..."

No one said a word, they just stared, so not knowing what else to do, Raif continued.

"... Defined as the ratio of the circumference of a circle to its diameter, Pi is a simple enough concept. It doesn't matter what size the circles are. But what's so fascinating is that it turns out to be what's called an *irrational number*, meaning that its exact value is unknowable! Computer people have calculated billions of digits of Pi starting with 3,141.5926 and so on – as I said before – but because no recognisable pattern emerges, we could go on calculating forever into infinity…

"In other words, the Hourglass is transcendental…"

Raif ran out of words as he realised he'd rendered his audience dumbstruck.

"Apparently I have a photographic memory and I do quite like mathematics… astronomy too… and astrology… quantum physics is fun too – once you get the hang of it…?" he stammered, testing the water. "But I like clocks best…" He rallied. "Well, the concept of time actually…"

Gideon spoke first which was just as well since the other two were rendered speechless. "Well… I think you're a remarkable boy who carries great knowledge. All I was going to say about the Hourglass – and this seems rather basic by comparison – is that the Hourglass is recognised as being an entity in itself, hewn out of the very fabric of folklore until it evolved to have a very real physical presence of its own. In other words, the symbol became the reality."

"I understand that," said Raif with enthusiasm, "and because synergy needs to be maintained between order and chaos, it has to be turned to keep the world turning – so to speak…

"… Oh, and you need a Foundling too – me – to do it!"

This final revelation of his understanding caused everyone to smile and Raif felt happy that for now at least, he'd been able to share his understanding of what was going on. No one had contradicted his theories although he still had a great many questions to ask, not least what would happen if the Hourglass *didn't* get turned. He decided to risk it.

"If the Hourglass didn't get turned, would it set in motion something like in my vision of the waterspouts… like I just read in that book? Would stuff like that happen and be cumulative and multifaceted, growing and multiplying until all that was left would be chaos?"

Uncannily, the question was right to the heart of the matter and was the one question it would be difficult to answer.

Gideon sighed and did his best to furnish Raif with an answer. "It's impossible to know what would actually happen because as far as we're aware it's never happened before… and we have no knowledge of what might have happened prior to 3,141 years ago…"

"3,141.5926," corrected Raif, "to be exact."

"Whatever," continued Gideon and Raif could see he was anxious not to lose his thread. "All we know is that according to the *Prophecies* it's come close once or twice and now – following the terrible tragedy of Canatu's death and there being a full blood moon coinciding with the summer solstice – we're going to have to be extra vigilant…"

"And there's Darke…" added Motto. "Now he's escaped Carcerem he's also out there somewhere…"

"Darke?" snapped Anakee and shot him a look. "What about Darke?"

Raif felt the earth stand still as Anakee looked firstly at Motto and then at Gideon. Everyone froze.

"Answer me!" she bellowed.

"I'm so sorry," said Motto. "I didn't mean to say…"

The look on Motto's face said it all. "You had to find out sometime but not like this…"

"Is it true? Has he escaped?" Anakee glowered, this time looking directly at Gideon, her face wreathed in anguish. Raif went and stood very closely next to her as if by doing so he'd be lending his support.

"I'm sorry but yes. We've only recently found out – he tricked us, he tricked all of us…"

She didn't want to hear any more – she simply couldn't take it – so she ran.

She ran out of the hut and into the woods. Motto leapt to his feet to go after her but Gideon stopped him. "No, leave her for a while."

"But it's my fault. I didn't want her to find out like this."

"There was no easy way. However she found out, it was always going to be painful."

"Shall I go and talk to her?" volunteered Raif who couldn't bear to see his new friend – his new sister – hurting so much.

"No, not yet," said Gideon gently, his voice strained with emotion as he too was only just coming to terms with what Pythia had told him. "It's a lot for her to take in but I'll talk to her in a while."

'I'd rather go after Anakee…' is what he wanted to say but he knew Gideon was right. She needed a little time for the terrible news to sink in.

13

Anakee stopped running and collapsed beneath a huge, spreading oak tree. She looked for the moon but there wasn't one. There weren't any stars either – of course not. They were between worlds in another dimension that was a sort of no man's land that she'd never been to before so the sky was as alien to her as her surroundings. She didn't care, she didn't care about anything anymore.

"Are you alright?"

Raif stepped out of the soft half-light and, without waiting to be invited, sat down beside her. She pulled away angrily. "You shouldn't be out here!" she scolded.

"Would you like to talk about it?" he asked.

Anakee didn't answer. She just clasped her knees under her chin and ignored him but Raif didn't seem to mind that.

"I'll just sit here, then. I'm used to the silence of solitude and after all that's happened recently, it's quite nice just to sit here… with you."

Anakee turned towards Raif, her face streaked with tears. "There's not a lot to say really," she said. Her voice was tired and defeated.

"Then tell me about Canatu," he said softly.

Anakee turned her head away again and said nothing but Raif waited; he waited patiently as if lending his silent support and didn't move until, eventually, Anakee turned back towards him.

"Ahhh... Canatu... my beautiful baby sister," she said with warm reminiscence. "Do you know, I prayed every night for a sister and then – one day – I had one. I couldn't believe it. It was like a miracle. I only had brothers, you see, and it was always such a *fight*. Everything was such a fight – for food, for space, for attention – but you found you didn't really want attention because it was so often the wrong sort, so you learned to become invisible. It was different with Canatu. Mum was too busy and I think she was tired of having babies, so it fell to me to take care of her and I loved it."

"Whereabouts did you live?"

"London. The East End. Up in a high-rise, number 38, and the lift was always broken so I had to carry the pushchair and her! It didn't matter though, she wasn't heavy."

"And how old were you when Canatu was born?"

"Dunno... seven? ... No, eight – 1976 – I remember it was a really hot summer but it was when Canatu was two that I met Pythia. I think she saved my life."

"What happened?"

"Well, Canatu was in this baby buggy that folded up. I got it from the charity shop and it was blue and white striped plastic and really light. It was great! Anyway, I was walking through the underpass and this gang of lads – and two girls, would you believe – thought it'd be cool to take this buggy and make it into a sort of skateboard. Well, Canatu was screaming, I fought back and it all got nasty. I grabbed Canatu and got a kicking trying to shield her, then suddenly, there was Pythia in a big blinding light. Of course, I didn't know who she was then, but I know this: all those thugs were permanently blinded from that day forward."

"Gosh! Then what happened?"

"Nothing really. Pythia told me who she was... some kind of High Priestess but, you know, we got a lot of weirdos around there – druggies mostly – and she told me Canatu was special and I said I knew she was special and that she'd better back off."

"And did she?" Raif was obviously enthralled by the story.

"It was odd. The big light went out and she stood there – Pythia that is – looking like just an ordinary woman out shopping. She wore this grey coat and carried a shopping bag. You wouldn't have looked at her twice. She said we should go to the chemists to get my cuts seen to then she said she could really do with a coffee."

"And did you? Did you go with her?"

"Yes, of course. Canatu stopped crying the minute Pythia got near to her and she was really kind. We bumped into each other quite often after that, and over the course of time, she told me about Canatu being the Foundling – she told me what the Foundling *was*, for a start – and she told me all sorts of things about the universe and about this magical thing, the Hourglass."

"Do you want to tell me what happened? You know... with Darke?" asked Raif tentatively and once more Anakee fell silent as if trying to muster the courage to go over it yet again. But would that be so difficult seeing as for the past five years she'd gone over it day after day after day trying to make sense of what happened? Trying to *understand*.

"Not really, but I will." She sighed with a heavy heart. Her voice was now numb and heavy. "I didn't really know my dad, none of us did, and around that time my mum fell in with this crowd – the Lee Bridge gang I think it was called – where they all took drugs and felt angry. I bunked off school as much as I could to take Canatu to pre-school and pick her up after but sometimes I couldn't, so Mum took her with her and that's where she met Darke. When she was five she started infant school, but she changed. She was always bright and happy before but then she started to get anxious and withdrawn. I thought it was just her settling into her new school, but it wasn't. It was Darke who – looking back – had sort of become obsessed with her, always wanting to play with her and buy her presents…"

Anakee stopped and put her head in her hands. "I told Pythia and that's when Gideon got involved but we didn't see it. We didn't make the *connection* with Darke. Darke behaved impeccably and, in fact, he drew back and we didn't hear of him for a while until the day it happened. I went to pick Canatu up from school to be told she'd already been collected. We searched, the police got involved and two days later she was found in the canal surrounded by a shoal of dead fish…"

Raif couldn't speak. Neither of them could as they shared the tragedy. He put his arm around her as she cried quietly.

"I will always be here for you," vowed Raif, wiping his eyes too. "And we will find and punish him. I give you my word."

"That's what the Collective said," she replied and sniffed loudly. "They said to the police it wasn't a civil matter and they had the authority to take care of it. Darke was captured, tried and banished to Carcerem – an apparently inescapable prison planet on the edge of the galaxy. A living death rather than a quick one, the punishment befitting the crime, that is. I wish they'd just executed him."

"Me too," muttered Raif with adult venom in his voice.

Anakee felt better having shared the recollection of her tragedy. Raif was the same age as Canatu would have been and now he had taken over the destiny that would have been hers, she felt an affinity with him. She also felt fiercely protective.

"Are you two okay out there?" called Motto from the hut.

"Yes," replied Raif, reluctant to go in but Anakee thought otherwise.

"You go," she cajoled. "I need a bit more time on my own."

"If you're sure…"

"Yes, I'm sure. I'm fine."

Raif went in, leaving Anakee who was far from *fine*. She summoned up a picture of Darke in her mind – something she hadn't done for a long time – because the image of him disgusted her.

She'd found out in the ensuing years that Darke originally came from another planet within the galaxy. This wasn't unusual and was quite acceptable, and in fact, quite a large percentage of the population had originated elsewhere.

He'd come from the little-known planet Oberronex – a volcanic salted swamp environment – which had long since disintegrated and, despite controlled modification, Darke hadn't adapted too well to the earth's environment. His skin felt tight and prone to splitting.

He had a lithe, eel-like body, muscular and strong like a prehistoric form of a shark. The evidence of two pairs of dormant gill slits was scarred across his chest and it was the adaptation to lung function that gave him problems breathing.

As a consequence, he constantly drew on an inhaler and wheezed audibly. He had a skin one didn't want to touch. It was as if he'd once had a form of chronic psoriasis, which had left a residual coating – like an oiled dust – which when touched would cling afterwards and feel unpleasant.

His head was broad and flattened with a short, rounded nose with prominent nostrils, which were prone to flare easily when angered. He didn't appear to have much of a neck and his shoulders sloped, giving him a sloth-like appearance, although this couldn't be further from the truth as he was fast and active, making quick sudden movements as if foraging.

Like his name, Darke's eyes were dark too. Black. Dead and fathomless, quite large and oval-shaped giving him a curious Mongolian appearance. His jaw was his most remarkable feature. Long and jutting, it had no soft flesh around it. It was just hard, tight and cruel with small, sharp grey teeth widely spaced but seldom seen as Darke rarely smiled.

To distract from his physical shortcomings, she remembered that Darke always presented himself in exquisitely made handmade suits impeccably coordinated with the right accessories. She always thought this a little incongruous considering the neighbourhood and Anakee could never decide if it was his physical attributes that caused her such revulsion, or the smart suits that hid the reptile beneath. What she hated about him too was that he was unfathomably and consistently rich. This was due – although she didn't know this at the time – to the visionary powers of prediction integral within the gems he'd allegedly brought with him.

When Pythia had informed her about the new Foundling – about the boy Raif – the Collective had no hesitation in agreeing that Anakee should be the one who should collect him and deliver him to Gideon. It was agreed that Raif couldn't be in better hands and it was felt too that her involvement would be a small but valuable step in the healing process. Or so it was thought.

When Anakee stepped back into the shepherd's hut she looked more composed and despite being a little shaky, she held herself well. Raif wanted to rush and throw his arms around her – they all did – but instead, they waited for her to speak first.

She smiled weakly at Raif first and beckoned him to come and sit beside her and although addressing him directly, she was making an announcement to the whole room.

"Raif, I have to go now as my task – my great pleasure as it turned out – was only to deliver you safely to Gideon, which I have done. The revelation that Darke has escaped from Carcerem is highly disturbing, so I need to go and see Pythia right away. I'd like to have stayed with you awhile longer, I'd like to have seen Dina who I haven't seen since… you know… it happened but I can't."

"I'd like you to stay too," said Raif and he took her hand.

"I can't. You know I can't. Not now." She smiled and squeezed his hand in return. "But listen to me, you must put all this business about Darke out of your mind and concentrate solely on the job in hand, which is to meet up with Dina and turn the Hourglass. When… and only when this vital ceremony has been completed… can we turn our attention to hunting down and destroying that monster for good."

As she spoke, the image of Canatu's lifeless body crowded her mind. Her little sister's small frame lapping amongst all the flotsam and jetsam that gathered in the pockets of the dirty canal. The dead fish sacrificed around her. The finality of it all and not a mark on her.

The consensus was – at the time – that perhaps she'd taken her own life, but it was later decided that Darke was the culprit and he was brought to account. As it was Collective business much of the enquiry was held behind closed doors as a public outcry would have drawn attention to matters which were best left unspoken.

What was strange, however – and throughout the ensuing years no explanation had yet come forwards – was that the *Prophecies* stated that on death, the Foundling should be cremated. Not so with Canatu.

For some inexplicable reason, the burners refused to ignite regardless of the number of attempts so, on the Collective accepting this as an omen, Canatu's body was entombed.

Anakee shuddered visibly at the memory as a new fear gripped her. Darke had been convicted for the murder of Canatu because she was the Foundling. What if he was now plotting the same fate for Raif. "You must hurry!" she said urgently before turning her attention to Gideon. "And you must take care of him, both of you – all of you – do you promise? Do you all promise?"

"I give you my word," said Gideon solemnly.

"Me too," chorused Raif and Motto together.

"Pythia will know when the Hourglass is turned. Tell her we'll come to her then, and I will deliver Darke to her."

Anakee nodded and got to her feet and walked towards the door. Raif walked with her.

"I left a pebble in the bark of the tree we came out of so you'll know which tree will take you back," he said helpfully.

"That's wonderful but I don't think I'll need it." She smiled and turned to see Henry Mullet, back in his tweeds, standing next to Gideon.

"Henry will take you back," said Gideon and almost as soon as he'd spoken, both had gone.

14

After Anakee had left Raif couldn't help but feel abandoned. It was a feeling he knew only too well and he wasn't going to let it take hold. Anakee wouldn't have wanted that so, taking back control, Raif turned to his emotional failsafe – the subject of clocks.

"I was telling Anakee about my collection of clocks," he informed Gideon bravely. "I collect clocks, you know. I've got hundreds, well maybe not hundreds, but lots of them and I got this really special clock when I was five from my uncle Frank who died and it's gold with a boy warrior on it and I met him – I met him twice – his name's Spiritas…" Raif faltered and stopped as both Gideon and Motto looked at him intently. "What is it?" he asked.

"You've met Spiritas?" said Gideon. What new revelation was this boy going to come up with?

"Yes, the first time was when I was five. He took me to a desert and let me ride a huge giant tortoise as big as a tank and explained that time and distance are not always what you think. I ended up in a big glass jar that I now think had to be the Hourglass, but I didn't know that then."

Raif paused to see if they were going to laugh at him. They didn't, so he continued.

"Then I met him again at Mr Khan's Furniture Emporium and I think he may have blown the ceiling up because Anakee told me he's not very good at... err... Tesseractic travel but I'm not sure he did because Mr Khan didn't mind a bit because he'd created this beautiful mural which was all blue and sparkling and Mr Khan was *really* pleased. He said he was *over the moon*."

Raif wasn't sure if he should say anything about the paper plane Spiritas had made for him, which was now safely in his pocket. But he decided he should.

"He made this and gave it to me," he said and took out the paper plane and offered it for inspection. "He said I should tell you Spiritas made it with some old manuscripts which were all over the floor and that you would understand."

Raif handed over the slightly crumpled plane and Gideon straightened it out. His eyes lit up in amazement and a big smile spread across his face.

"There's more going on than we realised," he said ruefully. "Now you keep that safe because you never know if and when we might need it."

Despite the absence of Anakee, the mood had lifted as talk turned to the next stage of their journey. Motto meanwhile had prepared a proper boy's meal of sausages, beans and chips with a brand-new bottle of ketchup taking pride of place on the table.

Motto had honey, served in a bowl, with a large spoon to scoop it up with.

"I'm a honey monster," is all he offered by way of explanation.

"We'll take the truck," said Gideon between mouthfuls. "Now then, Raif, as you seem to know so much about

Ruralactic travel, how much do you know about the *Localeactic* means of transport?"

Raif paused as he dipped a particularly large chip in the ketchup – he hadn't realised how *hungry* he was – and, scanning his memory, couldn't say he'd ever even heard the word.

"Nothing," he confirmed then added, "but I'm sure you're going to tell me!"

Motto meanwhile felt it was time for him to take the floor. "Err... before you wade into all that mumbo-jumbo about inter-dimensional travel and eye-ology, I think you should see this. Although I say it myself, it is rather spectacular."

Motto stood up and cleared a space around him. "Watch..." he said.

Raif's mouth fell open and the last of his chips remained untouched as he witnessed Motto's incredible transformation – his morph – from man to bumblebee and him landing lightly on the table.

"What d'you think about that, then?" he said in a voice that although a little... buzzy... was still perfectly audible. "And that's not all. I can be made to measure!"

And with that, he reduced himself to the size of the tiniest fly to then become a rather alarming man-sized bumblebee. "And I can go bigger..." He laughed. "Much bigger!"

"No!" shouted Gideon, enjoying the fun.

"Amazing!" said Raif and he laughed. What on earth was he going to be confronted with next?

"I deliver shooting star wishes," Motto embellished as he flew around the room and landed on Raif's shoulder. "And unlike my friend here, I can come and go *anywhere*!"

Gideon laughed at his friend as once again Motto resumed his human persona, leaving Raif with a million questions to ask.

"Not now, we need to get going," said Gideon, "but in the fullness of time, we'll tell you all we know. Are you okay if we take the truck?"

Raif had never ridden in a truck before and when he approached the dented, scratched, beaten-up and muddied pick-up truck it was like a child's dream come true.

"I don't mind at all!" he exclaimed with his eyes lighting up and a big grin spreading across his face as he clambered into the front seat and made a space between the heaped ropes, wires, clocks and junk. He couldn't wait to get going.

"Ready?" said Gideon as he climbed in next to him and put the key into the ignition and the engine roared into life.

"I'm ready!" said Raif. "I'm ready for anything!"

"Don't forget me!" shouted Motto in mock panic and he jumped in just as Gideon slammed the gears into low box. Whooping joyously, they rallied off at a perilous speed through the dense woodland.

They left the woodland tracks behind and cruised along the open road through the clear indigo night that would soon give way to the shining promise – or perils – of a new day. While they travelled, the three of them bumped and jostled in the front seat, telling stories about faraway places.

Raif listened while Gideon told him about the birth of the universe and the way it all fitted together. He expanded, too, on a version of their place in the overall scheme of things.

"You see, there's more than one dimension. It's a question of perception. Who's to say what's the here and now when, equally, it could be the there and then," remarked Gideon.

"Or when or if?" added Raif enjoying the adult conversation.

Motto listened but drifted off when, inevitably, the conversation steered towards clocks.

"I can tell you all sorts of things about clocks," began Raif, "like… did you know the first pendulum clock was invented in 1656 by Christiaan Huygens and from then until the thirties it was regarded as the world's most accurate way of keeping time?"

"No…" said Gideon slowly, "I didn't know that…"

"And did you know that all twenty-four GPS satellites are equipped with atomic clocks capable of getting the time stamp to a location to the 100 billionth of a second?"

Gideon laughed. "No, I didn't know that either. But what I do know is that you have a great future in front of you and I'm very happy to have you on board."

Raif could have chattered on about clocks for the entire journey but he knew from experience that to go on for too long would become tedious for the listener – well, that's what his dad had said – but there was something else still on his mind.

"You know when you were saying if the Hourglass didn't get turned it would probably mess things up for a bit… you know, the hens would stop laying and the moon would sulk… and you were being daft…"

"Yes?" said Gideon slowly and he wondered what this line of thought might be leading to.

"Well, you said the weather could become unpredictable – which it would if the cycle of the moon was messed up – so wouldn't that lead to catastrophic natural disasters and phenomena like we've never experienced. Wouldn't it be chaos, like it said in that book?"

Out of the mouths of babes… thought Gideon in wonderment but he didn't say it.

"Yes…" he said instead. "But like I said, we cannot predict chaos otherwise…"

"… it wouldn't be chaos!" finished Raif. "Would you

like me to tell you about my recurring dream about the waterspouts now?"

Gideon nodded; he was keen to know as much as he could about this gifted child.

"It was very clear, and I've never forgotten it," began Raif shyly, and he went on to explain in great detail about the boy in his shorts kicking the football and breaking the window and the wind getting up and the waterspouts...

"... and there were all these waterspouts taking the water up and through the atmosphere where they all shattered and disappeared like fairy dust!" he explained breathlessly, obviously affected by the recollection.

"But..." he added, "I don't believe it. I can't help but have the strangest feeling that this wouldn't happen...

"I think it all depends on how you look at things and I think...

"... I think I'm looking at it the wrong way up?"

Gideon listened. Motto had woken up and listened too and both remained silent while they absorbed what Raif had said.

"What do you mean *the wrong way up?*" asked Gideon.

"Well, it's like this, waterspouts could be a really good visual example of the extremes which could happen. An example of the sequences of events that could ultimately lead to chaos. I think it's called the *butterfly effect* leading to the *domino effect*. I don't actually think that the world will be destroyed by waterspouts, but I do think it's the simplest way of showing that we're all dependent on water. Take water away – either up through the atmosphere or down through the ground – and we would all perish. I think my vision must be some kind of premonition or warning, don't you think?"

"I don't know," replied Gideon, keeping his eyes and attention on the road ahead. "In truth, I have never considered the presence – or lack of – water as any kind of issue. We take it all for granted but if you're saying you believe that chaos would tip the balance to such an extent that water – drinking water that is – became a rarity, whoever had control over this life-sustaining commodity would indeed have Power Absolute."

What Gideon *didn't* say to Raif was that he had the very sure conviction that it was the Hourglass itself that had chosen Raif and had also chosen to bestow this vision and conclusion upon him.

15

As far as Dina was concerned, she was dead. Smashed to pieces on the rocks that carpeted the Great Chasm. Rocks, sharp and jagged, that had willingly reached up to impale her. She had to be dead because she was five years old again, talking to her mother, or rather her mother was talking to her, scolding her for venturing into a holloway and for not looking where she was going.

"Corpseway, not holloway," Dina corrected, now thinking the former wholly appropriate and it occurred to her too – as she was thinking and not having been dead before – did you actually carry on thinking when you were recently dead, at least for a while after anyway?

She decided not to pursue this line of thought when shocking pain abruptly put paid to that. Ahh... but didn't the presence of pain mean she wasn't dead, although considering her predicament, it wouldn't be long in coming.

Opening her eyes proved difficult as both were badly bruised and swollen but she managed – just – and instead of the hues and patterns she would have expected to come into focus, she encountered nothing but darkness and wondered for a moment if she'd gone blind. It was a different sort of darkness to that of night; this had permanence and a density that gave it a physical weight, and with this heaviness came a feeling of oppression.

Very slowly, Dina tried to move. Tentatively at first since as far as she was aware, she was still impaled on the rocks. Her fingers explored the black air but rather than finding damp rock or grasses, she found a smoother, rather warm rock not unlike pumice stone.

"Oh no…" she groaned as the rumours of demons, devils and the undead crowded into her mind but distressing as these were, this wasn't what gripped her. It was the fact – the fear – that she'd fallen helplessly into a fault.

A fault was an accidental crack in the earth's crust which provided access to and – more worryingly – exit from other dimensions. Remember the filo pastry. The landslide which had caused the whole face of the landscape to slip into the sea had also created the Great Chasm and its inaccessibility had denied access on the part of the Collective for inspection, let alone remedy or exorcism. With no steps having been taken to stem this rupture, who knew where it might lead to? Or what might venture out of it?

A smell of sulphur confirmed her worst fears and she knew it would only be a matter of time before demons – or should she say, *creatures, not of this world* – would sniff her out like hungry rats and devour her. She had to move away from here, even if it risked further damage to herself, but bones were broken, and her left ankle had swelled alarmingly. She tried to move – she really did – but she had no strength. She was helpless. There was nothing she could do other than make a valiant effort to resist as the drift towards the grey blanket of sleep pulled her towards oblivion.

Death would probably come within the hour and she wondered which would take her first. Would she die as a result of her injuries or would she suffer a far worse fate if the demons arrived?

And they were coming. Scuttling and prancing, darting in and out of the shadows hardly able to believe their luck! These small, alien creatures were no real threat to her as they nipped and licked but she knew the commotion would soon attract more sinister adversaries and she knew too it was time to exit her tired and broken body before anyone of them could claim and possess her life force.

She watched what was going on with her peripheral vision and elevated herself to a place where she felt no pain as she concentrated on the beautiful light that had appeared and was hovering above her. Willingly, she floated towards a world far preferable to the world she was currently departing and she felt she suddenly had time – all the time in the world – to consider both her life and her failure. Apart from the usual ups and downs, her life had been good, and it was just a shame it was being cut short…

Her failure to retrieve the Hourglass, on the other hand, was catastrophic, unthinkable even, and to give up without a fight was just appalling. What on earth was she thinking of!

And with that, any thoughts of a 'higher plane' were dismissed as she came crashing back down to earth with all the pain, misery, stench and darkness that went with it.

"I'm not going to die!" she said defiantly and resumed full consciousness as the creatures were now upon her jostling and snatching, vying for a handful – a mouthful – of her precious life force. They didn't often get the opportunity to feast on a soul that'd come back – a treat indeed – but what they hadn't bargained for was that it was *her* soul which she wasn't ready to surrender easily.

"Get away from me!" she spat, flailing around in the darkness as they nipped and scratched at her. "Be gone!" she commanded, flinging one after another at a wall she couldn't see while all the time knowing these were probably only the forerunners of more ferocious adversaries to come.

Then, almost as quickly as they'd arrived, the impish creatures vanished. The temperature – hot and sulphurous – dropped suddenly creating a ghostly chill as a dark enveloping shadow fell across her.

This is it... she thought and resigned herself to the darkness.

16

Mercifully perhaps, Dina had passed out, but she regained consciousness only to realise that some foul repulsive monster was pressing down on her face and, much to her disgust, his tongue was wrapped around her tongue. She fought, she tried to bite. She gagged, tasting bile in her mouth. She kicked and struggled all to no avail until after what felt like a lifetime, the monster withdrew, and she could see through her swollen damaged eyes a blurred image of the creature that had violated her. It was twice the size she was, if not bigger. Swathed in rags that billowed a cloud of heavy red dust – the colour of red oxide – its skin was coarsely reptilian and of a similar hue. Perhaps humanoid in its initial design, it had mutated – or not evolved (devolved?) – to be closer to dinosaurs than man. It was an aberration indeed but what she found incongruous were its eyes. Small, bright and mischievous.

She didn't move, feigning death although that probably wasn't far off. The creature watched her as if lost in thought. Through bloodied eyes, she stared in disbelief at the manifestation which now loomed before her and involuntarily she took a large pitiful breath. "No!" she screamed defiantly, and with one last almighty effort, she clawed at the face looking down on her. Her hand caught one of the soft cheek pouches that hung on either side of his face and in doing so caused it to rip and disgorge an iridescent bright green fluid. The creature's three-fingered hand flew to its face. It roared at her in a language she couldn't understand but it would have served no purpose anyway as it took hold of her foot and, like some trapper or hunter, began dragging her towards the craggy opening in the grey flint. The pain was indescribable but then cutting through came the vibrations of a continuous low snarl. Dina thought it was either the sound of her own blood pounding in her ears or the sound of something far worse, if indeed there could be anything worse than the predicament she was currently in. She conceded her own failure. She would not permit being subject to any more torment, nor would she allow herself to be taken hostage. It was her fault – her failure – and she had to die *now* and at her own hand... She scrambled about for her penknife.

It was some time later when Dina looked up at a gap in the dappled canopy. It had created a pretty haloed effect that she felt bordered on almost being ecclesiastical and, truly, she felt quite moved. Under any other circumstances, it would have been wonderous but then, as the *here and now* kicked in, she became horribly aware that whereas the red-oxide monster had seemingly vanished, a new foe had beset her since she was now at the mercy of – and beneath the dripping jaws of – a ferociously large black dog. She didn't move a muscle while she took stock of this new predicament. The good news was that there was no evidence of the previous violating monster and, optimistically, she presumed this new peril had snatched her for his own gratification, namely lunch. Hardly good news she thought as wearily she conceded she had no appetite for further conflict. In short, she was fresh out of fear and loathing, so adopting the role of spectator she assessed her mounting degree of hopelessness and welcomed this feeling of detachment.

Dina hadn't found her penknife. She hadn't died and although death was still surely imminent – only this time at the jaws of this big black dog – she didn't feel any of the things she thought she'd feel when faced with the inevitability of certain death. She didn't feel fear; she couldn't run so all she could do was accept, wait for those massive jaws to crunch her bones to splinters and listen to the silence. And what a lovely silence it was. She had no idea how long she'd remained in this state until one by one, like some kind of miracle, the sound of birdsong found its way into her subconscious.

First came the call of the blackbird, strong and clear, followed by the robin and the wren. A chaffinch joined in only to be ousted by the staccato panic of a pheasant suddenly roused from sleep. After a moment the harmonies reunited as sparrows, crests and warblers joined in until a crescendo was reached by celebrations of the song thrush joyfully welcoming the dawn of a new day as all the other birds had no choice other than to join in out of pure exuberance.

Dina would never forget their performance. It made her spirits soar. Higher and higher she soared with them above the canopy to a place that was blindingly light and so breathtakingly ethereally enchanting.

It was wonderful. She felt no pain; she felt immense happiness in an enveloping peace as she drifted weightlessly in golden fields. Hot, sweet air fanned her cheeks and then she realised – as the pain returned – she wasn't dead.

She didn't open her eyes. She wanted to stay and make the most of this wonderful place and she thought that if she kept her eyes shut, the pain would go away, and she could stay in this place for all eternity.

But the truth was, she couldn't. Curiosity began to take hold, as too did the resignation that she may as well get this carnage over with. Dina opened one eye just a fraction and the scenario presented gave no cause for encouragement, since standing astride and almost above her remained the vigil of the ferocious black dog. She connected this with the *hot sweet air* she'd experienced earlier but what puzzled her was that in her experience, she had never associated dog breath with the word *sweet*.

Local rumour and hardened folklore had told many tales of this terrifying creature. For a dog he was huge. The size of a young steer, lean and muscular with an oversized head like a mastiff and eyes that glowed yellow in the shadows. It moved with the slow stealth of menace with short, pointed ears, sharp and attentive that twitched at the slightest sound.

A wet mouth slathered froth around jaws big enough to devour a child and around his thick neck he wore a collar studded with strange discs and symbols. He was a spirit creature said to be an omen of death and although the sightings were few, the accounts of his atrocities were many, with fearful protracted stories fuelled by flagons of cider bravado being graphically recalled throughout the long winter nights.

Dina had no recollection of what happened next. She didn't know if it was hours, days or perhaps even longer when she awoke to find herself lying on a soft bed made up of scented fern and rabbit fur.

The swelling had gone from her eyes and she was patchworked into a curious assortment of improvised bandages clumsily holding a variety of poultices. The ferociously large black dog was sitting on his haunches watching over her.

It very quickly became apparent that the black dog had no intention of devouring her. On the contrary, he'd confronted the creature who, in such an ungainly manner, had attempted to drag her into what she'd later regard as *the Gates of Hades* and he was, it would appear, entirely responsible for her improved state of well-being. Each observed the other and neither moved nor uttered a sound until Dina found her voice.

"Thank you," she said. "I take it that had you desired to tear me limb from limb, I wouldn't be sitting here swathed in these… what are they?"

"Poultices," the black dog replied in a deep, calm voice. "I have special skills in the practice of healing."

Dina nodded and accepted this information but still felt it wise – for several reasons – not to make any sudden moves, although she did manage to sit up.

"Excuse me asking, but are you the so-called Beast of Bowminster? The Girt Dog, the Hound of…"

"Yes," he replied wearily. "The Black Shuck, Cu Sith… It goes on, but one gets used to local notoriety. Sometimes it's even rather useful."

Dina smiled. It was no surprise that she was able to communicate with this mythical beast. As a general rule, she much preferred birds and animals to people.

"Well, that's folklore for you," she said philosophically, "I think it'd make me want to be even more ferocious!"

And she feigned a growl, held up her bandaged hands and managed a small laugh which dissolved into a cough.

"How are you feeling now?" he asked. "You've been through a really terrible ordeal."

"Much better and entirely in your debt," she responded, then asked, "May I know your real name and purpose?"

"Lenken," he replied. "Pythia charged me to take care of you if and when the situation arose."

"Well done, Pythia, and thank you, Lenken." Dina smiled weakly and as she recalled the recent sequence of events a great weariness enveloped her. "I really need to rest now but then I think we have a great deal to talk about." And with that, she lay down beside him.

17

Over the next couple of days, Dina marvelled at how her broken bones and wounds were healing. It was little short of a miracle in so short a time but Lenken explained how he too had knowledge of holloways – these shortcuts to faraway places – and about the magical flora and fauna growing within them. He explained his knowledge regarding their secret uses and application of the many rare plants, and even the more commonplace species, for their use in homoeopathic healing. Plants such as aromatic arnica with the sweet essence of pine sage to calm her trauma. Comfrey, also known as knit-bone and bone-set, to mend her fractures quickly. The anti-psionic marine sponges to mend her skin and keep her warm when her body could not. Aloe vera – which he had to go a little further afield to source – to soothe and make her whole again.

He explained too how, using his own saliva, which coming from a supernatural creature was magical in itself, he'd made compresses and poultices and applied them to her during her delirium. He'd bandaged and splinted her using leaves and twigs from the woodland and he'd watched her, fed her, washed her and had talked to her constantly in his deep, gentle voice to stop her from quietly slipping away. His words melted into her subconscious so that when she awoke, she felt at peace and less daunted by the task ahead of her. It couldn't get any worse, and what was such a comfort was that she now had Lenken and with that warm thought wrapped around her she increasingly felt really ready for anything.

"Can you tell me more about what happened?" she asked, eager to put together some of the missing pieces.

"Would it do any good to speculate or dwell on what has passed?" he asked. "You know what happened and to know more would serve no purpose. Would it not be better to leave it that you are fortunate to be alive?"

Dina hesitated but held her ground. She felt almost embarrassed by her ordeal and disgust at how – and why – the creature had engaged with her in such an unseemly manner.

"I need to know."

"He was using the universal language," Lenken conceded. "Surely you must know of it?"

Of course… Of course she had, but under such circumstances, it seemed so wrong. So invasive. "A joining of tongues…" she breathed and was sickened by the mere thought of it. "Not like that! It's… supposed to be consensual. It's a ritual performed while adhering to very strict rules of protocol…"

"You were hardly in any state to adhere to any strict rules of protocol and he just wanted to find out what he could about you. I don't think we should be worried unduly, but he will now know about the Hourglass and about your feelings towards Darke."

"Who was he? Where was he from?"

"I didn't get much chance to see him, but I'm sure he was from the dimension known as Camarthon. A parallel universe to our own but, sadly, it's a dying dimension and there are only a few pockets of colonies left. It is said the king – the ruler – is a peacemaker and has existed alongside earth for many thousands of years but I fear the colonist you encountered was probably Gwalch, who canvases more progressive views."

"And that green stuff? What was that?"

"Nothing. Just plant extract. They're dependent on it as an essential food supplement. You see, the inhabitants of Camarthon cannot tolerate UV light and as their dimension now is little more than a dust bowl, they've had to travel further afield to find food. They've had portals to our world for… I don't know… thousands of years and we've co-existed peacefully for all this time. They come at night to forage and this fault – this portal – is only one of many worldwide. They harvest the extract… you know the saying '*you must eat your greens…*'? Well, that's what they're doing. They extract it from the plants, mainly weeds, and especially stinging nettles, then carry it in their face pouches – rather like bees, actually – and return home with it. No harm done."

"So, the stories of demons, devils are really just these creatures… harvesting?"

"Not altogether, because we get many other strange visitors too, but they certainly make up a few."

"If there are so many faults – portals – why don't we stray into their dimension?"

"Simply because in order to go somewhere – to go anywhere – one needs to know where one is going. Only a very few, even those within the Collective, have even heard of Camarthon, and with what little we know about it, who would want to!"

Dina shuddered at the thought that if it were not for Lenken, she could have been lost to the mysteries of

Camarthon. "Do our people ever stray into these or other portals by accident?" she asked.

"Unfortunately... Yes. And quite often. Look around any town or city and you'll see the posters proclaiming *Missing Person*. Draw your own conclusions but it's very sad... heartbreaking. Many have befallen this fate, although, thankfully, I have to say, not all of them."

Dina was moved by this account as she recalled seeing one such poster in the Co-op only recently. She was ashamed because she couldn't remember what the missing person – a smiling photocopy of a happier time – looked like.

"But we're not concerning ourselves with these creatures for now. We must concentrate on retrieving the Hourglass," said Lenken, getting to his feet. "There'll be time enough to dwell on what took place here when our task is done."

18

It was agreed that despite her injuries not yet being fully healed, it was imperative they continued with all due haste. The fall had delivered her to just above the shoreline, and much as she scanned every inch of the cliffs looming above them, she could see no sign of where she'd been. With the early light of dawn on their side, they could make reasonable progress along the beach regardless of the height of the tide, and although the terrain was rough with large rocks often barring their way, these were nothing to the deadly grey mudslides which could swallow them in seconds.

"Stay close to me," said Lenken.

The black cliffs, almost vertical at some points, hovered above them and every now and then a small rock would tumble randomly. The sea was calm in the flat white light and an offshore wind provided a stillness as step by step they made their way eastwards.

"I must rest," said Dina, sinking back onto a large rock, taking the opportunity to examine the angry florid swellings beneath the improvised bandages. Lenken did his best to tighten the leaking poultices but he could see that the arduous climb down to the shoreline was taking its toll and he was concerned that fever could set in.

"Mr Cuff showed me a way up there," she said pointing at the steep sides of Chapel Rock, offering no explanation as to who Mr Cuff might be. "He said at low water there are rocks just beneath the surface which serve as stepping stones. After that, there are footholds but…"

"Rest awhile and I'll make a harness," ordered Lenken. "It will be much better if I can carry you." And he set about selecting driftwood and gathering the springy saplings which grew sparsely just above the tide line.

"The seawater will do your wounds good," he encouraged as he fitted the makeshift device around her and gently towed her into the water. The stepping stones were there, just as Mr Cuff had predicted, and although the water soon became waist high, it was clear enough to see them, flat and reassuring, marking a passage through the waves. They were making good progress but gradually the waves got stronger and a swell began to build.

The sea, previously flat and calm, began to drag – in out… in out… Each time, the waves became a little bigger and little stronger until Dina found herself struggling.

"We're almost there," encouraged Lenken, straining to keep them both upright until a seventh wave crashed over them and flung them hard against the rock face.

"Lenken! I can't hold on!" Dina shouted through the surf as she scrabbled for a foothold, but the wind had changed and a sudden storm took hold as white horses reared, whinnied and then broke over them.

For a moment she was lost but then she appeared again, gasping for breath as Lenken pounced forwards, grabbed her in his jaws and flung her onto a small ledge.

"Hold on to me!" he called as he dragged her through

the surf, lashing out with his powerful tail at the seagulls that dived and shrieked as if it was all a game. They'd tasted blood and delighted in seeking out and pecking at her exposed flesh until, without warning, the sky darkened.

From out of nowhere black storm clouds gathered, and like great blocks of cement being hurled across the sky, they clashed and shattered. Each thunderous engagement sending shock waves through the strata. The sea rose and frothed even higher as giant waves reached out to take her while the watching wind reached a hysterical crescendo. A terrifying banshee frenzy.

Dina was lifted clean out of the water by invisible hands and hurled towards the rocks. With only seconds to spare before impact, she was again snatched and pushed roughly into a vertical crevice in the cliff face.

"Don't move!" roared Lenken as he barricaded himself in front of her. There was nothing more they could do. Fork lightning struck within feet as if to taunt him – to test him – but he didn't flinch. He just snarled and snapped at the storm as if he'd rip it to bits if it dared come closer.

But it was just a summer storm that vanished almost as quickly as it had arrived and soon it was as if it had never happened. The only spectacle was a flock of cormorants that dived in vertical formation only to reappear moments later each with a large tentacled squid fighting in its beak. Then almost as a ritual, each victim – each catch – was thrown expertly into the air and caught – like a circus act – by synchronised wide-open beaks and swallowed in a macabre wriggling animation. Dina couldn't help but empathise with their fate and drew parallels with herself and the red-oxide monster, but then they too were gone, and the only sound was the plaintive call of the skylark.

The sea had lifted them to safer ground. In fact, it had lifted them and dumped them like flotsam to over halfway up the seaward side of Chapel Rock where a wide path, further aided by small wooden steps hewn into the rock face, made the rest of their arduous journey easy. The early morning sun shone on her face and she breathed a great sigh of relief.

19

It was amazing sitting high up and isolated on Chapel Rock. The panoramic view of the sea rolled out in front of her from east to west, and even though she felt like she was flying, she felt grounded. All that had happened to deliver her to this spot — this here and now — paled into insignificance as if a distant recollection of something that happened to someone else. *Trauma displacement*, she thought and locked it away in a box and then, for the first time since Dina could remember, she felt well again. The pain had gone, she could breathe great gulps of fresh sea air and her strength had returned. She sat up abruptly, charged with new vigour, and looked around. The sun shone and had warmed her and she was bathed in a feeling of optimism. Lenken was sitting apart from her. Watching. Forever watching.

The plateau they found themselves on was only small, measuring some eight hundred metres across. They could see the small, ruined temple teetering on the edge, the land around it long since slipped and eroded. Dina knew they were still far from safe. These cliffs were prone to sudden and frequent falls happening without warning other than a heart-sinking rumble followed by a sharp staccato crack.

But the cliff didn't fall, and the ground remained stable, and as they approached the ruined temple, they came across a shallow pool of oozing thick blue lias. Liquid stone would best describe it.

"Be careful," warned Dina. "These are treacherous quagmires which will drag you down in minutes."

Lenken nodded. He was well aware of the dangers but was also aware of the healing properties they offered too.

"Please, sit for a moment?" he asked. "Your wounds are all but healed but it's the scars on your soul – the wounds you *can't* see – I need to attend to."

Dina didn't argue and sat patiently while Lenken set about making a concoction using the blue lias, his own spittle and the sap of a few carefully chosen plants which clung to the banking. He applied the sticky balm to her forehead.

"That feels good." She smiled.

"Let it penetrate and be healed," he said hoping, but not saying, that the balm would at least go part way towards exorcising the trauma of her recent experiences.

They continued on their way and Dina's close encounters were all but forgotten – the work of the balm perhaps – and the day seemed perfectly normal again or as normal as it possibly could be under the circumstances.

"Here we are," enthused Dina as they arrived at the ruined temple.

Obscured only by a few windswept trees, each tree etched and bent like weathervanes due to the constancy of the prevailing winds – winds which had momentarily ceased – the small derelict chapel, so humble in its presentation, presented itself as the hallowed resting place of the Hourglass.

It was nothing to look at, just the remains of a washed flintstone chapel with a jumble of gorse, ragwort, brambles and nettles growing in and around it.

But the area around the ruin crackled with magic. It was steeped in folklore. It was reputed to be inhabited by woodwoses – hairy humanoid creatures and gossamer-winged wisps and although they remained unseen at this time, shadows and whispers reassured Lenken they were there and ever vigilant.

Dina looked around but now she was here, how would she know exactly where the Hourglass was hidden? Having never been called upon to perform this task before, where was she supposed to look?

And it occurred to her, too, that she had no idea what the Hourglass looked like, other than – presumably – an Hourglass, but how big was it?

She turned to fire these questions at Lenken but hesitated. He looked tired. No, he looked drained. Exhausted, as if every fibre of his body had been put into fighting a cause that she had no idea would – in time – become realised as only the beginning.

"I can manage now," she said gently and stroked his noble face, "and you know I need to do this alone. The journey back will be much easier with Pythia watching over me and of course… I'll have the Hourglass. I am forever indebted to you not only for saving me but for restoring me. I simply cannot thank you enough."

And with that, she threw her arms around his neck and hugged him.

Lenken understood. "It was a privilege," he replied and hooked a disc from the sleeve of his collar and gave it to her. "If you ever need me, use it to call me."

A sudden noise caused Dina to turn sharply but there was nothing, and when she turned back to say farewell, Lenken had gone. The space he'd left behind was enormous.

20

She walked towards the ruined chapel trying to keep an open mind, dismissing the questions which were crowding in on her. As no one in her lifetime had ever *seen* the Hourglass and there was great debate – great division – as to whether the Hourglass was just folklore jiggery-pokery or if it really did exist, it didn't make Dina's resolve any easier. But such thoughts were distracting as well as disquieting, so she chose to ignore them as they served no useful purpose. Her knowledge of animism – the belief that objects, places and creatures all possess a distinct spiritual essence – assured her that it would be the Hourglass who'd find her, not the other way around.

Still, she speculated about what size it might be and what, other than glass, was it made of? How would she carry it? Would she be able to carry it? Should she move it at all?

But all this was becoming increasingly academic as she could see no sign of anything that looked remotely like the Hourglass – or how she perceived it might look. Within the ruins, there were the remains of a porch, a low wall or two, long fallen into disrepair, and some lumps of stone which may have once been part of a window.

Dina sat on the nearest low wall and leaned against what was once probably the original altar. The two blocks of stone she leaned against were of a different colour to the rest, because whereas all the other walls were made up primarily of grey flint, this small insert of two stones, each measuring no more than half a metre, was smooth and golden. Not being able to help herself, all Dina could think of was that they looked like two deliciously large pieces of fudge pressed into the wall.

Tentatively, Dina touched them. These two flat stones didn't feel like fudge; they felt like sandstone because, indeed, that's what they were. The indigenous stone that made up that part of the coastline – deep yellow ochre in colour and smooth like packed sand. Dina rubbed the palms of her hands lightly over the lower stone. It felt raspy like rubbing your hands on a fine coir coconut matting and it made her fingers tingle. She pulled her hands away but found she couldn't, and what's more, she didn't want to. She couldn't resist. It was a nice feeling, like scratching an itch, and the more she rubbed, the more intense the sensation became.

But what had she done? The golden surface started to disintegrate. It was no longer stone, it was sand! Just sand packed into the wall and now it was falling. First, just a few grains trickling through her fingers; then, as it picked up momentum, it began to pour, dry and uncontrollable. Impossible to catch, to stem or to halt.

Dina fell backwards as the sand engulfed her, getting into her eyes, her hair, her clothes and her wounds. She felt like crying, there was no more fight left in her. She looked around frantically for Lenken and cried out his name, but he had gone – he was no longer there – and still the sand kept on coming.

Then something hit her. It was quite sharp, the corner of something perhaps, and the roaring sound stopped, the sand stopped, and it seemed to Dina that for one single moment, the whole world stopped too.

She looked down and saw, half-buried in the sand, something that resembled a Moroccan lantern. Only it wasn't.

It was cylindrical, about eighteen centimetres in diameter and maybe forty centimetres in height, not including the large ring at the top used for carrying.

The dull and tarnished filigree metalwork wrapped around it was intricate and fascinating. Beautifully handcrafted, and the two-tiered top – like an ornate roof with a lookout tower – was equally intricately crafted. Beneath the filigree metalwork was glass of the most delicate shades and hues, which although it appeared virtually clear on first inspection, spontaneously caught the colour spectrum, choosing either a hot or cold palette seemingly at will.

Dina picked up the lantern and the sand around it shimmered then fell away. She held it up to the sun and marvelled.

There inside was the Hourglass.

Like an adrenaline rush, Dina felt a great power surge coursing through her veins and she rather wanted to hear a multitude of angels singing because that's what it felt like – enthralling. It was true! Hallelujah! The Hourglass exists and it had found her! Instinctively, she looked around to see if the discovery had been observed, to see if demons or woodwoses or any other force or creature might materialise to snatch it from her, but nothing did and only a light breeze whispered. Strangely, she felt safe and strong and even if some evil force had materialised, she felt she could take it on – she could take on anything. Such was the transmutable power of the Hourglass.

In her state of heightened awareness, she examined the relic in her hands and trembled. She wanted something to happen, and surely after 3,141 years, something should happen? But there were no singing angels. No shaft of light breaking through the clouds. No opening up of a brave new world. No multitudes praying. No proclaiming pilgrims.

She continued to stare at the relic in her hands until it occurred to her. It was just so *ordinary*. Unremarkable and dull, even. The sand from out of which it came lay in heaps and drifts but already it was dissipating as the wind picked up, sweeping it up and over the cliff to return to its origin in the sea. She looked at the wall again and the two slabs of sandstone – the fudge – looked just as they'd done before. She touched them gingerly, afraid she'd disturb the surface and fearful of what she might bring to the surface, but nothing moved, and her palm didn't itch. She wondered fleetingly what would happen if she touched the upper sandstone, but her instinct told her to leave well alone. She continued to stare at the Hourglass in its tarnished and dulled container for a while longer until it dawned on her. The beauty of it all was that it *was* so… so… unassuming. Dina laughed as she realised. In such a dulled and dormant state, what better way to survive than by being unnoticed!

With this understood, she still felt highly respectful – even more so – but at the same time, less in awe in its presence. She examined it further. It was heavy, but she could lift it using the ring on top. Except for a small light emitting from the centre, which had no discernible source, it was quite dim inside the lantern chamber, but she could see the Hourglass well enough. She fiddled and looked for a catch to open the casing and found there was none, but through the lattice casing, she could just see the sand formed into a natural pyramid within the Hourglass, the most part being in the bottom chamber. She noticed too that there were still grains of sand waiting to fall, although these didn't move as they were locked in some kind of suspended animation. Dina shook the lantern gently. Nothing happened. She shook it again and tilted it on one side but nothing changed as the contents remained unmoved. This was very odd and although Dina knew it was possibly a foolish thing to do, she tipped the lantern upside down impetuously, yet still the sand dispersion remained unchanged.

Dina righted the Hourglass and was satisfied. It would seem that whichever way the lantern was turned the Hourglass within – and more importantly, the contents – would remain a law unto itself.

Or so she hoped.

From one of the many inside pockets in her jacket, Dina produced a nylon, postage-stamp-sized bag printed with flower motifs, which opened up to be more than ample to carry her cargo. The Hourglass fitted well into this small bag and now she had to get home with all due speed. She was sure she hadn't been followed and she thought wryly she'd challenge anyone to have made the journey she'd just endured and come out in one piece!

She retraced her steps down the roughly hewn steps and was pleasantly surprised to find that they spiralled around right down to the water's edge. It must have been low tide – a spring low tide – since the flat stepping-stone rocks were now clearly visible and proud of the water – a far cry from what they'd been when they'd begun their ascent. She alighted on the shoreline and, with no small measure of trepidation, braced herself for the arduous trek back the way she had come.

She turned to take one last look at Chapel Rock, standing alone like a single tooth in an old person's mouth, and noticed a patch of greenery – or maybe it was just a gorse bush – growing a little above the waterline.

I wonder… she thought and retraced her steps.

It wasn't there before. It cannot have been there before, or maybe she'd missed it in the storm. If it was what she thought it was, why hadn't she come this way? Or somewhere along the way, had she taken a wrong turn? Maybe when she fell…?

It didn't matter. To Dina, it was unmistakably a holloway and wherever it led it would surely deliver her from this place, so without more ado she pulled her jacket around herself, clasped the Hourglass closely to her chest and boldly stepped forwards. She gently slipped into what appeared to be a rabbit run and allowed thoughts of *Alice in Wonderland* to run unfettered through her mind as she shut her eyes and awaited what might be on the other side.

Dina emerged and looked around. She knew most – if not *all* – of the holloways in the area but this particular one was new to her. True, she didn't usually venture this far from home since she had no cause to, other than to pick sloes in the autumn, and she was therefore relieved to find it was quite lovely and very unlike the holloway that had delivered her to the Great Chasm.

Dappled light filtered through and lit her path. The way was clear of brambles and although quite small and narrow in places, it soon opened out into a tunnel-like path sunk below the level of the land. Slabs of sandstone, chalk and greensand lined the sides and had eroded in places to expose the varicose roots of ancient trees while naturally seeded hazel and ash paraded unabashed, creating a pretty canopy of shadowy green luminosity. A natural spring trickled to form puddles and when she splashed it on her face the water felt clear and pure. The blue indigo mud with which Lenken had anointed her clouded the water and left her hands, face and clothes streaked but she didn't care. She felt wonderful. Clean and refreshed.

21

The holloway disgorged Dina next to the main road, just near the bus stop. It was only ten minutes or so until the bus – a number 56 double-decker – came along. Fortunately, Dina always carried her bus pass in one of her numerous pockets and she was doubly pleased to find a five-pound note had fortuitously slipped inside it. The day was most certainly looking up.

Dina always regarded going on a bus as a bit of a novelty – a bit of a treat really – so she bounded up the stairs to the top deck and saw that the front seat was empty. In fact, the whole bus was empty apart from a single female passenger sitting a few rows back.

Just as Dina lurched past her, the bus had cause to brake violently as a young deer leapt into its path. Instinctively, the other passenger sprang to her feet to see if the animal was hurt, just as Dina went flying. Both women collided heavily and the nylon bag with its precious contents went scooting under the seats.

Being the younger and more agile of the two women – and also eager to help – the younger woman was quick to scrabble under the seats to retrieve the nylon bag but much to

Dina's horror the younger woman appeared to have become transfixed. The bag had fallen open and all the younger woman could do was stare at the Hourglass within. What was worse was that the Hourglass then emitted a beam of pure white light aimed directly at the younger woman's forehead.

How long this penetrative beam remained can only be conjecture. It could have been for a mere fraction of a second or, equally, it could have been for an entire lifetime. It could have been that time was suspended for a massive 3,141 years but whatever it was, Dina feared there would be consequences.

"I'll have that if you don't mind!" she squeaked trying to control the hysteria in her voice as she grabbed the nylon bag and did her best to conceal the contents. The bewildered younger woman took a deep intake of breath and stood up abruptly as she crashed back into the here and now.

Dina was quick to compose herself and helped the younger woman sit down. She was feeling decidedly awkward about the encounter and was sure the younger woman would be feeling likewise – both reeling from the shock for entirely different reasons – and what didn't help the situation was that they were now sharing the same double seat. Dina desperately wanted to remove herself from the situation, but it would seem rude and entirely unnecessary (and suspicious) since she found herself occupying the window seat and having only a few stops to go. She would just have to sit it out.

"I hope there is no damage done," ventured the younger woman in a charming French accent just as the bus lurched again. This caused both to grip the rail instinctively and, momentarily knocked off guard, each turned to gaze at the other. Their eyes met and a mutual curiosity sparked.

Dina didn't usually take to people. On the contrary, she did everything she could to avoid them, preferring, as she did, the company of birds, animals, plants and clocks, but she sensed something about this woman was different. For a start, had the Hourglass made a connection with her when it zapped her with that beam of light? Or was it just taking a look at her? She hadn't been zapped when the Hourglass was first uncovered so she decided upon the latter…

Well. That's what she hoped.

Although Dina did all she could to avoid further eye contact – she did all she could to avoid any further contact of any kind – she had been struck by the impression that the young woman sitting next to her was extremely beautiful.

There was something feline about her and it was probably because she was so feline – so cat-like in her manner – that Dina felt an affinity. Her eyes were the clearest blue and fathomless, her hair sleek and golden, and everything about her was manicured. She was so… graceful and even though she carried a rucksack and wore a tie-dye tee shirt with jeans that had more holes than substance, she radiated an aura of *haute couture*.

Dina's admiration for such presence must have been obvious since she then became aware of her own complete dishevelment and shifted uncomfortably in her seat. She stole a glance at the younger woman just as the younger woman did likewise, and realising a stalemate, both women picked up on the undisputed contrast and laughed.

"I see you have been busy doing country things," said the elegant young woman and she extended her hand. "Véronique, pleased to meet you."

"Yes," replied Dina, not giving her name. "I'm err… a botanist" is all she could think of. "It's very hands-on."

Véronique accepted this explanation.

"And what do you do?" asked Dina in an attempt to avoid disclosing any more information about herself.

"As little as possible." Véronique smiled. "I travel... I have, as you say, *itchy feet* and I look always for beautiful things. You have a beautiful object in your bag. May I see it?"

"Errr... no," said Dina with finality, clutching the bag to her chest. "It's nothing... it's... very muddy..."

"I do not mind that! I work at the *Université Paris Descartes* and the students bring me many strange things. Please, let me see it."

"No!" snapped Dina rather too sharply, then she quickly changed her tone. "No," she said more gently. "I have sentimental reasons... It would be too painful... my mother's ashes..."

"Oh... I am so sorry, I understand. My mother too – *je suis très triste.*" Véronique nodded and mercifully (for Dina) changed the subject to more general conversation. Dina feigned interest by nodding in all the right places while Véronique chatted on about her reason for being there and the backstory regarding her mother. She listened while é explained that although her recently deceased mother was English, she'd spent most of her life in France and she had come to England only to finalise her mother's *affaires*.

"I've not been on an English bus before," she confided. "I feel very much like a tourist, but my mother always said it is a beautiful coastal route, so I felt it was my duty to take this journey for her. Do you understand this?"

"I most certainly do. Your mother would have liked that and what a wonderful way to remember her by," said Dina kindly and lending her support further by pointing out various places of interest when all the time all she could really think about was the precious cargo now seemingly welded to her chest, invisible beneath her muddied clothing.

"This is my stop," announced Dina and she scrambled to her feet. "It's been so nice to meet you."

"*Mon plaisir aussi!*" Véronique smiled warmly as they shook hands. "Maybe we'll meet again?"

Dina muttered some inaudible platitudes, disembarked and, as the bus drove away, sighed a great sigh of relief. That had been so stressful! After a near-death experience, demons, a giant dog, bad omens, a near-drowning and shifting sands, then actually finding – and holding – the Hourglass, the last thing she needed was a casual conversation with a complete stranger.

Her nerves were jangled and she simply couldn't wait to get home. A double, if not a treble, sloe gin loomed largely and became very high on her list of immediate priorities.

Still reeling from the extraordinary effect the curious artefact had had on her, Véronique examined her forehead when she got back to her hotel and confirmed no visible evidence. She'd been aware of a strong beam of light but couldn't be sure it had been of any significance. It could've been just a shaft of brilliant sunlight reflected through the window and to think it was anything produced by that… that artefact… would simply be preposterous and yet…

She wondered instead if she might have bumped her head when she went skidding under the seats because there it was – in the centre of her forehead – a pain that didn't actually hurt. It was a pain she could better describe as a *weird sensation*. It was like a tingle and if she shook or turned her head suddenly, she glimpsed stars, only they weren't stars like when you bump your head, these were *real* stars. What Véronique would come to realise was that in those few moments, she had glimpsed the entire universe. She'd experienced a profound connection and she knew that although she understood none of it – yet – she'd stumbled upon her nemesis and it would change her life forever.

Fired by a burning curiosity, Véronique opened up her laptop and searched her files to see if she could find any reference to the symbols she'd caught sight of when the bag containing the lantern had rolled along the floor. Had it really emitted a beam of light or had she just imagined it? Now she thought about it, there had been another kind of light too – a most extraordinary luminosity – that had come from within and extinguished almost immediately the moment she'd grasped the bag but it was odd – very odd – because it had emitted a tangible energy, like a force field. It was a magnetism she'd picked up on but she didn't know what it meant. The arrangement of symbols troubled her too since they were like nothing she'd ever come across before.

Pondering, she slumped back in her chair and took stock of her room. The hotel was rather nice. It was elegant, probably Edwardian, with old-world charm and many original fittings. It was central to the town but higher up and overlooked the sea and had a magnificent view of the harbour below, and the coastline, to both the west and east, stretched in an arc as far as the eye could see. She decided not to go down for dinner and instead take something light in her room as her flight back to Paris was early the next morning.

She was perplexed about the symbols she'd seen emblazoned on that old lantern. Not knowing what they were or what they related to gnawed at her, and what was worse, nothing she'd ever seen had been even vaguely familiar. She thought too about the dishevelled lady on the bus and decided there was a lot more to her than met the eye. She had a knowledge about her – a wisdom – and those marks on her face and hands looked like newly healed wounds that were once quite serious, and those smaller ones…? Were they bites? Tiny incisions that were still festering and could have only come from something like a rat, but all that aside, why was she so secretive about some old lantern?

With these thoughts computing and cross-referencing in her mind, Véronique looked out along the coastline and wondered where such a person – such an eccentric – might live and what it might be like. The more she speculated, the more curious she became, and as it was in Véronique's nature to be inquisitive – and ostensibly she had nothing else to do – she spread out the map of the area that had been amongst her mother's things, and with a glass in one hand and a pen in the other, she circled a radius of ten minutes on foot from the bus stop where Dina had got off and began looking.

Half an hour later she picked up the phone and made a call. "*Je veux changer mon vol pour Paris…* I would like to change my return flight to Paris."

22

It was now several days since she'd returned from her ordeal and Dina could safely say she felt fully recovered. She had no idea how many days she'd actually been away, not that she gave much thought to conventional time. Everything was the same as when she left except, oddly, the clocks had all stopped at around midnight (or noon?).

Her first priority was to decide on where to put the Hourglass and she conceded that much as she would have liked to have placed it centre stage on the mantelpiece, that would be a very bad idea. Instead, she identified as suitable a large, sturdy, red-painted blanket box, apparently once used for pantomime props, which she'd acquired due to her fondness of the colour, and that would do nicely.

Dina was pleasantly surprised to find there were still some props in it. Aladdin's lamp, some pointy slippers and armfuls of silks and drapes, so she felt that hidden in there the Hourglass would be safe, incognito and very much at home. Her only concern was that it might catch fire but the light it had been emitting previously had since gone out and the lantern – the Hourglass – looked much like any other old piece of pantomime junk.

Before putting it away for safekeeping, Dina examined it. What fascinated her was that no matter which way the Hourglass was turned, the contents within the Hourglass – the tiny grains of sand – remained unmoved. It put her in mind of the Greek inventor Philo of Byzantium who'd invented the gimbal by coming up with the ingenious eight-sided inkpot. It had an opening on each side, which could be turned so that while any face was on top, a pen could be dipped and inked yet the ink would never run out through the holes on the other sides. This was done by the suspension of the inkwell at the centre, which was mounted on a series of concentric metal rings so that it – the full inkwell – remained stationary (and upright) no matter which way the pot was turned. Brilliant!

But Dina couldn't see any concentric rings. She couldn't see anything that could be deemed in the least bit mechanical, so she happily concluded the device – the caging – had to be nothing more than a work of pure magic.

She placed the lantern containing the Hourglass in the red box (making sure it was upright just in case) and closed the lid. She then found and placed a potted geranium on top of the red box and patted it for good measure.

It was early evening later that day when the strains of Scott McKenzie's classic song 'San Francisco' floated on the air…

It could only be Gideon. They hadn't actually seen each other since Canatu's entombment, when he'd looked so defeated. So lacklustre and broken. Now, as he rattled and skidded to a halt just a little too near her dilapidated conservatory, he was a very different man. He'd got his roguish smile back; there was an air – new confidence – and a determination about him. The music died abruptly when he turned off the ignition and he all but fell out of the truck. Without ceremony or waiting to be invited, he picked Dina up and swirled her around.

"Put me down!" she scolded. "Whatever next!"

Motto eagerly followed, taking his turn to sweep Dina off her feet. "You didn't expect to see me again so soon!" He laughed. "But you did it, didn't you – you brave clever girl – you got the Hourglass?"

"Put me down!" protested Dina laughing and squirming. "Yes, I did and I'm telling you it was no easy task!"

And then she caught sight of Raif watching from the truck with a bemused look on his face.

"And who's this?" she asked, knowing exactly who it was as she tidied her hair and straightened out her snagged cardigan.

"This is Raif, our new super-star."

Raif emerged grinning from ear to ear. It was obvious he'd been having the time of his life rallying through the countryside as his eyes were shining and his face flushed.

"Hello. Yes, I'm Raif – the new Foundling," he said enthusiastically if not a little shyly, giggling at Gideon who was making faces at him. "Watch him! He's crazy he is! We were going through this gate and he didn't even stop! He went straight through it! Honest!"

Everyone laughed. "And I'm Dina," said Dina putting her arm around the boy. "Come on, let's get you all inside."

The mood was jubilant. While Dina busied herself finding cups and plates, Motto took charge in the kitchen, making toast and finding jars of honey and anything that could contribute to their celebrations. They'd done it! Everything was in place for the Turning and all they were waiting for was for the Hourglass to tell them when. Gideon chopped firewood – because it was there – and Raif helped by loading logs into the basket. It was a quintessentially idyllic scene. Nothing could possibly go wrong.

23

Darke, meanwhile, was unaware of the developments that had taken place and had no knowledge of Dina and her encounter. He had yet to locate the boy Foundling, but it would only be a matter of time, and when he found the boy, he'd find the Hourglass. An elaborate search was in motion and all he had to do was wait but the waiting didn't come easily to him.

Feeling both troubled and impatient Darke paced the chamber within the main hub of his principal operation deep below the Arrid Sea located in an almost forgotten region of western Asia. It was ideal for his purpose and, if all went well, this prototype – arguably, his experiment – would be the first of many strategically placed operations around the world designed to do the same thing.

He'd chosen this location primarily for the rich source of the precious blue crystal on which he was so dependent and because it was suitably isolated and remote while being abundant in pure clean water. It was an inland sea which, before the controversial dam was built, was constantly fed by both snowmelt and precipitation from faraway mountains. Using this ready-made resource, he'd built an impressive processing plant beneath the desert and had systematically contributed to reducing the sea to two-thirds of its original volume.

This grand theft went largely unnoticed due to Darke's manipulations, which feigned a major water diversion project of which its backing and purpose were skilfully clouded by political shenanigans. As was Darke's intention, the ecologists blamed the dam for the alarming depletion of the water levels while carefully placed bribes kept all discussions non-conclusive and nicely circular.

The damage caused was irreversible. Climate change and drought didn't help the situation and as over a third of this sea, previously one of the four largest inland seas in the world, disappeared, the outcome was devastating. The receding levels left huge plains covered in salt and toxic chemicals which were picked up and carried by the wind as lethal toxic dust. People died or were left with cancers, lung disease, or disorders of the liver, kidneys and eyes. The high salt content of the dust melted the parent glaciers while there was not enough moisture in the air to replace them. Children died. Whole generations died. Crops were destroyed. The fishing industry was devastated, and huge ships lay scattered and land-locked, rusting and bleached in the interminable heat.

Huge natural aquifers stored the water deep underground while processing plants beneath the desert syphoned the water from the deepest part of the ever-depleting seabed. Sophisticated processing plants, funded by money being no object, performed their magic then expelled the toxic waste through outlets along what was once the pretty shoreline, and internationally, no government batted an eyelid.

The consequence of his actions provided an example. Tangible, real-time evidence of what would happen in a terrifyingly short space of time should water be strategically withheld. He would drain the rivers, empty the reservoirs, stem the tides and show the world the error of its ways. The fate of the world was already sealed by global warming and, with false modesty, he liked to think all he was doing was hastening it. That he would achieve Power Absolute and be released from the strangulation of Order only served to sweeten the nut.

Satisfied all was well, Darke faced the vast plate glass wall in the private inner sanctum of his operation and allowed himself a small thrill of accomplishment as he gazed into the clear, blue fathomless water beyond. It gave him great comfort to feel this weight of this water around him. The aquifers – of which there were many – were almost full to capacity and the time was now approaching to go to the next stage in his madness – his announcement to the world that the apocalypse was approaching and that he alone held the key to survival.

His polished shoes clicked on the marble floor as he crossed the room towards a recess which was little more than a corridor leading only to a smooth, alabaster white wall. Darke touched the wall with the flat of his left hand and, effortlessly, the wall slid sideways to reveal a chamber that was in total contrast to the clinical minimalism of the room he was exiting. This was a very different space. It reeked of evil. Hideous gargoyles festooned the walls in uncouth poses surrounded by talismans, forbidden teachings and artefacts. The rock out of which this chamber was hewn dripped a rust-like fluid akin to blood and fed the greedy mould and fungus that festered in abundance. Candles dimly lit this godless place, casting morbid shadows that enacted murderous and obscene scenarios, while the dank cold air evoked feelings of desperation and drowning.

On the dirt floor, drawn out in lime, was a five-pointed star; a pentacle with a single downwards-pointing spoke represented the carnal *ungodly* side to mankind. From a shrine cut into the rock face, Darke selected a single blue crystal roughly the size of a tennis ball and threw it into the centre of this symbol.

24

It had almost been too easy taking the Hourglass. It was never Véronique's intention to steal it, merely to borrow it, so she could have time to examine it properly. She'd contemplated simply asking if she could take it for examination at the Université Paris Descartes – just for a few days – but there was something about the dishevelled lady, the lady known to her only as *the botanist*, that told her hell would freeze over before she'd let it out of her grasp.

But she kept an open mind and decided she'd see what happened when and if she found the remote cottage where she was sure Dina lived.

Wearing walking boots and the proper attire for rambling (Véronique thought she ought to look the part just in case), she parked the small Renault she'd hired in a National Trust car park about a mile or so away and set off on foot. It was a beautiful morning, one of those mornings with a clear, blue sky that promised rain later. A dirt track with two deep furrows either side of a vivid ribbon of grasses and weeds led down into woodland and Véronique was relieved she'd left the car where she did. The wood was magical: tall silver birch swayed in unison with pine and the sunlight sparkled as it sought to find her. As she descended deeper, the light deserted her, and instead, the screech and complaint of now indigenous guinea fowl, peacocks and pheasants took precedent and this alarmed her. Would they alert Dina as to her presence? She continued but now more cautiously and came to a gate which had long since given up being any kind of barrier. Véronique slipped through it and the dirt track she'd been following petered out to become more of a rough pathway overgrown and overshadowed by lilac, dog roses and, on one side, an enormous fig tree.

A collection of dilapidated outbuildings in various stages of decay cluttered what may have once been a pretty courtyard. Tiles were missing – walls were missing! – and sheets of corrugated iron, burnt orange in colour and gossamer-thin in places, encouraged weeds to flourish. The house itself wasn't much better. It would seem the ancient thatch had simply got too heavy for the rafters and had sunk, much like a deflated soufflé. That, or it just got too tired of keeping up appearances. The windows were small and deeply recessed, due no doubt to the thickness of the walls, and none matched with the other in terms of size or degree in disrepair. The door leading off from the front porch was the only anomaly since it was made of oak and studded with large metal rivets meaning it would be impossible to break down but why would one bother? Looking at the dust and bric-a-brac congregated on the floor, it would seem that the door was left permanently open.

Véronique hid behind the slouching fig tree and waited. She was still in two minds as to whether she should boldly just ask to borrow the artefact for the purposes of examination, but no, she knew there was a lot more to all this and she *had* to find out what it was. Presently, Dina emerged from the cottage, carrying a large basket cradling a variety of forks and spades. She was wearing stout gloves and muddied boots so – fortunately for Véronique – it was fair to assume she was off to do a little gardening or, at least, some summer harvesting. The tops of tall runner beans were just visible to the left of the house, indicating a vegetable garden, and sure enough, Dina set off in that direction along an overgrown path and through a small gate with no latch. It made a loud rusted scraping noise when she opened and duly closed it behind her, and Véronique made a mental note of this.

She approached the house cautiously and knocked lightly just in case there might be someone else inside. There wasn't, although it was dark by way of contrast. It took a moment or two for Véronique's eyes to adjust to the darkness and all the time she felt she was being watched. She continued nevertheless – after all, she'd come this far – and just as her eyes were becoming accustomed to the gloom she all but jumped out of her skin as Mr Cuff sounded the alarm and Mr Bath of Cirencester quickly followed suit. Véronique froze as this great cacophony of sound thundered out. Surely Dina would come running? The silence that followed was almost as loud as the incessant striking, but no Dina appeared as Véronique held her nerve and ventured further in along the low beamed hallway which revealed a treasure trove of antiquity and artefacts. Her feet were soundless on the stone-flagged floor as she examined every surface, all of which were cluttered with things that had either eyes or history. The walls too were heavily occupied, hung with rescued taxidermy – the accidents in life unable to let go – from wild boar and roe deer to foxes and badgers. Thick velvet curtains gathered dust around birds flocked together on a well-worn Persian rug and piles of books, tottering nervously, defied the laws of gravity. Glass-fronted cabinets were crammed with even more treasures and a lumpy leather sofa, scorched on one corner, languished dangerously near the inglenook fireplace where logs the size of breeze blocks were still smouldering.

Véronique's heart sank. Where would she begin to look for the artefact she'd taken such risks to find? Not daring to touch anything for fear of betraying her presence, she surveyed the room critically. She noted the two longcase clocks that had caused her to jump out of her skin previously, and in an act of getting her own back, she stared at them defiantly. This was when she noticed that unlike most of the room, the clocks displayed no evidence of dust.

In this room with an open fire, everything was of course covered in a light film of dust but not so the clocks. It was as if Dina's ritual was not only to wind these clocks but to dust them too. She looked around for anything else that might be dust-free and came upon a large red box. The potted geranium which sat on top of it looked incongruous. It was remarkably fresh and colourful and Véronique deduced that nothing this fresh and as vibrant could survive for more than a day or two in such a dark and smoky atmosphere. With her pulse racing, she quickly and deftly removed the potted geranium and lifted the lid. There it was – the Hourglass – nestled in yards of tasselled silk.

25

As soon as Darke had entered the secret chamber and cast his offering of the blue crystal he felt calmed and soothed. This was a place – a private sanctuary – steeped in magic that was accessible only to him and where he could cast off his worldly shackles to indulge in a higher plane. Protected by the talismans festooned around him, Darke stepped into the five-pointed symbol scratched out in lime and began his transcendental journey. It was a journey he'd taken many times, and although it was risky, the rewards far outweighed any possible consequence since it enabled a myriad of astral destinations to fall within his grasp. In his intense meditative state, Darke could be released from his worldly shackles and travel freely to other planets and dimensions where he could gain knowledge and insight while revelling in the delights that an earthly existence denied him. Extreme gratification – both physical and cerebral – was more than enough reward for the risks taken.

"What is life without risk to sharpen the senses?" he maintained as he endeavoured to push the boundaries even further.

But Darke knew there was no risk – other than to that of his own sanity – seeing as he never left the confines of his refuge, only travelling these vast and fantastic distances in his head. Likening the experience to that of a spell – and it was a spell – to that of being the singular occupant in an opium den, did it matter what was deemed real and what was not?

However, this time something was different, but having embarked on his journey, he couldn't yet turn back. If he did, he'd risk disrupting the time ripples and could end up anywhere. This time… this time… it wasn't all happening in his mind. Things were happening around him that were both tangible and physical and there was nothing he could do about it. And, to his dismay, he too had changed. He'd gone from the suave impeccably dressed man he presented to the world to become a much smaller, hunched individual who, given different circumstances, could only be regarded as pitiful. This wizen, stooped figure carried an air of self-loathing as he found he'd been stripped of his finery with this replaced by the filthy, coarse grey issue of his prison clothing. The identity DM48775/02L indelibly machined into the thick canvas. Wildly, he looked around for someone to blame, someone to talk to – even someone to help him – then made a futile attempt to leave the symbol.

"I wouldn't do that if I were you," said a voice with no origin. Darke looked around frantically and then with horror realised that if he'd succeeded in leaving the five-pointed symbol, he would have been plunged into a bottomless space. An abyss with no sides or substance. Anti-matter, a black hole. It made no difference what it was called.

A High Order Demon was seated on his haunches at the far end of the most southerly point of the five-pointed symbol. Hideous, scaled and easily twice the size of Darke, he appeared unconcerned – relaxed even – and curling his serpent tail around and under, he rose up and walked around. Wherever he walked – and it was a menacing stroll – the ground beneath him moved to accommodate his direction. Wisely, Darke remained rooted to the spot.

"Who are you? What are you doing in this place?" challenged Darke.

Having proved his superiority, the demon moved towards Darke and resumed his squatting position. As he moved his grotesque head closer, Darke had no choice but to inhale his dank and putrid breath.

"I am Breaffen, High Order Demon of the Underworld," he breathed with a voice hollow and rasping. "And I am to believe you summon demons?"

Darke said nothing. Yes, he'd successfully summoned demons before and had been very much in control but this demon sitting before him was completely out of his league and he was at a loss as to what to do or say next. What had happened?

Breaffen answered for him. "No, you did *not* summon me – you have come into *my* domain, not the other way around – and it is me who has dominance here."

Darke attempted to speak but was silenced.

"You have no voice here – you are nothing – and you cannot cajole, threaten, promise, implore, beg, trick, scheme or entice. I know who you are, what you have done and what you desire. You trifle with demons, attracting only the weak or the stupid, although I must congratulate you on what you have achieved.

"Calling upon and stupefying a demon into assuming your persona while you made your escape was clever…"

Breaffen was referring to the ingenuity Darke had shown in escaping Carcerem, the prison planet. It had taken many months and failed attempts but in the end he'd triumphed.

"… and using his demon gate. How many planes and dimensions did you need to cross to reach here?"

As he spoke Breaffen moved to within inches of Darke's face and looked quizzically. With his great savage jaws, he could easily have bitten Darke's head off, but he didn't. He waited.

Darke didn't answer.

Breaffen released his stare and changed tack. "So, you've studied the *Alternate Prophecies*…"

Darke still didn't answer.

"You made a pact… to deliver the prophecies… why?"

Still no response.

It was a game of cat and mouse. Darke knew that this intruder had the upper hand, but until he knew more about how this formidable demon fitted into the jigsaw, there was nothing he could do. His best hope was to remain passive.

Darke hadn't expected it when Breaffen pounced and pinned him to the floor.

"*What is your purpose?*" he roared. "*Why did you enter this gateway?*"

Darke didn't speak, he couldn't, as Breaffen's horned hands were gripped tightly around his neck. His eyes bulged and his breathing became erratic

"Chaos…" was the only word he could manage.

Breaffen released his grip and stepped back, enabling Darke to regain some of his composure. This sudden assault had badly shocked him, making him aware of his own fragility and mortality. He could now so easily be dead, so why wasn't he? Darke felt a wave of anger build inside him. It was anger built on injustice since, surely, they should be on the same side.

Feeling more certain of his ground, Darke nodded an acknowledgement of his foe's dominance although the gesture was almost imperceivable. He didn't take kindly to this brand of condescendence – or assault – and longed to fight back. But he didn't.

This higher-ranking demon had come uninvited. Darke had entered the five-pointed symbol with the sole purpose of exploration and self-gratification, not to be humiliated and possibly annihilated by the abomination before him.

His previous experience with demons had been limited to those creatures from the spiritual realms of Abademean, eager for the mischief of discord, whom he could manipulate for his own purposes, but this apparition before him was quite a different matter.

Darke chose his words carefully and made a conscious decision to reveal his strategy. "I don't know who you are but am I to be honoured by your presence? Or afraid? Throw me into the abyss if that is your wish but I do not believe you have come here merely to dispose of me. Undoubtedly, your knowledge and power far exceed anything I have yet encountered but from what you have witnessed, you'll know that I am committed to the testaments of the *Alternate Prophecies*... I am here to fulfil the prophecies of Gyre – the second coming – and to put into play a new historical cycle of chaos. You'll know of the Collective, a powerful adversary, but know this too: their Foundling Canatu is dead and with that, the Turning, which is imminent, will fail."

"But what of the new Foundling?" enquired Breaffen.

It quickly became apparent to Darke that this powerful entity knew as much if not more than he did about the Collective and as a consequence about their role and the imminent turning of the Hourglass. Breaffen meanwhile appeared amused while he watched Darke fit the pieces into place.

"You don't know… do you?" He laughed. "You don't know that the Collective are aware of your escape. You only know that they have a new Foundling – a young boy that goes by the name of Raif – and you may already be too late!"

It was evident that Breaffen enjoyed seeing Darke visibly shocked. He could hear Darke's mind saying, *Is this a trick? A lie? And if so, a lie to what end?*

"So why are *you* here?" ventured Darke at last. "Why should you come?"

"Because you need me. Because, as it stands, your whole strategy is flawed. You're making assumptions and, worse than that, you're underestimating the cunning and intelligence of the Collective! And what of the new Foundling and the Hourglass? You had no idea that they're already assembling; I know this! I have eyes and ears in places you wouldn't think possible. It is as if I can walk amongst them!"

Breaffen didn't tell Darke that he had allies who could do his dirty work for him. It was enough for Darke to know he had a special insight which Darke did not.

"Without me, you will have already failed in your mission. You need me," said Breaffen enjoying his dominance as he played his trump card.

"The Hourglass is vulnerable, and I can tell you of its whereabouts. Take it by whatever means, and I will deliver the boy Foundling to you."

"And why… why would you do this?" asked Darke.

"Because we have a common objective and if we succeed, we will enter a new era with all the opportunities that would bring…"

Darke responded to the use of the word 'we'. "So, are you suggesting we collaborate?" he ventured.

26

The following morning, Raif was delighted to have the opportunity to examine Mr Cuff, who stood shoulder to shoulder with Mr Bath. To see one longcase clock was a joy in itself, but to see two standing together was a rarity and an opportunity not to be missed. He examined both clocks closely.

"May I?" he asked politely, and Dina nodded as he scanned the faces of both and opened the doors to each and peered inside. "Why is this one not ticking?" he asked of Mr Cuff. He could see it was fully wound and there was no apparent reason why his pendulum would give up after only one or two movements; why he chose to remain silent.

"I don't know but he can be rather moody," replied Dina. "Otherwise he's in fine fettle and very level-headed. I know, I used a spirit level."

"That's probably the problem," Raif smiled and noticed a small wooden wedge under one of the feet; he gently removed it. Mr Cuff seemed to sigh as if at last someone had understood his discomfort as he listed slightly to the left, away from Mr Bath. It was only a fraction, but it was enough. Confident that all would be well, Raif set his pendulum swinging.

Everyone watched as Mr Cuff ticked stoically for one minute until one minute turned into five.

"Maybe upright for Mr Cuff isn't the same upright as it is for us," ventured Raif, and all smiled at the profundity of Raif's simple statement; there were parallels to be drawn with the current fragility of the universe. But the spell was broken when the fire crackled into life and Raif turned the conversation to his own collection of clocks, choosing to bombard Dina with his little-known facts.

"Did you know that with the invention of the pendulum clock in 1656, Christiaan Huygens increased the best accuracy of clocks from fifteen minutes deviation a day to around fifteen seconds a day?" he said. "And did you know too that due to changes in local gravity, a pendulum clock that's accurate at sea level will lose nearly sixteen seconds per day if moved to an altitude of 4,000 feet or more?"

As always, Raif imparted clock data when he was happy or nervous and it would seem that right now he was experiencing both these confusing extremes of emotion. Dina took his hand and invited him to sit next to her. "You're obviously very knowledgeable about clocks – and time – and this may have had a bearing on you being chosen as the Foundling but listen to me... It's not just about time. And as you've just demonstrated, it's about balance and maintaining the right balance, because without it, we don't have order and within the framework of order we can have good triumphing over evil and right getting the better of wrong. Fair against unfair. Light opposing the darkness. All these things, the yin and yang which describe how seemingly opposite or contrary forces may actually be complementary, interconnected, and independent in the natural world, and how they may give rise to each other as they interrelate to one another..."

Raif listened intently to all that Dina was saying. So much so, it rather unnerved her, causing her words to trail off as Raif took over. "So, we must just be mindful that order has to take precedent over chaos otherwise chaos – which is a necessary and highly creative force – could not exist."

"Exactly!" Dina smiled. "Now, let's go and fetch the Hourglass."

27

It was with little ceremony that Dina led them all to the big red box. She removed the geranium placed on top of it, and even took care to reposition it on the window ledge on the southern side where it would get the most sunlight. Trembling with excitement, she lifted the lid and gently rummaged through the yards of silk to find the Hourglass wrapped within but found nothing. Puzzled at first because this didn't make sense, she went through the silks again but this time a little more frantically until the entire contents of the red box were scattered all over the floor.

"It's not here," she said in almost a whisper and fell to her knees as if a thunderbolt had hit her.

Everyone looked. Could she have been mistaken? Was there another red box? Was she sure? Had she had visitors? Had she been out? Anything suspicious?

Dina thought over her actions of the past few days. She'd hardly slept, and when she had done, it was next to the red box on her lumpy old sofa covered in a patchwork quilt, and even then, she slept with one eye open. No one had called, she hadn't been out, and she wasn't mistaken as to where she'd hidden it.

Apart from Lenken in the Great Chasm and the demons who'd had almost snatched life from her, she'd seen no one other than the bus driver, who'd hardly noticed her, and...

"Véronique!" she exclaimed, and the realisation was so intense, she reeled dizzily. "How could she?"

"Verra... who?" asked Gideon with concern as he helped her to a chair.

"Véronique. The elegant young lady on the bus."

Dina had to think quickly while she re-enacted the encounter. "She was just a passenger... the bus lurched... she helped... she was so pleasant?"

Dina's words stumbled to a halt as she flash-backed to being thrown forwards as the bus lurched, the Hourglass falling and Véronique possibly – possibly – getting a glimpse of the Hourglass before she could fully conceal it again. It was now so *obvious*. Why hadn't she realised the danger? But this woman – this Véronique – didn't know her... she wouldn't know where she lived?

"It wouldn't be difficult," said Gideon quietly when Dina had calmed down and they could think logically. "She knew where you'd got off the bus, you were on foot and, looking at you, you could only be living somewhere... err... rural. Put it this way, you wouldn't be hard for her to find."

"It's not your fault," said Raif kindly, putting his arm around her shoulders. "My dad told me that there's no such thing as coincidence, so maybe this was supposed to happen. You know, part of *the bigger picture*. He was always saying things about *the bigger picture* and I never really understood it until now."

Words of comfort indeed and from one so young. Dina recalled that the only time she'd left the house was to shoo away the peacocks and pick some beans.

"She must have been watching and came in then," said

Motto, deducing it was luck – or just bad luck – that she'd chosen to look inside the red box before Dina returned. But no matter, they had to deal with the situation they were faced with and needed to know all they could about the mysterious Véronique.

"She was very charming, extremely elegant and beautiful," recalled Dina. "Half French, I believe, and very open – in fact, I have to say she was lovely; intelligent, articulate and committed to her work, which she said involved a lot of travelling."

"Did she get to see the Hourglass?"

"I don't think so… it all happened so fast. But maybe…"

Dina thought about them both scrabbling under the seat then Véronique's persistent curiosity. "Yes, she did see it," she confessed quietly and realised how much in denial she'd been about the whole incident.

"I should have realised the danger and made the connection," she added glumly.

"Let's stick with what Raif said," said Gideon. "We've no time for recriminations. What else did she say?"

"That she had rooms at the Université Paris Descartes – she helped out there…"

"Meaning she's an academic, not a thief, so let's hope she's merely taken the Hourglass to examine it out of professional curiosity!" interrupted Gideon. "She didn't dare ask you because she knew you would've said no!"

"And she can't do any harm," added Motto. "No one can turn it – only you and Raif here – and besides, she'd never manage to open the casing… am I right?"

Dina thought about the intricate filigree casing that contained the Hourglass and nodded.

"So, what do we do?" continued Motto, looking to Gideon to see what he would say.

"We must get to Paris and to this Véronique by the fastest means possible!"

For a moment, Dina felt her spirits lift, only for them to be dashed again. "Surely, we don't have time?" she said in little more than a whisper. "Firstly, we have to get there and find this Véronique, then find the Hourglass and then settle on a place where the Turning can take place. It's impossible…"

"Yes," said Gideon, "it would be impossible under normal circumstances, but we don't operate under *normal circumstances,* do we?" And with that he put his finger up to his left eye. "Remember *ti evah seye eht?*" he said, and Dina managed a small laughed.

"Come on everyone… hurry. Into the truck!"

28

Safely back in her rooms at the Université Paris Descartes, Véronique clicked on her Daylight Omega 5 magnifying lamp and scrutinised the Hourglass. Seeing the mysterious symbols and hieroglyphics cut into the intricate latticework – but now greatly magnified – still offered nothing more towards helping her understand or translate. Neither did this scrutiny offer any clues as to how the outer casing might be opened. Like a treasure so near yet so far, the Hourglass remained untouchable within.

Just as Dina had been, she was intrigued that however much she turned and tilted it, the tiny grains of sand – the contents – remained unchanged and independent in its own glorious suspended animation. She tried, and tried again, until in sheer frustration, she shook the Hourglass violently and instantly regretted doing so.

"What am I doing?" she said out loud, amazed at her uncharacteristic lack of patience. She already felt bad about taking the Hourglass in the first place – even though she had every intention of returning it – but not being able to place it, date it or even find out anything more about it only added to her guilt and, ultimately, her frustration.

She was out of her depth and she knew it. Her arrogance and *bon chance* had got the better of her and as she looked around her rooms within the grounds of a little-known division of the Université Paris Descartes where she rubbed shoulders (sporadically) with archaeology and ancient artefacts, she felt an overwhelming despondency. The facilities at her disposal were basic, to say the least, but she knew – she just knew as she rubbed her forehead – something remarkable had happened, but still, she'd made no progress in deciphering anything significant that may have provided clues as to what the Hourglass was or where it came from. She remained none the wiser as to what it was made of or its purpose. It was an enigma – just an unidentified relic – and this bugged her. She couldn't consult her colleagues for fear of being found in possession of borrowed (stolen?) goods, and when she did come across something that could be even remotely useful, she unexplainably found it difficult to retain the information – even to write it down – yet alone find it again amongst her copious notes. It was almost as if this *object* didn't want anyone to know about it. As if it had a life of its own.

Her train of thought was interrupted by a knock on the door and this rather startled her because she rarely had visitors. Quickly, she hid the Hourglass in one of the many designer carrier bags she happened to have to hand and pushed it out of sight under the table. Fortunately, for the time being, it had ceased to glow.

"Come in," she called questionably, and a hooded young man entered. He was impeccably dressed in a simple, hooded, navy-coloured tunic and bowed politely. He didn't speak.

"*Comment puis-je vous aider?*" she asked in French. English was her native language but while in France she felt it appropriate to try and speak in the language of the country.

The hooded man didn't answer and instead reached inside his tunic pocket and presented her with a small laminated card with a message – printed in English – which said:

Hello,
    My name is Fouad. I am a deaf-mute meaning that I can neither hear nor speak. To communicate with me, please write your message down and I will respond likewise.
    Thank you.

Véronique acknowledged his crisp courtesy and accepted the small notepad and pen he offered to her. She thanked him and, using the pad, asked how she could help. With written pleasantries exchanged, Fouad turned to a page in his notebook where his note had already been written.

Mademoiselle Véronique,
    If you would care to, please accompany Fouad to where I have a limousine and driver waiting to take you to the restaurant 'Le Restaurant de la Mer' on Boulevard Diderot. I have a table for two reserved at 1300 hours. The maître d' will escort you to my table.
    Do not be alarmed. I have valuable information regarding the artefact you recently acquired in England and have a proposition to make.
    D.

For a moment, Véronique didn't quite know what to say to this stranger, so feeling flustered and profoundly guilty, she busied herself tidying things that didn't need tidying. Who was this person and how did he know about the artefact hidden under her table? She was at a loss as to what to say.

Fouad waited patiently and looked dutifully down at the floor. She read the note again. She knew of the restaurant on Boulevard Diderot although she'd never been there. It had three Michelin stars with a waiting list that went on forever, so it was impossibly out of her league. A limo waiting? She looked up at the clock on the wall; it had just gone twelve so there was just enough time to get there if they left now. How clever to give her no warning; how astute to know she acted on impulse.

"I'll get my coat." She gestured rather than writing it down.

29

To make enough room for them all in the front of the truck, Motto assumed the persona of a bumblebee and settled comfortably in Dina's beret. They set off (presumably) in the direction of Paris, which gave Raif cause for concern. "I haven't got a passport," he announced, terrified that this revelation might mean leaving him behind.

"Neither have we." Gideon grinned. "But the route we're taking wouldn't have much call for one. Don't worry, all will be revealed!"

They took the B358 (or was it 9?) and, in what seemed like only a matter of minutes, pulled into a perfectly square, gravelled car park. With the exception of the entrance and a narrow path leading out, it was completely surrounded by dense, almost tropical undergrowth.

Gideon steered the truck into the banking at the far corner and applied the handbrake. "We'll walk from here," he said.

They ascended the narrow path in single file until they came to a flat, much broader pathway. It too was cut into the undergrowth and had steep, almost perpendicular verdant sides out of which grew great clumps of fern such as hart's tongue, spleenwort and shield. At the far end was the entrance to a large cave, partly camouflaged by trailing flora, and as they approached they could see the way was barred by stout railings where, languidly, a cold mist escaped from out of the inky blackness within.

Gideon stood closest to the railings and kept his back to them as he muttered with whoever stood unseen within the cave until a clawed hand appeared out of a ragged dust-covered sleeve, released the chain and opened the gate.

Once inside, the first thing that hit them was the icy dampness. It was dark too – proper dark – with the way lit only by tiny candles. Raif watched his breath billow as they all kept closely behind Gideon as he led them deeper into the cave. Eventually, bar a few stumbles, they came to a more open area that was obscurely lit but light enough for them to see they were in a rough-hewn cave where the stone around them was either infinitely high or so low they had to stoop. From the plateau where they stood, they had multiple choices as to which way to go next.

"What do we do now?" asked Raif.

"We wait."

The chamber they were in was devoid of anything other than stone. "It's called freestone," volunteered Gideon while they waited. "It can be cut in any direction and while it's in here it's soft and malleable but turning as hard as granite once it's outside. All the great churches and cathedrals are made out of it... It's magical, you see..."

"The same stone that housed the Hourglass," said Dina as Raif ran his hand over it and felt that it did indeed feel soft and almost velvety to the touch. It was a lovely colour too. Almost creamy.

But then Raif noticed more of a chill in the air as a draught was created out of one of the tunnels; he couldn't tell which. This draught became a breeze which became a wind which started to rather frighten him.

"Keep your feet together, your arms by your side as we all hold hands and lean back," shouted Gideon, barely audible above the wind. "And Motto, hang on to your hat, or rather Dina's hat. See you all on the other side."

Because Gideon had made it feel like it was the most normal thing in the world to do, Raif didn't question or argue. He stood between Gideon and Dina and held their hands tightly. Keeping in step, they entered the enveloping blackness which was soft to the touch and slimy.

"I'm now going to treat you to the wondrous delights of *Localeactic travel*," said Gideon, letting go of Raif's hand for a moment. He touched his left eye and recited the same words he'd spoken to Dina earlier, "*Ti evah seye eht.*" He spoke these words three times while looking into the blackness with his other eye then took hold of Raif's hand again. "Let's go!" he added. "Now arms by your side and hold tight!"

Raif had no choice but to lean back. They started off slowly at first but then gained momentum to reach lightning speed, going faster and faster down and around invisible bends. It wasn't dark anymore, but it wasn't light either. It was sort of like flying down a translucent tube, which flashed and glowed like the Northern Lights. Raif thought he *should* be worried and a bit afraid, but he wasn't. It was the big dipper, the helter-skelter at midnight, and such good fun he almost wanted to shout 'Wheeee…!' as they rounded every bend.

The journey ended when they gradually levelled out and slowed to a halt as their feet lightly made contact with the ground as if they'd been hang-gliding. Raif became conscious of the air, which was musty and damp, signalling they were still somewhere underground. It was pitch black, but arrows of light pierced through a large circle just above their heads.

"We're here!" said Gideon, although he wasn't exactly sure where 'here' was and he studied the circle above him. "Raif, can you give me a hand?"

Gideon put Raif on his shoulders and asked him to push. The circle, which was some kind of manhole cover, moved easily and Raif had no problem in pushing it aside. What greeted Raif was not what he'd expected, and he didn't like it at all.

30

Sitting at his reserved table — the reservation being a permanent arrangement since he enjoyed a particular recessed table — Darke, with his immaculate tailoring and private manner, appeared outwardly much as any other successful businessman might. The only clue to him not being of this world was psoriasis evident on his hands and face although careful lighting did much to detract from this affliction. He was too rich for anyone to notice anyway.

Comfortable in his favourite restaurant, Le Restaurant de la Mer, tucked away just off the Boulevard Diderot and a stone's throw from the Seine, he came to this restaurant whenever he was in Paris. He sat at exactly the same table near the heavily curtained window, surrounded by the intimacy of old oak panelling and away from the eyes of those who might find him 'curious'. He'd made an arrangement with the management to have this table always available to him and paid a handsome price for the privilege — money being no object or obstacle to him. His menu varied little. A dozen native oysters and perhaps a little raw octopus and he always declined any vegetable content or garnish. Occasionally, he'd toy with steak tartare, but it was usually returned untouched. He didn't drink alcohol, preferring spring water, and he always insisted on a bowl of sea salt being present. His guests, on the other hand, were encouraged to drink and dine like gourmets.

Darke's phone trembled inaudibly indicating a message. He glanced at it and a trace of satisfaction shadowed his face fleetingly. Today – as planned – he'd be joined by a woman.

When his interview with Breaffen had concluded they'd more or less reached an agreement whereby they would collaborate. Breaffen had told Darke that the Hourglass was in the not altogether reliable hands of a woman called Véronique here in Paris – the woman who was about to walk through the restaurant door.

Véronique arrived and was ushered to his table. He didn't stand up but motioned for her to sit down. She hesitated, slightly taken aback by a presumed lack of manners, but she had a choice – either to go or stay.

She chose to stay.

"You have an item of merchandise which is of mutual interest," he stated as his opening gambit and pierced her with his cold, black eyes.

31

With a little help from Gideon, Dina hauled herself up into the passageway to join Raif. Gideon followed and carefully replaced the manhole cover.

"Shouldn't we mark it in case we have to go back?" said Raif, not liking the feeling of the place. He felt an alien, evil presence which greatly unnerved him and the distant rumble of trains and steady drip of black water did nothing to endear him to the scenario.

"That's not the way back, as you cannot undo what is done," said Gideon gently, aware of Raif's alarm. "But don't worry, we'll soon be out of here."

"Where's here?" asked Raif, hoping Gideon wouldn't detect the tremble in his voice.

Before Gideon could answer, Dina called. "Over here! There's a narrow staircase but be careful. The steps are very steep and not that sturdy. Hold on to the handrail."

Sadly for Raif, the wooden staircase only led downwards towards more absolute blackness, but Gideon rummaged around in his pocket and donned a head torch. This slightly erratic, singular beam of light cut through the blackness, much like a ray of hope, and Raif found that he felt less afraid.

In fact, they all felt the release of tension, and with renewed courage, they continued their descent, first following their own beam of light until, further along, their passage was lit by perpetual tar-fuelled torches, which better illuminated the way.

On reaching the bottom they found themselves in a large chamber.

"What was this place?" asked Raif again.

"We're in the catacombs below Paris," said Dina, unsure as to why they should be here. Surely they should be in the grounds of the Université?

Motto metamorphosed to his human form and, fascinated, studied the walls. "Look at this," he marvelled. "Look at the walls!"

Raif looked closely and was horrified. The hall and gloomy passageways that led off were made up of bones – human bones – thousands upon thousands of them. Reportedly, the remains of over six million people.

"They call this the '*Barrière d'Enfer*'," said Dina, pulling her coat around herself. "The Gates of Hell," she added in little more than a whisper.

For some reason, they must have encountered a glitch or some kind of psychic intervention as they now found themselves deep into an ossuary with no obvious way out. In these depths, one could feel the very fabric of the darkness as the heavy silence was broken only by the gurgling of a hidden aqueduct and the echoing sound of scurrying rats. Gideon held up his torch to read the inscription on a stone portal '*Arrête! C'est ici l'empire de la Mort!*' (Stop! This is the Empire of the Dead!').

Gideon gazed – they all gazed – and Raif held on tightly to Dina's hand, pulling himself closer to the security of her warmth. It was a depressing spectacle. In the flickering torchlight, the stacked and embedded skulls and femurs constituted endless walls. Hollow, empty eye sockets absorbed the light and in return cast their own watching shadows. Broken teeth and shattered jaws grinned as if darkly amused by their mutual plight, and as the light flickered, so the skulls performed their macabre dance.

"Do you *now* think we should turn back?" urged Raif, disturbed by what he saw.

Dina squeezed his hand and held it firmly. She rummaged in her pockets and found the remains of some extra-strong mints. "Here, share these with me and let's think only about what's happening in this very minute," she advised. "We'll be out of here and on our way in no time."

Dina wasn't altogether sure about having had a recent near-death experience with demons and she too felt the ominous presence of danger – and of death.

And then Raif heard something coming. He strained his eyes into the darkness but could see nothing. All he could hear was the sound of muffled feet marching and the steady creak and rattle of wheels turning.

"Quick! Back to the main chamber," instructed Gideon with some urgency as he herded them all in front of him. "Whatever it is, we mustn't let them see us!"

Raif shuddered as he pressed his back into the wall, conscious of the skulls surrounding him and being acutely aware that his was the only face that bore flesh. He felt panic rise inside his chest but knew he couldn't cry out.

Not knowing what else to do, he covered his eyes with his hands and imagined himself to be somewhere else as the tramp, tramp sound of the marching feet demanded he remained. Rooted to the spot.

He watched through the gaps between his fingers and was horrified to witness a mournful procession of grey, ragged people trudging past, hauling black cloth-covered wagons. It was the epitome of absolute misery.

"They're the Ossurmen," whispered Dina, moving closer to Raif. "The Lost Souls... plague victims mainly but also victims of murder and injustice. These pitiful creatures then becoming vulnerable to unearthly predators who literally ripped their souls out."

Bubbling over with questions he couldn't ask, Raif was forced to remain silent while the procession passed. The idea that your soul could be ripped out filled him with a new horror.

"Unearthly predators that condemn their victims to an existence in Perpetuity – another dimension you really don't want to go to," she continued. "They recognised the soul was pure energy and developed the ability to simply reach into the chest cavity and take it. You've heard the expression '*ripping your heart out*'?"

"Yes."

"Well, it's very much the same thing."

The very thought caused Raif to ashen and sink back even further into the wall so that he became just another one of the skulls that surrounded him, but he was aware, nevertheless, he was the only one that was flesh and blood.

Suddenly – and quite dreadfully – everyone disappeared and Raif found himself alone. The grey procession was thankfully now some distance away but a young girl, who was trailing some distance behind, stopped and looked at him. She was younger than him, about five years old, with large jade-green eyes that radiated sadness. She was grey – grey all over in grey rags – and it was as if she'd been dipped in a grey slurry, which had long since dried.

"Can you see me?" she asked and smiled, reaching out her hand.

Raif didn't know what to do. "Yes, I can," he replied levelly and, summoning all his courage, he reached out his own hand.

Her touch was icy and as a contact was made a charge went through him that he'd never forget as he saw images of death, deceit and abandonment.

"I am Canatu and your destiny is to rescue me." She smiled, appearing not in the least bit troubled by her current predicament. "I was cheated of my birthright and you – you who have taken my place – are charged with the task of redressing the balance or the future of mankind will pay dearly." And as each word was delivered, she began to fade to become dust but before she did so, she made one last request.

"I want you to solemnly promise, with your word, that you will do this for me. Do I have your promise?'

Raif nodded. "I solemnly promise," he repeated as Canatu was rendered to dust and once again, he was alone and rooted to the spot.

"There you are!" said Gideon crashing in on him. "You must stay close," he scolded and began guiding Raif back towards the others but Raif resisted.

"I saw her! I saw Canatu and she spoke to me! She really did! She said I have to save her We must save her... she's with the Grey People!"

And with that he slipped from Gideon's grasp and ran headlong back into the darkness, leaving only the sounds of scurrying rats and their own footsteps. The cold damp air clung like chilling despair when a shattering cry broke the silence.

Screeching like banshees and with a voodoo-like clattering of bones, tibia and fibula crashed and smashed, filling the air with a drumming, tuneless rhythm. Fleshless skeletal fingers reached down and plucked Raif out of the darkness, carrying him aloft by the shoulders of his red jumper.

He screamed and, amidst all the pandemonium, all he could do was to close his eyes to the horror as he was tossed and swung like *pass the parcel* from one pair of fleshless hands to another. Each swing carrying him further away down the endless corridor.

Gideon, followed frantically by Motto and Dina, ran after him jumping and clutching at the air, but try as they may, they just couldn't grasp him. They simply couldn't.

And then he was gone. Catastrophic. They stood there frozen in disbelief with their hands over their mouths and eyes wide open and staring. This cannot be!

And then they heard it. Like an approaching train coming towards them, a blood-curdling sound followed by a howl when from out of the darkness, Raif was dropped to the floor.

Out of the suffocating darkness, something or someone had forced the bones to release their prey and it occurred to none of them – because why would it – that this had been a first (failed) attempt by Breaffen to snatch the Foundling.

"Raif! Raif! Speak to me!" Dina was crouched over him, cradling him in her arms. He looked up, dazed and frightened as he re-orientated himself to his surroundings.

"I saw Canatu," he said. "I spoke to her then she turned to dust then they took me…"

"I have no answers for you… yet," said Dina softly. "But whatever, we must get out of this place."

32

WHEN VÉRONIQUE RETURNED TO HER ROOMS, SHE checked to make sure the artefact was still in the carrier bag where she'd left it. It was, and now she had a great deal to think about. First, she had to decide if she was more scared than exhilarated. That was a difficult one because what she *actually* felt was highly flattered and jolly pleased with herself, never mind also contemplating being unexpectedly extremely rich!

If she accepted Darke's proposal – and she knew there was no way she wouldn't because apart from anything else, thoughts of her jealous, manipulative mother were never far from her mind and what a comeuppance this would be, albeit posthumously. What a feather in her cap and it was just a shame that her mother wasn't still alive to seeth at her success. To envy her achievement! Privately, she had to admit that she hadn't been left with many choices, not if she wanted to continue living for a while longer, but she wasn't going to let that tarnish her current euphoria. She would have to accept his proposal and go along with it. The only thing that niggled her – that nibbled away at her conscience – was that she didn't really deserve to profit from all this. Technically speaking, she'd stolen the Hourglass not knowing either its purpose or its value. Sure, she'd only actually *borrowed* it but now here she was about to hand it over to this mysteriously rich, rather revolting stranger in exchange for a dream life. It was such a dilemma but no dilemma at all. She was already in too deep. Right up to her wilful pretty neck.

When she'd said she *worked* for the Université Paris Descartes that wasn't altogether true. More like she'd *come to an arrangement* with them. She rented the rooms she was now standing in as an exchange for helping out on occasion if there was an event or help needed. She'd been allocated the rooms mainly because no one else wanted them, apart from a visiting stray cat who called in on her from time to time. The apartment – such as it was – was a basement. It was archaic, but the cloistered atmosphere suited her and, more importantly, the rent was low and the thought of actually being able to pay her rent, and the arrears, made her smile. Now, with the eye-watering sums Darke had offered, she wouldn't have to worry, not that she ever had done.

It had all happened so fast. Véronique was still extremely shaken by the remarkable – and unexpected – interview and was still trying to process the enormity of his proposal. She'd always dreamed of uncovering something or somewhere rare and priceless and had pursued a sporadic (when not distracted) career in archaeology in the hope of (maybe) one day striking gold. It would seem – now – that she had.

Darke had been quite clear with both his proposal and instruction, and such was his manner and directness, Véronique had no cause to think he'd have any ulterior motives. He may have found her attractive, but he gave no inkling in that direction and even if he did – and she shuddered at the thought – she could take care of herself.

"*What should I do?*" she said, addressing the Hourglass which she'd placed on the table in front of her. At first, and as expected, the Hourglass was non-responsive, although the light within that hadn't glowed for some time sprang into life. Encouraged by this development, Véronique stared into the light and then – allowing herself to be guided as if transfixed – she turned her attention to the hand-painted box on the mantelpiece. The box containing her Tarot cards.

Feeling extremely excited by what the Hourglass was obviously... *obviously*... guiding her to do, she opened the box and took out the pristine Tarot cards which had only ever been touched by her. She shuffled them, cut them and turned the top card over. It was The Moon. It showed a full moon above a desert with two pointed mountains in the background indicating either a dried-up river bed or sea. Two wolves – one was black and the other white – howled at each other. To either side, there were the remains of a temple and in the middle, an oasis of blue sparkling water. A crab on the bank indicated the water to be of some considerable depth.

Crikey! thought Véronique and she looked at the ticket and the bundle of documents Darke had given her. The ticket granted her open passage on Darke's private jet and the destination was Uzbekistan. Encouraged by this, she dared to do a more complete reading.

Darke. Was he good or evil? She turned The Devil card and that spoke for itself because he must surely be the devil or at least in league with him. She knew it meant feeling trapped too and she certainly felt that. Could he be trusted to have told her the truth? She turned The Sun card which told her he would as he'd have no cause not to do so. She could give him the Hourglass, join him later and maybe find out why such a dull old relic meant so much to him.

She then thought, rather guiltily, about Dina. She was such a nice lady. Mad as a hatter no doubt but there was something about her. She turned over The Queen of Pentacles and was happy to have it confirmed that Dina was indeed a good and powerful force. She turned The Page of Wands where the page with his staff looked inwards across a blazing desert and this told her she must let Dina know where she was going.

33

Véronique was about to replace the Tarot cards into their box when the Hourglass, through no fault or contact with her, fell over. Instinctively, she reached out to save it crashing to the floor and, in doing so, dropped the Tarot cards which scattered randomly. Or did they? As she crouched down to gather them up, she noted six had landed face down and formed themselves into a neat row. Now the chances of this happening by accident were pretty remote, *and as there's no such thing as coincidence*, it meant that this phenomenon warranted further investigation.

Setting her mind to be as open as the sky, Véronique turned over the first card which revealed a man. The Hierophant. He was sitting between two pillars – the same as in The Moon card – reading a large, heavy book; his left hand was raised with two fingers together as if in benediction. He too was in a desert.

Véronique turned another card. She needed to know why this person was so important and if he was a force of good or evil. She turned The Magician and knew there and then that whoever this man was she'd have to find him as surely he was integral to the plot. Whatever that was.

And what of this adventure which was about to unfold? What would be the outcome? She turned over another card with this question in her mind and revealed The Judgement card. She turned over another and revealed The World...

She turned the fifth card. The Knight of Wands. This told her that things were going well. In fact, better than expected and that she was charged with energy and purpose. Finally, she turned the sixth card. The King of Wands. This card simply told her she had to take action which was exactly what she wanted to hear.

34

Empowered by this new wisdom, Véronique returned the cards to their box, but instead of replacing the box on the cluttered mantlepiece, she put it in her bag. Always a good idea to carry guidance, so much better than a map.

Almost wistfully, and certainly fondly, she looked around the rooms that had become her home. Soon she'd be speeding to the other side of the world to work in an environment where Darke had indicated money and facilities would be no object, whereas here – in stark contrast – this humble basement apartment hadn't changed much since its inception in and around the early 1900s.

With all the imaginings of a true romantic – Véronique often went off on flights of fancy – she said goodbye to the original *art nouveau* wallpaper, unmistakable in its symmetry. She ran her hands along the heavy shelves that lined the walls with all manner of bottles, books and alchemy. She listened (and laughed) at the noisy intestinal pipework that snaked the ceiling as it picked its way around a large unadorned light bulb too dim to work by.

Fondly she rearranged the unused alchemy, the ammeters and the ancient desk globe that she'd never bothered to throw out, leaving too the brass balance scales, the gaudy molecular models and the bizarre collection of anatomical instruments that sat alongside all manner of hourglasses, sandglasses, magnetic compasses and spirit levels. These dusty artefacts, so comfortable in their original environment, didn't seem to mind the intrusion of the present day and happily rubbed shoulders with the minimal technology Véronique had introduced. They didn't seem to mind the hangers hung with designer dresses. At least they were second hand. And the umpteen pairs of shoes that littered the floor only served to make the place feel lived in and then there were the books – so many books of every description – that dominated her space, her kitchenette, her bed and even her bath, such as it was…

'*I'm inviting you to be my personal assistant…*' Darke had actually said these words – more or less – when at last he'd got a word in edgeways.

"Huh… I don't believe a word of that!" she said to the feral cat who'd slipped in through the window to see if any food was in the offing. "If he wanted '*an assistant*', with his money he could afford ten of them… twenty! Top people too, not me… so why me?"

The cat merely yawned.

"And he could have just taken it," she continued, checking as she spoke to make sure the Hourglass was still under the table where she'd replaced it and was thankful it was. "I suppose if he'd stolen it, it would be fair to assume I'd call the police… even though I probably wouldn't seeing as I'd only *borrowed* it in the first place. But Dina would and I'd be in the doghouse and no one would think of chasing off to Kazakhstan or wherever it is he's gone to and… but that doesn't work, he probably owns the police anyway."

"Where's the catch? What's his angle?" She thought but didn't try too hard to find one. The cards had told her what to do and now she couldn't wait to get going. What she *didn't* know was if she'd turned over just one more card, she would have been given the answer. The cards would have come up with The Ace of Coins which would signify a gift, money and the answer to a prayer. Unbeknown to Véronique – but very much known to Darke – it was decreed in the *Alternate Prophecies* that the Hourglass could never be taken or stolen. It could only be bequeathed as a gift since to do otherwise would unleash one thousand years of woe on the perpetrator and Darke certainly wouldn't want that. It was fortunate too that Véronique (as the Hourglass knew only too well) had only borrowed it.

She decided – finally – she had no choice. For whatever reason Darke wanted her to be with him and he wanted the Hourglass. This was her big chance, and probably her only chance to be someone and she certainly wasn't going to pass it up.

"It's a can of worms," she said, laughing, to the feral cat, and both contemplated a can of worms from entirely different perspectives. "Did *curiosity kill the cat?*" she asked as she held the cat to her face. "Or did it embark her on an amazing adventure? What do you think, eh? Pussycat?"

She'd chosen the latter. But by way of hedging her bets, she decided she'd leave a note for Dina just in case she showed up. Just in case she'd made a gargantuan terrible mistake and needed someone like Dina to come to her rescue.

She began to throw things into – and then out of – a bag and thought as she did so. He obviously liked her. He liked her enthusiasm – her knowledge – of ancient writings and artefacts and she felt she'd made a good impression. He'd handed her the dossier and documents which were now on the table in front of her and matter-of-factly told her that he'd issued credit cards in her name – with no limit! – he'd put a substantial amount of money into her bank account and that when she was ready she should ring this number and board his jet to Uzbekistan where a car would be waiting...

But what of this mystery man the Hourglass had gone to so much trouble to identify? The Hierophant. Applying her knowledge – and she had to admit, with a giant leap of faith – she fired up her borrowed laptop and entered what details she had. She deduced this mystery man would be a man of learning and expert on ancient artefacts. He'd be some kind of mentor. A teacher or a spiritual or religious advisor. She also decided – and this was a wild card – he might be some kind of trader.

"How am I doing?" she asked the Hourglass and the Hourglass lit up. In fact, every time she went along what she thought was the right path, she imagined it rewarded her with a little glimmer of light. When she took what was obviously the wrong path, it duly remained glumly in darkness.

It took a while to whittle down all the references. There were so many of them but feeding what information she had into her laptop her SEO eventually gave her a shortlist of six. Six became four, four became two, and then, there he was. Mr Khan, a dealer in ancient artefacts and curio. His website proudly emblazoned his Furniture Emporium and the picture showed him proudly standing beneath his blue-domed ceiling.

What clinched it was when she enlarged his somewhat crude publicity, she spotted something in the left-hand corner.

"Ahh... What have we got here?" she said to the now absentee pussycat. "If I'm not mistaken, isn't that a rather faded poster of the Hierophant."

"Yorkshire," she read, taking down the address details. "I've never been to Yorkshire but as they say... there's a first time for everything."

One last thing bugged her. Armed with new information (although she argued it was only a lead) should she take the Hourglass to this Mr Khan and risk losing it, or should she stick to her original plan and hand it over to the mysterious and rather formidable Mr Darke? The cards had told her that was okay to do so but in her heart of hearts, she still had her doubts. The dilemma brought to mind the TV quiz programme her mother had always liked and had often quoted. *Take Your Pick* with Michael Miles. It was from the early sixties but it seemed as fresh today. The lucky (or unlucky) contestant was invited *to take the money or open the box...* The box could contain *tonight's star prize*, or equally, it could be a booby prize. Véronique frowned as she thought about her mother and could hear her hissing 'take the money... take the money, you stupid child!' Her heart whispered she shouldn't, but her mother shouted she should and Véronique – being a typical victim of conditioning – never dared to argue with her mother.

35

A SILENT, SLEEK BLACK LIMOUSINE CRUISED UP TO THE annexe of the Université Paris Descartes and delivered Darke precisely on time. Véronique was waiting at the far corner of the quadrant, sheltering under a large umbrella since it was now raining and, carrying the Hourglass in an innocuous-looking Dior carrier bag, she looked for all the world like a chic Parisian who'd merely been out shopping. Darke alighted, and without ceremony, she handed the carrier bag to him. He gave the contents a cursory glance, his face betraying no emotion as he acknowledged receipt by giving an almost unperceivable nod of approval. The boot of the car opened automatically, and he placed the Hourglass inside. When it closed, it didn't make a sound, not even a click.

The door on the left-hand side was opened by a uniformed deaf-mute and Darke disappeared inside, the darkened windows rendering it impossible to see him. The car didn't move and neither did Véronique until the window behind which Darke was seated silently scrolled a third of the way down. Darke didn't look at her. "I will see you in Uzbekistan," is all he said.

36

Having found their way out of the catacombs, which turned out to be surprisingly easy, something as unglamorous as a taxi delivered them to the Université Paris Descartes. It was deserted, the students, fortunately, being on summer recess, although the downside of this was that there was no one to ask where (and if) Véronique might reside.

"Surely there's a registrar or some kind of a caretaker?" said Motto and he was about to take flight to recce the grounds when a large, mottled cat rubbed itself affectionately against Dina's leg.

"Well hello, beautiful," purred Dina and the cat purred back. "Do you know by any chance where we might find Véronique?"

The cat hesitated for a moment. It wouldn't do to appear too compliant with a total stranger but as there was an obvious affinity – and as it was so pleasant to converse properly with a human *who understood* – he confirmed he'd be delighted and nonchalantly led the way.

He led them through the corridors and into the courtyard. He led them up three flights of steps and then down four, if not five. He took them through the gardens, through the cordons, through the orchard and across the quadrant, until finally, they arrived at a tall stone building on the perimeter of the grounds where there were some railings and steps leading down to a door. Dried leaves had collected into the corners of the vestibule and wild buddleia played host to bees. Motto emerged from Dina's beret and was instantly attracted to such a culinary display but resisted by taking refuge in his more human form.

The cat disappeared. Gideon knocked, and as if to welcome them, the door swung open. In her haste, Véronique had forgotten to lock it.

"I'll go first," said Dina. It was right she did so since it would be far better for Dina to confront Véronique alone rather than them all crowding in mob-handed.

Taking one cautious step at a time, Dina entered and listened to her footsteps on the flag-floored corridor worn and polished by generations of perhaps more legitimate traffic. She squeezed past the bicycle with its wicker basket and negotiated the bins, the bags and paraphernalia that always littered this type of temporary accommodation. She pushed open the inner door which was slightly ajar. Everything was as Véronique had left it – a light carelessly left on and a half-finished coffee leaving a ring-mark on the painted kitchen table. It was as if Véronique was still in the room. But she wasn't.

"We're too late," said Dina dolefully when the others joined her. There were discarded clothes everywhere and it was apparent that a bag had been packed – and then re-packed – several times but the biggest shock was the large mirror which leaned precariously against the wall on the mantelpiece. It carried the single word *'SORRY!!'* hastily scribbled in pink lipstick.

"Is she saying that to you?" ventured Raif, accepting, like the rest of them, that her absence was likely to be permanent.

"I think it must be," said Dina. "Who else!"

Hoping to find some kind of clue as to where Véronique might have gone to, Dina sifted through the jumble of maps and documents littered across the table. Véronique would have known she'd come after her — that she, Dina, would eventually be standing here — so was this *evidence* left for her on purpose or was Véronique just careless?

Dina smiled. No, Véronique wasn't careless, this was intentional. Punctuated by question and exclamation marks, arrows and circles, the documents strewn across the table looked random, but on closer inspection, they were in fact quite systematic. Everything pointed to the little-known Arrid Sea located somewhere within the desert wastes of Asia.

"So, what now?" asked Motto.

"We accept the worst," replied Gideon. "She's gone, she's taken the Hourglass and we have no choice but to assume that Darke has either taken her or she went willingly. I have to say it would appear she went willingly… they don't usually give you time to pack a bag."

Dina's heart sank. This was all her fault but now — now of all times — wasn't the moment for recriminations or to give up. "You and Raif will have to go after her," she said, calmly mustering all the courage she could find. "There has to be a reason for all this, but for the life of me, I don't yet know what that is. We must keep positive. Why has this happened?"

There was no point in depressing herself further, so gathering up the few bits of information that may prove useful, she took a last look around the room then followed the others out into the sunshine. It had been raining and now the sunshine presented them with a refreshed and more optimistic world.

The quadrant was deserted which was just as well since their party of four presented a strange mix of characters.

Gideon dressed as ready for the great outdoors, Dina in her coats of many colours (and a beret) and Motto who in his black and yellow striped regalia looked more suited to a pantomime. Only Raif carried any semblance of normality in his jeans and red pullover.

Raif left them to talk and to decide what to do while he wandered over to the wall of some ruined building and listened to the skylarks. The mist following the rain had cleared completely, leaving a clear, azure blue sky, so shielding his eyes from the sun, he watched the birds dip, swoop and cavort as if they didn't have a care in the world. The warm sun, the clean air and the tranquillity had filled him with such calmness it was quite intoxicating. As boys do, he thrust his hands into his pockets and, on doing so, found the paper plane Spiritas had made for him from what seemed like a lifetime away. He examined it. It was a bit crumpled but surprisingly easy to flatten out so taking his lead from the skylarks that soared above him he launched it into the sky.

"What have you got there?" asked Gideon coming over, curious to see what Raif was playing with.

Raif explained how Spiritas had made it for him and had charged him to keep it with him at all times. "He said I'd be going on a journey and you never know… thou never knowest… when it could come… cometh… in useful. Or words to that effect."

Gideon grinned. In fact, he did more than that. He roared with laughter and shook his head. Raif watched dumbstruck at such unexpected behaviour. "Well done, Spiritas!" said Gideon, laughing, when eventually he could get his words out.

Intrigued, all three of them watched as Gideon placed the small paper plane on a flat piece of ground, being careful to brush away any bits of stone or gravel that might impede its passage.

"Now listen carefully," he said. "You remember what I told you about time, space and size all being relative?"

"Yes...?" said Raif slowly, already feeling worried about where this conversation might be leading.

"So, if you want this plane here to be big enough to take the two of us all the way to the Arrid Sea, we have to place it far enough away then walk towards it. Remember the tortoise in the desert? Yep, it's much the same thing but you have to make the mental switch. You have to concentrate. You have to believe."

Raif believed. He believed anything these days.

Having positioned the plane, Raif and Gideon then lay on the grass a fair distance away. They looked at the paper plane, which was now some way off, and yes... Strip away the preconceptions and the paper plane *was* as big – or as small – as any real plane on a runway.

"Hold that thought," continued Gideon, "then run with me towards it!"

They ran as fast as they could, keeping their eyes fixed on the plane, which got bigger as they approached. And more real.

By the time they reached it, the small, crumpled paper plane had become a very real two-seater bi-plane. They clambered into the cockpit, put on the helmets, which were there on the seats, and were ready to go.

"I believe... I believe... I believe...!" shouted Raif at the top of his voice as Gideon turned on the ignition.

Motto spun the propeller and within minutes the engine roared into life. "There's no room for all of us but make your way to Uzbekistan by whatever means!" shouted Gideon over the noise of the engine. "We'll meet you there. Don't worry – I'll find you or you'll find us! It's all part of a Grand Plan. I just know it! Keep the faith!" And with his remaining words being carried off by the wind, they careered down the makeshift runway and became airborne.

Soon they were high above the clouds and although Raif could hardly believe it – but he seriously kept on believing it in case he found they were up there at 5,000 feet and climbing sitting on nothing more than a scrap of paper! – he marvelled at the experience. He was amused that the fuselage still had the music score and graffiti – possibly in Italian – scribbled across it. For a nearly-ten-year-old boy, this was an adventure of a lifetime and Raif decided that he wasn't going to waste or miss a moment of it. He was afraid, of course he was afraid – he was terrified – but he had the failsafe of his clocks to block his fears.

"Did you know that a clock is defined as simply a device that tells the time. The term 'clock' comes from the Dutch word 'glock' and that Thomas Nash – an American – was the first clockmaker. There are all types of clocks which include an analogue clock, digital clock, sundial, sandglass – that's like the Hourglass – and that sundials were used to tell the time before the invention of mechanical clocks. The earliest use of sundials dates back to 1,500 BCE and an institution in Colorado created a clock that is used for internet time and it's so accurate it will not lose or gain a second in even twenty million years…"

Raif chatted on, having to shout over the loud noise of the engine, but for Raif, it didn't matter, it kept him focused. He accepted that Gideon probably caught only one word in ten. But that didn't matter either.

37

Darke landed at his private airstrip deep in the desert and his jet was then camouflaged beneath a huge hangar. He took the lift to his private quarters, carrying the precious Hourglass, and felt pleased with the outcome of the past few days. The most terrible experience with Breaffen had turned out well insofar as they were now in collaboration. Breaffen had been correct about the whereabouts of the Hourglass, which would soon be safely incarcerated within an impenetrable vault beneath millions of tons of stockpiled water. Véronique would – or would not – join him shortly but he was unconcerned either way since she'd already served her purpose. He rather hoped she would since she was both feisty and attractive, providing him with – whether she liked it or not – *entertainment*. He could always dispose of her later in this vast desert waste.

Everything was set. There could be no way the Foundling and the Hourglass could become united and the time of the Turning would soon pass.

Breaffen would deliver the boy Foundling to him. He would take care of the boy – in effect keep the boy alive – and in doing so, no replacement Foundling could come to the fore. With great satisfaction, it was what Darke liked to think of as a *win-win* situation.

38

When Raif and Gideon disappeared in their small plane up into the clouds, Dina experienced a profound sense of loss. It was an emptiness – an absence – she hoped she'd never have to feel again, but she took a deep breath and brushed such feelings aside. She had to.

"Will they be alright?" she asked. It was a silly thing to ask but Motto understood.

"It was a perfect take-off," he confirmed but already Dina's thoughts were directed towards more immediate matters. Namely, what to do next.

"I think we should contact Pythia," she said. It was the last thing she wanted to do but having recovered the Hourglass from its resting place – at no small risk to herself – and now this happening, she felt that due to the urgency, it was their only course of action.

"I think you're right. You wait here… I won't be long…" And with that Motto quickly morphed into his bumblebee state and disappeared into the undergrowth. He didn't even pause to sample the buddleia.

Rather than waiting around not knowing how long Motto might be finding Pythia, or even if she would be willing (or able) to volunteer any divine intervention, Dina thought she'd use the time to take another look around Véronique's rooms. She could have missed something and, besides, a cup of Earl Grey would go down very well. She remembered seeing an opened packet somewhere although there was no way she'd risk the milk and besides, she didn't take milk in Earl Grey anyway.

Not surprisingly, nothing had changed since she'd last been there other than her own attitude. Now the rooms seemed less hostile and had taken on a familiarity that she found almost endearing. She even caught herself spontaneously tidying up as if it were her daughter who'd left the rooms so untidy, but hastily, she checked herself. Such feelings belonged to another lifetime.

I could do with Motto here, she thought, steering herself away from maternal thoughts. Motto had exceptional eyesight having five eyes, three of which were normal plus two large compound eyes containing around 6,900 facets – meaning he could zoom in on anything that took his interest. Dina, on the other hand, had only her ancient eyes to rely on, which were further impaired by her vanity in refusing to wear glasses.

However, she had good instincts and from beneath the maps, charts and other regalia soon rooted out a blue Post-it with the hand-scribbled words '*An aquifer is an underground layer of water-bearing permeable rock, rock fractu…*'

"Why would she be interested in geology?" she wondered out loud.

The Post-it referenced photocopied notes explaining what an aquifer was. Nothing very exciting, just references to permeable rock, fractures and unconsolidated material, but what *was* interesting was that it made reference to a unique clutch of aquifers beneath the somewhat depleted Arrid Sea.

Thoughts of water prompted her to put the kettle on, then, having settled down to a cup of weak Earl Grey, she tried to make sense of the hurried scribbles that ranged from bits of shopping lists, remembered song titles, mundane 'things to do' lists and disjointed information referring to aquifers, with the ones located beneath the Arrid Sea taking precedence. Books – no doubt 'borrowed' from the library – were also flung open, illustrating aquifers located off North Africa, Oman, Libya, Israel and Wales, with even larger freshwater aquifers under the continental shelves of Australia, China, North America and South Africa. In fact, it would appear that there were aquifers everywhere.

"So, is this what Darke's up to?" she mused as pieces of the puzzle began to form a ridiculous picture. "Does he think... does he actually believe... he can have control over the key commodity we cannot do without? Fresh drinking water." Astounded, she all but laughed at the incredulous scale of his (obvious to her) psychosis.

The mottled cat whom Dina had met earlier strolled in. Being miffed at seeing no milk on offer, he registered his contempt by jumping up onto the table, where he commenced grooming, paying no heed to either modesty or inhibition. Annoyingly for the cat, Dina failed to register this anarchy and continued her investigations but if she'd been asked if she was glad of the company... she most certainly was. While she continued her investigations, she began to get a better picture of what Véronique was actually like. Obviously, she couldn't be all that bad because the cat liked her and various clues – like postcards, childish mementoes, flowers (sadly now faded and drooping) and several well-thumbed cookery books – told Dina that Véronique was actually quite a caring home-loving person. But there was something missing. There was something about Véronique that Dina couldn't put her finger on.

The cat used this moment of Dina's reflection to leap onto the mantelpiece, which despite being so cluttered, still afforded a safe landing spot. Instantly, Dina thought of Raif and Gideon and her heart wrenched, and these feelings of anguish weren't made any lighter when she again read the word 'SORRY!!' in pink lipstick. It still carried its poignancy, now if not more so.

Panther-like, the cat strolled along the mantelpiece, unconcerned as bills and papers fluttered to the floor, and remained unconcerned when a heart-shaped motif – also inscribed on the mirror in pink lipstick – became revealed by the disturbance.

Dina thought it was odd and she also thought it was odd that not only was the drawn heart pierced by an arrow, there were several other arrows too, all pointing in the same (downwards) direction. She poked amongst the cluttered papers and found, hidden, but clearly not that well-hidden because it was propped up, an envelope with her name on it. She opened it and read the hastily scribbled content out loud.

Dear Dina,

    If you're reading this – FANTASTIC!! It means you've found me! I knew you would!!

    Sorry I borrowed your hourglass (isn't it just amazing!) but I WILL get it back for you. I sort of let this man called Darke have it (it's a long story) and he's gone off to Uzbekistan(?) and I'm going after him. C'est la vie as they say!

    Love Véronique

    xx

    PS please feed Hercules (food in cupboard) the Bursar knows I'm away

Dina replaced the letter inside the envelope and put it in her pocket. She had mixed emotions ranging from acute anger to fear for Véronique's safety.

"What do you think, Hercules?" she asked, stroking him gently. Hercules didn't respond. He merely yawned.

"Ahh… there you are!" announced Motto, making her jump as he burst into the room in his human form. "I've seen Pythia and in view of what's happening, she's calling an Extraordinary General Meeting… Hello? Who's this?"

"Hercules. He's on our side." And she showed Motto the letter from Véronique.

"Hmmm…" said Motto.

Dina accepted it would take him a little time to become convinced that Véronique wasn't all bad but there would be time for all that later. Pointedly, Hercules rubbed up against Motto's striped legs and displayed far more affection towards him than he'd done towards her. However, Dina understood. She didn't need further convincing about the good nature of Véronique whereas Motto still needed working on.

"It's a cat thing…" she said to Motto, who clearly didn't know what she was on about.

Having left ample food open for Hercules, Dina and Motto emerged into the sunlight. The quadrant was still deserted and now there was a tangible stillness to the air. It was an incredible stillness that you could touch as if the air had turned into a clear viscous jelly, and as Motto waved his arm slowly through it, it shimmered and rippled.

It was just as well Dina had chosen to hang back because the ground began to erupt and rumble causing her to back away even further. Hercules was wisely nowhere to be seen. The transparent jelly-mass that surrounded Motto put Dina in mind of frog spawn in the way it moved and responded as he appeared to be orchestrating the animation. She deduced he must have encountered this vehicle before since he seemed to obviously be enjoying himself. Before long, the viscous air became settled then filled with a powerful low-register vibration, and as it did so, random stonework took shape until towering in front of them, stood a tall, impressive building.

First impressions put Dina in mind of a scaled-down version of Santa Maria del Fiore – a lovely cathedral she'd visited in Florence a lifetime ago – and although much smaller, it was nonetheless still awe-inspiring. It too had a dome, a tower and two huge bronze doors.

When the ground stopped shaking it felt like this fabulous imposing structure had been standing there for centuries. It was a beautiful building. The neo-gothic façade – like the Santa Maria del Fiore – was dressed in white, green and red marble and the two bronze doors depicted scenes of mythical encounters, both of which were familiar to her. An eight-pointed star joined the two doors and each emanation depicted an aspect of wealth: victory, patience, health, knowledge, nourishment, prosperity, mobility and monetary wealth. Above the door was a highly embellished plaque, also in bronze, where two overlapping squares made an octagram and clearly visualised the four elements of air, water, earth and fire.

The dome had eight radiating buttresses and was crowned with a large copper ball while the bell tower at the opposite end, being equally magnificent in its own right, was sturdy, square and much smaller by way of contrast. It felt separate as if it had been added on as an afterthought.

They entered through a small side door into the hallowed main chamber, which felt cool and silent as the light, filtering through the stained-glass windows, cast a palette of colour on the pale stone floor.

"Come, we have to report to a M Touraine," said Motto, leading the way. Curious as to who this M Touraine might be, Dina was keen to find out but was distracted when she reached the foot of a most peculiar staircase that rose large and twisting in front of her. They began their ascent only to realise they were actually descending. Or was it ascending? Around and around the cubist stairway they went, as if getting somewhere but, in this strange reality, getting nowhere. Dina found this fascinating and felt it was as if they'd entered the bizarre world of MC Escher, the master of such illusions.

"... *'The element of mystery to which you want to draw attention should be surrounded and veiled by a quite obvious readily recognisable commonness'*..." quoted Dina as she climbed, using the words spoken by the great man himself, and she decided this staircase certainly had a *recognisable commonness* and was not at all what it seemed.

"Ah... there you are!" M Touraine called, interrupting her thoughts as he appeared from out of the corner of this mathematical playfulness. He seemed genuinely pleased to see them and smiled broadly as he noted their fascination with the staircase

"It is geometric sorcery, *n'est-ce pas?*" he confided as if reading their thoughts. "It keeps the bad guys out..."

Motto took an instant liking to him whereas Dina was more cautious. There was an air about him that conjured authority and wisdom and a familiarity, although Dina couldn't place it. He had a strong, handsome presence and a quiet, commanding manner with an intelligence that would far exceed any expectations of Mensa.

"Let me introduce myself," said M Touraine in a soft voice with just a hint of an accent Dina didn't recognise. "My name is Monsieur Touraine – Michel – and I am the Grand Chancellor of the Collective. I am here to be of service to you but first a Special Assembly has been called. Please... follow me."

He led them back to the foot of the staircase, which had temporarily ceased to be a work of *geometric sorcery* and allowed them to ascend a single floor which led to the chancel.

39

Dina and Motto followed M Touraine through the large arched doorway that led to the centre aisle. Dina gasped when she looked up since the huge dome was bathed in an iridescent light, which apparently had no source. Natural pigments in egg tempera, gold and platinum leaf depicted a myriad of planets, stars and moons around a dazzling stylised central sun motif. Everything was moving – waxing and waning, shining and dying. Motto was evidently pleased to see that arcing shooting stars were included too, dancing around the meteorites which soundlessly crashed and burned. Had there not been more pressing matters to attend to, Dina could have stayed and watched with Motto for hours – spellbound.

Allowing them to linger just a little while longer, M Touraine took the opportunity to explain what was happening. "There will be eight representatives in total. Representatives have come from throughout the known universe, and most particularly, those from planets who'd also be adversely affected should we fail in our responsibilities, although it's likely that the entire gallery will be full to lend their support."

Leaving the fabulous dome behind, they entered the main gallery and, just as M Touraine had predicted, the tiered pews around the perimeter of the chancel were all full and indeed, it was standing room only for many of the attendees. After acknowledging those few who were known to him, he led them to a small antechamber where they were greeted by an official who, by the length of his beard and the depth of his wrinkles, put Dina in mind of an extremely ancient tortoise, but of course, she didn't share this observation. He and M Touraine were obviously old friends since a lot of handshaking and exchanges took place as absent-minded pockets were searched and the key found to unlock the cabinet predominant in the room.

Inside were hanging two garments, one for each of them, which were exactly the same as the one M Touraine was wearing over his suit, namely a floor-length buttoned tunic in a delicate shade of sky blue, a white surplice and, for around the neck, a small gold medallion on a long chain fashioned to replicate the sun, much the same as the sun motif in the dome.

M Touraine led them back into the main chamber and the hum of conversation hushed to silence. In the middle of the room, etched in gold, was an eight-pointed star. The Seal of the Prophets; the Star of Redemption and Regeneration.

High-backed chairs had been positioned at each of the eight points of the star and were occupied respectively by eight Collective dignitaries, similarly attired. Motto recognised one of them – Henry Mullet, the walrus from the Rune Inn – but no acknowledgements were exchanged. Dina and Motto were invited to enter the centre of the symbol, which was a four-pointed version of the larger one.

Pythia – the Deity, the High Priestess and Supreme CEO of the Collective within the (known) Universe – was waiting for them in the four-cornered diamond contained within the eight-pointed star. She smiled warmly and kissed each of them lightly on both cheeks and ushered each to take a corner then, on doing likewise herself, she turned and addressed the assembled.

"We have called this Extraordinary Special Assembly because the Hourglass is in great danger. If the Turning is sabotaged or unduly delayed it will evoke the writings from the *Alternate Prophecies*, setting in motion the foundations for a possible Armageddon… We therefore welcome into the circle Dina our esteemed Keeper and Motto without whom we could not do without…"

Murmurs travelled like a Mexican wave around the auditorium. The news had been broadcast that the Hourglass had been taken and the jury was still out as to how. And why? Foot-stamping – as if impatient for answers – followed and Pythia waited until the silence was restored before continuing.

"Hear this. Forces against which Dina had no recourse were already in play when the Hourglass was taken. Regrettably, they succeeded, but we now know and have word that our adversary is established in the little-known wastes of what was the Arrid Sea in Eastern Asia. At his hand, the waters of this sea have continued to recede, rendering the shores of this once great inland sea barren and poisonous… This fate could become our fate. Darke is behind it… And if the *Alternate Prophecies* are brought into play, then we believe that water – the lifeblood of our very existence – will be instrumental in being used as a weapon against us. The Finder and the boy Foundling are already on their way to the Arrid Sea with the intention of retrieving the Hourglass and completing the Turning, but we must be ready so we can be on hand to support them…"

Again, Pythia had to wait until more foot-stamping abated, and when it did, she turned to speak to Dina directly. "We have our own scriptures and our own history and for the past 3,141 years, generation upon generation has carried the story of the Hourglass. You, Dina – the Keeper of the Hourglass – have shown tremendous courage in risking your life to keep the Hourglass safe. You were right in challenging unknown circumstances. You were right not to expose the Foundling to the hidden perils of the Great Chasm. You were right to be guided by your own intuition. It was our founding prophet Aristotle who said, '*you will never do anything in this life without courage...*' and you, Dina... have shown such courage. You all but succeeded and even though the path may be difficult, we know the Hourglass is guiding us. All things are happening for a reason..."

"*All things happen for a reason...*" muttered the Assembly in response.

A mummer of approval rippled around the room which Pythia allowed to abate before continuing. At which point she turned away from Dina in favour of Motto who stepped forwards and took the floor.

"The boy Raif – the new Foundling, the Foundling who has replaced our sister Canatu – has visions," he announced loudly, and the Assembly hushed to hear him.

"Raif – the Foundling – has described in great detail the distortion of natural phenomena should the Hourglass fail to be turned. He has described fire, great winds and tempests resulting in towering waterspouts forming and multiplying, rising up through the atmosphere to shatter and disperse as if dust. Symbolic maybe, but link this to Darke having chosen to claim the waters of the Arrid Sea... it's right we should be alarmed. These things are set down in the *Alternate Prophecies* – the scriptures this boy had never seen let alone heard of – yet on seeing the book for the first time he could recite chapter and verse? He has seen the downfall. He has seen the devastation – the consequences – should chaos take precedence. I believe the *coincidence* of the Hourglass being snatched from us was nothing of the sort. On the contrary, I believe it is all part of some *grand design* instigated by the Hourglass itself with a view to bringing forth this boy as our new Messiah!"

Motto's outburst was greeted with thunderous applause as M Touraine ushered both Motto and Dina out of the circle.

40

Darke stepped back into the sterile minimalism of his fabricated world relieved that his unwelcome encounter with Breaffen was over. He'd emerged from the hellish gateway still feeling slightly shaken, although this soon dissipated when he glimpsed his ghostly reflection in the plate glass that contained his colossal watery abyss. Restored to his former immaculate self, he allowed an image of Breaffen to float before him while he recounted the last words he'd spoken to this new player. '*Because I'm the only way you can get to the Collective and consequently, the Hourglass…*'

So… what if an unholy alliance with Breaffen was formed? What benefit could it be to him? He had the Hourglass locked away in an impenetrable vault and Breaffen, for motives that were not yet altogether clear to him, had said he'd deliver the Foundling.

All he could do now was wait. Wait until the time of the Turning passed. The catastrophe would begin to unfold and there'd be nothing in its path to stop it.

Véronique loved to travel, so using one of the shiny new credit cards Darke had issued to her, it was no hardship to board a plane at Charles de Gaulle Airport and to land at Manchester Airport just a few hours later. She thought about Dina and hoped that by now she'd found her note, although needless to say, her thoughts weren't so much about guilt as about survival.

The hire car she'd booked in advance was waiting for her and it amused her that it was of the same type and colour as the car she'd hired when she went in pursuit of Dina – a small red Renault. She had no firm idea if she'd be going back to Paris before she set off to Uzbekistan, or if she'd fly directly from Manchester and, because money was no problem – thank you, Mr Darke – she'd see what the outcome with Mr Khan brought. How delicious to be free and with a credit card! Firstly though… some serious shopping! And Véronique certainly *knew* how to shop.

With her appetite for extravagance sated, driving across the moors to Strawberry Bridge was wonderful by way of contrast. She loved the vastness of the sky and the sheer emptiness of it all. Clumps of rough grass and reeds congregated on either side of the road while coal-dipped sheep watched in oblivion as she sped past the peat-brown reservoirs. There were no hedges or trees. Instead, there were the fallen remains of millstone grit, long since tired of standing, having endured for too long the depressing dampness of it all. She was unaware of the peat bogs which held secrets in their depths and unaware too that the weather could change in the blink of an eye. Which it did.

With her windscreen wipers on full blast, the cloudburst was swept from one side to the other as she drew up outside Mr Khan's Furniture Emporium. It was a formidable building and the word *grim* came involuntarily to mind. It was very much as she'd expected it to be – a tall, drab Victorian building that was probably once a wool or cotton mill. Like many of the other equally sullen buildings around it, the façade was etched black by years of industry while the roll-shutter door, fitted inside the far nicer original door and now propped open by a brick, told another completely different story. Inside it was true to its word. It was a real emporium, filled with junk, bric-a-brac and genuine antiquities randomly piled one onto another in true socialist ethic. She looked up and all but gasped at the mural occupying the ceiling. The wonderful rhapsody in blue shone and glinted as it caught the light, the mosaics and shards of glass refracting and changing as the sun periodically dipped in and out of the clouds.

"It is magnificent, yes?" said Mr Khan floating in psychedelic silks as he materialised through the brightly coloured stripes of a fly curtain separating his private space from the shop. "I find it is a great talking point...you know, it made the local press."

"Really," replied Véronique with all due enthusiasm.

"Free advertising." He grinned conspiratorially and tapped his nose. "It is of my own design inspired by the great Michelangelo." And he beamed as he awaited her compliment.

Véronique smiled politely. She didn't much take to his cheery disposition, finding it vaguely childish if not a little patronising. However, she needed to keep on the right side of him and therefore played the game.

"It is very beautiful," she confirmed. "And you have a wonderful treasure trove here," she added in her most coquettish French accent although suddenly feeling uncomfortable as she became acutely aware of the sightless taxidermy watching her suspiciously.

Mr Khan too became aware of this change, sensing she was no ordinary shopper or tourist. "Why have you come here?" he asked quietly.

This directness rather took Véronique aback and left her

feeling a little flustered. This wasn't helped by a large cloud crossing the sky completely changing the ambience of the room. Before, it was light and sunny. Now it felt threatening.

"I'm err… I'm looking for a clock – a timepiece…"

Mr Khan listened respectfully. "Do you see one in here?" he asked, well aware she was lying.

Véronique couldn't. She couldn't see *any* clocks apart from the huge longcase clock at the back of the room. Mr Khan followed her gaze.

"I'm sorry, it is not for sale."

"No… no… I was just admiring it. I'm actually looking for something smaller… something more specific…"

She turned to look at Mr Khan, who in turn held her gaze. What she was about to say was a gamble, but Véronique's whole life had been a gamble. "Look…" she conceded, "I don't want a clock but what I really need is for you – Mr Khan – to tell me all you can about the Hourglass. You see, I sort of borrowed it and rather foolishly, I let this man have it. I thought it was just some… artefact… but I'm finding out there's a lot more to it than that."

Mr Khan calculated what she'd just said. "One moment, please." He crossed the room and closed the main front door quietly.

Whoever it was he'd consulted, or wherever it was he'd gone to, Mr Khan returned in a matter of minutes. This rather perplexed Véronique because she distinctly remembered that the large grandfather clock in the corner had just struck one when he'd disappeared through the plastic stripes and now – as he reappeared – it was ten to three. But no matter since Mr Khan seemed almost jovial on his return and gestured to Véronique to sit down.

"What would you like to know?"

Later – and greatly empowered by what Mr Khan had imparted to her regarding the status, the history and the significance of the Hourglass – Véronique was reeling at the enormity of what she had stumbled across when, supposedly by chance (haha!), she'd boarded the very same bus as Dina.

Having taken a moment to absorb what she could about what Mr Khan had told her, she then asked about the boy. "You said the Foundling… Raif… has been called. Did he live here? Was he close by?"

"Of course. As a Shaman of the highest standing, I was enrolled to keep an eye on him and to provide the gateway, when the time came…"

He looked across at the huge longcase clock meaningfully. "He loves clocks, you see, and was very happy to climb inside that one!"

"He's not…?"

"No. He's long gone now but I would advise you to go and see his family. When you eventually meet up with him – as you no doubt will – it will be reassuring for him to know that you've spoken with his mother and therefore can be trusted."

Mr Khan then got to his feet and walked towards his colourful curtain. "One moment, please…"

It was again several minutes before he reappeared again. Véronique waited and again felt strangely *watched* as if she was being vetted in some way. She couldn't see any CCTV cameras, but it seemed nevertheless that there were eyes everywhere – as indeed there were. A pair of giant cockerels peered out from the recesses of a corner. Snakes, suspended in time, watched motionless, as if poised to strike. Ravens, crows and jackdaws congregated murderously, their sharp black eyes darting as if looking mindfully for death. Austere portraits of dignitaries, now long gone, stared down at her disapprovingly and it seemed that everything around her reminded her of Dina's house.

"I'd like you to have this," said Mr Khan on his return and he handed Véronique a small wooden bobbin similar to that as would've been passed through the looms when the cotton industry was at its peak. It was very slim and no more than four inches long in a purpose-made case. A small, hand-blown hourglass had been inserted into the central body of the bobbin and this contained fine blue crystals which flowed easily, like water, from one chamber to the other.

"It will have its purpose," was all he would tell her about it.

Having been given the address and clear directions to Raif's house, Véronique shook his hand warmly and left Mr Khan's Furniture Emporium as a far more enlightened person than the person who had entered. When she got outside, it had stopped raining.

41

Raif's house was a three-bedroom semi in a cul-de-sac. As it had started raining again – no, not raining, now it was pouring down – Véronique would have liked to have parked right outside but there were no spaces, meaning she had to park a fair distance away. As a consequence, when she arrived at the small front garden neatly planted with regimented roses, she was soaked through to the skin. Forlornly, she empathised with the crimson begonias dripping in the dark clay soil and felt a million miles away from the two ever-smiling plaster gnomes guarding a redundant sundial. She was here because Mr Khan had advised her to do so but what on earth would she say when whoever it turned out to be opened the door?

No acceptable answers came to her, so she rang the doorbell and heard a two-toned chime resound in the hallway as she awaited whatever presented itself to her next. "Hello?" enquired the lady who answered, peering around the door.

Véronique noted that the lady had a kind, soft face. She'd obviously come from the kitchen as there was a fine dusting of flour on hands she was still drying on her apron. She was only small, the other side of fifty, and if it was cake she'd been making, then she really shouldn't eat any more of it.

Véronique smiled her most winning smile. "Hello, I'm sorry to trouble you but I'm here about a boy called Raif – Raif Braithwaite. I believe this is his address. Are you by chance his mother?"

"That's right," smiled Raif's mum. "And you are?"

Véronique didn't answer straight away as she didn't want to talk out there in the road, so she leaned forwards and whispered loudly, "Look, I've just come from Mr Khan's Furniture Emporium – he said I should…" but she didn't get to finish.

"Oh, why didn't you say so?" scolded Raif's mum kindly and she ushered her inside, waving purposely to spying neighbours who may, or may not, have been watching. "Just look at you! You're wet through! Quick… come on, let's get you out of those wet things. You'll catch your death…"

These words. These few kind words cut through the thick layers of emotional armour that protected Véronique's fragile heart and rendered her helpless. Caught unawares, she had no time to summon her reserves or make a contingency plan. The sharp pain – a pain like no other – caused tears to well in her eyes.

"I wish I'd had a mother like you," she whispered as if making a confession, thankful that her sudden tears were quickly lost amongst the raindrops. Why had she never heard her own mother utter such simple words of kindness?

Pretending not to notice, Raif's mum squeezed her hand. "I'll call Raif down for you."

"But he's not here!" blurted out Véronique. "Mr Khan said he'd gone to do the Turning… He said he went via the clock…"

And as she spoke, she realised how bizarre she sounded. She also wondered if she should have imparted this information. Maybe – most probably – Raif's mum didn't know and would now be frantic – beside herself with worry – and would demand his return. She'd call the police! It was all her fault – again!

"Oh, I know all about that," Raif's mum said in her soft Yorkshire accent with no hint of alarm. She smiled. "But am I right in thinking you'd still like to meet him? Have a bit of a chat sort of thing?"

"Well... yes..." stammered Véronique, "but surely that's not possible?"

Raif's mum – who turned out to be called Vera – just smiled and called up the stairs. "Raif, love, there's a lady here to see you."

Raif ambled down the stairs, half leaning, half sliding on the bannister. "Hello," he said with an open face and grinned widely as he childishly proceeded to cross his eyes. Véronique was dumbstruck. Had Mr Khan got it wrong or... or had she misunderstood?

Raif stood there grinning while Véronique continued to stare open-mouthed...

"Have you come to take me away, ha-ha," he sang in mockery, "or to be bored by a boringly large collection of clocks?"

If this boy was Raif, and she had no reason to believe he wasn't, her assumption was further confirmed by the age-related photographs of him snaking up the stairs. But, if he was Raif, then he wasn't what she'd been expecting. True, he was the right age, but the boy Mr Khan had described was quiet, polite, studious and completely obsessed by clocks of every description.

"Actually, I hate clocks," interjected the boy impatiently. "Horrible noisy things with their incessant ticking, *tick... tick... tick... tick...* It's enough to drive anyone mad, and then they're always telling you off: '*You're late for this, you're late for that. You don't have time. Haven't you finished yet! What time d'you call this? What a waste of time! Sorry! You're timed out!* Shall I go on?"

"Ohhh... now stop that right now!" interrupted Vera and she wagged her finger at him before turning to address Véronique directly.

"This lad here isn't Our Raif. He's a... what d'you call it? A doppelgänger, that's it and he's only here as a decoy until Our Raif gets back..." She paused at this point and beckoned Véronique nearer as if to share a confidence. "It stops the neighbours talking. They'd only ask questions if they didn't see him but he's quite harmless... look... you can put your hand right through him." And to prove her point, she did just that.

"I'm sorry but I'm confused," said Véronique feeling rather faint having never encountered a doppelgänger before and certainly not in a place where it was considered perfectly normal. "Would you mind if I sat down?"

"Of course not, love... but first, you go on up and see our Raif's clocks. He'd want you to see them seeing as you've come all this way and I'll make you a nice pot of tea. Be nice to the young lady," she added sharply, speaking directly to the doppelgänger.

When Vera appeared again, carrying a tea tray heaped with home-made cakes, Véronique and the doppelgänger were getting on much better. Véronique had been fascinated by what he'd explained to her about other dimensions, namely a brief A–Z on parallel universes.

"Everything alright?" asked Vera.

"Fine," replied Véronique and she accepted the tea graciously as Vera settled herself on the edge of the bed next to her.

"Now then, love. Is there anything else you'd like to know?"

Where to begin... thought Véronique but she knew that even if she sat there for an entire lifetime, she'd never take it all in – least of all understand it – so she decided to say nothing. It was enough to know (and all she could cope with) that the excitable doppelgänger was nothing more than a blob of plasma – a non-biologically related look-alike paranormal phenomenon – and that he'd arrived here by travelling Tesseractically, which was how very clever entities passed between dimensions with references made to filo pastry(?). Raif – or should she refer to him as *Our Raif* – would be back shortly once the Hourglass had been turned (and the world saved from a chaotic future etc... etc...), meaning that the hyperactive doppelgänger could then go back to his own time and place. Talk about keeping up appearances!

"I need to get going," she said getting to her feet. "I have to go to Uzbekistan or somewhere like that to give Darke a piece of my mind and get the Hourglass back although not necessarily in that order... I fear I've made a terrible and catastrophic mistake."

"Well, I'm sure you'll sort it all out, and do take care. Right always wins over wrong, you know, because if it didn't, we'd all be sitting around making sandcastles," soothed Vera. "... Tell Our Raif you popped in and send him our love. Come and see us again when you're next passing."

Véronique once again felt a pang of emotion – why did she only feel this when people were *nice* to her? – but she controlled it and instead threw her arms around Vera's unsuspecting shoulders. "Thank you, thank you for everything..." And Vera had no idea what she meant.

42

M Touraine drove them back into Paris in his sleek black Jaguar. It effortlessly purred through the traffic as Dina dozed, secure in the comfort of the soft, enveloping seats. Motto, on the other hand, remained wide awake and eager to talk. It was such a relief to know what was actually happening – and that the Collective knew too.

"They'll be well on their way by now," he said referring to Gideon and Raif somewhere up in the clouds. "In fact, they're probably already there, knowing Gideon and his galactic shortcuts!"

M Touraine smiled. "Sometimes it's useful being able to step in and out of other dimensions but the tricky bit is knowing where and how to step back. All things being relative that is."

"Sure… but come on, Gideon's made crossovers more than once," responded Motto good-naturedly, although he did wonder why, at their latest departure, they'd ended up in the catacombs and he made a mental note to quiz Gideon about this the next time they were all together. "Will the temple now be a permanent fixture?" he asked, hoping to one day go back and spend time studying the fabulous domed ceiling.

"No," replied M Touraine as he indicated to turn left. "It was only a pop-up."

A small light turned from red to green signalling them permission to glide into the underground car park of the La Petite Chambre hotel. The hotel was small, but given its name, that was to be expected. Leaving the car in its allocated space they took the lift, and when they emerged in the foyer, they were greeted by the patron who was a thin, accommodating man carrying an inherent sense of servitude. Nodding and wringing his hands nervously, he appeared to be very much in awe of M Touraine whom he obviously knew.

"Would it be one, two or three rooms?" he enquired discreetly. "And how many nights might that be?"

"Three rooms just for tonight," confirmed M Touraine.

What Dina and Motto didn't know was that each of them could have had any number of rooms because this was no ordinary hotel since it expanded – or contracted – according to need. From the outside, the narrow façade housed a singular heavy black door with a neon sign above that permanently flickered *pas de vacances* (no vacancies) and it was squashed between two much grander buildings as if someone had decided to fill in the alleyway betwixt as an afterthought.

It was only a one-star hotel, but as M Touraine was pleased to point out, it was an eight-pointed star, which – like others in this franchise – signified it was exclusive to the Collective. He pointed out too, a small symbol like a badge which was a square within a circle, carrying a logo Dina obviously and instantly recognised.

The residents were an eclectic mix of members, friends or associates of the Collective originating from either this planet or other corners of the known universe. Such was the privacy – the exclusiveness – there was no need to keep up appearances and Dina soon became accustomed to the mélange of strange creatures going about their business or pleasures.

In keeping with the eccentricity of the clientele, the décor within the hotel was a riot of contrast and colour. Originally a whim of the eighteenth century, it had enjoyed the abandonment of the twenties, the freedom of the sixties until being brought to order by the onset of the not-so-naughty nineties. Nothing matched, everything clashed, and if it wasn't clashing it was fighting for the right to be there. In short, it broke all the rules and Dina loved it but much as she could have spent all day wandering the corridors and discovering what further delights and temptations lay behind the beckoning doors, she knew there was work to be done.

It turned out (fortuitously) that the patron – Claude, to those with whom he wanted to be on first-name terms – was a mine of information. This could have been due to having too much time on his hands and a vast library at his disposal. Or he was just incredibly brainy. Having decided it was both the former and the latter (the entire hotel was spotless) and knowing he'd been vetted by M Touraine, who'd confirmed his A1 clearance, Dina was confident she could trust him implicitly and was right to do so. He appeared delighted, if not extremely flattered, to be involved and listened patiently as she explained how and why they'd ended up at his wonderful hotel. Having told him about her encounter on the bus with Véronique she was eager to talk to him – talk to someone other than Gideon or Motto – about what was bothering her.

"On the bus, she seemed so pleasant. Open and friendly and such a sweet disposition. I got the same feeling when we visited her rooms and to have left a note for me was both kind and thoughtful."

"So, what is it that's bothering you?" asked Claude with enquiring eyes magnified through heavy brown framed glasses the colour of which exactly matched the colour of his moustache. She noted that his suit too was brown – brown suit, brown shirt and brown shoes. Only his psychedelic tie betrayed a possibly more bohemian side to his nature, and she found that endearing. It was useful that he spoke fluent English.

She showed him the letter Véronique had written and, out of an involuntary childhood habit, Claude flattened down his already flattened oiled hair as he read it. When he'd finished, he returned the letter and awaited her question.

"Why would she fall foul of the temptations proffered by Darke?" she asked. "I could understand if she'd been given no choice, if Darke had just taken the Hourglass, seeing as he knew of its whereabouts, or maybe killed her or threatened to kill her, but I get the distinct impression there was a *frisson* between them."

Claude said nothing as he appeared to inwardly digest what Dina had said. He was a scholar of many subjects, one of which being that of human behaviour and the principal reason he'd been elected by the Collective to manage La Petite Chambre Hotel.

Choosing his words slowly, Claude was careful with his answer. Dina was a woman of enormous wisdom and experience. She trusted her instincts and, by and large, she was invariably right. She saw there was goodness in Véronique even though everything seemed stacked against her, so… why the anomaly?

"I think Véronique is the consequence of an unhappy childhood," said Claude eventually. "A domineering mother probably… with her own issues."

Dina recalled her conversation with Véronique on the top deck of the bus and how – even then, after explaining her mother had died recently – Véronique had felt compelled to do her mother's bidding as if needing her approval.

"I think Véronique felt empowered by being offered such status as it would be a real poke in the eye for the mother. Also, she's young and pretty, so whose head *wouldn't* be turned? Just like the lovely *Marilyn*, she just wanted to be loved, and who better than by a rich and powerful father figure. I notice there's no mention of the father."

Dina was rather taken aback. She wasn't expecting this in-depth psychoanalysis, but it all seemed to make sense. "Thank you. I'll bear what you've said in mind," she said and really felt quite jubilant at the thought that, after all, Véronique maybe wasn't as bad as she'd been made out to be.

Not only was Claude good with people, he was good at organising and making travel arrangements, and he had arranged their flight from Charles de Gaulle Airport to Tashkent, Uzbekistan, scheduled for departure early the next morning. From there they'd be taking a small chartered flight to Moynaq, a hitherto unheard-of airport, which had required the pulling of several strings. The debate was whether or not Motto should go too, and if he did, should he travel as a bona fide passenger or as a bumblebee secreted in Dina's beret?

"I think it's a no-brainer that I should go," said Motto hotly. "Dina – as an eccentric lady of advancing years – will be more than capable of wrapping anyone she chooses around her little finger and with me incognito as a harmless bumblebee I can be on hand (within beret) to offer agility, invisibility, ingenuity and incredible eyesight. As I have said many times before, I can spy for her, I can eavesdrop. I can go places she can't go. I can disable anything mechanical or electrical. I can decoy and distract. Oh… and by way of a special dispensation… no one kills bumblebees and only a few are privy to the fact that I carry enough venom to immobilise an entire army!"

Dina had heard this litany on more than one occasion, but the words still rang true, and as neither Claude nor Dina could find fault with his reasoning, the arrangements were confirmed, and Dina was left free to devour the library and/or whatever else took her fancy.

43

Raif really liked being up above the clouds. He hadn't had the time or opportunity to see or think about the type of plane they might be in other than from when he'd watched it being childishly fashioned by Spiritas. Who would ever have thought they'd be flying in it! He knew that wasn't the case and that a real plane had been laid on for them – Gideon had said an Avro 621, whatever that meant – but he liked the idea of Spiritas and his illusions better. At least Spiritas and Gideon had been thinking along the same lines.

Gideon sat at the controls in front of him and the noise of the engines made it difficult to talk but Raif was glad of the opportunity to sit back and take stock. To him, the immensity of the sky and the quality of the light was so blue and so intense it took on an almost surreal quality. Everything achieved a startling focus unlike where he came from – Yorkshire – where the light was grey and defused; soft and rain soaked.

But soon they became enveloped in cloud and this changed the mood directing Raif's thoughts to his experience in the catacombs and his strange – and very frightening – encounter with the Grey People and his anguish at meeting

Canatu. Why hadn't they saved her? *Didn't they know she was there?* He recalled her words, 'I am Canatu and you must promise to rescue me', and he made a silent vow – there and then up in the clouds – he would do just that as soon as the Hourglass had been turned.

He thought about Darke too. He thought about Canatu as a happy, bonny five-year-old and Darke muscling in with his dubious motives, taking advantage of such easy pickings. Her vulnerability and poor Anakee… doing her best. He felt anger well inside him. It was deep-seated anger that enraged him and it was an emotion he'd never experienced before. Despite only being nine years old himself, this was a rage that belonged to someone far older and it empowered him. If he'd been a lion… he would have roared.

But for now, only the engines had the luxury of roaring and it was a good job they did as they carried him and Gideon towards a destination where he had no inkling as to the outcome. All he knew was that he had a purpose and that he had faith in the mysterious ways of the Hourglass. He knew to have faith. He knew he had to believe in that faith. He knew he'd been chosen and that at all cost, he had to survive, not least to rescue Canatu from her imprisonment.

Bringing himself back into the here and now, Raif realised he could not afford to dwell on things that were currently outside his control. What mattered was that he was alive and was about to become part of the greatest, most phenomenal ceremony ever, and even though he didn't really understand why he'd been chosen, he felt proud and privileged, nevertheless.

"I will give it my all," he vowed solemnly under his breath, and so lost was he in feelings of gallantry, he all but jumped out of his skin when Gideon reached behind and tousled his head.

"Where have you gone to?" he shouted amiably above the roar of the lions...

Having come back down to earth – although earth was still some 8,000 feet below them – Raif was eager to talk even if it meant shouting. "I haven't travelled much, so this is all very new to me," he explained loudly, and Gideon laughed and leaned over to speak.

"You do realise, or perhaps you don't," he said by way of reassurance, "that every night you unknowingly travel 858,240 kilometres around the sun and 6,256,000 kilometres around the centre of the Milky Way galaxy, so don't ever think for one moment that you're not already well travelled."

Raif pondered this amazing fact, and as he did so, he felt himself drifting. He desperately didn't want to sleep as he didn't want to miss a moment of this fantastic journey, but something was pulling him away from this physical dimension and catapulting him to another where he found himself experiencing the vastness of the universe. He was still conscious of the reassuring whirring of the engines and aware of the buffeting turbulence rocking, bouncing and sometimes even dropping them, but it was as if he'd been removed as translucent walls peppered with stars came at him at the speed of light as he simply flashed through them into another and then another dimension where everything was abstract and spectral and where there was no time to see or grasp what he was actually witnessing.

He saw glimpses of life – tiny cameos – depicting all walks and species of life. He saw strange landscapes and seas. He saw despair and disaster but also joy and exultation. He sensed the time and space. He sensed the vastness and his own smallness. His own humility. He understood but couldn't put it into words. He just understood and accepted that he wasn't capable of understanding, but just because he wasn't capable of understanding – his brain simply not being developed enough to comprehend – it didn't mean it didn't exist or wasn't wholly believable, and by virtue of this marvellous insight, he gained wisdom and foresight that would remain with him for the rest of his life. He saw how small he was in the overall scheme of things but understood that each one of us is as large and significant as the universe itself.

He saw too – and understood – the beauty and symmetry of Order. He saw the whole of the moon. He saw The Big Picture and how symbiotic relationships between all things provided continuation, reproduction and rejuvenation. He saw Chaos represented as the creative genius of the pack and that without it, the population of the universe would merely be puppets in a game, acting out a pointless charade. It meant that too had a place – a small, essential place but a place nevertheless – in the magnificent Order of Things.

Finally, he saw the Hourglass in an iridescent blue cave with a ceiling so high it was like a replicated bejewelled sky. It was both awe-inspiring and humbling. He knew – he just knew – it was the Hourglass, encased in its ornate lantern casing, even though he'd never seen it before, or even had it described to him. It had such a presence. He approached it slowly with all due ceremony, and as he got closer, so it got bigger until it was almost the same height as he was. A small catch held the filigree door shut and this swung open as he gently extended his hands. When he placed his hands around the top and lower chambers of the Hourglass and extracted it from its casing, such was the profound charge of pure energy manifested in light and sound, it caused Raif's hands to shake so violently he was afraid he might drop it. And then he did. Unable to hold it any longer, he watched in horror as the Hourglass fell to the floor and shattered into a million pieces.

And then darkness enveloped him. Lost was the dazzling light of clarity, replaced now by the vile absence of decency as Raif saw himself falling headlong. The darkness was succeeded by only more darkness until he felt himself being hurled into a sulphurous cave where he landed at the feet of a hideous demon who was laughing and laughing as if at some huge joke. He felt himself being cast aside with one sweep of the demon's serpent tail as he strutted arrogantly towards a pedestal where the Hourglass, once more within its filigree casing, was being stoned and tortured by a legion of smaller squabbling demons. It was chained immovably to a black rock and Raif could just make out, inside, a pile of shattered shards of glass.

It was unbearable. "*No!*" he screamed. "No...!"

"It's alright, Raif! Just hold on and brace!"

Raif snapped out of one nightmare only to find himself in another one as the light plane they were in veered dangerously towards the ground. The engine spluttered and caught, only to splutter again and fall silent. Raif couldn't help but think how lovely the sound of the wind was now that the engines had ceased to fire but realised such thoughts were born out of denial in its most crystalline form.

Gideon righted the plane as best he could and glided their descent, not knowing what would happen on impact. "We hit an ice storm," he shouted without turning his head. "It came from nowhere, with shards of ice like swords... ripped us to bits... the propellers too."

Looking down, Raif could see they were over sand, hundreds of miles of it, smooth and undulating. Fortunately, it was daylight with good visibility so there was a chance – albeit a small chance – of them surviving the landing.

Any hope of a reprise evaporated as Gideon and Raif careered headlong, out of control, towards the dunes. No last-minute hope that the engines would fire back into life. No 'wake up it was only a dream'. There could only be resignation and acceptance as the earth – the sand – came increasingly faster towards them. Rocks and scrub too came increasingly into focus and all Gideon could do was use brute strength and do his best to keep the nose up while they were delivered into the hands of fate.

"You've been very brave, Raif!" he called just before they hit the sand with such an impact it caused the broken plane to jump back into the air again as if in surprise, only to repeat this acrobatic move again and again, like a pebble on water, until they eventually slewed to a halt.

Raif's eyes were burning. He had sand in his eyes, his ears, his nose and his mouth. He was still strapped into his seat and couldn't move for the sheer weight of the sand on top of him, but more worryingly, he was sinking. "Gideon!" he called. "Help!" And he strained to turn his head only to see Gideon through the twisted wreckage – also still strapped into his seat – now either unconscious or possibly worse. Raif started to panic but the more he moved, the more the silent sand quickened and shifted, eager to swallow them both into its depths.

I must keep calm and think, thought Raif, taking deep even breaths. *What would Dad do?*

No immediate thoughts came to mind. Preposterously, Dad would have called the AA and he almost laughed at the idea. They were alone and lost in a desert and no one knew where they were. Slowly it dawned on Raif that there was actually nothing he could do other than stay very, very still and hope. Hope that either Gideon regained consciousness or that someone would come to their rescue. It was the hardest thing of all to do. Wait, keep still and keep faith.

He watched the day give way to dusk and was thankful that the scorpions, snakes and other survivors of the desert chose to ignore them at least for the time being. He was thankful for sleep as exhaustion took hold and, reluctantly, he succumbed. It was a blessed relief to let go as he sank below the weight of sand, too tired to fight a battle he couldn't win. Too tired to keep on hoping. Too tired to keep on fighting as he drifted like the sand towards a far better place…

But then… The sand was moving! The reality was terrifying! He hadn't actually believed it would come to this – that he would choke and die as the sand filled his lungs – but then he heard shouting in a strange tongue as strong arms gripped his shoulders. He saw a knife with a sharp shining blade coming at him and striking but he felt no pain as, roughly, he was heaved and cut free from his seat and dragged up to the surface with noise and urgency.

He was alive! But who were these liberators?

Cool water was poured on his face, making him gasp in shock. He looked around bewildered. Were they friend or foe these shrouded, turbaned men and what about Gideon?

"Save Gideon! You must save Gideon," he shouted hoarsely with a strength he didn't know he possessed as he tried to claw his way back through the sand towards what was left of the wrecked fuselage.

New arms enveloped and restrained him, holding him tightly. Gideon's arms.

"I'm here, we're safe. We've survived," he choked as Raif felt his grip tighten. "Look at me, Raif, look at me!"

Ashen and exhausted Raif turned and studied the face of the man who was holding him. He didn't trust anything anymore, least of all his own eyes. Was this just another mirage or vision?

"Yes, it's me, Gideon," he said softly and Raif, sensing his aura, felt relief and such gratitude it almost made him cry.

"I saw things," Raif said urgently, his face distorted by the anguish of recollection. "I saw the Hourglass… I did… really I did… and it shattered. I let it go! I couldn't hold on to it! We can't let this happen, we just can't. We've *got* to save it! We've just *got* to…!" And with the whole weight of the world on his young shoulders, he couldn't take any more and broke down.

"Shhhh…" said Gideon and he rocked him. "You're safe, but you must rest. We've survived – that's all that matters right now…"

But Raif didn't hear him as exhaustion took over.

44

Véronique returned to her little red Renault parked a few streets away and sat motionless behind the wheel for several minutes before putting her head in her hands.

"Are you alright?" enquired a passer-by. A lady, possibly one of the neighbours, who happened to be passing, was concerned at seeing Véronique's apparent distress. "Are you lost?"

Because the window was closed, Véronique couldn't hear what the passer-by was saying and fumbled to find the button to wind the window down.

"Are you lost?" repeated the passer-by, and in the few epiphanic moments it took for Véronique to come to her senses, wind down the window and comprehend what this stranger was saying, she knew absolutely what she was going to do next.

"No, I'm not lost and thank you for your concern. I just needed to think for a moment about the enormity of what lies ahead. I'm about to embark on an amazing adventure… Isn't that wonderful… and you know what else?"

The passer-by shook her head.

"I've already taken the money... but now *I'm going to also open the box!*"

Smiling and waving goodbye to the puzzled passer-by, Véronique drove off in what she hoped was in the direction of Manchester International Airport.

On her way she would ring the number given to her by Darke and, on following the explicit instructions given, she would board Darke's private jet where she would find she was the only passenger en route directly to Uzbekistan.

Everything went smoothly to plan – remarkably so – and as Véronique reclined in the unashamed luxury of Darke's private jet, being waited on by a detachment of polite deaf-mutes, she took time to reflect on the boy Raif.

The Raif doppelgänger wasn't in the least bit like the Raif Mr Khan had described. He was verbose and extroverted. Mischievous too and would no doubt be a keen practical joker. Also, he had a genuine dislike of clocks and no respect for time. And he was impatient.

The Raif – the *real* Raif – was supposedly quite the opposite. Studious as opposed to overtly athletic, unremarkable on the surface with a tendency towards shyness. The only extraordinary thing about him was his passion for clocks, his obsession with time and an aptitude for mathematics. It had to be said, his collection of clocks was impressive as he had dozens if not hundreds – from novelty clocks to more valuable pieces – of clocks of every genre and description, with the exception of a longcase grandfather clock, which she noted was conspicuous by its absence.

She wasn't sure if it would prove to have any relevance, but Mr Khan had also gone to great pains to emphasise Raif's background. Namely, his parentage. He'd told her that, by all accounts, Raif had been adopted at the age of two by an older couple who'd sadly lost their own son ten years previously – that would be Vera and her husband whom Véronique didn't meet. When it was announced that Raif was the new Foundling, the Collective went to considerable lengths to trace his real parents but had drawn a blank. All they could discover was that he came from St Winifred's Orphanage in Hastings and that all records surrounding the year of his arrival had been destroyed.

"So, we don't actually know where Raif came from..." mused Véronique thoughtfully, adding another piece to the ever-increasing puzzle while ordering a second (or was it third?) large gin and tonic.

On arrival at her destination, Véronique could see from the air that there was no evidence of a runway or indeed any buildings other than a small tower that was camouflaged to look derelict along with everything else in this desolate place. One would need coordinates to know where to land – or to know if it was even possible to land – but right on cue, just as the jet bringing Véronique to this strange country prepared for landing, the tarpaulins were rolled back and touch-down was textbook.

Véronique disembarked and breathed in the hot dry air which had a sharp chemical taste she didn't like. She covered her face with her powder blue, pure silk scarf and watched where shimmering in the distance, a sleek silver limo emerged from between the dunes and drove towards her.

"What on earth am I doing?" she questioned as the stark reality struck home and for the first time since this bizarre course of events had begun, she felt the first pangs of fear.

The limo pulled up and a silent chauffeur ushered her inside. It was cool and expensive. Shortly, they glided into a tunnel, the entrance of which closed behind them. Darke hadn't come to meet her and for that she was thankful. It gave her time to adjust, but adjust to what? Should she tell this man Darke about her encounter with Mr Khan? Should she tell him she'd met the boy who was – or wasn't – the boy Foundling? Should she let on how much she knew?

All these anomalies apart, what was really worrying Véronique was her role in all this. She'd given Darke the Hourglass, so was there anything else he'd need her for? Had he flown her out here merely to dispose of her? She concluded murder would be relatively easy out in the desert where no one knew where she was. She had no family to speak of and she was always travelling but what would be the point in bumping her off when she knew she could be *useful* to him. Building on these flimsy yet more positive thoughts she began to feel more confident. Darke seemed to like having an attractive woman around, and plainly, he didn't like being in the public eye, whereas she relished it. She was also an adventurer; she knew enough about history, ancient civilisations and, more recently, aspects of the occult to get by and she also had to hang on to the (private) notion that she was on a *quest* and this made her into something even better – a detective! Darke intrigued her and, giving rein to her overactive imagination, she could see herself undercover as his PA…

Continuing on this investigative theme, Véronique thought about their meeting in the restaurant – Le Restaurant de la Mer on Boulevard Diderot. It had been brief enough for Darke to impart scant details regarding his operation and for her to understand he was making preparations for something quite catastrophic. If nothing else, Véronique was a skilled interviewer and had gleaned that this *something* involved the storage of water. It hadn't taken her long to deduce that the only place one could store water would be underground. In a word, aquifers. Being Véronique, she'd read up on it, and being Véronique, she was right.

By the time she was summoned to Darke's chambers she was showered, changed and refreshed after the journey and ready to meet Darke full on. If it were to be a *do or die* situation – and she'd been in a few of those in her time – so be it. She took a deep breath.

"*C'est la vie!*" she breathed and remembered these were the last words she'd left on her note to Dina. *Let's hope she finds it*, she thought as she thought too about Hercules and as she put her hand on the door, she hoped that at least someone would remember to feed him.

45

Raif awoke just as the first fingers of dawn arced across the sky. For a moment he couldn't think where he was, and even on awakening, he was none the wiser other than realising he was in some kind of tent wrapped in a thick multi-coloured blanket that smelled funny and itched.

He shuffled himself towards the looped opening and pushed back the canvas to be greeted by nothing but desert. Sand dunes undulated elegantly and endlessly. It was a silent, ethereal landscape, beautiful in its minimalism and design simplicity, but Raif didn't see it like that. He simply equated it to the moors – the Pennines – back home. It shared the same characteristics in terms of scale and space. He felt attuned to the desert's unpredictability and the danger that lay in its vastness as he'd seen how, in the blink of an eye like a flash of temper, its mood could change then suddenly abate as if nothing had happened. Just as peat bogs could swallow and never leave a trace so too could these shifting sands.

The sun climbed in the sky and warmed him, and he felt good. He felt refreshed – invigorated – and recalled snatches of the events that had brought him to this place. Over to one side, he could see what remained of the plane, a mangled propeller still visible above the sand, and he wondered if he'd ever fly again. Being only nearly ten years old, and his mum and dad never having enough money – or inclination – for holidays abroad, he'd never flown before. 'Thurr's no need, lad. It's all 'ere, reight on't doorstep. We just need t' jump int car,' he could hear his dad saying, and Raif smiled at this recollection which seemed to echo out of a time and place so far away now.

If only he could see me now, he thought and felt the wrench of homesickness just as a youth with the most startling light grey eyes popped his head around the canvas.

"Your name's Raif, isn't it?" said the youth, who was a few years older than he was. "Hi... my name's Ganabek, pleased to meet you. We took shelter from an ice storm and saw your plane come down. It was quite spectacular watching you crash."

Ganabek then held out his hand and motioned Raif to do likewise. Not sure what to do – and feeling a little self-conscious – Raif hesitated but since he was in a foreign country... The boys locked hands. "I saved you so now you're my brother," said Ganabek solemnly, studying Raif intently with his incredible eyes.

"Errr... Well... thank you very much for saving my life," Raif replied, not sure whether he should bow or something but he felt extremely grateful, nevertheless. "I've... err... never had a brother before, so I'm honoured. One day I may be able to save yours... By the way, you speak very good English. How come?"

"My mother's English. She came here and fell in love with the desert and then fell in love with my father... or was it the other way around?"

"Ahh... you two have met," said Gideon striding towards the chattering boys, carrying a bowl of food, which Raif accepted graciously yet cautiously. He didn't know what it was – he didn't dare ask what it was – but although it was weird it tasted good as he realised how hungry he was.

"We're now brothers," said Raif happily between mouthfuls. "Ganabek saved my life when he pulled me from the wreckage... Did he save yours too?"

Gideon avoided the question. "Put it this way, we're both lucky to be alive and we're truly indebted to our new friends."

Now that Raif was awake, Ganabek's family came over to be introduced. Askhat and his wife, Sabina – who were Ganabek's parents – and Nuro with his wife, Masha.

"Let me look at you," said Sabina and she gently put her hands around Raif's face. Obediently, Raif stood there as she turned his head up to the sun. She studied him carefully then took hold of his hands and looked at his palms, his right hand proving to be the hand of most interest. After a while she let them go and turned to speak to her husband. Her tone was hushed yet troubled and Raif wondered what it was she'd seen in his hand that had concerned her. They were just hands... weren't they?

"I'm not sure but I think he carries the mark of the Hourglass?" she said, prompting Raif to examine his hands for himself. "Just below his index finger are two four-pointed stars. One etched above the other. He also carries the Masukake Line – the line of a conqueror – which may not be relevant outside Japanese culture, but I think it might be."

Raif saw no such symbolism, whereas all the remaining members of the small group of nomads became alerted as word went around that there was something special about these visitors who'd crashed out of the sky. They peered at Raif in some kind of curious wonderment and it made Raif feel rather uncomfortable. He looked at his palm again – he looked at both of them – and could see nothing to him that appeared out of the ordinary. Then, as the hum of speculation grew louder, Raif held out his hands and waved them, palms uppermost as if to show there was nothing there, but it only made the group surge towards him and he was glad of Ganabek who stepped forwards to stand protectively at his side.

"Stop! You're frightening the boy!" commanded Sabina in a language Raif didn't understand but got the gist of. A murmur of respect circled and having gained their attention, and their silence, she addressed the assembled.

"We have a boy here who is no ordinary boy. He and his companion are here as our guests and we must extend every courtesy to them. They were on a journey when – as you know – their plane was brought down by a freak ice storm. We must give them every assistance to enable them to continue. The Elders knew this was coming... that this boy was coming... it's in the boy's hand and it's in the *scriptures*..."

Again, a murmur went around, only this time it was more hushed – more reverent – as dark eyes looked out from their shemagh with a mixture of both fear and respect. What was Sabina saying, or not saying, to them?

"We must not speak of this. We must tell no one," she instructed. "It is vital that the boy Raif and his companion Gideon succeed in reaching their destination, so we will go with them."

The nomads dispersed talking and grumbling, not knowing which direction they would be taking or why. Whichever it was, it would be sure to be back into the depth of the desert, when before this, they'd been on their way to the markets. Still... Sabina had spoken, and she was the Wise One.

"What did you say to them?" asked Raif when he saw she was alone. "And how come you know so much about... I don't know... all that's happening?"

Sabina smiled. "You know they say *all things happen for a reason*? Well, that must be why I'm here. Don't tell anyone but I'm with the Collective. A sleeper, if you like, and we're everywhere. Just when you think nothing ever happens, the boy Foundling drops out of the sky and it was my son who saved him!"

"You know about the Hourglass?"

"Of course."

"And that we're on our way to find it after it was taken?"

"Well, I didn't know much about that bit, but it stands to reason."

"And you're going to help us?"

"It's what we're here for."

"Okay. Speak to Gideon and he'll tell you everything. He'll tell you about Darke and... stuff."

"Ahh, there you are," called Gideon, striding over. "I've asked Ganabek here to teach you how to ride a camel."

"A camel!" said Raif excitedly. "I've never seen one in real life!" And he couldn't wait to go and find them.

Ganabek laughed at his enthusiasm. "Come on, they're over there, but mind they don't bite or spit at you!"

Raif stood in front of the camel chosen for him and decided it was the strangest animal he'd ever seen. Like the rest of them, it was a Bactrian camel. A large, even-toed ungulate native to the steppes of Central Asia and an absolute *must* for anyone travelling any distance across the desert.

All the camels looked so funny... and furry! They had these beautiful dark eyes and an expression that seemed to be finding something constantly amusing. Raif decided this was possibly due to their peculiar shape, which to him was like a photo-fit picture put together by someone blindfolded who had no preconceptions as to what a camel should look like.

All the bits were correct and more or less in the right place but, somehow, still looked wrong.

"Can I stroke him?" asked Raif, completely fascinated.

"You mean her. Yes, you can try…" said Ganabek and Raif could see Ganabek was highly amused, not only to see how enamoured he was but that the feeling on behalf of the camel was mutual since the camel had evidently taken a liking to him. He explained while Raif listened and took note that, normally, camels didn't take to anyone new. Rather, they took a devilish pleasure in being antisocial but here… here was Margret… nuzzling Raif like he was her new best friend. Raif stroked her long neck as she kneeled before him, fluttering her eyelashes and making little grunting noises. Both seemed besotted!

Obediently, Margret allowed Ganabek to help Raif into the saddle. She struggled to her feet, being careful not to tip Raif off, and stood quietly while Ganabek explained how to hold on, how to ride with the rhythm, how to stop and how to get off.

"All they ask is to be treated kindly and be given a good night's sleep," he explained. "But be careful! Even though they're herbivores they'll eat anything – even your sandals – especially your sandals – and your tent!"

"And are these humps full of water," asked Raif, putting his ear to one of them.

"No." Ganabek laughed. "They hold fat to provide stored energy and they can go for ages without drinking. Did you know they can drink salt water too if necessary?"

Raif eagerly took all this new information on board, and on his command, which to Ganabek sounded more like a polite request, Margret resumed a kneeling position allowing Raif to slide to the ground. When he'd done so, he hugged her neck as if he'd known her for years.

"Now we must find you some suitable clothes to ride in," said Ganabek. "And you can tell me more about your mission. I know it's to do with an hourglass, but this is a really special one, isn't it? I heard them talking about it."

Raif seized upon any opportunity to talk about time and clocks and, more recently, hourglasses but for someone to actually *ask* him to talk about them was too good an opportunity to miss. Besides, Ganabek was now his brother so it was important he knew about these things. As Ganabek rummaged through the piles of brightly coloured blankets and rugs to find something suitable for Raif to wear while they journeyed, Raif settled down to decide where to begin.

"Well, I have quite a large collection of clocks for someone my age, but as yet, I don't own a longcase clock, which is my ambition…"

"Tell me about the Hourglass first," interrupted Ganabek almost immediately. "I've heard my parents speak of it, but they never say any more to me, telling me I'll know when it's time. I think it's time now. What is an Hourglass? Is it magic?"

Raif had to choose whether or not he should divulge all or part of what he knew, and he decided he should. They were lost in the desert, Ganabek had saved his life and if they didn't get to the Hourglass in time and from what Anakee had told him, it would be the end of the world anyway.

"Okay," said Raif and he began, but not having much of a clue as to what he would say the outpour that ensued was amazing – to both boys.

"Well, it's like this…"

And over the space of maybe an hour or so, Raif explained what even he himself didn't know he knew. It was because he was telling someone who really wanted to know. Someone who listened. Someone who had no preconceptions or motive to challenge or contest what he was saying. Fired with enthusiasm Raif explained that the Hourglass was designed to symbolise and demonstrate the vortex principle whereby different worlds, dimensions and galaxies can be connected via wormholes, and he went on to explain what a wormhole was. He attempted a potted history of the Hourglass and the significance of its shape and its relationship with infinity being two circles joined together. How one cannot have order without chaos although one can have chaos without order because chaos is the absence of order and this rightful balance – a co-existence – is achieved through the turning of the Hourglass.

Raif continued to chatter on and would have done so for hours, especially as Ganabek, having long given up sorting through blankets and rugs, sat spellbound.

"Sorry, am I going on a bit?" he enquired, not being used such a reaction when he went on (and on) about time.

"No... *no!*" said Ganabek, leaning back and making himself comfortable. "Please, tell me *everything!*"

"Well, there's not much more I can say right now other than the time for the Turning is coming up, and as it's turned out that I'm the new Foundling, it's up to me to turn it!"

Ganabek looked at Raif in sheer admiration. Raif could see he'd expected a simple one-line answer, not the torrent of factual information he'd just delivered, but he wasn't the only one to be dumbfounded.

Where did all that come from? thought Raif, also baffled by his own outburst. He didn't say all that did he? And anyway, from whom or where did it come from other than from the Hourglass itself?

He smiled sheepishly at Ganabek.

"I didn't know I knew all that..." was all he could find to say.

46

Véronique was delivered into sumptuous surroundings. A luxury apartment and, although she was slightly disappointed at having no windows and therefore no fantastic views of the desert, she did have an aquatic substitute where millions of gallons of illuminated water were contained behind plate glass. Coral, fish and sealife wafted and swam in harmony creating a calming effect that she found welcomingly restful.

Following her visit to Mr Khan and then meeting Vera and the doppelgänger, Véronique knew that she had made (in her words) a colossal, profound, catastrophic and dreadful mistake. She argued – in her defence – that she didn't then know all that *gobbledygook* about turning it and all that '*end of the world as we know it*' stuff. It was just some old lantern rolling around on the floor on the top deck of a bus. That this Mr Darke had shown an interest in it and had *just happened* to have offered her a job *and an opportunity to study it further...* was just professional prudence...

"No," she sighed. "You simply couldn't resist. You couldn't resist the money, the glamour or the opportunity... You're your mother's daughter alright."

And she felt ashamed. She felt bad. She felt frightened and she felt very glad she'd left that note for Dina.

But the damage was done, and all Véronique could do now was to do her best to get the Hourglass back and returned to Dina – if and when she showed up. Her only alternative, as she saw it, would be to retrieve the Hourglass and hijack the jet but never having hijacked a jet before (are they that difficult to fly?) she had her doubts as to her probability of success.

Eager to do something positive, Véronique ran a deep, hot bubble bath. She pressed a button to summon one of the attendants, who happily turned out to be the attendant Fouad, who she'd rather got used to, and scribbled a note on the statutory notepad.

Please take care of me because I am not a bad person. Please can I have a thin crust pepperoni pizza and a posh bottle of champers. Thank you x

After such a long day, Véronique was starving.

Wrapped in a huge white fluffy bathrobe and drenched in Chanel No 5, Véronique emptied the proceeds of her eye-watering Manchester shopping trip onto the floor and plugged in her (ready primed and installed) state-of-the-art laptop. The man in the store had been so helpful!

Cross-legged and comfortable, she chomped into her pizza, took several slugs of her Dom Pérignon and set to. The first (only) disappointment was that she could get any amount of information in but could get nothing out. It was very much one-way traffic. But who would she call? She regarded herself as little more than a common thief, and who would believe her or go to the trouble of finding her anyway?

She didn't really think it would be as easy as making a phone call, so instead she settled down to reference and cross-reference everything she could about the artefact, about the Hourglass within it and the hieroglyphics displayed within the latticework. She entered all she knew so far about the Collective and came up with only 'done by people acting as a group'. She entered Darke (very little came up) and asked about the Arrid Sea. She read up more about aquifers, about water – about the lack of it – about doppelgängers and other dimensions. About parallel universes. Paranormal goings-on. Sandcastles (in case Vera had been giving her a clue – she hadn't), until finally – finally – she started to piece it all together but only as asides, snatches, suppositions and seemingly unrelated facts but it was a start.

"It's all there," she said, leaning back and draining her glass. "I just need to process it…"

And she promptly fell fast asleep.

Feeling refreshed and newly invigorated, Véronique decided it was a whole new day – not that she could see any daylight – and she needed to instigate her first formal encounter with Darke. Rather than wait until summoned – thereby allowing him to appear in control, which of course he was but that was a *mind thing* as far as Véronique was concerned – she called for Fouad and scribbled down that Darke had sent for her and she had to go now… now being in an hour or so once she'd decided from her new purchases what she should wear. She chose a sharp little number – a cream suit with a pencil skirt and a lace top – by the designer Alexander McQueen that was both feminine and business-like. She teamed this with a pair of killer heels by Jimmy Choo and loaded her fingers with diamonds. Fouad used the waiting time to manicure her nails (and proved to have a real aptitude for it) and, although he could neither speak nor hear, he seemed to enjoy her chattering company.

Fouad led the way down endless tubular corridors until they reached a large singular white door. He pressed a discreet button and the door slid open. Darke was seated with his back to her and remained like that for the entirety of the interview, which turned out to be brief. His lack of acknowledgement that she'd even entered the room infuriated her.

"We need to talk about the Hourglass," she said vehemently. "I'd like it back!"

It would perhaps have paid Véronique to have thought about what she might say to Darke when she confronted him, rather than blurting out the first thing that came into her head. She'd be a dreadful liability to herself in a poker game.

Darke remained passive, with his back turned, and could only see Véronique as a reflection in the glass wall. She too could see both reflections and was further annoyed that this voyeurism allowed him to admire how superb she knew she looked without him having to acknowledge this face to face.

"Much as it may irritate you, and much as you would like to renege on your impulsive generosity, you cannot undo what you have done. You gifted me the Hourglass in good faith in much the same way as I recognised your potential and offered you gainful employment," said Darke coldly as he remained unmoved. "It is important to me that my employees are happy and well rewarded, and I bestowed on you the same privileges."

Darke pivoted his white leather chair to face her and still his expression remained unchanged. "You now have a choice," he informed her. "Either you enjoy my not-considerable generosity…" He looked pointedly at the weight of the small fortune that adorned both her hands. "And I can see you're happy to embrace excess as your prerogative... Or you can decline my hospitality and in doing so would most probably conjure your worst nightmare. I can assure you, there is *no* escape from here."

Véronique had to think quickly – very quickly. What she wanted to do was vent the boiling red mist that swam in front of her eyes and, with no thought for herself, rip Darke apart with her bare hands. But she would fail. She knew she would, and where did temper get anyone? Instead, she matched his cold stare with a stare of her own until, purposely, she visibly softened. He was a man – or a kind of man – after all.

"I'll think about it," she said flirtatiously, "... but I will want access to the Hourglass."

"All in good time," replied Darke and once more he turned his back on her. Véronique turned on her staggering Jimmy Choo heels and flounced out of the still-open door.

As soon as Véronique was back in her room, she ran to the bathroom and was violently sick. *Murder would be relatively easy out here in the desert where no one knew where she was...*

Her loathing for Darke – and for herself too, for her greed and stupidity – filled her with such revulsion that she threw her shoes and her diamonds at the wall in a demonstration of sheer frustration. She couldn't cry – she wouldn't do anyway – and as she sat there with her head in her hands, thoughts of revenge slowly began to replace those of despair. And when these thoughts became mixed with thoughts of justice, which then became tempered with the ingredients honour and truth, they stirred in her a cocktail that was as palatable as it was potent.

"This is only the beginning..." she realised as her own courage kicked in, then she felt that weird headache again. Why did it always come when she was in the throes of a crisis or dilemma? Right there in the middle of her forehead, it wasn't so much a pain as a tingle. In fact, it was the same tingling sensation she'd felt when she'd first laid eyes on the Hourglass all that time ago on the top of the bus.

"It's the Hourglass! It's talking to me!" she deduced, positively radiating with this momentous enlightenment; this epiphany caused her to feel happier than she'd felt... than she'd ever felt... in her entire lifetime. Without a moment to lose, she scrabbled around on her hands and knees amongst the papers and the boxes as she searched for – and found – her far-flung diamonds.

47

In the company of M Touraine and Motto, Dina enjoyed her perfect breakfast. Two warm croissants, a pat of Normandy butter, and a dish of home-made apricot conserve accompanied by endless cups of hot, strong coffee.

Their flight was booked, and it was agreed that Motto would fly incognito in Dina's beret, just in case they encountered the expected unexpected. The taxi to take them to Charles de Gaulle Airport was already waiting outside. Their ultimate destination was Central Asia somewhere on the border between Uzbekistan and Kazakhstan; they would be arriving first at Nu Airport then travelling to the diminished shores of the Arrid Sea and they couldn't wait to get going.

"How will we know where to find Gideon?" asked Dina.

"He'll find you," M Touraine assured her, and Dina didn't ask further. She knew Gideon would've done his homework, as well as knowing he knew far more about the matters in hand than he'd let on. It also reassured her that if the Hourglass had all the power it was purported to have, whatever unfolded, it would have a pivotal role to play itself. She allowed herself to feel a thrill: a tingle of both fear and excitement as she graciously accepted that they were embarking on a journey the outcome of which would decide the future survival and well-being of the universe. But Dina wasn't given to fanciful thoughts and any such indulgence would be misplaced at this critical time, so she reverted to being logical and pragmatic.

Their task was simply to find out what Véronique and Darke were up to and to take back the Hourglass. The rest would be up to the Collective. *If only it were that simple*, she thought but didn't say so.

"It's time you were going," said M Touraine, interrupting her thoughts. "I'll let Pythia know that you're on your way and she'll no doubt make contact one way or another." He reached out and kissed her hand then gently patted her beret in which Motto was already ensconced. "We will meet again soon." He smiled generously, and Dina hoped she hadn't blushed.

48

It was hot – amazingly hot – as Raif lay back under an awning, idly playing with the powder-dry sand running quickly and fluidly between his fingers. He took the oval silver box out of his pocket and for the umpteenth time since it'd been bequeathed to him by Uncle Frank all those years ago and examined it. He wondered – as he always wondered – why Uncle Frank had been so insistent he should have it, and why – try as he may, and as everyone else had done so, for that matter – hadn't he been able to open it? Even his friend Benny had suggested putting it in a vice and crushing it and they did try… But they couldn't even dent it.

It wasn't heavy, and it certainly wasn't solid because when you shook it, you could hear just the slightest, tiniest rattle.

It was smooth like snakeskin and nice to hold since it had no sharp edges. He examined the strange markings and made out moons, stars and lines creating spherical shapes layering into infinity.

There was writing too. Hieroglyphics. He liked the sound of the word more than knowing much about what the word meant and Benny had said it just meant 'scribbles' but he knew there was more to it than that. Maybe he'd ask Ganabek.

He looked across the deserted landscape. The plane they'd arrived in had all but disappeared having been swallowed into the drifting sand, and apart from their makeshift camp and the camels, there was nothing other than sand and more sand in every direction. He was beginning to feel uneasy and couldn't help recalling the visions he'd experienced recently. All had involved sand and, right now, that was all they had.

"What are you thinking about?" asked Gideon who'd approached unnoticed and looked at him quizzically.

"Sand," replied Raif truthfully, "and then more sand... I'll be glad when we can move on," he added, looking wistfully towards the horizon. He understood that Gideon hated this waiting as much as he did, but they had to listen to Askhat and wait for the remaining tribespeople to arrive. They had the scant supplies needed to go back into the desert subcontinent, but such was the unpredictability of the desert, it was always wise to have strength in numbers.

Raif shielded his eyes and scanned the horizon for the umpteenth time and saw only sand and sky. Or did he? He saw something shimmering in the distance. Was it a mirage he was experiencing?

He'd heard about such things and people believed they really saw things that weren't there simply because they desperately wanted to. But it wasn't just Raif, Gideon saw it too, and so did Ganabek and his family; they all saw it as it came closer and closer.

At first, it was a shimmering line which became two... no, four lines that dazzled. The lines were there one moment and gone the next but what remained was a dust cloud hovering above while carried on the wind was the sound of hooves pounding and the shouts of men. It was a wonderful sight as a whole entourage of nomads and tribesmen – dozens, if not more, of their fellow countrymen – rode purposely in their direction. Raif's heart soared as he experienced a joy unprecedented at the sight of them.

The relative quiet of their small camp was shattered by excitement and industry as Askhat greeted his people. Greetings were exchanged, news was exaggerated and, as the day wore on and dusk fell, fires were lit and camels seated.

Ganabek couldn't wait to show off his new friend – his new brother – and dragged Raif from one to another speaking excitedly as fast as he could amidst handshakes and exchanges of mutual respect with too many names to remember let alone pronounce correctly.

Raif was given a bowl to drink tea out of and he was careful to do exactly the same as everyone else. There was a lot of conversation between the men using the language he didn't understand but he didn't mind. He felt safe, at ease and part of a family. The camels watched as if on guard and the women glanced at him with respectful expressions, sometimes whispering behind their hands.

Suddenly being the centre of attention was quite exhausting for Raif who was used to taking much more of an *observational* role, so he was glad of the opportunity to step away from the spirited feasting to gather his thoughts in the relative tranquillity of the surrounding desert. Over the past few days, he'd developed an affinity with its enormity. He felt the same way about the universe.

Feeling a sudden chill in the air, he pulled a bright multi-coloured rug around his shoulders and took the small silver box out of his pocket. Much as he often did, he turned it over and over in his hand.

It was Masha, one of the wives, who passed by and noticed it first. She looked puzzled to begin with then gestured to Raif to let her examine it closer. She shrugged her shoulders, unable to throw any further light on it, but told her husband, Nuro, nevertheless. Nuro listened then got to his feet and came over. "I don't know how to open it," volunteered Raif, holding it out in his outstretched hand.

Nuro took it gently, almost reverently, and showed it to his fellows who joined him and sat cross-legged and conferred with him in a whispered debate.

Gideon noticed a crowd had gathered around Raif and came over to see what was going on. Askhat and Ganabek did likewise and on seeing the small silver box, they too were puzzled.

"It is a long time since I have seen one of these," said Nuro in broken English. "I believed there were none left. Until now. Do you know its purpose?"

"No… it was given to me by my uncle Frank…" replied Raif without hesitation. "After he died…"

Nuro examined the silver box and, just as Raif had done, turned it over and over in his hand. "Would you like me to open it?" he asked, his eyes transfixed.

"If you think that would be wise," replied Raif nervously and he shot a glance at Gideon, who delivered a nod of consent.

Nuro cleared a space around him and, with the middle finger of his left hand, made small circular movements on the central sphere that decorated the box. He traced the lines and jabbed at the stars. He muttered strange chants under his breath and his eyes, once soft and brown, became fluorescent as he looked up towards the coming full moon large in the east. Still he rubbed, ever so gently, and as he skilfully applied more pressure, so the edges softened and became malleable. The whole box appeared to melt and, like a flower, unfolded as the sides to the small box opened and fell away.

He placed the silver box in the sand and, with his finger, drew an eight-pointed pentagon around it. He then produced, from within the folds of his robe, eleven blue crystals. "These eleven stones are the link between the mortal and the immortal," he explained to Raif, who watched spellbound. "They are the link between man and spirit, between darkness and light. Between ignorance and enlightenment…"

"Between order and chaos," added Raif in a whisper.

The little silver box now appeared much bigger as indeed it was. The previously invisible lid clicked open, and in doing so, it was as if a colossal firework had self-ignited, disgorging a torrent of silver shooting stars; hundreds, if not thousands, of them showered into the night sky to perform a unique aerial display.

And that wasn't all. What followed was a ghostly menagerie of mythical celestial birds. Gossamer and transparent in their substance, they moved like waves of light floating and undulating as if in water, water which then became air as their new-found freedom prompted a spontaneous aerial ballet. Swooping and shrieking, their audience was captivated while the camels watched too. Unconcerned.

And then the spectacle was over. Like wafts of a morning mist with the sun close to rising, the phenomena evaporated and were absorbed – much as their plane had been – into the dunes. The small silver box now looked innocuous, and although it had more or less returned to its original shape and size, the lid was still open. Nuro picked it up and took out a tiny intricate clock, no bigger than a fingernail, attached to a chain so fine it felt like a whisper to touch. The hands of this clock were static with both pointing upwards to the roman numeral twelve.

"We've made ourselves known to the Celestial Messengers," he said gravely. "You might call them angels but whatever you call them they're the conscience of the galaxy and are on the side of right. If you ever need to call on them, place this tiny clock on a moonstone. But I give you a word of warning, never call upon them lightly or if there is a danger of your motive being selfish."

"I don't have a moonstone…" began Raif.

'Yes you do," said Gideon, stepping forwards as he pressed a smooth, pale moonstone into Raif's hand.

Nuro nodded, then, with all due reverence, replaced the tiny clock and clicked the lid of the silver box closed. He handed it back to Raif and placed both hands on the boy's shoulders. "You have power and wisdom beyond your years. Yes… you are the Foundling… but more than that, you are the Chosen One as it is written in *The Scriptures*. Chosen to deliver us out of darkness."

Reverting to the language of his people, Nuro turned and faced them. "Behold the Foundling!" he announced.

"Behold the Foundling!" responded the assembled.

As soon as the sun was up, the nomads struck camp and made preparations for the journey ahead. The mood was optimistic, jubilant even, and after the revelations of the night before and glad to again be journeying, Raif couldn't have been happier riding high alongside Ganabek, laughing and talking as their camel rocked and swayed sure-footedly through the dunes. No one noticed that one person was missing, because why would they? Who would notice a lone nomad who had turned up (fittingly) out of the blue and who'd disappeared again in much the same way? He'd been made welcome of course, such were the rules of open hospitality, but no one had enquired about who he was. No one gave him a second thought.

Whereas Raif was feeling carefree, Gideon was more pensive. He only had one path to follow – uniting Raif with the

Hourglass and completing the Turning – and as he rode, he had time to reflect on how he'd ended up on a camel in a desert with little or no idea as to where he was going. But the tribesmen knew. Like their forefathers, they had travelled this same path many times, only this time there was a new purpose.

Once, their path would have been along the shoreline of the Arrid Sea, waving to cousins and brothers as they fished, landing their catch of carp, zander, ide and bream with nets heaving. Once it would have been a thriving community teeming with people going about their business: fishing, farming, trading, surviving, living and simply *being*. It was harsh but they survived and, in many ways, thrived as the very nature of the geography around this vast inland sea softened the vicious Siberian winds in winter and cooled searing summer temperatures achieving a symbiosis. Yin and yang.

But that had all gone now, along with the ships that had once dotted the horizon, leaving weather patterns that only existed in the extreme. There was no sea – or precious little left of it – as the once 68,000 square metres of thriving productive waters had dwindled and the lakes within had all but disappeared, leaving only shallow strips of poison. A toxic salinity.

As they journeyed, the landscape became more and more desperate. The receded sea had left vast plains soiled by an alchemy of salt, acid and toxic chemicals, which the vicious winds picked up and carried, polluting the surrounding land, contributing further to the chronic lack of freshwater since the salt melted the glaciers, which fed the rivers, which fed the sea, and those too had all but gone.

"What happened here?" asked Gideon as the camels picked their way through the scarred wasteland, avoiding pillars of salt and rocky pitfalls. Like ghosts, they passed through the shadows of huge, rusted hulls – the hulls of stranded ships, abandoned and helpless, as the seas that were so vital to their purpose quietly and compliantly receded. It wasn't loud or dramatic, just litre-by-litre but on a grand scale. Quiet as a mouse.

"The sea went," sighed Askhat, sounding as hard and as unyielding as the landscape. "The rivers feeding the sea dried up. Dried up or, as some say, were diverted by the Superpowers. What difference does it make? We are poor and forgotten and much of our younger generations have taken off to work in the cities. There's no one left. There's no future here."

A silence fell. There was no cause for hope or optimism. No bright side. No silver lining. Askhat told it how it was with an economy of words befitting the landscape. It was the resignation of defeat that cracked his lips, burned his eyes and bleached his robbed soul. What in this forsaken place was happening?

49

Darke had a very different take on the landscape to the one Gideon was experiencing. He didn't care. It was alien to him anyway having come from a place – a planet – where his life, where life itself was essentially submerged, safe beneath the millions of tons of rock and strata that protected the life forms from the harshness of sunlight in a cool, silent world.

It was exactly this, his adaptability to hostile environments, that had saved him when he became interned on the prison planet. The fools for not realising! Within his purpose-built sanctum, he now took pleasure in adjusting the humidity setting to the maximum as he turned down the thermostat to just a couple of degrees above freezing.

A cold fish indeed, Darke was pale to the point of appearing bloodless and a light film of either oil or perspiration covered his face. His hair, what little there was of it, looked painted on. His breathing was laboured, and one could just hear – unless it was imagined – the fluid on his lungs warble. He thought about his encounter with Breaffen and how he'd known about his escape.

Safe from the dry arid wastes above him, Darke recalled

those desperate prison days with more than a degree of despair. Much as he liked the sound of dripping water, listening to its monotony day after day would be a sound that couldn't be endured. The only escape was death, or so it was thought.

Carcerem – commonly known as the prison planet – was chosen as a prison because it was isolated and consistent and didn't rotate. It didn't spin creating night and day; it just hung there. Sullen and overlooked. One side was searingly hot and uninhabitable. The other dark, frozen and equally hostile. The only place where any semblance of life was possible was along a thin grey north/south divide between the two extremes. Since this line was only a few kilometres wide, it was fit for purpose as a prison and to be incarcerated there was worse than any death penalty. There was no need for cells or chains. No need for guards either, as all inmates were tagged. All were assigned to the same fate serving life sentences until they died, which, luckily for some, was usually sooner rather than later since there was no point in survival. Survival simply equated to a prolonged death.

Many, if not most, took their own lives by throwing themselves off the rocky escarpment like garbage down a tip because that's what they were. Garbage. The thieves, murderers, rapists, dictators and war criminals rubbing shoulders with the terminally evil, the power-crazed and the heretical.

Food was dumped sporadically but if supply failed there was no recourse. No procedure for complaint. No rights. No human rights because no one within this prison qualified. The daily torture was the dripping water. The water coming up from an underground source, which then condensed onto the bare, roughly hewn rock. Without this resource, each inmate would have perished within weeks of arrival but with enough – just enough – food, they could live out this protracted death, although most died or chose to die. The stronger feeding on the weaker.

As there was no need for any kind of security other than remote surveillance, there was no need for restraint. The inmates roamed freely on the rock face, inhabiting pods, as they became known, that were fashioned as if for nesting seabirds but on a larger scale. Darke had chosen a pod that was set apart, high up the rock face and away from immediate predators. He chose it for its size, its location and its inaccessibility. Who would want to risk the arduous climb for food or company when he craved very little of either?

Darke had the advantage insofar as the planet he had originated from shared several similar attributes to that of Carcerem. Namely, it was a cold, water-orientated planet, where the inhabitants had adapted to this environment. Darke, being no exception, could sustain himself on an unpalatable diet of water slugs and other molluscs, which were plentiful in this, his current circumstance.

But it wasn't so much the location of his pod, it was the isolation. Prior to his imprisonment, Darke had studied the *Alternate Prophecies* and had become an active disciple. He had learned the secrets and power of the Hourglass. He'd learned the secrets of wormholes and access to other dimensions and was becoming practised at astral projection. So many skills, so many arts and such ambition!

Darke walked the path to enlightenment unceasingly in the deep recesses of his pod and in doing so was able to increase his knowledge as well as take respite in escapism – in mind if not in body – and during the course of doing so, he experienced visions. Visions of a future inspired by the

Alternate Prophesies and a future where – just as Noah had learned – the master card was water.

At first, his visions were sporadic. Fragmented glimpses of the future, but they were enough to educate him – to alert him – as to possible alternative destinies, and either by accident or design he stumbled into the annals of the Underworld and it was this association, coupled with his isolation, that provided hope for escape.

Darke became proficient at summoning demons, taking care not to be too ambitious since (as yet) he was vulnerable. He kept to only the lesser demons who were stupid and impressionable. His flattery won their trust and admiration. He singled out one particular demon and groomed him, inviting him 'to join him in experiencing the vast knowledge of the universe...'

After that, it didn't take long. With the stupefied demon dressed in Darke's prison issue attire Darke performed the dangerous ceremony that made them as one. It was a gamble but it paid off. With the two entities joined, and then separated, only one of them emerged from the pod – the bewildered, stupefied demon with Darke's clothing on his back and the tagging device embedded in his neck. It would be a long time before this substitution was discovered. The demonic gateway had been opened, and regardless of whatever fate might await him, Darke entered and vanished.

50

The change from picture-book sand dunes to the terrain they were now experiencing was quite a shock for Raif. He felt the misery and desolation. A constant wind blew what felt like acid in his face. He hurt all over but there was no stopping. No going back. There was nothing here, only rocks, sharp inclines and an endless horizon. Glimpsing out from beneath his blanket, Raif marvelled as they moved through the shadows cast by the giant hulls of rusted ships that littered their path and felt a yawning sadness too. How was this allowed to happen?

He would've liked to have asked Ganabek a million things, but any conversation would be impossible under such conditions, so he contented himself with trusting Margret to keep them safe as he leaned forwards in his saddle and accustomed himself to her rhythm. As he did so, the vision came to him again.

It was only a semblance of his previous vision, since this time it was he himself who was alone in the desert when he saw a boy – a barefooted boy in ragged shorts – and the boy tugged his arm, pulling and pulling, beckoning urgently for Raif to follow him to a tall derelict building. From nowhere the boy produced a football and grinning widely he made Raif watch as he positioned the ball and kicked it. The ball arced high in the air and both watched as it soared then, right on target, smashed through a top window, shattering the glass. The boy celebrated wildly, and the air was filled with the noise of a great crowd cheering a winning goal.

Raif experienced triumph like it was he who'd scored the winning goal and he awoke, disorientated yet elated to find they'd arrived at the rusted blue gates of a disbanded canning factory.

"We'll make camp here," instructed Askhat as he dismounted and ventured forwards with a few of the men to ensure it was safe.

The Canning Factory, so named because that's what was written above the wrought-iron gates, was once a hive of industry on the busy shore of the Arrid Sea. There were the remains of a small jetty, rusted capstans and perished fishing paraphernalia long since abandoned from when the sea receded. There were no people, no animals and no birds. Only insects and flies. Incongruous in its stranded isolation, the Canning Factory hadn't succumbed to the ravages of wind and weather as much as the other buildings that leaned towards it as if for support. Most were devoid of roof or timber whereas the Canning Factory, although damaged, had remained more or less intact. The large iron gates – a pretty shade of cerulean blue still evident – barred their way but one push was enough to ease them open, creating the sound of metal upon metal. There were no signs of recent occupation, only scrub and tumbleweed, blown sand, more salt and rock. The camels surveyed their destination and registered no surprise.

By now, Raif had lost all sense of time as one day had drifted into the next with any brief interludes of sleep adhering to no set discipline. However, sleep was the last thing on his mind since he was eager to explore. Although derelict, the Canning Factory appeared sound and all the canning machinery, benches and storage were intact as if the workforce had simply upped sticks and left. Jackets and overalls still hung on pegs, and although rusted and stagnant, water was still evident in the kettles.

In readiness for the night, they found hurricane lamps and kerosene that only needed straining. Askhat and Nuro unloaded the camels and made camp, foraging for firewood which was in plentiful supply. Ganabek, who couldn't stand still anyway, was itching to explore and ran off in the direction of what might once have been a storehouse, and although Raif ran along after him, he hesitated. The nature of the building brought to mind the building in his vision.

He followed but, once inside, Ganabek was nowhere to be seen. By way of contrast to the bright sunlight outside it was dark and silent. There was nothing apart from the pin-sharp shafts of light streaming in through the partly opened door and the cracks in the walls and he half expected the boy in ragged shorts to jump out at him. But he didn't.

"Are you in here?" he called. "Hello…?"

Still nothing, just darkness and a stillness that was palpable. After the noise and bustle of the journey, Raif stood and listened to the silence. It was beautiful – it was golden – but then, cutting through came the sound of a clock tick… tick… tick… tick… but the more closely Raif listened (and knowing a thing or two about clocks) he realised it wasn't tick… tick… Rather, it was *drip… drip*. The sound of dripping water.

It was impossible to know where the sound was coming from since it resonated off every surface – it seemed to be all around him – and unless it was his imagination, it was getting louder. Raif began ransacking the junk on the floor, never once thinking the smart thing to do might be to call Ganabek or Gideon, but what if he was just imagining it? With his fervour exorcised, Raif stood perfectly still again and listened. He followed the logic of his ears and sure enough – under a piece of the roughly hewn board stacked around it and a pile of old rags heaped upon it – he discovered the source of the sound.

It was a well. Raif could make out it was a fairly deep well because rather than the water being fathomless in an inky darkness, it was faintly luminous and iridescent.

Hardly able to contain his excitement – the water here being more precious than gold – he looked around for some kind of container that had a handle and a length of rope that wouldn't break. Having found both he tentatively lowered his makeshift bucket into the waters, scooped up what he could and hauled it to the surface.

He sniffed the water, which looked perfectly clear, then tasted it cautiously. It could so easily have been caustic, salted or even poison but it wasn't. It was cold – but not too cold – sweet and delicious. Still acting with caution, Raif poured it over his hands then couldn't resist rubbing it into his dusty hair. It was the most wonderful feeling he'd ever experienced, and it would be a memory he'd carry whenever he showered for the whole of his life.

He poured the remainder of the contents over his head and joyously laughed out loud as he filled the bucket again, this time pouring it all over himself before drawing another bucket, full to the brim, and running to show his find to the others.

Meanwhile, Raif wasn't the only one to have come across treasure. Ganabek had returned before him, carrying armfuls of rusted tins of every size and description, and eager hands were already prising them open, delighted to find that although the labels had long since perished, the contents were unaffected.

"And it's not just fish!" said Ganabek, excitedly sorting through the tins at breakneck speed. "Tinned fish, of course – dozens of them – but tinned peaches, tinned pineapple, tinned potatoes, peas, corned beef – more tinned fish – tinned beans, tinned meat, tinned tomatoes, tinned everything!"

Raif watched smiling and waited for a break in the excitement before stepping forwards with *his* prize. "And guess what I found…" He grinned and when he had everyone's attention, he picked up his bucket and poured the entire contents over his head. Everyone gasped in shock and horror. Water – such a most precious commodity – couldn't be wasted in such a way!

"Don't worry." Raif smiled. "I've found an unlimited supply where this came from!"

The evening was given over to feasting. The fires were lit, music played, and the tins were opened and decanted, displaying their exotic contents. Nuro and Sabina used the flour they'd brought to make flatbreads, and everyone washed and drank the cool clean water with no regard to economy. Even the camels took great draughts on board until sated.

Feeling extremely happy, Raif wandered off around the makeshift campus. The air was still, and a vast sky canopied above him. It was so large and so clear it all but took his breath away. He thought about all that had happened and was still happening when he saw a shooting star and instantly thought about Motto.

"I wish Motto and Dina were here," he said wistfully, not knowing the implications of what he'd just wished for. It seemed so long ago when they were all together in…

where was it? Paris? And he was just thinking about all his new-found friends when it occurred to him that in all the excitement, he hadn't seen Gideon for quite some time.

51

Motto would've given anything to be with Raif in the wide-open spaces of the desert, rather than being incinerated in the hot black hole of Dina's beret. But he didn't dare come out seeing as the airport they'd arrived at was teeming with large flying predators of dubious origin no doubt eager to snack on the prized morsel of a bite-sized bumblebee.

Unfortunately for Dina, these annoying predators had become aware of Motto's whereabouts so made repeated forays in her direction, causing her to flap and protest loudly as if the journey alone hadn't already been bad enough. Even she, who had endured far worse circumstances, had to admit it was rather a rough passage as they were dipped and buffeted with lightning storms and turbulence the likes of which she'd never encountered before. It was almost as if the forces of nature had been trying to prevent them from reaching their destination.

It was daylight when they arrived, and the heat hit Dina like a brick wall as she emerged, blinking, from the small light aircraft. Only a handful of passengers disembarked – a couple of dazed and preoccupied gap-year students who quickly dispersed leaving only Dina looking awkwardly conspicuous.

The airport she'd found herself in could hardly be termed international. She'd transferred several times during their arduous passage to eventually arrive at Munayayne Regional Airport, which was little more than a strip of sand-on-rock. The larger rocks had been removed to facilitate the runway and to provide the foundations for a couple of improvised shacks huddled either side of it. Ripped plastic carrier bags served as wind indicators and Dina noted with approval that corrugated iron and/or cardboard were popular choices for roofing material. Some of the other dwellings may have had previous lives as caravans and there was no doubt that the central building had once been a cargo ship, although only the hull remained. The entrance – through the bilges – displayed a large crack and a faded sign with an English translation underneath reading '*Arrivels and Executive Lunge*'.

Shooing away the carrion who'd perched watchfully, she entered the cavernous darkness and was relieved to find that the roof – the upper deck – had rusted away sufficiently to allow some sunshine to stream in. However, within these dusty sunbeams were more of the hungry carrion hovering restlessly as the news went around telepathically (or via pheromones?) that the fat prize within her beret was, as yet, still unclaimed.

In defiance – the predators being rather large – Dina secured her beret with a floral headscarf, found in a pocket she didn't know she had. She was beyond caring what she looked like and challenged the small man who approached her to make comment. He didn't. He merely stood there in his well-worn shiny suit – incidentally, several sizes too big – and looked down nervously at his shoes. He was reluctant to make eye contact.

"This way please," mumbled the small man gesturing towards a makeshift neon-lit office. Although it was without a porthole or window, it had instead a large, rusted hole that offered a view of the runway and the barren shimmering desert beyond. The makeshift office led off from the main concourse – such as it was – through a mazed (amazed) suspension of lethal wiring where baited conduits tangled like weighted cobwebs. Dina thought it little short of a miracle that anyone survived the electrified passage as she ducked her head and kept both hands firmly in her pockets.

Believing that the small man in the oversized suit only wished to be helpful, Dina dutifully followed him into the office and took a seat having first checked for snakes or scorpions.

"Your luggage will be delivered to you shortly," the small man informed her. "Welcome to my country..." he added as if being prompted by some imagined autocue.

He barked a more confident instruction in a language Dina didn't understand to one of three airport employees. The small plane they'd arrived in had since taken off again leaving her single bag – aptly, a rather faded carpetbag in deference to *Miss Marple* – sitting conspicuously on the runway in readiness for one of the three employees to retrieve it.

In the interests of good manners – *one should always be an ambassador for one's country* – Dina took the opportunity to thank the small man using slow deliberate English, causing the small man to break into a radiant smile that vanished almost instantly as if he'd remembered some terrible misnomer or procedure. It proved the latter.

"Please wait here, I have to make a telephone call," he said as he hurried out.

As far as Dina was aware, all their paperwork was in order – Claude, the patron of La Petite Chambre would have seen to that – but the waiting was nevertheless uncomfortable. She fidgeted. She didn't like red tape or officials, especially those in shiny ill-fitting suits. "I'm not terribly good when it comes to bureaucracy," she confessed to Motto in her beret, looking like she was muttering to herself.

"Me neither," buzzed through Motto.

Her impatience prompted Dina to think about what they'd be doing or where they'd be going next. She'd assumed hotels with lots of vacancies rather than a barren wasteland, and what about Gideon? Where was he?

She left these thoughts stacked in her mental in-tray and smiled when the small man in his ill-fitting suit returned. He smoothed his oiled hair nervously and looked even more stressed than he had before and made no reference to the call he'd just made. He needlessly shuffled the papers on his desk and cleared his throat noisily.

"Welcome to my country," he repeated stiffly as if reading from a script. "What is the purpose of your visit?"

Dina was sorely tempted to tell the truth… *'We've come here to retrieve the Hourglass, complete the Turning and save the world – if not the entire universe – from imminent Armageddon'*. But she decided such sarcasm – such truth – might prove inadvisable. "Camels," she said instead and, keeping an absolutely straight face, added, "Bactrian camels. Don't you think they're quite adorable?"

The small man looked unsure, as if not knowing how to respond to this information. Had Dina been a fly on the wall earlier – and she shuddered at the thought of how many flies there were on the wall alongside the many other unknown winged species – she would have heard how he'd been told to report anyone speaking English who seemed even vaguely unusual and to detain them under any pretext until someone from the Higher Authority arrived. As he looked now at this eccentric woman in a beret, Dina certainly fulfilled the criteria. That was the purpose of the call. Now it was a matter of waiting.

Making frequent references to an obsolete tide table, referring to a great many files obviously unopened for many years, the small man protracted the response regarding camels as long as he could. When he felt he could sustain this stalling no longer, he asked another question. "How long do you intend to stay in this country?"

"That largely depends on the camels," replied Dina, passing the baton back to him while continuing to gaze with a doleful expression.

Unsure as to how he should proceed, the small man in the ill-fitting suit was visibly highly relieved when one of the porters knocked and whispered urgently that a man had arrived looking for an English woman who was probably wearing a beret.

So great was the small man's relief to be relieved from this responsibility, he didn't question how this could have happened so quickly in a country where nothing happened quickly. He didn't think to remember whether or not he'd mentioned a beret when he'd made the call.

"I have to pass this matter over to the authorities," said the small man officiously. "There is nothing to worry about."

Hurriedly, he got to his feet and made ready to greet this anticipated official. He'd expected a man, not unlike himself, being similarly attired, not the tall, handsome, ruggedly suntanned man with strange eyes, one being slightly different to the other, who swaggered in wearing the comfortable robes of the desert.

"Ahh..." said the tall man and he smiled as he took great purposeful strides forwards and looked intently at Dina.

"The lady in the beret!"

Having signed for his cargo (Dina), the tall man escorted Dina out of the airport and towards the camel waiting in *Arrivels*. Contrary to what she'd told the small man, camels were *not* wholly adorable in Dina's eyes, but she was deeply grateful for their transport, nevertheless, as clasping her carpetbag, she clung on somewhat inelegantly. She was happy to be in the safe hands of Gideon and even happier to be taking the back seat.

When they were a sufficiently safe distance from the airport and beyond prying eyes, they dismounted. Dina flung her beret into the sand and scratched her head in a gesture of ecstatic freedom. Motto too was delighted to be released.

"It is so wonderful to be out of there!" he exclaimed as he assumed his human persona. And as he stretched and breathed in the hot air, he vowed never again would he spend even five minutes in Dina's beret. He was desperately in need of sugar, and to add to his joy at being free again, Dina rummaged in her bag and found him a much-appreciated jar of honey.

"So, you're the man from the Higher Authority." He laughed between mouthfuls as Gideon unravelled the dusty shemagh tied around his face.

"Well, not exactly, but we'll be long gone by the time the real henchman turns up."

"I hope the small man doesn't get into too much trouble," said Dina, feeling he was rather the victim of their duplicity.

"He'll be alright," Gideon reassured her. "People in shiny, ill-fitting suits always are…"

52

The man from the Higher Authority and his cohorts were local ruffians recruited by Darke solely for the task of apprehending anyone suspicious – or English – who arrived at Munayayne Regional Airport. The small man in the shiny, ill-fitting suit was interrogated, and despite everyone's best efforts, they got nowhere.

"He specifically asked for the woman in the beret," explained the small man for the umpteenth time while he described Gideon as best he could. "He was very clear about this…"

"What beret?" said the man with sharp features, losing patience, not really knowing what a beret was. He nodded in the direction of the two thick-set men who'd accompanied him and left the room. Obviously, someone had got there before him and his task was to now inform Darke.

"It's of no consequence," rasped Darke using the small microphone concealed by a diamond in his immaculate suit jacket. He touched his ear and the conversation was terminated in much the same way as the man in the ill-fitting suit would probably soon be terminated.

Judging by the description given, Darke knew this strange

woman would have been sent on behalf of the Collective, and that being the case, who was she and who too was the mystery official who came and gathered her up? But for now, it was of no consequence and whereas he'd have preferred taking the woman and conducting the interrogation himself, all was not lost. His *fortress beneath the sands* was virtually impenetrable and in such a hostile environment so bereft of shelter, he would soon learn of their whereabouts. Besides, with so little time left, the presence of the Hourglass would soon flush them out.

"But where's the boy? Surely, he must be with them?"

Darke suddenly felt weary. His plans and ambitions were so close to reaching fruition, he was impatient for the drama of the next phase. It was the waiting that was getting to him. After all the long years that had rolled from centuries to decades, years to months, it was now down to days and possibly only hours. Like eggs ready to hatch or a baby ready to be born, it was a finite time and he only had to wait. The time of the Turning would arrive, the Foundling wouldn't be there to perform the ritual and a devastating new era would begin.

And reaching for the *Alternate Prophecies*, he turned to Revelations. What he liked was its similarity to Revelations in *The New English Bible* where in verse 21 both began with the words '*Then I saw the new heaven and the first earth had passed away, and there was no longer any sea...*' He'd seen to it that there was now precious little of the Arrid Sea left and that made him feel good. Like he was playing his part.

He perceived that once the hour of the Turning had passed, the Hourglass would be rendered as nothing more than a pile of glass fragments, trapped forever within its lacy prison. But he knew there would be a bigger, more profound sign. A spectacular sign. A sign that would herald the beginnings of the chaos to come, and this excited him.

The *Alternate Prophecies* had proclaimed (and the gist being) this would come as a great whirlwind that would gather detritus from all four corners of the world and culminate in a dense, black funnel-shaped cloud. It was further written that this phenomenon would multiply exponentially until their numbers reached 3,141. These would be seen descending from the sky and moving rapidly over the seas, gathering up water, from out of which other black funnel-shaped clouds would form randomly – or in other words, chaotically. When the saturated descending clouds coupled up with the equally saturated ascending clouds, the column between would become four or six metres in diameter. As these protracted due to the sheer weight of water, so they would collapse to devastating effect. Like a pot thrown by an inexperienced potter, centrifugal force would be lost and thrown out of kilter releasing immeasurable torrents of water. Tsunamis would register worldwide, and the knock-on effects of chaos would begin.

What Darke rather liked about the poignancy of this prediction – apart from revelling in the annihilation it would wreak – was that the very shape of this phenomenon closely replicated that of an hourglass…

It was cool in his palatial living quarters, which were coordinated in minimal tones of grey and white. He didn't want walls; he wanted space – acres of it – with nothing to interrupt the clean lines. There were no pictures, no objects, no furniture other than a central desk and a white leather chair facing a vast blank wall. He sank into the white leather and pressed a concealed button that caused the blank wall to silently rise slowly to reveal, once again, the inner wall of plate glass behind which was a vast subterranean world stretching through countless underwater corridors where surreal arches and towering stalagmites melted into an infinity.

Lit by pockets of sunlight which punctuated the surface, the water contained therein was so clean and clear, you could see fathoms of unaccountable depth.

A far cry from my previous existence, he thought with no small measure of satisfaction and shuddered as his mind flash-framed images of life – if one could call it life – on the prison planet. The misery of Carcerem.

53

Having survived her first meeting with Darke on his home ground, so to speak, Véronique took comfort in still being alive – at least for the time being – and for being returned to her sumptuous apartment rather than being thrown to languish in some prison cell. Darke obviously liked her…

This was a *Positive Thought* she decided to hang on to even though in reality (what reality?) it was probably far from the truth. More likely she was just an amusement. An audience so he could see how big and powerful he was.

"Whatever… so be it." She shrugged as she ran a shower and gave herself to the sparkling waterfall. The soft cool waters felt delicious, and as she stood there, she began to formulate a strategy. *He's obviously mad,* she thought, *and he's a narcissist – big time! Psychotic too with definite delusions of grandeur. He has an acute inferiority complex due most likely to his chronic psoriasis and like me – like anyone come to that – he probably just wants to be loved.*

Pleased with her thumbnail analysis she was grateful once again as she recalled her sporadic education. It had been an exceptionally cold winter and, par for the course, she had no money, so that nice professor… Albert something… had allowed her to commandeer the radiator during his lectures. If he'd lectured in – say – economics, she'd no doubt have learned a lot about money management, but he didn't. He lectured in psychology and now, being here swathed in her enormous bath towel, contemplating what it was that made Darke tick, she was jolly glad he did.

Now she knew Darke or at least thought she did, she no longer felt so afraid of him. Or so in awe of him. Or so intimidated by him. She knew he was dangerous, even more so if her analysis of his personality traits was right but *knowing thine enemy* is usually half the battle. Her priorities were to (a) stay alive, (b) find out where the Hourglass was kept, (c) escape (with the Hourglass) and (d) give the Hourglass back to Dina.

As lists of priorities go, it seemed reasonable. She decided it would be okay to keep the diamonds, but she'd leave the credit cards, maybe just hang on to one of them, as he'd no doubt put a stop on them anyway. Maybe she'd keep the shoes too as he wouldn't be able to take them back.

The next thing that crossed her mind was Raif. Vera had said – or was it Mr Khan? – that he'd gone off after the Hourglass. Did that mean he'd show up here? And if so, how would he get here? Or was he heading for some special place, meaning she'd better get the Hourglass back to Dina *tout de suite*?

Whereas before, she was just beginning to feel more in control of events, her old friend *anxiety* decided to give her a visit and she felt her spirits sink. Who was she trying to kid? If she'd known all this was going to happen and it was going to end in such complexity, she'd never have got on that bus. In fact, she rued the day she'd promised her mother she would, knowing now – as she did then – that her mother didn't really give a monkey's. It was just a passing whim to demonstrate (on her deathbed, would you believe!) that she could still have fun manipulating her silly daughter. And it worked. Of course, it worked!

Véronique sighed heavily and felt glum... but she never felt glum for long and quickly brightened when, in an instant, she decided to lay all blame on the Hourglass itself. She told herself she believed – *she truly believed* – that the Hourglass had engineered all this – probably centuries ago – and had compelled her to be in that place, at that time, and to come back for more.

"This is why I have the headache!" she announced as if that in itself was proof enough, and happily rubbing a central point on her forehead, she poured herself a generous flute of Bollinger.

Accepting that the premise was perhaps a little farfetched, if it made her feel better and what harm could it do? After all, she needed all the encouragement she could get, however tenuous it might be. Staying with this optimistic theme, she took stock. She'd already pulled off item (a) on her list – staying alive – so moving on to item (b): find the Hourglass. Where to begin...?

54

WHY IS IT THAT THE SOUND OF A MOSQUITO ALWAYS gets louder once one has tuned into it? This was a really loud buzz and, annoyed that he couldn't locate where it was coming from, Raif flapped and swatted irritably, pulling, as he did so, the rough blanket over his head.

"Well, that's a fine way to greet a friend who's travelled halfway around the world to find you," grumbled Motto good-naturedly as he hovered.

Raif snatched the blanket off his head and leapt to his feet. "Motto!" he exclaimed wildly, hunting around for his friend. "I made a wish – a shooting star wish – that you'd come and here you are! Errr… Where are you?"

From folds within the tent Motto appeared as a bumblebee and instantly transformed to human form. As he did so he performed a silly pirouette. *"Tra-laaah…"* he sang melodically, "… wishes *can and do* come true!"

Raif was overjoyed to see his friend, and this was made even more so when, moments later, Dina charged into the tent and spontaneously scooped him up in a bear hug.

"It's lovely to see you too," Raif reciprocated, hardly able to breathe, noting how surprisingly strong she was, and felt slightly relieved when she eventually released her grip.

"I am *so* very happy to see you." She beamed, rather embarrassed by her open display of affection and thankfully for Raif one bear hug was evidently sufficient.

Later, over a supper of tinned delights that were still in plentiful supply, Raif gathered with his friends around a blazing fire under the canopy of stars. Talking nineteen to the dozen, he listened and joined in as each recounted their respective journeys and the encounters that had led them to this time and place. Raif paid no heed to what lay ahead, wanting to just enjoy the moment and the circumstance of them all being together again. The only one missing was Anakee, but as much as she was in Raif's thoughts, now wasn't the time to feel maudlin.

Dina and Gideon, however, descended into deep conversation leaving Raif to chatter to Motto. "I found this amazing well... would you like me to show it to you?" he asked excitedly, already getting to his feet.

"Isn't it rather late?"

"No! There'll be no time tomorrow. Come on!"

As Raif clearly wouldn't take no for an answer and as there would be no way of dissuading the boy, Motto conceded. "Lead the way," he said good-naturedly.

"I love it here," confided Raif as they walked through the long shadows past the derelict workbenches. Past the troughs and shelves where the doors – thrown open or merely rotted on their hinges – swung slackly to reveal their plunder. Rows and rows of tinned everything, most of which would probably turn out to be fish.

"I feel like I'm part of a family," he continued quietly, taking Motto's hand. "Like I really belong."

"You *do* belong – we *all* belong somewhere – it's only a question of finding out where and recognising it," said Motto and he squeezed Raif's hand in return.

As Raif approached the well through the gloom his attention was drawn to an eerie blue light emanating from within the depths casting ghostly dancing shadows onto what remained of the roof. And the emanating light was getting stronger. Through the rafters, where the roof was missing, the sky, by way of contrast, maintained its steady blackness and bore no signs of dawn. The heavy canopy wasn't yet ready to succumb to daybreak, rather it served as a spangled backdrop for the waxing moon that felt so close, he could almost touch it.

Raif viewed the well cautiously. Obviously, the light hadn't been there before, and he – as too undoubtedly was Motto – was curious as to its source and cause. It was therefore with some trepidation that he peered over the edge of the roughly hewn stones not sure what, if anything, to expect.

It was beautiful; mesmerising. The entire cavity was filled with a gentle undulating light that circled and rippled in a kind of hypnotic vortex. It wasn't hostile in any way. On the contrary, it was strangely inviting.

"I'm going in there!" said Raif impulsively, pulling off his shirt and shoes.

"Are you mad!" exclaimed Motto, and in a gesture of panic he covered his ears and ran around in a circle. "No… really, that's *not* a good idea. In fact, I think it's a very *bad* idea, so let's go and get Gideon first…"

But it was too late. Raif was too quick for him and, poised on the edge of the stones, a slight tilt forwards was enough to deliver him into the luminance of the silky blue water beneath. "I won't be long; I just want to see." He grinned, breaking the surface just before he took a deep breath and swam headlong downwards.

Speechless, all Motto could do was stare at the spot where Raif had been only seconds ago. Why hadn't he managed to stop the boy? Whatever possessed Raif to be so foolhardy? Where was he? He couldn't see him...

Should he go after him? No. First... stop... Think.

He couldn't go for help, there wouldn't be time; if he followed, how would they get out without a rope...?

"Get a rope! A rope, a rope!" he wailed helplessly and frantically looked around to find one.

55

Swimming through the sparkling clear water was a wondrous experience. It was like flying in a vast cave where stalagmites and stalactites created a hushed and holy cathedral-like environment. Raif had made a mental note of where he'd come in and was mindful that he could only hold his breath for a matter of a few more moments. He was just about to turn around when something caught his eye. The source of the blue light was coming from above – just above – the surface. He had a decision to make. Either swim back to the well *now* or make the decision to surface.

Being a nearly-ten-year-old boy meant he hadn't yet learned *cause and effect*, so of course he chose the latter, not even thinking about the consequences of gambling (with his life!) that it was indeed the surface and, as such, there would be fresh air on the other side.

Gasping great gulps of air, Raif was more than relieved to be right as he found himself in a large underground chamber. Shards of blue minerals that Raif would later learn were cavansite, barite and azurite and other more precious gems like aquamarine and sapphires made up the substance of the cavity. It was these elements catching the light of the waxing, fast-approaching full moon that created the light, which, as the moon moved along its trajectory, was already fading. Raif looked around. Was there any other way out?

As the water began to darken, it felt colder and far less inviting. He took a gigantic breath, plunged beneath the surface again and realised it would be harder than he had thought to find his way back to the well. Just as a tingle of panic gripped his heart, he saw a rope swaying in the light current just ahead of him.

Oh... thank you, Motto, thank you! he thought, feeling overwhelmed with gratitude as he quickly swam towards the swaying rope and grabbed it, enabling Motto to haul him up.

"Don't you *ever* do anything like that again!" Motto said angrily when Raif was safely restored to dry land.

"I'm sorry, but for some reason, I just *had* to," replied Raif not even understanding himself what had compelled him to do such a foolhardy thing, and with hindsight, he realised how dangerous it was.

Motto softened visibly at seeing Raif so sorry and pursued the scolding no further. "Anyway, you're safe... how did you manage to stay down there so long?"

Still rather ashamed of his foolishness, Raif was nevertheless in wonder of what he'd witnessed. "It was incredible down there!" he said. "It's like dozens of football pitches all joined together and going on for miles and miles. There's no bottom, or sides – just an infinity of fresh clean water. This strange blue light is amazing too. I'd never have found the air pocket without it and what made it happen, what made it blue, was this blue rock stuff – like a mineral, so it was like glass – and when the moon came round, for just that short while, it shone directly through it. It was dazzling, like some kind of energy, then it all faded and was gone again.

"Err… Thank you for the rope," he added sheepishly. "I wouldn't have found my way back without it."

"That's okay, I'm not ready to lose you yet. And what about this chamber you found? Could you get out? I mean, was there any other way out?"

"No, I didn't see anything, it was all just this blue glass stuff. But there might have been a passage at the far end and I'm saying that because I'm sure – I'm really sure – I saw something moving at the end of it. I saw it just as the light was fading. Should we go and tell Gideon?"

Motto thought for a moment. "Let's get some sleep first. It won't be long until daybreak. We can talk about this later when everyone's rested."

"Where's Raif?" asked Dina, emerging from Raif's tent trying to conceal the strain in her voice. She wasn't one to panic, believing there was a rational explanation for everything, but she'd already searched high and low for him. His bed, such as it was, had been slept in but other than that there was no sign of him.

"What is it?" asked Motto, newly roused from sleep. "What do you mean where's Raif? In his bed, surely? Or maybe with the camels?"

"No, he isn't. He isn't anywhere."

Motto, now on his feet, hopped from one foot to the other with both hands on his head in sheer panic. "He *must* be? Have you looked? Have you looked everywhere…?" Then he faltered and his face paled. "Have you been to the well? We went there last night… maybe he's gone back there…"

"No, we've searched everywhere."

Motto saw no point in telling about Raif entering the well, or about the blue light. It would only confuse matters, and besides, it would have faded by now. Anyway, Raif wouldn't have gone there alone. He wouldn't have entered black water.

"He must be *somewhere!*" he said just as Askhat burst in.

"One of the camels is missing," Askhat announced gravely.

56

Darke had endured a difficult night. His eyes, although cold, were rimmed red, and his skin, never good at the best of times, had developed cracks and pustules where the psoriasis had become particularly virulent. It was caused primarily by Darke's poor adaptation to this different environment and made worse by his meddling with astral projection; his skin had mutated to not develop or rejuvenate properly – the skin cells growing faster than usual and therefore not developing as they should. The stress of his visions, his cause and his ambitions, plus the problems he was now encountering, all contributed to fuel his discomfort.

Wearing only a shift of light gauze, Darke prostrated himself on a bed, the ingenuity of which meant his body was supported only at a few key points, giving the impression of him floating. Even so, the light gauze stuck and crisped where the weeping lesions had split or burst open.

The Blue Light. What a blessed relief. It was the blue light created by the abundance and particular combination of sapphire, moonstone, calcite, barite, cavansite, azurite, blue quartz plus his most prized aquamarine that had first convinced Darke to choose this particular geographic location. He could have chosen any one of the worldwide locations colonised for his purpose but only this one had an abundance of a rich seam of the healing blue crystal.

Of course, the sea was paramount as too was its remoteness in his ambition towards power but power – Darke accepted – was useless if you're dead. He had found that the ideal wavelength of the blue light could activate a rejuvenating natural healing process and harvesting that light ensured Darke would continue to be very much alive.

The fabulous encrusted blue ceiling adjusted remotely to find the right refraction of the sun, and when it did, the room was blasted with intense blue light. Darke closed his eyes and basked. The mirrored surface beneath him ensured too that every part of his body was penetrated.

And while suspended in this self-induced catatonic state, Darke opened his mind and explored how the demon Breaffen might serve a purpose.

He hadn't had a visitation from Breaffen for quite some time now but that was no bad thing. He had the Hourglass securely locked in a vault deep within the desert beneath them and there would be no way anyone could take it or even get near it. And certainly not in the time there was left. This thought cheered him as he rose stiffly from his bed. He breathed in and, although his chest bubbled and rattled, he felt rejuvenated after his session.

His thoughts turned to the whereabouts of the boy Foundling as he chose a tailored lightweight Ermenegildo silk and wool suit in dark grey. All his bespoke suits were dark grey. Likewise, his shirts, shoes and accessories carried labels like Hermès, Duchamp and Savile Row.

Dressing slowly and deliberately, he took care not to disturb his lesions, concealing all but his face and hands. He'd once considered wearing gloves but decided that would draw attention to, rather than distract from, his condition. There were no mirrors, as Darke had no desire or inclination to regard his own reflection.

Having dressed to his own satisfaction, Darke was content to continue his waiting vigil, amused only by the fathomless wall of water held behind the plate glass, so it was with some measure of surprise when his vigil was interrupted. Soundlessly, one of his deaf-mute manservants entered and passed him a note requesting his presence on Level Five. He was further surprised because to Darke's certain knowledge, he'd only fabricated his fortress to Level Four.

Darke stood in front of the lift that accessed all floors, pressed the button and stepped inside. The interior, finished in brushed aluminium, only permitted a ghosted reflection of him as a blur, which he studied with feigned interest as if to pass the time and appear normal. He didn't issue any further instructions or press any more buttons. The lift would take him where it would. Or would not.

The movement was slight but apparent, and after a short while, the door duly opened to reveal a darkened space not dissimilar to that of uninhabited office space, only there were no windows. The lighting – such as it was – had a thirty wattage LED utilitarian feel that glowed slightly greenish and was concealed along the prefabricated wall panels. Alternatively, the place could have been mistaken for a deserted underground car park as it was also rather grubby. But it didn't matter. It was just an observation.

Darke stood there and took stock while his eyes adjusted. His senses on full alert. Nothing came at him, greeted him or alarmed him other than silence and the all too familiar cold smell of damp.

At the end of the room there was a rectangular bench-like table draped with a black cloth, the purpose of which was to conceal the content beneath. Darke approached with a measure of caution, although this wouldn't have been apparent by the sound of his footsteps as he crossed the empty floor space.

Click... click... his footsteps echoed with the confident regularity of a metronome.

Inwardly he raged. How could this space – this level – have been created without his knowledge? But through his rage it occurred to him, and this was more worrying, that perhaps none of this related to the physical plane he currently inhabited? That this was another dimension he'd been delivered to unwittingly. Or maybe it was a vision. A hallucination and he was in fact still lying beneath the healing light of the blue crystals. In the far recesses of his mind he knew he was losing the ability to distinguish between reality and fantasy, but it was cold in here, and such was the clarity, he could feel and smell his own breath. This reassured him as he approached the draped black cloth, took hold of the hem and paused. Then with a flourish, like a magician at a magic show, he whipped off the cloth and gasped audibly at what lay underneath.

57

"I'LL JUST TAKE ASKHAT AND GANABEK," SAID GIDEON, and the boy Ganabek swelled with pride at being chosen to ride alongside his father. Although he was a few years older than Raif – and in his culture almost a man – he was still a boy nevertheless and as he and Raif had become good friends – brothers even – it was right he took part in the search.

"Whoever's taken him can only be a few hours ahead of us and Darke will be behind it all," added Gideon. "We'll head for Vorzo Island and just hope the winds don't whip up."

Askhat agreed and instructed his men to scout the more immediate surrounding area for any signs they may have missed.

Dina accepted it would be impractical for her and Motto to go too. "We'll maintain base camp for when you return with Raif," she faltered as Gideon put a gentle arm around her shoulder.

"It'll be okay," he reassured her softly. "We'll find him and bring him back."

Having been loaded with essential supplies and the parchments relating to the area that Gideon had been studying earlier, the waiting camels shifted impatiently, for once eager to be off. But already the air felt hostile, laden with a presence that didn't bode well. A slight breeze rippled the canvases causing tiny bells around the silks to shimmer and tinkle as if in warning. It was a hot wind, scorched and toxic, which didn't belong to the untainted promise of a new day.

Neither Gideon, Askhat nor Ganabek made it to Vorzo Island. It was still called an island even though the sea around it had long since dried up, leaving salt flats strewn with nothing but the evidence of death. The wastes between offered no protection from the storm that came upon them and raged horizontally, biting into their faces, which, if exposed, would be etched to the bone within minutes. A small rockfall forming part of the peninsula saved them since they were able to crouch – huddle – until the storm abated. Then suddenly, almost as quickly as the sandstorm had arrived, it moved on. Like a whirlwind, a dust devil, or a tornado even, it passed, leaving them blinking in the harsh sunlight.

"Come and look at this!" called Ganabek, raking in the sand. The consequence of the storm had caused drastic changes to the topography of the landscape and, in doing so, had revealed a shape that was smooth and rounded with the sheen of metal that was completely incongruous to the rusted armatures and carcasses strewed around it. The storm, sudden as it was, had brought about this re-formation, and had it not done so, they'd never have come across this metallic hump

Gideon examined it. "It looks like some kind of ventilator," he concluded, marvelling at the fact that had they not sheltered in that exact same spot, they'd never have stumbled across it.

Recalling the mantra *there's no such thing as coincidence* he knew their find was worthy of further investigation.

So, they dug. The top layer – the crust – was hard and unyielding, being made up of chemicals and compacted salt, but when Gideon broke through the surface, he found the sand beneath soft, powdery and quite easy to work. Scooping out the dry sand surrounding what he'd decided was a ventilator, he exposed a flat area of some two metres square just below the surface. Like the rounded pipe, this too was of a dull grey metal. There was no hatch or doorway, but as Ganabek dusted away the fine sand, tiny grains fell into otherwise invisible grooves only made apparent when the sun was behind them. But there was a blade too. It ran invisibly around the perimeter of the central symbol and was razor-sharp. Whether or not it was some kind of booby-trap, Ganabek didn't see it and exclaimed only when blood ran down his arm from the cut – like a grass cut – it made on the flat of his hand. He assured Gideon that it didn't hurt until, wiping the blood off the supposedly flat surface, it left a trace in the intricate markings rather like ink on an etching plate.

Ganabek's father, Askhat, viewed the effect curiously. Unable to yet read or even decipher what the markings meant – the legibility still being too sporadic – he drew a knife from his belt and cut his own finger, letting the blood drip and collect in the tiny grooves. He spread the blood over the circular markings, wiping it clean again as he did so.

Now they were able to see the markings more clearly, it became apparent that the symbols were similar to those found on Raif's silver box – the one Nuro had opened – and it would seem they were becoming clearer and more distinct as the tiny veins filled, spread and joined as if at their own volition. Almost as if it was completing its own picture. More and more elaborate it became as the three of them watched and said nothing.

"What does it mean?" asked Ganabek, breaking the silence.

"We're here at some kind of entrance," said Gideon, who had been studying the other parchments Askhat had brought along. "And this symbol is the key if only we could decipher it."

They fell silent as they all studied the parchment in front of them which offered up no further clues until Gideon started chuckling. "Of course!" he exclaimed, looking at the procession of stick men, the circles, swirls and hieroglyphics. "It isn't a key – it's a map!"

58

When Darke snatched away the black cloth, he didn't expect to see the limp body of a nearly-ten-year-old boy. Pale and motionless, his flawless complexion was translucent as if carved in alabaster and such was the aura of his sheer purity it struck a note even in Darke's cold heart. In fact, such was the presence this child radiated, Darke could hardly bear to look at him let alone touch him for fear of soiling the epitome of such exquisite innocence.

What have I done? What am I meddling in? were the involuntary thoughts that crowded his head, and for a split second, he viewed himself shamefully as some kind of mad deranged beast, until a low growl snapped him back to this nightmare reality.

"I give you the Foundling," said Breaffen as he stepped out of the shadows. His arrogance carried an air of pride in both speech and manner as with a sickening gesture that was both outrageous and inappropriately fatherly, he caressed a blackened fingernail across Raif's forehead.

Darke was rendered speechless. Assuming the boy to be dead he frantically scanned the options. It was catastrophic!

It was debilitating. It was his years of careful planning thrown into chaos, which was ironic seeing as his ultimate goal was to aid and abet the implementation of chaos.

"Not like this!" he spat, completely beside himself in fury. "The boy had to remain alive or they'd find another! And then another!"

And with eyes bulging, he momentarily seized Breaffen by the throat only to immediately let go as he knew such a gesture would be both futile and dangerous.

Breaffen meanwhile looked astonished if not highly perplexed.

"I needed the boy alive," said Darke icily, his composure returning. "I have my reasons…"

Breaffen continued to look at him quizzically before bursting into a mocking, hideous laugh. "He isn't dead!" he exclaimed. "He's merely suspended in an induced sleep. How else would you suppose I'd transport a wriggling, protesting, loud child… hmmm?"

Darke didn't answer. He couldn't. His relief that the boy wasn't dead was profound in itself and now he felt foolish. Inept at jumping to such a quick conclusion.

"I said I'd deliver the Foundling to you and I have done so," continued Breaffen, "and now I have another proposition to make. You give me the Hourglass."

As if Darke hadn't had enough shocks for one day, this latest proposition was profoundly preposterous. Was Breaffen mad? Surely, he was, but to make such a suggestion was outrageous. "Go on…" said Darke, playing for time and endeavouring to hide his effrontery but using the opportunity too to learn more as to Breaffen's reasoning.

"It seems to me that we follow the same objective, which is to destroy the power of the Collective and to fulfil the prophecies as laid down in the *Alternate Prophecies*. Power for you and the ability for me and my kind to roam free again to enjoy… shall we say… more earthly pleasures."

Darke didn't disagree and continued to listen.

"It seems… how do I put it… *dangerous*… for you to have both the boy Foundling *and* the Hourglass. Even if you succeeded in keeping both apart until after the time of the Turning has passed – and I really do think you underestimate the tenacity and resourcefulness of the Collective, particularly when cornered – you would always have the worry of having overlooked some small but important detail. Some get-out clause. Something in the small celestial print."

"So, what are you suggesting?"

"I'm suggesting you entrust the Hourglass to my care. The Underworld isn't another dimension, it's accessible to those who know the path. It's part and parcel of *this* world and no one… no one… enters with a view to getting out again expecting to be the same as when they went in. If I become the custodian of the Hourglass, the fate of this planet will be written forever. Enter the circle and deliver the Hourglass to me but don't leave it too long. The Collective is already here and will soon be baying at your gates. Be warned, if you are going to act, act fast." And with that he was gone.

Darke looked down on Raif's translucent face and experienced a feeling he'd never known before. Was it regret? Or sadness? Whatever it was he didn't like the curious pain it stirred within him.

Weighted by these troubled feelings he gathered up the boy – light as a feather – and almost as if preparing to make an offering, he walked with funeral dignity towards the open lift door, which silently closed behind them.

59

It was a profound moment for Véronique when Darke entered her apartment unannounced, carrying the limp body of Raif. Instantly, her hands flew to her face in shock.

'*Raif!*' she almost screamed but didn't. A sixth sense, deep in her subconscious, reminded her that although she knew so much about the child being presented to her – and indeed had had tea with his mum and met whom she now firmly believed was the boy's alter ego – Darke had no knowledge of this. As far as he was concerned, she knew only (a little) about the Hourglass and nothing about the Foundling.

"*What on earth has happened?*" she cried out instead with justifiably genuine emotion and, without waiting to be asked, snatched the boy from him and gently laid him on the bed.

"Who is he...? Is he... is he dead?" she choked, rehearsing her words before she spoke them, terrified she'd let slip she knew him. She stroked his forehead while anxiously – desperately – looking for any signs of life. Also, she knew she had to keep herself together while she navigated through this nightmare.

"Who he is, is none of your concern. He's not dead but he's been given a strong sedative and I'm led to believe he will eventually wake up. His name's Raif and I need you to take care of him. Send for me when he's conscious."

Darke took one last look and turned to go. "Fouad will attend you and do not let anyone other than me or him into this room."

As soon as Darke exited the room Véronique fell to her knees and embraced Raif in a gesture of instinctive maternalism. She held and rocked him, devastated by the thought he *could* have been dead, and it was her meddling that had brought about these shambles. Full of remorse and ashamed of her very existence, she clasped Raif to her neck and held him as she wept, vowing from the very depths of her soul that she would trade her life for his (if it ever came to it), when she hesitated as she became aware he was struggling to breathe.

Instantly, Véronique shot backwards and Raif – looking uncertain as to who might have instigated the embrace – remained sitting with his eyes transfixed on the floor.

"Where am I?" he asked, his eyes wide and frightened.

"You're safe," replied Véronique softly, "and I'm going to take care of you... Raif."

She waited a moment to allow her words to register and for Raif to take a tentative look around the room. And at her. "My name's Véronique..." She cooed gently.

"Oh no... Not Véronique!" exclaimed Raif in dismay while shrinking back as far away as he could from her.

Véronique chose not to register this rebuff and continued to maintain a friendly disposition. She knew she'd move heaven and earth to take care of him and he just needed a little time to understand this. "Yes, I'm afraid so." She continued to smile and then, in a moment of inspiration, added brightly, "I've met your mum."

60

With Raif's suspicions regarding Véronique having abated, they soon became friends. They exchanged accounts of the long journey that had brought them both to this same place, while unbeknown to either, and through many layers of rock and sand, Gideon, together with Askhat and Ganabek, was examining the grey flat surface they'd uncovered following the sandstorm.

Gideon – in fact, all of them – had tried to find a way of gaining entry but without success, until Ganabek traced the slightly raised, razor-sharp perimeter of two small circles. "I think I've got it!"

Very gently so as not to cut himself, Ganabek found the six points where two triangles crossed the circles and identified the symbols representing two eyes. One of them was raised slightly higher than the other and when he pressed its outer perimeter it tilted ever so slightly and sure enough, the metal grey platform duly tilted inwards and downwards, providing a ramp down into a dimly lit passage.

After taking only what they needed and releasing the camels to make their own way back, they began their descent.

"Let's hope this leads to Raif," said Gideon grimly, knowing they were fast running out of time. And options.

The passage had obviously been man-made, albeit crudely, and this led down a long gradient where it opened up eventually to a myriad of caves and tunnels. Although dark in some places (Gideon was glad he'd supplied everyone with head torches) mostly the caves were lit by light breaking through a largely translucent canopy high above him. From where he was standing, it was difficult to determine what this canopy could be made of, but he suspected it was mainly salt. He was mainly right.

The blood-rubbing they'd taken proved to be very useful since, as Ganabek soon discovered, certain markings on the map corresponded to small markings at the entrance of the passageways, signifying the right way to go. Or so Gideon hoped.

As the map began to make more sense to him, Gideon could see – and Ganabek agreed with him – that they were in a subsidiary tangle of small caves. The passages leading off mostly led nowhere, other than more deeply into the honeycombed walls, and others led to what would be best described as an artery. This artery then developed to a larger principal artery and – according to the map – became part of a formation not dissimilar to that of an octopus laid out in the sun. In any event, all avenues led to this central main complex.

As far as Gideon was aware, they'd remained undetected, and with the aid of the map, Askhat led them through what felt more like tunnels until all three of them emerged into an open, top-lit cavern and were confronted by a large, lavishly decorated door built into the rock face that was seemingly unguarded. There was no doubt about it. This door was the door identified on the map as being in the central point of the octopus.

"And my bet is… Darke's on the other side of it," said Gideon. "This is thousands of years old and must have originally been the gateway to some ancient kingdom."

"Now it's Darke's kingdom," added Askhat sagely.

"Yes, he must have built the complex around the existing foundations." And for a moment, Gideon admired Darke's ingenuity.

Gideon knew of the door but not of its whereabouts, so historically, this was a real find. The intricate gold leaf depicted the god Janus – the god of the doorway – holding the keys to the power of opening and closing.

Above this depiction was a dragon: a winged serpent. Originally, this fabulous creature was wholly beneficent as the manifestation of life-giving waters, seen here as the serpent with the breath of life depicted as a bird. It showed the sky gods and their earthly delegates, and it became ambivalent as water was shown to be both constructive and destructive – the fertilising rains following thunder or, contrarily, the destructive forces of lightning and flood.

Askhat traced his fingers along the hieroglyphics and read what words he could out loud. "… Something… something… being interchangeable representing the unmanifest. Chaos. Untamed nature. The hurling of the thunderbolt or striking by lightning is the change from the unmanifest to the manifest… it can be two-sided, either as a rain god or an enemy of the rain god, preventing rain from falling…"

Gideon waited as Askhat read silently for a few moments before getting back to the thread.

"… Ah yes. It's associated closely with the sea, the great deeps, the mountain tops and the clouds and the solar eastern region."

"Does that mean the dawn?" asked Ganabek.

"I don't know what it means," replied Askhat. "All I know is we need to get this door opened. Any idea anyone?"

They didn't see or hear them coming. Being so absorbed in examining the great door, they were unaware of the silent guardians that materialised out of the surrounding walls. They failed to notice the drifting sand which moved as if to accommodate and assist.

Perhaps they'd been there all the time – on display yet cleverly camouflaged – only now they were moving, homing in on their prey with surprising speed and agility. Giant scorpions, some over several metres in length, numbering four, maybe eight, converged in a well-rehearsed manoeuvre to take their strategic place on the battlefield.

None of Gideon's party stood a chance. These formidable armoured giants with dexterous crab-like pincers arced their tails – their deadly stings – like ballerinas. If they hadn't been so deadly, their performance could only be described as elegant – poetic even – and certainly worthy of applause for their sheer synchronisation and precision.

Gideon thought, as the giant sting hovered above him, poised ready to strike, what a shame it was that their mission would fail. That he had failed.

He didn't care about his own life, but his heart wrenched when he thought about Raif. It's odd how time stands still when death is imminent, how so many thoughts flash with such clarity. He saw – in the blink of an eye – the journey they'd been on together and a future which now held nothing more than desolation. He saw wasteland and desert, flood and famine. He saw despair in the eyes of children. He saw dictatorship and cruelty at a level hitherto unheard of. He looked across at Ganabek, frozen in time and stricken with terror as his father, Askhat – also in a motionless pose – reached out helplessly to shield and protect his son.

What a tragedy. Never for one moment had he considered failure as an option as he let out an anguished cry for the fate of a young boy called Raif. A cry for the loss of his friends and for the fate of humanity. He felt shame at his own failure, at his inability to protect and safeguard as was his duty. At least the beautiful death would be swift.

61

Dina was struck by a terrible sense of foreboding. It was a premonition so powerful and debilitating it caused her to stagger and, for a moment, almost lose her footing. She saw the wives glancing and whispering and could see they were afraid. She knew they would've seen such visitations before, but perhaps never in a foreigner, and she was grateful that they would know not to touch or interfere.

Checking herself, Dina mumbled a quiet excuse and left the compound, letting herself out through the rusted blue gates towards an endless shore belonging to a sea that no longer existed.

The sun was low in the sky, but it wasn't yet dusk, and she welcomed the cooling breeze on her flushed face. She knew something catastrophic had happened or was going to happen and felt powerless.

She thought about Raif and her heart ached. She'd lost all track of time and, with no word from Gideon, she feared the worst. Dina didn't often feel defeated. In fact, other than during her ordeal in the Great Chasm, she couldn't ever remember a time when she did, and far from her sinking into defeat, she conjured up the opposite effect.

With her *no-nonsense* attitude restored – sentiment and woolly-minded thinking could wait – she decided that if there was ever a time when she'd need Lenken it was now. Something catastrophic was going to happen.

"If there was ever a time when I really need you, it's now," she called into the desert breeze. But her words were lost and didn't even echo because there was nothing out there to pair an echo.

From around her neck, she took the disc which Lenken had given her – the one from his collar – and squeezed it into her palm. It felt warm and comforting. She rubbed it gently with her thumb. In doing so, she hoped Lenken would appear – like a genie out of a bottle – but that was fantasy wrapped up in her own wishful thinking. She held her breath, hoping, but nothing happened. Nothing changed. And the desert sea went on endlessly.

After a while, Dina gave up and returned to rejoin the others. On seeing Motto, who looked up anxiously, she searched his face as if to say, 'any news?' only to see a reflection of the same question. No news, no sightings. Nothing new to report.

There was nothing she could do other than wait. "Tell me more about the well," she asked Motto.

"There's not a lot more I can say than what I've already told you," he replied.

"But tell me again… how long was Raif down there and what did he see? Do you think this air pocket, or whatever it was, could have led anywhere?"

"He was only down there for a matter of minutes and I think this air pocket was just that. One of many."

"You said he thought he saw something moving?"

"Possibly but unlikely. The light was fading – rapidly – so it was more like a trick of the light. Look… if you think that's where Raif went, forget it. If I hadn't been there with a rope to haul him out... put it this way, he won't forget that in a hurry."

"Yes... you're right. I just wondered..."

"Clutching at straws, more like. Get some rest. Over the next few hours anything could happen."

Like a fly on the wall, if only Dina could have seen him. Far from being abandoned in some prison, or suffering a fate she couldn't even dare contemplate, she would have seen Raif sitting cross-legged eating a giant pizza laughing and joking with Véronique. Similarly, Véronique would be sitting opposite in the same state of dishevelment with both behaving like a couple of kids without a care in the world.

Raif having got over the initial shock of finding himself in Véronique's care and Véronique having finally convinced Raif she'd suffered a lot of bad press and that she *actually* wasn't all bad, the two of them got on like a house on fire. They chattered and exchanged adventures, aware initially that Fouad stood silently in the corner with his eyes cast downwards, but after a while, they became freer with their conversation. Véronique assured Raif that he couldn't hear them anyway. Occasionally Fouad would circuit the room picking up clothes and clearing plates and Véronique would give him notes asking if he was okay, but other than this, they more or less forgot about him, accepting him as part of the furniture.

As Véronique watched as Raif explored her laptop, she was *amazed* by the changes in herself. Previously, she'd had no fondness for children; in fact, she wouldn't even acknowledge them as children, seeing them more as irritating and highly uninteresting young adults, and the thought of having one of her own – or spending time with anyone else's offspring – was entirely abhorrent to her. However, when Darke had dumped Raif's seemingly lifeless body in her arms, some kind of miracle had happened. Her heart broke. It shattered into a million pieces as she clasped the boy to her and looked down at his fragile, innocent face. The joy she experienced when she realised Raif wasn't dead was an emotion she'd never experienced before and, like a pride of lions or a pack of wolves, Véronique instantaneously bonded with this helpless child. Her previously dormant undiscovered maternal instinct became so strong it would have equalled that of any mother polar bear, orangutan, penguin or elephant. It shocked but also exhilarated her, and for the first time in her life, she felt she had a noble purpose. The care and nurturing of children (who were not necessarily her own).

Leaning on her elbows, she smiled as she watched Raif surf the keyboard with his eyes wide open, full of curiosity as he absorbed fact after fact. Between them, they'd learned all they could about the mythology surrounding the Hourglass, the *Alternate Prophecies* – although there was very little on either of these taboo subjects – the history and the underground geography of the Arrid Sea, and anything that related or contributed to the mysterious depletion of the sea levels. What was interesting too was that according to Wikipedia, Darke didn't exist.

"Tell me again about how you were captured," said Véronique, confident that Raif was now strong enough and sufficiently removed from what must have been quite a trauma for him. Reluctant at first to tear himself away from the screen, Raif knew it was important to know who – or what – was behind his capture.

"I'm afraid it's all a bit patchy," he said.

"Don't worry, patches have an uncanny knack of knitting themselves together." Véronique smiled. "What was the first thing you remember?"

Raif looked at Véronique while he thought. She was so nice. After the horrors of his ordeal, to wake up to this... to this angel... where he felt safe and cared for was like a dream he didn't want to wake up from.

"The first thing I remember was the smell. I think that's what woke me up because it was so strong, I couldn't breathe. It smelled like rotten eggs and I know that because one of Mr Carson's hens had laid eggs in the hedge and I broke one. It must have been months old! Anyway, it made me retch and that's when I saw him – or it.

"At first, I thought it was some kind of goat sitting up on its hind legs because it was very hairy, then I realised it couldn't be because it was far too big. It had eyes like a goat – the pupils more rectangular than circular – and they were horrible. I shouted at him to go away but he just dribbled as he came towards me, which was when I saw he had a tail which was ridged like a dinosaur or serpent. I shouted as loud as I could for the others to wake up, but no sound came out, then he pushed me to the ground, and I thought I was suffocating, I really did..."

Raif fell silent. He didn't want to appear upset in front of her.

"Then he made me swallow this yellowish stuff, but I pretended I did and managed to spit some out. It was vile but then I woke up here."

"It must have been terrible for you," said Véronique. "We'll take a look later to see if we can find out more about this *rotten egg*, but I think what we need to do now is figure a way out of here." She knew without trying that the door to her apartment was locked.

"I need to think," she said and, clearing a space on the floor, adopted an entirely unnecessary yoga position. She put her hands in prayer pose and closed her eyes while she composed herself, took stock of the situation and hoped a plan would come to her. It didn't, so she had another idea and took out her Tarot cards, but since they told her nothing specific, she decided to look only at the practicalities.

First of all, she was fairly certain no harm would come to Raif – yes, she was sure of that – but she was expendable, so bore that in mind. Also, she knew too much, and she didn't have much time. Turning her thoughts now to the resources at her disposal, these were mainly confined to knowledge and right now she didn't need knowledge. She needed something far more practical.

"Now I wonder what this can do?" she pondered as she opened her eyes and reached across for her fiendishly expensive Loewe handbag, out of which she took the small bobbin containing a miniature hourglass that had been a gift from Mr Khan.

"Have you ever seen one of these before?" asked Véronique handing the bobbin containing the miniature hourglass to Raif. He examined it carefully, turning it this way and that, then holding it up to the light…

Which was when Fouad – like lightning – came to life. He grabbed the bobbin, concealed it in his tunic and resumed his statue-like pose only seconds before Darke barged in.

"You were supposed to notify me the minute the boy woke up," he fumed and looked suspiciously at Fouad.

Véronique had to think quickly. "He *has* only just woken up!" she stormed. "He was… starving!"

Much to her relief, Darke seemed to accept this explanation. It was plausible and, as they were surrounded by half-eaten pizza, it was obviously truthful. Seeing Darke again brought Véronique crashing back down to earth; her previous euphoria shattered as her loathing for him mounted.

"This is Darke," she said icily and put her arm around Raif protectively, "the person I was telling you about."

Tousled and red-faced, Raif dropped the cushion he'd instinctively picked up as a weapon and stared at Darke defiantly. With his cold black eyes, Darke stared back, and Véronique could see him waver as if there was something in Raif's younger eyes that unnerved him.

Darke disengaged and turned towards her. "You will remain here until further notice." That was all he said. He turned and made towards the door, which was when Fouad stepped forwards.

This is it! thought Véronique. Even though she hadn't yet found out if the bobbin was anything more than a trinket or novelty, she was banking on Mr Khan having given her something that would one day get her out of a jam. What bothered her too was her deceit could mean her having written her own death sentence.

It was therefore with bated breath that she watched Darke and Fouad exchange sign language and notes, and when satisfied, Darke nodded and left, locking the door behind him. Fouad assumed his statue-like pose.

"Well…?" said Véronique clearly. "Why didn't you betray us?" She knew no other way of saying it.

Fouad looked up, and for the first time since they'd met all that time ago in her basement apartment, he smiled and removed his hood, and in doing so looked completely different. "Because I'm going to help you," he replied, and after taking the bobbin from beneath his tunic, he handed it back to her.

62

Restless, ill at ease and still haunted by her premonition of death, Dina wandered out into the desert to find solitude. She hoped solitude would enable her to think more clearly, but think about what? Her frustration at being stranded here, her inability to do anything about it or castigation about her part in all this? If she could (do anything) it'd make no difference anyway unless she had a magic wand... or Lenken. Idly, she sifted the sand through her fingers, noting how hot it was on the surface yet how cold just beneath. She let it mingle, thinking how cathartic it felt until she became aware of no longer being alone. Was it a sound or a smell that had alerted her, or was it simply hope that if she closed her eyes then opened them again, she'd see Lenken sitting there?

He was. He was there but he wasn't sitting. He was poised and ready to pounce, which is exactly what he did, rolling Dina over and over in the sand.

"Lenken!" she squealed. "Lenken... You came!" she repeated, overjoyed at saying his name, and threw her arms around his neck.

With greetings exchanged, they sat and watched the dusk descending. The sky streaked hues of blood-red, gold and orange as she told him about Raif's disappearance, and how Gideon had gone after them with Askhat and Ganabek but as yet, they'd had no word. Then she told him about her terrible premonition. It was a premonition of death. But whose death?

"I have no pictures in my head to give you. No signs or symbols. Nothing. Just a terrible oppressive blackness…"

"Well, I'm here now," said Lenken, replacing the disc Dina had used to call him back into his collar. "I'll stay with you now until this matter is finished…"

"One way or the other."

Lenken turned and put his huge paws on Dina's forehead. "I need to know about your premonition and hope we're not too late."

Dina sat very still while, telepathically, he connected. She couldn't see it – no images flashed in her mind – but he could. And he stiffened.

"Please go and join the others," he said quietly, "and make preparations to leave at short notice. I have work to do here and I must do it alone."

Dina returned to the Canning Factory, leaving Lenken alone in the desert as the sun sank below the horizon. There were no hills in this desert sea but there were the rusted hulls of ships, long since abandoned, and Lenken chose one – the remains of a tanker by the look of it – sticking out of the sand with its bow pointing skywards. It must have been scuppered to have ended up this way, presumably to make removal of its cargo easier. It was a forlorn, depressing sight which prompted a great sadness in him.

But it was fit for purpose, so with long strides and

little effort he scaled the rusted carcass and sat poised on the prow. He was rewarded by a panoramic view of the landscape, and Lenken – with his sharp eyes – could see a faint glimmer of light on the horizon, which, as the evening light faded, grew brighter. *That's the place*, he thought. *And we still have time.*

Almost as if he were beginning a stage performance – which in many ways he was – Lenken meditated for a moment then rose to his full height and began. From small introductory guttural sounds, the volume increased until he produced a sound so haunting it could chill the blood of ghouls. It was an anguished howl. A cry that evoked terror, fear at its most desperate. He howled as if for all the sorrows of mankind.

Everyone within the Canning Factory heard it, stopped what they were doing and shivered. Even the camels stopped chewing and instead laid down their heads and mewed submissively as, still, the dreadful lament continued delivering its relentless instruction to the desert sky. Touching the souls of those still living and those a long time dead. Only Motto recognised the call but didn't know to whom or for what purpose. He said nothing.

And then it began. The sand around the derelict vessel started shifting. Sinking and swirling as it gained momentum, growing and falling into macabre shapes until tottering, collapsing and re-forming, it fell again. Each time, each effort grew bigger and more substantial until the sand towered into a great mass and held.

Lenken had summoned the Sandman, but who was he? To Motto, he was the thimble of dust that willed children to sleep when called upon to deliver wishes. Equally, he was a force so mighty he could move mountains. One couldn't put a finger on it because as soon as one tried it was gone or changed. He was the content of the Hourglass, the shifting sands that maintained the Grand Order by virtue of being the embodiment of Chaos. He was there to protect and to serve Pythia.

When the roaring died down it was replaced by more undulant tones. The shifting sands of the Sandman conferred with Lenken, not with words but with eerie banshee-like utterances, which were quite beautiful although unintelligible to anyone other than the two of them. The Sandman, now made manifest as a mass of swirling sand, constantly moved and swayed like a sandstorm. His face was distinguishable one moment then lost the next.

Lenken climbed down from his makeshift lectern and headed out across the desert with the huge moon bright in the sky keeping pace with him. The Sandman followed, creating a sandstorm like the wake of a ship, zig-zagging this way and that to maintain his momentum.

Lenken had been right. As he approached the small escarpment, he could see it was an entrance – the same service door Gideon had stumbled across – and it was still open. Flattening himself against the rock face, Lenken stood to one side and signalled to the Sandman. It was all that was needed. Lenken turned his head to the floor as the Sandman, screaming like a hurricane, and with all the speed and devastation of a hurricane, poured his fury down into the passageway.

It all happened so quickly. One minute Gideon, Askhat and Ganabek were staring into the face of certain death and the next they were lying in the aftermath of what? A sandstorm? But whatever, the mangled carcasses of the monstrous scorpions lay broken and lifeless around them.

"What happened...?" said Ganabek, getting to his feet and observing the carnage around him. Rocks, debris, and dismembered scorpion parts were strewn about in the sand and Gideon – as much as any of them – was as mystified as to what had taken place as he was. It was like a bomb had gone off yet none of them was hurt.

It was only then, as the dust was settling, that Gideon saw something move within the dark recess of the cave. Eyes glinted, reflecting the torchlight beam momentarily before extinguishing. "Stay back…" he instructed, his hand instinctively on his knife as he ventured forwards.

Leaving Askhat and Ganabek at the Great Door, Gideon probed the darkness as he ventured deeper into the cavern. He could smell the warmth and the damp smell of an animal then heard the sound of a low guttural growl. A growl he recognised.

"Lenken! I might have known!"

Lenken, sleek and shining, stepped into the beam of Gideon's head torch. "Dina knew you were in trouble," he said.

Gideon tried to recall what had actually happened but could only come up with there being some kind of dust devil that was sufficient to cause such carnage but which had nevertheless left them unscathed. He thanked Lenken, knowing he was responsible for such a timely intervention.

Lenken nodded. "You must go. And hurry. There's nothing more I can do here other than tell you that to open the Great Door you need to align the stars. Tell Askhat, he'll know what to do." And he melted into the darkness as if he'd never been there.

"What was it?" asked Ganabek when Gideon reappeared.

"The cavalry," he grinned, "and I'll explain later but first… Askhat. We need to align the stars."

After examining the Great Door more closely, Askhat selected two cylindrical motifs off-set against each other which carried the markings of the god Janus holding the keys against a backdrop of stars. Carefully he rotated these cylindrical discs until all the stars within aligned, then *click*, the Great Door clicked open.

63

Motto didn't quiz Dina when she returned from the desert. He knew something had taken place since he could sense Dina's restored inner calmness meaning that whatever danger had been out there, it had passed and those whom it had threatened were safe. *Was it Gideon or Raif?* he wondered. Instead, and to keep the mood light, he chattered to Sabina – Askhat's wife – who was curious to learn more about the Collective.

"I've only really met one of them face to face and that was Pythia," she explained, "although I did have an audience with the Elders when I was recruited. It was all beards and hearing aids… are they all like that?"

"Not so!" Motto chuckled, enjoying a tin of peaches in syrup. "The robes – yes – but that was only for your inauguration. Normally, they like to meet in somewhere like a village hall or community centre. In fact, they actually call it a Parish Meeting, and it's in a different place each time."

"And what about the members, the council?"

"Hmm… well… they come from all walks of life – planets too – and it largely depends on the agenda to decide who's best to attend. You'll be called one day."

Sabina beamed at the prospect. "And what about you? How do you fit in?"

"Me?" enquired Motto, giving in to another tin of peaches. "I deliver shooting star wishes... amongst other things. I'm here one moment and gone the next. If you like, I have a passport to the entire universe, and I like to think I have a special place in what's known as *The Overall Scheme of Things*."

Dina came over and smiled at his openness and listened as he explained the Collective's ingenuity. About how many parish councils, village councils, committees and societies there were. All low key, all under-rated and all well... boring. As was the intention, trying to track them down would be like trying to find a needle in a haystack.

Satisfied to have learned more about the Collective, Sabina went about her chores, leaving Dina and Motto alone. "Have you had any word from Anakee?" asked Dina, helping Motto with the peaches. Although Dina didn't know Anakee personally, she knew of her insofar as she was Canatu's older sister and had been devastated to learn of Darke's escape from Carcerem.

Motto shook his head. "Not directly. Not since I last saw her when she delivered Raif to Gideon and learned about Darke but a little bird told me she's with Pythia as we speak."

It was the hardest thing in the world for Anakee to leave Raif when she did. She knew he'd be safe in Gideon's care and even though her job was done she wanted to stay, nevertheless. She wanted to see this thing through. But then all that changed. Knowing Darke was out there meant she had to see Pythia and find out why and how. She was furious! Why hadn't Pythia told her?

She'd wasted no time. Just as Gideon had said he would

be, Henry Mullet Broadbent was tweeded up in his best Harris waiting for her when she'd emerged from Gideon's hut. Being at the centre of the universe – one of the many crossroads between dimensions – meant it wouldn't have been easy (if not nigh on impossible) for her to have found her way back on her own. She was relieved to see him.

"Keep a hold of this neckerchief and don't look back," he had advised, holding tightly on to the other end. "Maybe you might want to shut your eyes too."

Maybe Anakee *didn't* want to shut her eyes, and by not doing so she witnessed a journey very much as Raif had done racing through galaxies, constellations and time warps as if travelling through a timeless kaleidoscope of smoke and mirrors. It was wonderful and she didn't really want it to end.

"I do apologise for the journey having taken so long," Henry gushed when eventually they landed, "took a wrong turn somewhere along the line… got a bit flummoxed."

Anakee didn't feel it had taken any time at all but later found out what should have taken minutes had actually taken days (no wonder she was starving), but looking on the bright side, it hadn't taken years – or centuries… if it had she worried that she'd have been nothing more than dust!

Henry deposited Anakee in the garden of one of Pythia's many earthly residences. As the High Priestess of the Collective, she had access to many grand residences scattered throughout the world. Occupancy was conducted via word of mouth, with strictly no paperwork, relying on the '*it's who you know*' protocol rather than conforming to any formal arrangement. It was a global network – a highly successful *understanding* – of which La Petite Chambre was a good case in point.

Pythia, in keeping with her standing and being a Deity in her own right, had chosen somewhere far grander than the likes of La Petite Chambre. She had taken residence in the Abbey: a magnificent 900-year-old former Cistercian monastery set in 1,600 acres of prime farmland, which more than provided her with the space she needed.

She had agreed to meet Anakee whom she'd receive in the library. Pythia's greeting had been strained, Anakee was on the defensive and the conversation had been heated.

"I thought you of all people would understand!" bleated Anakee. "Darke's responsible for the death of my sister and now he's free! Why didn't you tell me?"

"Because what good would it have done?" said Pythia icily, not looking away from the index of books she was scrutinising. "You would have reacted, just like you're doing now, when we have far more pressing matters to attend to."

"You mean more important than the murder of my sister?"

"Yes... I mean no, of course not. It's just that it's a matter of priorities. We can't change what's happened but we can and must retrieve the Hourglass as our first priority. Otherwise... well... he will have won."

"Won?"

"No... yes... Look... I knew you'd be devastated – understandably so – but right now there is nothing we can do about it. I'm disappointed that having placed Raif in your care, you chose to abandon him at a drop of a hat. In fact, I believe it was here in this very room that you begged us to entrust the boy to you... the boy who'd been found to replace... I'm sorry... but to replace your sister. We are all devastated by her callous death, but it was precisely because you convinced me – you convinced all of us – that you were the one person, head and shoulders above anyone else, who had the strongest motive to ensure that the new Foundling, this innocent child, *the one who stepped in to take your sister's place*, would be safe and able to play his part in this continuity."

"I thought he'd be safe with Gideon..." countered Anakee.

"You thought nothing of the sort!" Pythia snapped back. "Your judgement was clouded by the selfish motivation of revenge. Vengeance isn't yours, it's mine!"

Anakee stared at Pythia with an ashen face. This wasn't what she'd been expecting. She thought Pythia would sympathise, she'd *understand* that if Darke was free it was right for her to go after him. *"He murdered my sister and now he's free!"* she argued, feeling her mind closing down, jarring with conflict and disbelief, hardly hearing the words still falling from Pythia's lips.

"... We felt you were the one we could trust the most, the one who would defend Raif with her *life* if necessary and look at what happened? Seduced by revenge, you didn't give the boy a second thought and now the boy's missing and for all we know he could already be dead!"

"That's not fair! I wasn't even there!" protested Anakee timidly.

"Exactly!" retorted Pythia and returned to her books. It was clearly the end of the interview.

64

Dina found it difficult – nigh on impossible – to be confined to the Canning Factory, unable to help or at least do something, so it was a welcome respite when Motto suggested they should follow on in the direction Gideon had taken.

"It would save time if he didn't have to come back here for us," he argued weakly, "and besides, he may need our help."

Dina didn't need any convincing and immediately began making preparations to leave at a moment's notice – if not sooner – and she didn't even seem to mind the prospect of sitting astride a camel for however many hours it might take. Motto shared this same buoyancy and was openly jubilant at the thought of seeing Raif and Gideon again.

Keeping their farewells brief, Motto and Dina set off into the desert. The Canning Factory had only just fallen behind the horizon when Motto was suddenly gripped by an excruciating pain, which caused him to fall to the ground.

"What is it?" exclaimed Dina, rushing to his aid, but Motto couldn't speak. All he could do was clutch at his head, as if it were ready to burst, and curl himself into a ball.

"Leave me!" he shouted in anguish. "Go... please... go back to the factory."

"I'm not leaving you!" protested Dina but she had no choice as Motto morphed into a bumblebee and was gone. It happened so quickly. Dina's words carried across the desert and with no one to receive them – to absorb them – they trailed off and fell to the deaf ears of the landscape. Why would Motto do this? What unseen force had gripped him? What was so important he would abandon her, now of all times? *There must be a reason – there's a reason for everything*, she thought silently and took comfort in her own wisdom as she held down her abject feelings of abandonment. *I must keep faith and allow events to unfold*, she thought silently to herself and drew strength from her stoicism.

Rather than go back to the Canning Factory, Dina sat alone in the sand for the second time since she'd arrived in this hostile landscape. She wondered how much more she could endure. Raif had been taken, Gideon was missing, and now Motto had deserted her, for what reason she didn't yet know. It seemed they were no closer to finding the Hourglass and they were being overwhelmed by adversaries known and unknown.

She breathed in deeply and savoured the beautiful shades of dawn as indigo gave way to shades of pink which then blushed stronger until the sun, dazzling in its re-birth, spilt into the sky. She thought wistfully of her garden in all its lush greenery and longed to be home amongst the roses and hollyhocks. She thought about the joy of grazing in her vegetable garden while there was still dew on the ground and felt tired. It all seemed such a long way away as she got to her feet and felt the heat of the sand.

It wasn't far back to the Canning Factory and Dina chose to walk rather than negotiate how she'd clamber back onto the camel unaided. It was nice to walk. At home, she always walked when she needed to think and here was no exception. Her thoughts brought her to what Motto had said about the well and how Raif had been compelled to investigate. How he'd possibly found a way through to whatever lay beneath.

She arrived back at the Canning Factory and, rather than joining the others, made straight for the building that housed the well, taking care no one saw her. Shutting the door on the beautiful morning, she peered down the well into its inky blackness. Her heart sank. Surely Raif would not have climbed in. It would have been madness, but just as she turned to go, the sun rose infinitesimally higher and it was enough to introduce the first rays of light through the delapidated remains of the east wall.

As the sun rose, so the light grew stronger as it refracted upon the blue stones embedded along the circumference of the well. And as the light, like a wave, travelled downwards in accordance with the sun's trajectory, so a faint blue tinge started to emanate from deep within the still waters. It grew steadily brighter.

Just as Raif had been, Dina felt compelled to climb in, and she hoped the water wouldn't be too cold. It wasn't and, in fact, was rather pleasant, so she quickly discarded her sandals. The rope Motto had provided was still there and she checked to make sure it was tied securely. If she was wrong in what she was about to do, she may as well have a plan B.

Over the time she'd spent with the nomads she had, by degrees, shed her practical, rural clothing – clothing more suited to foul weather, brambles and downpours – in favour of the flowing desert attire as worn by the women. Dina had to admit it was extremely comfortable and had decided this is what she'd always wear once she returned home. Even when visiting the Co-op.

Therefore and needless to say, she found swimming (treading water) in this attire made her feel both graceful and aquatic, so after a few attempts to build her confidence and get used to the feel of things, she was ready to take the plunge. She took a deep breath and disappeared beneath the silky blue surface. The water soon stilled and several minutes later the surface remained unbroken. She didn't reappear.

65

Following her interview with Pythia, Anakee didn't know what to do or where to go. She felt confused and as she turned over in her mind what Pythia had said she experienced a feeling of mounting guilt. Pythia was right. She should never have left Raif. She shouldn't have lied when she'd said her job was done. Panic and an overwhelming sadness gripped her. The Abbey, which had felt friendly before, now seemed to shun her. All the staff had gone, so she could wander at will through the historic rooms with their high ceilings and unsmiling portraiture knowing no one would come to help her or enquire. No one to care, least of all Pythia.

She wandered aimlessly from room to room, eventually finding herself in the garden walking through the formal rose gardens down to the lake. A welcome breeze fanned her face and it made her long to be free, to be rid of this place this world… this pain.

She slumped on a bench by the side of the lake, threw back her head and from the top of her lungs expelled the heartfelt words, "*I wish I was dead!*"

Feeling better at howling such a release, Anakee kept her eyes closed, not realising in her anguish that she had uttered these words at precisely the same moment a shooting star arced across the sky.

Motto, still in the guise of a bumblebee, was trying to find his way through the endless corridors, desperate to locate Anakee's precise whereabouts. He'd had several shooting star alerts since he'd joined the quest to find the Hourglass but none had proved time-sensitive. In fact, most would-be recipients would have already forgotten about them and, anyway, they could all be dealt with in the fullness of time. This one was different. This was an SOS of the highest and most urgent order and more than that, it had come from Anakee, so it was little wonder he'd reacted so violently.

But right now he desperately needed honey – or, better still, nectar – and he headed for the garden where he found roses… hundreds of them and drank heavily. How he'd managed to arrive at this place in such a short space of time would be something he'd ponder during the long winter evenings. True, he could materialise virtually anywhere, and sometimes at remarkable speed, but in doing so – and doing it too often – certainly took its toll.

The sweet nectar worked wonders to revive him but, still feeling rather dizzy, he decided he'd make better progress if he resumed human form. Besides, he could see zealous cleaners arriving and the last thing he'd want would be to encounter a toxic cloud of fly spray. The nectar was great as a pick-me-up but now he needed sugar – vast amounts of it – and he headed for the kitchen.

It didn't take him long to find out that most, if not all, of the rooms were unoccupied and he had no idea that Pythia was temporarily in residence. The place had a deserted feel that rather unnerved him, so he headed below stairs where industry replaced grandeur as staff went about their chores.

No one took any notice of him – an art he'd perfected during the course of his very long life – and it was almost by accident that he saw one of the cleaners carrying a tray upon which was a mug of tea surrounded by a few biscuits and, thankfully, a sugar bowl heaped with his salvation. He took a chance that the tray was for Anakee.

"I'll take that, she's a friend of mine, and by the way… thank you. She's had a pretty rough time."

"I don't know who she is," said the cleaner, willingly handing over the tray. "I found her curled up in a corner and she wouldn't speak, so I thought I'd wait until the office opened… Didn't see the need for the police, well not until the morning…"

Motto thanked the cleaner again, and as soon as she'd resumed her duties, he downed the contents of the sugar bowl in one. It would buy him twenty minutes or so, time enough to find his next sugar hit.

He knocked on the door indicated by the cleaner. No response but he didn't expect one. What he didn't expect either when he opened the door was to see the pitiful sight of Anakee, normally so crisp and tidy, so *in control*, now wretched and dishevelled, curled up in the farthest corner of the room, her knees clasped to her chest. She was rocking gently. All the time she hummed quietly to herself, but he didn't catch the melody.

It was difficult to know how to approach her. He didn't want to frighten her but neither did he have time to coax her and gain her confidence. "Anakee, my darling. You poor child… It's me… Motto," he said quietly.

Anakee turned towards him quizzically and, on recognition, momentarily betrayed joy at seeing him, only for this to cloud as she again withdrew into herself. "Go away!" she muttered dully at him. "Pythia's right. I've messed everything up."

Motto settled himself on the floor beside her and leaned against the wall. He wanted to sit next to her rather than opposite to make them equal. Like friends, which of course they were. "I'm afraid I can't do that," he said. "You made a shooting star wish and it's my painful duty to carry out that wish. That's the way it is with shooting stars."

"What wish?" asked Anakee, recalling very little other than her misery.

"You said, '*I wish I was dead*'."

Anakee thought about this. "Well, I do," she said uncertainly. "It would be better for everyone."

"... But not necessarily for you."

"I don't matter."

"I think you do."

"I don't, so just go away."

Motto sighed, they were going around in circles. He was duty-bound to carry out that wish and it seemed pretty certain Anakee wasn't about to retract it – not that that would have made any difference.

"Look," he said kindly. "You made the wish, so I've got to carry it out... Is there anything you'd like to say... you know... before?"

"Just get on with it."

"Are you sure?"

"Yes."

"Well, if that is your wish, so be it." He sighed heavily but added, almost as if it were an afterthought (but wasn't). "But you know... in my long experience, I've learnt that shooting star wishes are all about interpretation..."

"Meaning?"

"Did I ever tell you the story about the boy and the yellow bicycle?"

Anakee said nothing but with her hands over her ears

she listened, nevertheless. She listened while Motto related the yellow bicycle story and others besides insofar as things are not always what they seem and slowly, bit by bit, word by word, he managed to cajole her into a more positive way of thinking.

Patiently, as if they had all the time in the world, Motto talked and Anakee listened until such time she answered back. She disagreed. They debated. They argued until in the end they were laughing and teasing, and Motto knew he had the Anakee he knew and loved restored to him.

"So what do we do now?" asked Anakee, feeling a whole lot better as she got to her feet and smoothed down her tousled hair. "Do I still have to die?" she enquired, thinking she'd better make sure.

Motto smiled and shook his head. "No. I think you've already managed to kill off the broken Anakee – the one curled up in the corner full of despair and self-loathing – so let's get the reborn Anakee out of here, but first… I really do need to find some sugar!"

66

When Darke locked the door behind him and left Véronique alone with Raif and Fouad, she wasn't quite sure what to do next. Should she trust this Fouad? *Did she have any choice?*

"I didn't like *him* much," said Raif, referring to Darke, then he turned his attention to Fouad. "Thank you for not saying anything... I mean I know you can't speak – or hear – but you did. You can? Oh dear..."

Both Fouad and Véronique laughed.

"Yes, how come?" asked Véronique. "I thought you were one of his trusted servants or whatever it is you call yourselves."

"I was. And as far as Darke is concerned I still am but since coming here I've learned a lot about Darke and his ambitions and it's fair to say we err... differ on many fundamental levels."

"What do you mean?"

"I'm an ecologist. He's a destructionist. As part of my thesis, I came here to study the disappearance of the Arrid Sea and found out Darke was behind it all. I don't know much, but what I do know is monstrous."

"But I thought he only employed deaf-mutes. That being the case, how did you manage to get in?"

"Easy. It's only acting. I used to play statues in the Piazza. You know... you stand there for hours and people throw money at you. When you've done that for a few hours every day, playing a deaf-mute is easy. I was a statue of a Roman soldier."

"I know a soldier, but I don't think he's Roman?" piped up Raif thinking of Spiritas.

Véronique warmed to the young man. He seemed genuine. Just a nice-looking young man, full of dreams and aspirations – not dissimilar to her student friends at the Université de Descartes – and it wasn't as though she was awash with options.

"Okay," she said. "Have you ever heard of the Hourglass?"

"You mean the one all the fuss is about? The one locked in the vault?"

Véronique wasn't often stuck for words and she wasn't going to let this be a (rare) case in point. "That's right," she said evenly as if it was the most normal conversation in the world, "and as you probably know – as you've probably *eavesdropped* – we have to retrieve this Hourglass, return it to its rightful guardian and in doing so allegedly save the world. Now then, do you know, firstly, how we can get out of here and, secondly, can you lead us to where the Hourglass is being kept?"

Unfortunately, Fouad fell at the first fence since it was beyond his powers to even open the door.

Véronique then wondered – but didn't say so – if this young man would prove to be of any use to her at all. These idealists often lacked practical skills and, sadly, any vestige of common sense but, to his credit, he had infiltrated Darke's world *and was still alive*, so, for now, she'd reserve judgement.

Instead, she turned her attention to the bobbin Mr Khan had given her. She examined it closely, scrutinising the miniature hourglass contained within. She turned it this way and that and watched the tiny grains fall from one chamber to another. Nothing happened. She shook it; she rattled it. She even threw it like a dice, but still, it remained unremarkable.

"I think it's an egg timer," offered Fouad helpfully.

"No it isn't," countered Véronique, who refused to believe Mr Khan would pass her off with a novelty. Didn't he take her *seriously*?

Defiantly, she stared at the tiny hourglass within its bobbin casing and conjured an image of Mr Khan. In her mind's eye, she could see him in his Furniture Emporium putting the kettle on when – much to her surprise – he turned and spoke to her as if she were standing next to him.

"You're supposed to use that only in an emergency," he said sternly then paused as he rinsed out his cup and continued with his tea-making ceremony.

Véronique was initially completely taken aback but remained undeterred.

"Well, I think this is an emergency!" she retorted without hesitation. "Raif's being held prisoner – as too am I – the Hourglass is locked in some vault and if we don't get out of here soon it's all going to be too late!"

Mr Khan suspended his tea making and looked at her sharply. "Give me one moment, please." And he was gone. Véronique couldn't understand what on earth had just happened when a small polite cough made her turn to see Mr Khan, with his ankles crossed, calmly seated in the chair in front of her. "You were saying?" he said patiently.

Véronique had learned not to be surprised by anything anymore, so Mr Khan's *manifestation* was no exception. After all, she'd only recently had a long and lucid conversation with a doppelgänger. Raif and Fouad, on the other hand, were gobsmacked.

"Raif... I believe you know Mr Khan," she said, sounding rather as if she were at a conference or garden party.

"I sure do!" exclaimed Raif, obviously delighted at seeing his friend and mentor. "Fancy seeing you here!"

"He's only a... err... manifestation," said Véronique, eager to take charge. "I asked him to come..."

Mr Khan didn't object or contradict her. On the contrary, he agreed absolutely. "That is right. Véronique informed me you needed me, so here I am. Please, would you bring the bobbin to me... and hold it for me too.

"It's rather clever," he explained as he ran ghostly fingers over (and through) it. "You know the expression '*I think therefore I am*'? Well, this operates along the same principles. If you want it to be a light, then it's a light. If you want it to open doors, just let it know which one. If you need to find your way, it will guide you. If you need to find friends, just say who. All you need to do is think it and mean it."

"Wow..." said Raif.

"Cool..." said Fouad.

"Thank you," said Véronique as Mr Khan faded.

67

Darke was keenly aware of Gideon's presence within the compound. After all, it was he himself who'd lured him, but no matter; Gideon would wander these tunnels and passages for days, and with this thought in mind, he relaxed a little, although his intuition – that tiny voice – told him something wasn't right. He was irritated that the scorpion guards hadn't dealt with Gideon as intended and was curious too as to how, not only had his guards been defeated, he'd also succeeded in breaching the Great Door. It was a glitch, that's all. A temporary setback, which was irritating but manageable, and besides, now wasn't the time for speculation. The time for the Turning was drawing ever closer and while there was still much to be vigilant about, the underlying strain was causing him problems. He was experiencing an overwhelming weariness as if all his energy was being systematically drained.

He stood for a moment and looked – for the umpteenth time – into the vast glass wall behind which his ambition was contained. The colossal volume of cold unyielding water. He needed to recharge. To prepare himself for whatever eventualities lay before him and was sufficiently *compos mentis* to know he'd need all the strength he could muster.

Ritualistically, Darke prepared himself for his purpose-built altar and offered himself up to the blue light. Almost immediately he fell into a trance-like state and a vision came at him like a freight train. Such was its speed and ferocity, it was loud and terrifying as he felt himself being dragged down and ensnared by hands he couldn't see while millions upon millions of gallons of water crushed down on him. He was being crushed in space but space that was solid.

With a sharp intake of breath, he sat up with a start. The shock made him wheeze as if choking – he didn't dare use the word 'drowning' – and it took a moment or two for him to regain his composure. The vision, dream, insight or whatever it was had unnerved him, but it had served to kick in his very practised instinct for survival. He would ensure his house was in order and he would agree to Breaffen being the custodian of the Hourglass.

Véronique continued to stare at the place where Mr Khan had been for quite a few moments after he'd gone as if to use the time to gauge whether or not this encounter had been an extreme case of autosuggestion on her part or merely a huge cosmic practical joke. With this in mind, and feeling a little foolish as a consequence, Véronique stared pointedly into the fullest chamber of the tiny hourglass and – if the truth be known – did her utmost to stifle a small giggle. But she went with it and, as instructed, visualised the door to her apartment unlocking. It was all terribly serious as Raif, on cue, tried the door, which, much to her delight, opened as if it had never been locked. She did the same thing again only this time, instructing the door to be locked. And it was. Locked. Unlocked. This was all very encouraging.

Autosuggestion, magic or merely a whole different set of rules that she was fast coming to accept, Véronique decided that now wasn't the time to question or probe the reasons why. It worked and that was enough for her. If she could get them out of the apartment (which she'd proved she could) could Fouad lead Raif to the vault? Yes. Could Raif gain access to the Hourglass? Unlikely, but worth a try.

She had a plan and this excited her. She would distract Darke for long enough to enable Raif and Fouad to complete their mission, and in order for her to fulfil her role in the offensive, her thoughts turned towards her choice of wardrobe and this excited her too.

With no time to lose, preparations were made. Fouad communicated to Darke that Véronique had requested an urgent audience and advised that such a meeting would be *significant* since she was keen to offer him a proposition the details of which she wouldn't disclose.

Two deaf-mutes duly delivered Véronique to Darke's inner sanctum. There was no protest or resistance on her part, so restraint wasn't necessary. She arrived composed and elegant in an Alexander McQueen cream tailored suit, comfortably wearing spiked stilettos. Her hair was newly styled, her nails manicured, and she simply looked fabulous. Darke – who appreciated such grooming – couldn't help being impressed, particularly as he noticed too that she wore diamonds on both hands and a great many of them.

He poured her a glass of Dom Pérignon Rosé and one for himself. They chinked glasses and she noticed that although he brought the glass to his lips, not a drop was imbibed.

"So, what is your proposition?" he asked, adopting the manner of a convivial host, and although Véronique found this quite sinister, she was ready and prepared to play up to it. She knew he cared not what her *proposition* may or may not be since he'd be bound to ignore it anyway. What he liked – and what she knew he wanted – was the audience of her company. She was his entertainment until such time she became problematic.

"I've come to ask that you let me and Raif go free," she said getting straight to the point. "You have the Hourglass and Raif is no possible threat to you. If you don't let us go, they'll come for him – they're probably here already – and together with the might of the Collective, they'll crush you…"

"Ahh… So, you've been reading up on the Collective," replied Darke evenly. "No doubt they'll try but they won't get here in time and when the time's passed – what then?"

Véronique contemplated drawing him out regarding the vast supplies of water he held. Using long words she wasn't sure the meaning of, she wanted to confront him with his rapidly deteriorating mental health but it would be a dangerous path. To her, he was obviously quite bonkers and, as such, probably wouldn't respond well to being told this. Instead, she remained pleasant and steered Darke back to his relationship with the Hourglass. She was eager anyway to know as much as she could about his motivation and his distorted vision of the future.

"Okay… So, just supposing that the Hourglass doesn't get turned," she challenged, "seeing as you're no doubt going to kill me – or at least try to – you may as well tell me. Does the world get plunged into darkness? Are we thrown into a biblical flood with the pestilence of epic proportion as whole civilisations are wiped out by earthquake and tsunami?" She paused for dramatic effect. "Are we *all* going to die?"

Véronique was aware she was pushing the boundaries, but she *had* to keep him talking. He took the bait. It was almost too easy but that's the way it was. That's the way it was with all psychotic narcissists.

"No. Initially nothing will happen," he replied in a matter-of-fact tone that Véronique found chilling. "The sun will continue to rise and set, the moon will continue its usual trajectory, the tides will ebb and flow, and the weather will follow the patterns of logic determined by pressure and season. All will seemingly be as it was before, but the wild card of unpredictability will be incubating the chaotic wantonness of extremes."

"Extremes? In what way?"

Véronique sat back and sipped more champagne. She could see she'd hit the spot insofar as Darke was set to indulge – given the (rare) opportunity – in what he liked to talk about most. After years of isolation, it was stimulating to have an exchange with an intelligent individual – particularly one as attractive and engaging as she was. She was sure too that he must be regretting that soon he'd be attempting to terminate her but he'd be making the most of it in the meantime. Almost as if on cue, he poured her more champagne.

"Extremes of phenomena are part of the day to day but without control – without order – they would go wildcat," he continued amiably. "Imagine a small volcano, there are so many which erupt occasionally, but in doing so the devastation is localised. Now imagine an eruption a hundred times bigger that prompts a chain reaction."

"Are you talking about the... what's it called...?"

"The Butterfly Effect?" said Darke finishing her sentence. "Yes, as my vision will verify it is precisely this seemingly innocent phenomenon that will bring about the ultimate destruction of this planet as we know it and bring about the opportunity for the changes as made testament in the *Alternate Prophecies.*"

He waited for a response but Véronique said nothing. She knew he was looking for some clue as to the extent of her knowledge. She didn't let on that she had, in fact, come across various references to the *Alternate Prophecies*, although these were so shrouded in contradiction and secrecy, it was difficult to get a handle on not only their authenticity but also their credibility.

Darke watched as she shifted uncomfortably in her chair. She had considered and possibly accepted that there were many highly far-fetched stories and claims in the Bible that did nothing to rock faith, so why not be as equally open-minded about an alternative doctrine? Whatever. She would give this thought later but for now, she was enjoying the exchange and wanted to savour what little time she had left. "So, a volcano will wipe us all out?" she continued. "Like it did in Pompeii but triggering a chain reaction?"

"It won't be a volcano," said Darke, "although that could follow as the earth's crust re-aligns and settles. It will be a tornado – a colossal waterspout – which will come from the humblest of beginnings as a boy, idly playing with a football, inadvertently smashes a window."

Darke went on to describe, in detail, his vision of the waterspouts and how these mutated and multiplied, taking up seas and vast areas of water to leave devastation on a scale unimagined before.

Véronique settled in the white leather chair and crossed her long, elegant legs. She extended her glass in a request for more champagne and prepared herself for the long haul. "So really, you see yourself as some kind of Saviour…"

68

The water, tinged with blue, was crystal clear and Dina felt like she was flying, swooping and gliding between rocks like mountains with plains that stretched out far beneath. The water was of a similar temperature to her own – maybe a few degrees cooler – and the coolness made it delicious after the heat and dryness of the desert. She was aware she only had a limited amount of time underwater, and if she didn't come across an air pocket soon, she accepted she would drown. However, she felt no fear. She had faith.

There was a spot directly ahead of her where the light was brighter, although she couldn't tell how far above her it might be. Regardless, she swam towards it – she had no other option – and broke the surface gasping. It was only a small chamber – like an oasis in the rock – and the entire cavity was encrusted with rocks, crystals and minerals of every hue from the blue spectrum. From amethyst to aquamarine.

Treading water, she took in her surroundings; it was all so amazingly beautiful. She saw a semi-submerged ledge, an overhang of sorts, and she'd need to crawl along it, coming up for air – so to speak – periodically as and when it dipped below the waterline. Being naturally sure-footed, she edged her way along sometimes above the water and sometimes just below it until she emerged into an immense empty cavern.

Dina looked up into the giddying empty space. An industrially large pipe on the opposite side was disgorging an unending quantity of water into a holding tank for what could only be the next aquifer waiting to be filled. It would be a bit of a climb – but not a difficult one – to reach what she could see was a precarious roped walkway snaking around the perimeter.

"I think I've found my way in," she said to herself with no small measure of satisfaction and put her best foot forwards.

It wasn't a difficult climb. In fact, it was easy when compared to the treachery of the Great Chasm, although she wasn't quite so keen on the roped walkway which swayed and frayed as she minded her footing. But she made it and took the first entrance she was presented with, which led her into the main plant.

It was very noisy. Pumps and turbines whirred and hummed incessantly along, seemingly, miles of pipework. The light was dim, so it was hard to make anything out properly, but as dials and pressure gauges meant very little to her, she concentrated only on finding the way out. A few uniformed operatives absorbed in monitoring the procedures were dotted here and there but no one saw her and there were no guards. She chose an exit door nearest to her and slipped into what looked like a service track. It was hewn out of the rock, lit by arc lamps hanging at intervals and it led – so she hoped – to the hub of Darke's main complex.

There was a notice sellotaped to the UPVC glass door of Mount Joy Village Hall. It said 'Roving Ramblers Society. Extraordinary General Meeting 10.30am (today)', and as the local time was 10.32, it meant the meeting was already in progress. Representatives from the Collective were duly assembled, and all were suitably attired in stout boots, lightweight waterproof jackets, map pouches around necks (where necks existed) and bobble hats...

Pythia – similarly attired for the occasion – chaired the meeting. She banged the table to call them to order as she didn't have much time. "Thank you for coming here at such short notice. I have it on good authority that Darke is indeed in possession of the Hourglass and that Raif, the Foundling, is also his prisoner. We are unsure as to the whereabouts of Gideon but no doubt he won't be far away. Or let us hope so. I am of the opinion that our intervention is necessary, and as such, I need a show of hands to enable sending in our Armed Forces..."

The assembled took a moment or two to confer and there followed a lot of head nodding and grunts of approval. Arms of varying lengths and sizes (and numbers) were duly raised, and the motion was passed.

"Thank you," said Pythia crisply. "Make the necessary arrangements and we'll reconvene on Golden Cap. You will be notified as to when... Any questions?"

Without waiting for any questions to be asked, Pythia closed the meeting. This meeting still holds the record for being the shortest committee meeting on record, lasting precisely 3.14 minutes.

69

Raif and Fouad knew they didn't have long to locate the Hourglass. For every minute Véronique was risking her life buying time for them was a minute closer to Darke realising he'd been duped. And then the unthinkable consequences. Raif had been hotly against the plan but was forced to agree since as things stood, there was no other way.

"Come on… this way," said Fouad, locking the door behind them. With Fouad's knowledge of the complex and with the help of the bobbin co-navigating and opening doors, they found their way to the vault. It was a large, steel, impenetrable door displaying no lock or visible means of entry.

Raif's heart sank. "Even if we could open it, surely it would set off all the alarms," he said despondently. He'd seen many films where the robbers got caught – or at least didn't get far – because the alarms had gone off.

"I didn't think of that…" said Fouad.

"Nor did I," said Raif.

Two heads are normally better than one but, in this instance, neither could come up with a solution until Raif had the dawning of an idea. "Didn't Mr Khan say, 'to find friends, just say who'? So if the Hourglass is my friend, and I truly believe it is, can't I just say take me to my friend the Hourglass?"

Fouad didn't answer. How could he? Logically, Raif was right but surely it meant stuff like turn left here, right down there and keep going. Being transported through plate steel was a little more... ambitious?

"We won't know if we don't try," said Raif. "You wait here, and I'll be back in a jiffy."

Before Fouad could assemble any kind of argument advising otherwise, Raif locked his psyche into what he kindly referred to as *the novelty egg timer* and made his request. To be fair, it took a few moments for the request to be processed but processed it was and Raif found himself in a tall, circular room, which apparently had no door. It was rather like a tower with a constant light source coming through the glass-topped ceiling high above him. He wasn't sure if he might be underwater because the light seemed to ripple and refract. Sometimes it changed into an aquamarine blue and at other times it became the soft green colour of jade.

Central to this room was a pedestal. It was about three times Raif's height, maybe a little more, and was also circular, and whereas the walls of the vault were decorated with extravagant mosaics and friezes, the sheer smooth surface of the pedestal was remarkable for its plainness. The Hourglass – still in its ornate and engraved casing – was atop this pedestal, magnificent in its isolation.

There was no way Raif could examine the Hourglass more closely as it was way out of his reach and the smooth sides of the pedestal provided no opportunity for purchase. He looked around the vault for anything he could use to climb up on but there was nothing fit for purpose, only a hard bench secured to the floor that was too far away anyway.

Raif sat on this bench and stared up at the Hourglass. He wondered but doubted if he had enough room to make a run for it. If he simply *threw* himself at the pedestal to gain enough height to clamber up it, he might gain enough height just to grab it. He tried and each time just ended up sliding to the floor again.

So he gave up this idea and, instead, returned to sit on the hard bench where he looked up and stared intently at the Hourglass. All the while he thought about what Spiritas had said to him and could hear him saying it... over and over. *'It's all about believing...'*

So Raif started believing. "You believed a paper plane could bring you here, so believe you can move the Hourglass..." he chanted quietly over and over and over.

It was at this moment with his hands outstretched, palms upwards, that he recalled what Sabina had said. Something about lineage and being the Chosen One. He called to mind, too, the small silver box. Keeping one hand extended towards the Hourglass – for some reason he felt it important to maintain the connection – he ferreted in his pocket with his other hand and pulled out the box. The lid clicked open willingly and as expected – or rather, as hoped – another drift of ghostly Celestial Messengers rose up and shimmered before shrouding the Hourglass like a morning mist. As they did so, Raif willed the Hourglass towards the edge of the pedestal and held his breath while the Messengers took over and gently lifted it up.

For a while, nothing further happened, but Raif didn't give up. He stayed focused on that one single thought until, almost undetectable at first, the Hourglass began to show signs of life. Slowly, it began to pulse, radiating shimmering sound waves that emanated rhythmically from deep within; waves that took on the same colour and tone as the blue-green water above.

And with that the Hourglass moved, safe in the ghostly hands of the Celestial Messengers. It was very slight, to begin with, but it *did* move. It moved closer and closer towards the edge in Raif's direction while he continued to look and continued to believe until – when it was right on the edge of the pedestal – the celestial hands let go, the balance was tipped and the Hourglass careered headlong towards the stone floor.

If there was ever one single memorable catch (or save, or goal, or shot) in a boy's life this was it. Why it all happened in super-slow motion, Raif would never know, but he got to his feet, threw himself to the floor, rolled (probably twice), held up his arms and in his outstretched fingers caught the Hourglass.

Véronique was acutely aware that her life could be terminated at any moment. Darke hadn't poisoned the champagne – she hadn't missed the fact she'd been the only one drinking it – because now, the best part of a bottle later, she'd already have been a goner if he had. She mused as to her exit. Perhaps it would be a small pistol to the head but decided that would be far too messy. He wasn't the sort to clear up after himself and he'd hardly want one of his servants to know about it. Feeling more unsure of her ground she was noticeably more guarded as she distanced herself from him and scrutinised his every move, watching for anything that could herald her demise.

Her gradual change in behaviour seemed to have alerted him since whereas before she'd made such an effort to appear *interested* in him and in his ambitions, now her behaviour was more reticent. She'd feigned being so attentive – even supportive – of his ideals but now she was wondering if she'd gone too far. Surely... surely... he couldn't think she meant it? That he was beginning to think – and she gagged at the thought of it – that there could be a future for them…?

"Look… I hope you don't think…" she began and that was enough. The suave nonchalance that Darke had been practising vanished in an instant and, whether or not it was the champagne that gave her clarity of vision or merely female intuition, she watched as his paranoia took hold. She knew he no longer saw her as the interesting coquettish woman she'd so cleverly presented. Now he would question why she'd seemed to relish this exchange when now, she so obviously did not. Why she was drawing out the conversation when it was suddenly so apparent to him that she loathed him. Why was she toying with him? Why she was keeping him talking…

He became gripped by a fury, like a child's sudden tantrum, and she hadn't expected him to move so fast or so suddenly. She didn't see the micro-thin wire he pulled from out of his sleeve and only became aware of it when he raised his arms and lunged.

But she was quick too – and prepared – although she hadn't planned on her passion for diamonds proving to be so useful. As the wire was about to make contact with her exposed throat her hand flew up and it was the diamond cluster on her third finger of her right hand which snagged the wire and prevented it cutting.

"*Raif!*" she screamed as she fell to the floor, resisting the wire Darke was still holding… which suddenly went slack.

At the sound of the boy's name, Darke glanced up then stopped in his tracks. Momentarily, he forgot all about Véronique wrestling on the floor and stared in disbelief. It wasn't seeing Raif that caused him to drop the wire and fall back, it was seeing Raif holding the Hourglass.

With equal fury at witnessing Darke's assault on Véronique, Raif roared with wild eyes and a red face. "*Leave her alone!*" he thundered.

Véronique had already scrambled to her feet. "Let's get out of here!" she said grimly, grabbing Raif's hand and running towards the door only for their path to be blocked by Fouad.

"Stop them!" shouted Darke hoarsely before realising a deaf-mute couldn't hear or speak, so in an absolute rage he resorted to sign language, frantically raising and flapping his arms.

While Fouad feigned confusion and made a clumsy show at being overpowered as he pretended to apprehend them, Véronique and Raif, still clutching the Hourglass, ran for all their worth. Soon the guards arrived together with more deaf-mutes and, amidst all the mayhem, Fouad was well placed to frantically point them in the opposite direction to that of the direction of their intended quarry.

70

"What's that?" said Gideon and he stopped dead in his tracks as he motioned Askhat and Ganabek to pull back. They were in one of the main service routes, which so far had remained deserted, but now an elongated shadow approached and bobbed along on the ceiling.

"Shhh…" motioned Askhat silently and drew his knife. Just as the intruder rounded the corner, Askhat lashed out but found himself being slammed against the wall with *his* knife now against *his* throat as Dina deftly disarmed him.

"Askhat!" she pronounced and dropped the knife.

"Dina!" responded Askhat in equal surprise.

She retrieved the knife and gave it back to him. "It's nice to know the skills are still there," she smiled, "and how perfectly wonderful to see you."

And then she saw Gideon. Words wouldn't come to her when she saw he was safe. He was alive and had survived her terrible premonition.

Gideon was overjoyed too. "How did you get here?" he asked, giving her an unexpectedly large hug before pulling back. "Hey… you're all damp? How come?"

Dina explained about the well and about how Motto

had been suddenly called away. She told him too about the premonition. "I thought you were... you know."

"Yep, it was a bit close at one point but we're okay. Now tell me, do you have any news on Raif?"

71

Véronique, now hot and dishevelled, very much regretted her earlier choice of high stilettos. She collapsed into the sand, pulled them off and threw them against the rock face. Whereas it was easy for Raif – being a bouncing nearly-ten-year-old with boundless energy, able to cover any amount of distance – for Véronique, it was one hundred per cent physical and therefore exhausting. She added near strangulation and having downed the best part of a bottle of champers to her defence.

They'd travelled a myriad of capillary tunnels that had got increasingly smaller and the previously provided lighting had long since given up; she relied now on the bobbin, which Raif was happy to hold aloft. With no sign of Fouad, she had no coherent idea of where to go. She couldn't ask the bobbin to direct her since she had no idea where to go other than '*not here*' and that would hardly constitute a workable instruction. Besides, she wouldn't dream of leaving Fouad behind and was anxious for him to catch up.

"Come and look at this!" called Raif.

Reluctantly, she got to her feet and followed the light source around a large rock to where Raif was standing in a high and spacious cavern. He was transfixed, staring into an extremely inviting, luminous blue lagoon.

Véronique didn't need an invitation. Half running, half limping, she stumbled to the water's edge and slipped her feet into the delicious water.

After setting the Hourglass down, still in its latticed casing, between them, Raif pulled off his trainers and joined her in putting his feet in the water. Neither of them spoke. There was no need to.

Was it by chance, bearing in mind there's no such thing as chance since *all things happen for a reason*, or was it due to some divine intervention on the part of the Hourglass that Gideon and Dina, having told Askhat and Ganabek to return and wait for them at the Canning Factory, had decided to remove themselves from the beaten track? Rather than continuing forwards, Dina had had an overwhelming compulsion to turn left, then left again, and again, and again. Gideon, knowing better than to question these instincts, had kept faith and had allowed Dina to lead the way. Smaller and smaller the passageways became – and darker and darker as head torches were switched on – until they came to a strange blue light emanating from the recesses of the rock face.

It was no great surprise to Dina to find herself in *an extremely inviting luminous blue lagoon*. What did surprise her, however – what actually made her jaw fall open – was seeing Véronique quietly sitting on the other side of the lagoon with Raif sitting to the right of her and the Hourglass nestled between them. It looked for all the world as if they'd been awaiting their arrival.

72

Something caught Raif's eye. He looked up and across the blue lagoon and saw Dina and Gideon looking back at him. He wasn't sure if it was some kind of mirage again. Or maybe a trick of the light brought on by wishful thinking. He'd learned through the course of this incredible adventure to not always believe what he saw, so was this yet another trick? Another test?

No. It was nothing of the sort. Dina waved her arms frantically and called out to him while Gideon wasted no time in wading into the water, taking great strides towards him. Dina eagerly followed suit as Raif did likewise, beside himself with joy as they charged towards each other This was no mirage or wishful thinking! Here were his friends – they'd made it!

Véronique remained where she was and watched the happy reunion, and as if to lay claim – to send out the signals to show she was neither afraid nor intimidated – she pointedly put a protective arm around the Hourglass.

This gesture didn't go unnoticed by either Dina or Gideon who approached Véronique with a measure of caution. Dina and Véronique recognised each other immediately and a cursory nod was exchanged between them. Gideon was more forthright in his contempt, refusing eye contact with a scowl firmly fixed on his face, leaving Raif to make the introductions.

"This is my friend Véronique," he volunteered, a little out of breath when they'd all clambered out onto the same waterside. "With the help of Mr Khan and Fouad, she got us out. She's really brave…"

"Oh… I wouldn't say that, but yes, if you say so." Véronique smiled openly as she got to her feet and extended her hand. "I'm so terribly pleased to see you all."

There followed a bit of an impasse. There was so much to say but no one knew where to start so Véronique continued. "Before you say anything and pass any kind of judgement of me I'd just like to say I'm sorry I took the Hourglass – at the time I didn't know what it was – and I think you should know too that according to Mr Khan, he believes the Hourglass compelled me to act as Darke was already coming for it. I merely scuppered his plan…"

"Huh!" snorted Gideon.

Véronique chose to ignore him by turning to Dina directly, holding the Hourglass in her outstretched hands. She smiled and held her head up, aware of the brevity of what she was about to say. "In the midst of all this I made a four-part plan," she said royally. "First of all, stay alive, which so far I've managed to do (just). Find the Hourglass, and believe me that was no easy feat. Escape with the Hourglass – obviously with Raif too – and may I just add he's been amazing. And finally, return it to you – to Dina – which right now I'm very relieved to do so."

And with all due ceremony, she passed the Hourglass over to Dina who accepted it graciously and with no small measure of relief. "… And now I'd really like to go home," she added to lighten the mood as she was afraid she might burst into tears.

Dina accepted the Hourglass graciously and smiled. "I knew you weren't all bad," she said warmly. "Thank you and thank you for taking care of Raif too."

It was a defining moment. Like the end of a long journey where each had taken their own path to reach a common goal, and with that goal having been reached, there was a sense of triumph – a sense of relief. Everyone fell silent at this pause for reflection. Even Gideon held his counsel...

"Errr... hello?"

Their moment was shattered by the introduction of a fifth person. Gideon snatched up the Hourglass and put himself between them and the intruder but there was no need... It was Fouad.

Véronique was so incredibly pleased to see him – on several counts – and didn't hesitate to lay claim by throwing her arms around him. It meant he was safe, or at least as safe as any of them were. She liked it too that he swelled the numbers in her popularity stakes and, most importantly, if anyone knew the quickest way out of here, it would be him.

"This is Fouad," she announced. "We have a lot to thank him for."

Raif was delighted too that his friend – *their* friend – had escaped Darke's clutches and wanted more than anything to show him the Hourglass but there wasn't time so, instead, chattered on about who and what Fouad was and all he'd done for them.

"I managed to throw them off the scent," said Fouad when he eventually managed to get a word in edgeways as he anxiously looked over his shoulder. "But they'll soon catch up with us. We really do need to get out of here... fast!"

And it was almost as soon as Fouad had said these words that the Hourglass began to show signs of life as a light pulsed like a heartbeat from within. Placing the Hourglass on the floor for a moment, they all watched in wonder as the light emitted a presence that touched each one of them as if it were casting a spell. It looked bigger too. In fact, as one looked at it, it just seemed to grow bigger and more imposing as it resonated a tone that was almost inaudible but at the same time all-consuming, creating a thrill – like butterflies – and an immense sense of calm and well-being.

Gideon leaned forwards and traced his finger around the circumference of the latticed casing and, in doing so, opened a tiny window that Raif was sure hadn't been there before. Looking inside, he saw the interior surrounding the Hourglass itself was bathed in warm light that swam and danced over the surface of the glass and inside – inside the Hourglass itself – a light with no obvious source lit up a landscape of sand with no horizon. They could see the last few grains of sand falling from the top chamber into the bottom chamber in exaggerated slow motion, leaving the multitude of tiny grains free to mingle, drift and settle.

"We don't have much time," said Gideon grimly. "We need to get out of here and back to the Canning Factory."

73

Fouad was at pains to explain it'd be far too risky to stay where they were for too long as Darke would have gone all out to seal the compound and search every inch. If he was dangerous before, now he'd be doubly so; desperate and unpredictable. His mercenaries – and they'd no idea how many there might be – would have been called out to join the guards and the instruction would be that no one, probably not even the boy, could be taken alive.

"We can't wait and risk turning the Hourglass here. We have to get back to the Canning Factory," said Gideon before turning to Fouad. "Is there any way out other than via the well?"

"I don't know about the well," replied Fouad, "and as for other ways, they'll all be heavily guarded, but I have heard of a place, a sacred temple, that belonged to the Old World... mind you, it's only a story."

Gideon thought about the Great Door where they'd encountered the scorpions. It was obviously not part of Darke's complex but if this temple *had* existed – and this door would have been linked to it – it would have made practical sense for Darke to take advantage of its location. There were so many tunnels and passages too, Darke couldn't have created them all. There'd have been no point.

"They say it's within a Mana Cave," Fouad volunteered as an afterthought. "And that if you go in, you never come out again… well, that's what they say."

Now, this wasn't quite so encouraging. Fouad was right, a Mana Cave was a sort of no man's land between the Underworld and the Celestial. A mingling of the yin and the yang where neither discipline took precedence. In a Mana Cave, anything could happen: '*may the best – or worst – man win*'. An unknown quantity between good and evil left free to fight it out.

Gideon was aware of the dangers, and of the risk, but other than the well, he didn't see they had any other choice. If the Mana Cave could lead them to the Great Door, they could find their way out.

"We can't even think about going back via the well," said Dina despondently. "For a start, it would mean going back into the complex – that is if I could find the way – and even if I did and we managed to evade the guards, there's no easy way through the water. We'd never make it… we just wouldn't."

"So it's decided then," said Gideon, turning to Fouad. "Can you take us there?" he asked. "Do you know where it is?"

Fouad shook his head. "They're only stories passed down through generations and no two versions are the same," he said ruefully. "I only half-listened anyway as I'm sure they were only ever told to frighten children. Like bogeymen."

Nevertheless, having seen the Great Door Gideon was convinced a Mana Cave existed. They would have to risk it. Whatever the dangers.

Véronique had been listening and was puzzled. "You don't think the Hourglass itself is behind all this?" she asked. "That we've been led here to end up at the Mana Cave to fight some battle blahh blahh... I don't know – what do I know – but first there was the incident on the bus, then we all ended up here and now we're trapped with our only option being to find this spooky cave place."

"Maybe," said Gideon, delivering her a withering look, "but aren't you forgetting one thing? We don't know where it is or how to find it..."

"I can find it."

"How?"

"With this!"

Véronique held up the bobbin – 'the novelty egg timer' as Raif affectionately called it – and both Fouad and Raif burst out laughing.

"Of course!" said Raif. "It's how I got into the vault! Véronique... tell them about Mr Khan, about what it can do. Honestly, it's brilliant!"

Gideon was (or chose to be) a little sceptical about the capabilities of the small hourglass within its wooden casing, while conceding (arguing in his head) it had, however, got Raif into the vault and – against all odds – they were all here.

"Take us to the Mana Cave..." instructed Véronique and she waited. Nothing whatsoever happened.

"Take us to the Mana Cave, please..." she corrected.

"I had my doubts..." began Gideon just as he heard a tremendous *crack*! The rock face to the side of him sheared off and fell in a neat slice revealing a narrow passageway.

"*Even though I walk through the valley of the shadow of death, I will fear no evil,*" recited Véronique to give herself courage, and without waiting to be asked, she led the way.

It was a single winding path that was light in colour and, as previously experienced, all hewn out of salt. They had no need for head torches since a soft viridescent light penetrated the ceiling high above them, likening it to walking through a narrow ravine – a fault in the strata – meaning the only way to go was forwards since going back wasn't an option.

74

As Fouad had warned, Darke had assembled not only his guards but had called up his mercenaries too. They were his most senior personnel, numbering around twenty and from all different ethnic backgrounds and origins, including some from other parts of the universe. All were dressed in simple, dark grey uniforms and there was no distinction in rank.

Like the rest of his *entourage*, they were primarily deaf-mutes, or the equivalent thereof, with some impediment in speech and/or hearing because he didn't want – or need – conversation. He just wanted obedience. He also wanted a troupe of soldiers who had a common bond in their affliction who would benefit greatly from their loyalty to him. Many had been cast out by either their families or society or had missed out on an opportunity, so recruitment was only a matter of locating, training, and providing a generous fiscal reward.

Darke took his place on the lectern and motioned them to stand at ease and give him their full undivided attention. He addressed them, but rather than using words they could not hear, he produced a scale of clicking sounds which were outside the (human) 20–20,000Hz range. Pre-administered implants had facilitated the ability to register and interpret these vibrations.

The audience was brief. Under no circumstances could the intruders be allowed to escape or be captured – all must be dispatched with their bodies brought to him for verification. The boy to be no exception. The Hourglass must be retrieved and brought to him just as soon as it was in their possession.

"Send in the scorpions," he clicked then added, "and whatever else it takes."

Despite the entire complex being on lockdown with every single one of Darke's guards, mercenaries and staff posted on full alert, there had been no sightings. It was if Raif, Véronique and whoever else they'd met up with – if indeed they had – had just vanished along with the Hourglass.

Should he just give up? Should he accept that the Collective had won and that within the coming hours or days the Hourglass would be turned and his whole ambition would lie in shreds? Time – or rather the lack of it – was all he had left. There was still a chance he'd succeed in their capture, but these odds were depleting by the minute as it would only be a matter of them lying low until the appointed time presented itself. How could he prevent them? The boy was of no consequence to him now – he could perish with the rest of them – but how to scupper the Turning now they held all the cards?

And what of the demon Breaffen? During their last encounter, Breaffen had proposed that *he* should have the Hourglass to incarcerate it forever in the Underworld and to have it as a… a hostage too, was a nice touch. But having decided it would be prudent to do this, what would he say to Breaffen now? Now both the boy and the Hourglass had been taken from him.

Darke pulled up the hologram that mapped his underground complex. First, he identified the dam built by the superpowers to divert the main arterial rivers which had previously fed water to the sea. It would be easy to destroy as the charges were already in place in readiness for his eventual departure. Then he assessed his many aquifers, most of which were filled to capacity with his prize of clean, clear water. He thought logically, and the solution was simple. He'd flush them out. In effect, he'd drown them. He'd blow the dam while at the same time disgorging the aquifers into the tunnels, the passageways, the purifying plants and the pumping stations. The sheer weight of displaced water would do the rest, destroying the service stations, the living quarters and everywhere else with the exception of his own module, which would remain safe and untouchable. Safe due to its proximity – independent and already deep underwater.

The irony of this *physic* pleased him, and it also offered a ray of hope. If the Hourglass became lost under tons and tons of water, so be it, he had the resources to retrieve it. But more likely, Raif and his comrades would do everything to save it, and if and when they did, he'd be ready.

It was without regret that with the exception of himself, everyone would perish. To his mind, he merely saw this as an unavoidable consequence, and as his army of mercenaries, guards and servants meant nothing to him, it could almost be convenient to lose most or all of them. All were expendable – and replaceable – and besides, he had control of other strategically placed aquifers he could relocate to and recruit from.

"To use a local colloquialism, it isn't the end of the world," he said wryly to his ghostly reflection and afforded himself a shiver of pleasure at the inevitability of it all.

He liked to stroke the cold glass wall and visualise the fathom upon fathom of water contained behind it. He found it reassuring. This wouldn't be the first time a flood had purged the earth and he called to mind how closely this flood – his flood – paralleled the story of creation; a cycle of creation, un-creation and re-creation where the ark – Noah's Ark in this instance – had played a pivotal role. Such was his madness he was able to draw parallels where he could equate his place of safety and control – his free-standing, independently powered module – to that of the Ark, and as if for confirmation he recalled the Old Testament passage that had made such an impression on him.

> *The universe as conceived by the ancient Hebrews comprised a flat-disc-shaped habitable earth with the heavens above and Sheol, the Underworld of the dead, below. These three were surrounded by a watery 'ocean' of chaos protected by the firmament – a transparent but solid dome resting on the mountains which ringed the earth. Noah's three-decked ark represented this three-level Hebrew cosmos in miniature – the heavens, the earth and the waters beneath. God created the three-level world as space in the midst of the waters for humanity. As in Genesis 6–8, he fills the space with waters again, saving only Noah, his family and the animals with him in the ark.*

He needed to make contact with Breaffen. Better he found out from him directly that the Hourglass had eluded him, despite his best efforts, rather than Breaffen draw his own conclusions. He was going to flood the entire complex too, and while he had no regard for Breaffen, he felt it would be in his own interests to keep him on side by informing him of his intentions.

It was therefore with some reluctance that Darke approached the small alcove with its sheer plain panel and entered his own private hell hole. He felt the familiarity as soon as he entered and made his offering of the blue crystal. He stepped into the five-pointed symbol scratched out in lime and began his transcendental journey.

In his intense meditative state, Darke was released to travel freely, only this time, he had an objective – Breaffen – as he wanted to seek him out rather than it being the other way around. Taking care not to breach the five-pointed symbol, since to do so would mean entering an infinity via a black hole presenting no certain way back, Darke searched for Breaffen, calling him up as he did so.

Breaffen duly appeared much as he'd done so before. A scaled epitome of evil with his serpent tail wrapped around his gnarled clawed feet.

He sat on his haunches at the far end of the most southerly point of the five-pointed symbol and watched while multiple gossamer layers of Darke amalgamated and re-assembled – layer upon layer – to form one coherent body. It took a moment for Darke to take stock of where he was when he saw Breaffen. Neither of them spoke as speech wasn't necessary.

75

Raif was aware of a tension between Gideon and Véronique. It was understandable seeing as Gideon saw Véronique as being largely responsible for their current circumstance, although, in Raif's view, he felt it unjustified. Gideon just didn't know Véronique as he did. However, he knew enough about adult fallouts not to intervene and contented himself with walking this perilous path towards an unknown destiny. Now was hardly the time or the place for a full-blown row – or to kiss and make up – so he turned his thoughts to following Gideon and wondering when they'd get there.

"How will we know when it's time for the Turning?" he asked Dina.

"The Hourglass will tell us," she replied brightly and Raif found this instantly reassuring.

"And if we *are* being guided, I'm sure the Hourglass will wait until we arrive in the Cave," added Gideon. "And look, I think we're coming to the end of this."

Raif looked ahead, and rather than seeing light at the end of the tunnel, it was the other way around, since the track they were on led only to darkness.

"We must all stay close," said Gideon, addressing them as he positioned himself in the lead again and Raif was glad to note that Véronique hadn't been excluded.

As they continued to follow Gideon, the pathway split into many dimly lit tunnels all leading more or less in the same direction. There were many twists and turns, dead ends and possible ways to go as he led them deeper and deeper into the caves. Was it this way or that? Or was it they had actually arrived?

They reached a dead end. "This simply isn't *possible?*" said Véronique. "We wouldn't have been led all this way to find ourselves in a cul-de-sac."

"Who said we were being led!" piped up Gideon hotly. "You're the one who jumped to conclusions…"

"… and you were very happy to follow!"

"That will do!" said Dina sharply. "Now listen… I was wondering the same thing, why follow a road leading nowhere when it occurred to me and like I'm always saying…"

"*Don't all things happen for a reason?*" piped up Raif, finishing her sentence.

"Like in synchronicity?" asked Fouad who, being very much the student, was into this kind of stuff.

"Yes. And far from leading us down the *wrong* path, I think we're being guided very much along the *right* path. I think the Hourglass has taken control and our job is to recognise this and go with it."

"Let's take a closer look at the wall," volunteered Raif. "I'll start at this end."

The ambient light was very poor, coming only from cracks in the concave ceiling above them, but it was enough to make out the unusual perpendicular contours. Dina stepped forwards and ran her hands over the smooth rocks in much the same way as she did when tracing openings in new and existing holloways. She took her time to think logically about their immediate circumstances.

She didn't know – none of them knew – that had they taken any other route, they would have circled back to the main complex and into a carefully orchestrated trap. She didn't know either that it hadn't taken Darke long to figure out that she and Gideon had also penetrated the complex and he had surmised their most probable escape route. Something, and Dina could only think it was the Hourglass, had prevented them from going that way. She thought too that so often when coming to a crossroad or a choice, the decision to turn either left or right – to take the high road or the low road – could result in a life-changing difference. Between life and death. Between meeting someone who would change your life forever or never meeting that person. Musing on this, Dina let her thoughts wander. *'If I hadn't gone back for my raincoat, it would've been me in that car accident'* or *'if I hadn't got off the train at the wrong station, I'd never have met the man who's now the father of my five children.'* She liked the idea of life throwing the dice and could have dwelt on this train of thought further when she was interrupted by Véronique.

"Over here!" she called. "Come and look."

The sheer rock face she was referring to looked solid enough from a distance, but as one got closer it became apparent that far from being solid, the wall was a series of perfectly matched shutters that created the *illusion* of being one solid mass. The space between the first few shutters was very narrow, but subsequently, the gaps increased to a point where it would be possible to slip through. This was strange in itself but what was even stranger was when Gideon switched on his head torch and shone it into the depths, there was no beam or passage of light. In other words – and the only way to describe it – the beam of light travelled only a matter of centimetres before being totally absorbed by the blackness.

"I think we can say we've arrived at our Mana Cave," said Gideon and Dina noticed the tremor in his voice. "And all we have to do is make it through to the other side."

He set the Hourglass upright on the ground, clearing away any stones or debris from the area immediately around it, and then, with great care, laid the Hourglass, still in its latticed casing, on its side. Normally – as had been proved by all those who had tried – the Hourglass always remained upright regardless of the circumstances. It merely adjusted its size to fit. Not so in this instance.

For the first time ever, they witnessed the Hourglass within the casing becoming horizontal. When it had settled, it started resonating a pulse of light that travelled around the figure eight-shaped Hourglass circumference. Faster and faster it travelled until it became nothing more than a blur.

"I give you infinity." Gideon smiled as he picked up the resonating Hourglass – still on its side – and walked directly towards the shuttered wall. "Follow me…"

76

GOLDEN CAP, SO NAMED FOR THE GOLDEN GREENSAND rock which crowned the uppermost part of it, was the highest point on the south coast of England, standing 191 metres above sea level. Bordering Stonebarrow to the west and Thorncombe Beacon to the east, this steep-sided, flat-topped cliff had an almost vertical drop down to the beach along from which the eighteen miles of Chesil Beach began its elegant arc eastwards to conclude at Portland. It was a sacred place and was where the Collective now met to summon the Armed Forces.

As long as they were mindful of keeping well away from the edge, their chosen summit was ideal for their purpose. It formed a large plateau providing a commanding panoramic view, yet at the same time the peculiar geography could conveniently make it isolated and largely inaccessible. Any walkers who happened to stray in their direction were inexplicably gripped by a change of mind and re-routed with absolutely no recall as to why.

Those members of the Collective who'd been summoned arrived stoically attired in the practical, unassumed costume of country folk. This was partly in a bid to blend in, and therefore to not draw too much attention to themselves, but mainly because it was quite a climb to the top of Golden Cap and most – if not all – were not in the first flush of youth. Henry Mullet was one of the members called to task, and having walrus in his genes, he found the climb difficult but not insurmountable.

Pythia, who could come and go anywhere on account of being a Deity, was already there, ready to meet them as they appeared out of the clough.

Out of deference to the occasion, Pythia handed out white surplices, which, somewhat dubiously, were a little too much like tablecloths but served their purpose, nevertheless. These were worn – after a fashion – over their more practical garments so that now – in robes that billowed and mimicked the clouds rushing by – they were majestic and formidable.

The seven members of the Collective formed a circle around their High Priestess Pythia, who drew herself up in preparation for the summoning. Her poise, striking good looks and air of a higher intelligence belied any age she might have chosen to be. Timeless would best describe her, although of late a shadow had fallen across her face.

She knew the potential catastrophe that lay before them was their (her) fault and this peeved her. What also peeved her was that she wasn't used to being *mortal* for such a long length of time and she longed to get back to being ecclesiastical. There was much to be said for being lighter than air.

She – that is, they – had been too quick to assume no one ever escaped the prison planet Carcerem, least of all Darke. What troubled her too was that initially, she'd made no direct connection between the dwindling of the Arrid Sea and Darke's preoccupation with the Hourglass – why would she? The two entities bore no relation to each other; they were worlds apart.

Now they all knew, only too well, that rather than attempt to take control of the Hourglass – what would be the point when only the Keeper Elect and the Foundling could perform the Turning ceremony – Darke's purpose was simply to *prevent* the Turning. Now it seemed so obvious but as for the role the Arrid Sea played, this was still baffling. All she knew was that he had to be stopped.

Pythia called the assembled to attention. Not being one to mince her words or use a hundred when five would do, she was impatient to get all this over with.

They all knew why they were there anyway. "This whole situation has got completely out of hand," she barked. "We have no recourse other than to destroy Darke once and for all! Call up the Armed Forces – the Vitiators – call them to arms!"

Every member of the assembled amalgamated psychically and honed their thoughts to one pure objective. Then, no sooner had Pythia's instruction thundered out from Golden Cap, the sky – like the onset of a freak summer storm – darkened and turned sulphurous as the wind picked up. The sea, flat and calm only moments ago, swirled and boiled to the colour of blackened jade while white horses charged and clashed. The air became oppressive and the heavens opened.

With as much ceremony as they could manage in their wet surplices, the members of the Collective worked together to build a pyre of holy laurel leaves, which had been carried to this place for such an occasion. They were sprinkled with rare incense and a casket of the purest Himalayan glacier water. An umbrella was found, and beneath it, clashing two white flints together, the appointed pyrogenists produced a spark which lit the spill, which lit the pyre, which burned brightly for a moment before smouldering an acrid green vapour.

The rain stopped, and taking a replicated Hourglass no bigger than her hand, Pythia held it aloft in the billowing vapours and cleanly broke its neck. The tiny grains of sand – little more than dust – fell from both chambers into the pyre and the Summoning began. To those unfamiliar with the proceedings, it was terrifying.

The beach to the east was deserted. It arced into a perfect crescent with nothing to mar, spoil or interrupt the vista, and although it was made up of small pebbles on the surface, beneath it was sand to an unfathomable depth.

To the west rose the daunting and unstable blue lias cliffs. Constantly shifting and crumbling, they were veined with rivulets of perilous grey mudslides capable of devouring anything in their path.

The cliffs were weakened by these slippery rivulets; a loud crack followed by an unmistakable rumble would herald a rockfall, causing dragons and monsters long since deceased to be exposed. The shocked souls of these suspended creatures would then be laid bare. Skeletally, perfectly preserved.

Pythia selected the crumbling cliffs of blue lias first. The wind blew gently, whispering in and out amongst the dead grasses, as if telling of what was to come. The most predominant mudslide, barely imperceptible in its passage, ceased its slow journey to the sea and waited just as Pythia was waiting. Only the seagulls hovered and sniggered until they too fell silent, aware of some dreadful premonition.

Like the lights going out, the sky filled to the colour of slate and large drops of rain – pitter-patter – splattered the earth staining dove-grey to black. It happened without warning. A whip-like crack – a shrill thundercrack – caused the startled seagulls to scream and scatter as a great shard of black rock weighing many hundreds of tons slipped off the cliff face and smashed onto the beach.

Fed by the torrential rain, the gentle mudslide resumed its passage and picked up the pace as it morphed into a heaving retch of thick sludge which was swelled further by more mud that disgorged out of the newly exposed wound. Heaving and spewing, weird shapes and indistinguishable monsters were created, culminating in what looked like a giant sea serpent, which wailed desperately before dissipating into the waiting waves.

Then a calm pervaded. The wind dropped, and the sky lightened with the sun almost visible like a shining orb through the thick mantle of dense cloud. The beach to the east, by way of contrast, looked tranquil in its stillness as the waves ceased their agitation and gently lapped instead. But was it so still? Or did the beach murmur?

Pythia turned her attention eastwards and held out her arms, her fingers splayed and stretched, then, as she clapped her reaching hands, the beach erupted into thousands of snakes. Sidewinders came first, rippling like camouflage, followed by all manner of other snakes and vipers – horned vipers, desert kingsnakes, weird cerastes and Mojave greens all writhing and moving with impatient purpose.

Next came the Sandman himself in much the same manner as he'd become manifest to Lenken. Dust Devils spiralled and amassed, falling and re-grouping until the weight of sand held. Suspended and organic. Entwined within its own body, a singular death worm hovered, as too did other mythical creatures summoned to the cause.

Land crabs, scorpions, lizards and reptiles of every description were recruited just as the impenetrable fog – a massive and engulfing sea fret – lifted. The beach, once so static and tranquil, was now a heaving mass of crustacean and slither eager to be away from this place of council. The Sandman rose up like a crescendo to the full height of Golden

Cap, dwarfing Pythia with his enormity, when from out of the still-smouldering pyre, a new element emerged that did far more to shock Pythia and the Collective than the theatre being enacted before them.

An apparition of Canatu appeared within the viridescent smoke. She wasn't ten years old as she would have been had she'd lived. She was five. Her ghostly image was just that of her face and it was large, larger than the Sandman in fact, but it was her expression more than her size that chilled Pythia and indeed, struck remorse into every member of the watching Collective. She looked so pitiful.

"Why did you abandon me?" she asked, her wavering voice sounding distant and broken. "I don't want to be here, it isn't fair… it just isn't fair…"

Pythia tried to speak but couldn't find the words. Or rather, no sound came out as she gazed upon Canatu's beseeching face; such a beautiful face, such an angel. "We couldn't find you, we tried…" she managed at last but already the image of Canatu was fading until it became indistinguishable from the clouds and was blown away on the breeze.

"Find me…" were the last plaintiff echoes which resonated around the clifftop.

And then she was gone, and everything ceased. The Sandman, blown into a million fragments, was carried off on the wind, and the rippling creatures – the snakes and the vipers – became still and invisible again. Acting as one, and with east joining west, they knew what to do. The gulls returned and it was as if nothing extraordinary had happened.

Pythia was deeply perturbed. Why didn't she know? Why hadn't she persevered? Why, when all around were so taken up with grief, herself included, didn't she think? "Canatu isn't dead… she's trapped in Perpetuity," she said, realising the huge implications. "Find Anakee and send her to me."

77

Had Raif not had such blind faith in Gideon, he would have thought twice about walking into what appeared to be a solid wall, but it wouldn't be — it wasn't — the first time. When they'd travelled... What was it called? Localeatic... err... Localeactically (or was it Tesseractically?) and ended up in the catacombs, it was really good fun and he recalled Gideon blithely saying it was about dipping in and out of other dimensions as the quickest way (the *only* way) to get to certain places.

"Here we go again," he said, then noticed Fouad looking none too sure. "Don't worry. The Hourglass has created an infinity bubble for us. We're quite safe, but if it'll make you feel better, stay close to me."

Much to Raif's disappointment, the whole experience was nothing to write home about. It was about as exciting as standing in a room, turning the light off then switching the light back on again to find yourself standing in a different room. It took seconds or, who knows, it could have taken years, only no one looked to have aged that much.

The Mana Cave, to an untrained eye, looked much like any other cave might in this vicinity but there was a line

– a line in the sand – that Gideon was hesitant to cross. It was little more than a ripple, but its rigidity was sufficient to prompt him to investigate further, and true enough, it was revealed as much more than an arbitrary mark and Gideon knew that. He brushed the sand aside carefully and traced the line to its farthest point, crossed another line on the way until it reached the edge of what could only be a curve and angled back. Just as he'd suspected, it was a pentagram – a reversed or *inverted* pentagram – which confirmed it to be a satanic device. This didn't bode well with him since he feared, and was right to fear, that the Mana Cave they were entering was already charged with all manner of opposing influences.

Mana was closely linked to the doctrine of animism, so this, coupled with an inverted pentagram, could only mean that if the Hourglass had to be turned in this place then it was more than likely that the forces of evil would already be stacked against them.

He had no choice: he had to risk entering the pentagram. "You go ahead and make preparations," he said to Dina quickly, taking care that none of them even came close to the markings on the floor.

"Be careful," said Dina needlessly while she recalled what she could think of which habitually possessed Mana. "I don't know what it is you may encounter but beware of '*startling manifestations of nature, curious stones, animals, human remains, blood, thunderstorms, eclipses, eruptions, glaciers…*' You may even come up against a manifestation of the devil himself."

Gideon accepted her warning then waited until they'd rounded the corner before entering the pentagram. As soon as he did so, his senses were filled with the deafening sound of a bullroarer, and while this didn't bode well for him, he remained steadfast.

Before taking his place in the centre of the pentagram, Gideon removed a small, embroidered bag from around his neck and hid it in the rock face. Satisfied it was safe, he then removed his outer garments, assumed an asana (a sitting yoga pose) and closed his eyes. The blue light which targeted him was no ordinary light, it was energy – pure energy – and Gideon feared its power, acutely aware of the risks he was taking by even being in this place.

Opening his eyes again, he took from his now discarded jacket pocket a plain, narrow collar made of soft leather and secured it around his neck. Then, from around his right wrist, he unwound a gossamer-thin chain made of platinum, which extended no further than the width of the pentagram, and fastened this firstly to the collar around his neck and then to the protruding rock face. He tested it to make sure it would hold fast.

Again, Gideon closed his eyes and breathed evenly until he'd achieved a meditative state. Whatever it was that came for him didn't come with carnival or anthem, nor did it skulk in the shadows. It came like a chill. A simple absence of anything good and it weighed heavily, sapping any will to stand up and fight. What's the point… we're all going to die.

But not so Gideon. He strained on his lead, his face distorted in pain brought about by an inner turmoil as forces stronger than he crowded in on him. He needed to fight but not as Gideon and while the evil amassed and crushed around him, he raced in his mind to find what he could become to defeat this hidden enemy. Skipping through the dimensions at lightning speed, Gideon reached out to the entire galaxy and through all the constellations until he found what he was looking for. He looked in the constellation Centaurus – the location of the Hourglass Nebula some 7,000 light years away – and identified the configuration of Taurus and within that he found *Ophiotaurus*. An undefeated beast from Greek mythology (*Titane*). Fittingly, it was a shocking monster, born out of Chaos by Mother Earth, who was half-bull, half-serpent. Having survived his entrails being torn out in a previous existence, he would be in no mood to be trifled with by the likes of perpetrators who may have similar designs. In short, he would be only too happy to let Gideon temporarily occupy his terrifying, most formidable frame.

Having identified Ophiotaurus in his mind's eye with no objections raised, Gideon then had to endure the agonising process of possession. Firstly, his shoulders imploded only to re-form as a singular muscular neck, which became part and parcel to a powerful body rippling with the taut muscles of a fabulous bull. Stamping hooves capable of crushing any head replaced hands and pawed the dust while horns tipped with sapphire prepared to toss and gore. Gideon bellowed in anguish as his legs gave way beneath him and instead a mighty serpent's tail took their place, whipping and severing anything in its path. When at last the transformation was complete, Gideon would never be more ready to face any foe. "Show yourself!" he commanded, now fully assumed as Ophiotaurus, with the lead – now a massive chain – still holding fast around his straining, powerful neck.

78

"What *is* this place?" breathed Raif when the passageway they were in opened up to become a dome-shaped cave containing a crystal-clear blue lagoon, not dissimilar, although much smaller, to the one before. Above them was an iridescent canopy of blue crystal. The place was magical. All around them was a powerful omniscient presence as if something much bigger and more august was watching over them.

As the light above him crackled and refracted Raif found a central place for the Hourglass and set it in the sand. All regarded it solemnly.

"I know it doesn't look much right now," he said, pulling up the sleeves of his red pullover, "but it changes... it changes all the time." True, it didn't look very inspiring. It had reverted to looking like nothing more than some old lantern one wouldn't give a second glance to, but then, if one looked closely, there was a faint glow beginning inside. A glow that was getting brighter.

And it didn't stop getting brighter. Soon its iridescent light filled the cave, shone through the clear water of the lagoon and, in doing so, lit up an underwater wonderland rippling with light and sparkle.

"Is it time?" asked Raif.

"Yes, it's time," breathed Dina, shielding her eyes. "I don't know why and I don't know how and I don't know a million other things other than knowing in my very soul – my very being – that it has to be turned and it has to be turned *now*. Otherwise, it will all be too late."

Véronique and Fouad exchanged glances. They'd hardly said a word since setting off along the path to the Mana Cave where everything had gone from being fantastical – a dream even – to becoming something frighteningly real. "Look... would you like us to go?" she said tentatively. "I mean... you know... this is, like... private and we shouldn't..."

"Be quiet," said Dina, although not unkindly. "If it wasn't for you, and you too, Fouad, we'd be in a right pickle, so give Raif a hand here so we can get on with it."

"Shouldn't we wait for Gideon?"

"No," responded Dina quickly. "We cannot wait for anything now."

"Do you think he's alright?" Véronique asked Fouad when they were out of earshot. She'd picked up on the strain in Dina's voice, and even though she held little affection for Gideon, she was concerned.

"I'm sure he's just checking the place out. I mean, it is all a bit weird..."

"You stay here and look after Raif," said Véronique, cutting across him. Her mind was obviously made up. "I've got a bad feeling something isn't right. I won't be long. Promise."

79

Gideon, in the guise of Ophiotaurus, lashed out with his powerful serpent tail and smashed a break in the circle. In doing so, and he knew *exactly* what he was doing, he enacted a manoeuvre that would force his opponent – or any abomination that could lay claim to be an ambassador of evil – to show itself.

When Breaffen appeared before him, Gideon had no inkling as to whom this might be and/or how it fitted into the scheme of things. He had no idea that the creature before him was a demon of high caste, whom Darke had conspired with to bridge the Underworld and the earthly ethereal plane. He didn't know that this creature was ready and in waiting… waiting to tip the pivotal Mana balance within this cave towards his leanings. Gideon had never even heard of Breaffen.

Habituating between this world and the Underworld, Breaffen could dominate and wreak havoc without being seen or detected. An invisible silent killer, like a virus. But – by Gideon breaking the circle – the demon was made manifest, and not only that, so too were many other parasitic demons who crowded and heckled, all of them manic and excited to be free – a development Gideon wasn't expecting.

And so, they came at him. Breaffen, the high caste demon, led the assault and, on seeing Gideon tethered, was lured into a false sense of security. Gideon cowered, seducing Breaffen into believing the kill would be easy, but he was ready for him. The trap was set.

Breaffen lunged but misjudged his opponent's agility and fell afoul of Gideon's massive horns as his powerful hooves rained down on him. In truth, they were well matched but with Gideon being chained it would seem Breaffen had the advantage. Not so... as Breaffen was soon to discover. As Gideon retreated to the edge of the circle, the chain went slack – slack enough for Gideon to loop it around Breaffen's head then hurl himself to the other side of the circumference. Gideon had to hope the chain would hold. It did, for it was no ordinary chain, and with Breaffen's startled head all but severed, his dismembered body collapsed. Lifeless.

Dismissively, Gideon raised Breaffen up as if weightless and tossed him out of the pentagram into the waiting abyss. But it wasn't over yet. Breaffen's exit had only cleared the way for the eager pack that followed. Demons and gargoyles fallen from Grace jostled around him. Winged and horned with bulging eyes and protruding tongues, they appeared initially perplexed but then gleeful at seeing a tethered adversary – such a prize! Gideon knew they carried the ability to possess him; to take possession of his mind and feast on the knowledge contained therein. He'd remain safe from such an invasion while he remained in the circle but that wouldn't stop them from devouring his spirit.

Large feet carried the pack forwards and gnarled grasping hands with long yellow fingernails reached to grab and throttle. Toothless mouths grinned horribly, dripping and salivating, as they fell on their prey.

But Gideon was poised for the assault. His serpent's tails lashed them aside out of the pentagram and, squealing like rats, they were banished to eternity. Those who escaped were either impaled or trampled as the chain held and Gideon still remained within the now bloodied circle. He ripped out their throats and tore them limb from limb, yet still they kept coming out of the shadows like lemmings over a cliff. Leaping and grasping in a frenzy of killing, one after another joined the carnage shrieking and howling until a great pile of ripped lifeless bodies lay heaped around him.

Gideon, exhausted yet triumphant, shook away the blood and stinking mucus and gathered the last of his strength to deliver a single anguished note of closure.

In response a bell sounded. Sombre and even, it tolled as it heralded the hour of the Turning. It had no source, yet it could be heard in all four corners of the earth.

Gideon panted heavily. At the sound of the bell, any evidence of the inverted pentagram reverted to dust and those dead remained lifeless. The onslaught of demons turned to stone. He'd done what he could in the time to redress the balance in this sacred place, but would it be enough?

He closed his eyes and scanned countless inner horizons to confirm it was safe to resume being Gideon again, then he shuddered. His former persona took over, and wounded and bloodied, he sank to the ground. He released the collar and chain, relieved that it had held. It would be too awful to even contemplate where the evil might have taken him had it not, as with shaking hands, he returned the gossamer chain to his wrist and the collar to his pocket.

His wounds were extensive but mainly confined to flesh wounds. Many were superficial bite and scratch marks although some ran deeper. Wounds inflicted by demons were unlike any other wounds – even a scratch could cause sepsis within hours – and some of the deeper ones were already beginning to fester and smell putrid. Bundling up his clothes and anxious to be reunited with his friends, he was stopped dead in his tracks.

"What on earth happened to you?" Véronique stood there, hands on hips, awaiting an answer. He was a pitiful sight.

"What did you see?" he replied in a desperate half-whisper, unable to disguise the panic in his voice.

"What do you mean?" flared Véronique, visibly shocked at seeing Gideon in such a state. "I didn't *see* anything but what I *do* see is the outcome of one hell of a fight. Was it the mercenaries... or, dare I ask, something worse?"

"It is not your concern," Gideon retorted wearily. She obviously hadn't seen what had gone on within the pentagram as it was enacted in an entirely different dimension, but he was on his guard, nevertheless.

"It happened back there," he lied. "It's over now, so please leave me be."

"No chance!" she said briskly, taking full advantage of his weakness. "We need you, or should I say Raif needs you, so let's get you cleaned up."

Leaving Gideon no choice in the matter, Véronique helped him to his feet. She didn't enquire further or ask why he was all but naked, being more concerned about the extent of his injuries. She didn't make reference either to the intricacy or symbolism of the tattoos that covered eighty per cent of his body.

Taking his weight, she began leading him back to join the others, pausing only when they reached the far side edge of the crystal blue lagoon.

Véronique took his bundle of clothing, bloodied and soiled, and dipped it in the cool water. Gently, she applied the damp cloth to his wounds and the effect was both instantaneous and miraculous. As she dabbed and wiped, so the wounds faded, but rather than comment on this, Véronique chose to show no sign of surprise or delight. Indeed, she showed only indifference to Gideon being made whole again.

"I must ask you to say nothing of this," he said curtly. "But there's one more thing I need to do, and I don't need you here. Please leave me."

Véronique nodded, any kindly feelings she may have been nurturing towards him waning rapidly. "Do what you must," she snapped back at him before turning on her heel and leaving.

When Véronique had left to rejoin the others, Gideon crossed his feet and outstretched his arms. In a strange tongue, he recited an ancient text as he gently submerged himself in the water. His body was healed but now – more importantly – it was essential to cleanse his mind and soul. He also had to do something about his disproportionate resentment towards Véronique.

With Raif's help, Dina chose several of the blue rock crystals that were lying around and encouraged Fouad to do likewise. Together, they set them in a circle, and whereas before the crystals were dimming as the day outside gave way to dusk, now they held their light and, if anything, shone brighter.

They decided to set the Hourglass on one of the larger blue crystals that had a flat, smooth surface. When Fouad tried to lift it to move it into place, it was surprisingly heavy but suddenly – when Raif lent a hand too – it became as light as air as if the crystal itself had joined the effort.

In its tarnished lantern casing, the Hourglass still looked less than impressive, although Raif had been intrigued by whichever way he turned it – upside down or sideways – the Hourglass within always remained the same way up; the sand falling steadily and evenly from the top chamber to the lower one.

Surreptitiously, Véronique re-joined the group. They'd all been so absorbed in the Hourglass, they'd hardly noticed she'd been missing.

"Everything alright?" asked Fouad.

"Yes, I found Gideon. He was just making sure we weren't being followed."

"And were we?"

"In a manner of speaking but it's okay now. He'll join us shortly."

"Oh! There you are!" called Dina when Gideon appeared looking much as he always did. "I think we're just about ready."

Gideon shot a glance at Véronique, who instantly looked away and busied herself with something trivial, but she watched, nevertheless, as Gideon passed a small, embroidered bag to Dina, who accepted it graciously.

He kept that well hidden, she observed silently, not having noticed it amongst the garments she'd salvaged. Again she felt peeved. Why did he constantly annoy her?

Dina took centre stage and, very gently, traced around the latticed casing with her two middle fingers and found a small catch none of them would have found in a million years. She synchronised this with a similar catch on the opposite side as she closed her eyes, bowed her head and spoke barely audible words, chanting these in a strange tongue. Carefully she then lifted the top part of the casing away.

With the Hourglass now freed, Dina removed from the small bag an elongated liturgical vestment – a stole – a narrow band of embroidered material depicting symbols of the Hourglass and the Trident of Siva – a symbol of his threefold character as creator, preserver and destroyer. Also depicted were the seven candles symbolising the sun, the moon and the principal planets shining out of the darkness of Chaos, while blue yin-yang symbols decorated the fringed and knotted ends of the vestment. Wrapping this around the narrowest part of the Hourglass, Dina remained in prayer.

Holding hands with Gideon and Véronique, who were on either side of him, Raif watched intently, not daring to move and hardly even daring to breathe.

After removing the Hourglass from the lower part of its casing, Dina placed it on the stone.

"It's wonderful!" whispered Raif… captivated.

80

Darke seized his chest and stumbled a few steps as a great bolt of energy drained out of him. Like switching to emergency power, he was quickly restored, but what had *caused* this power drain that had affected him so acutely? Could it be the approaching hour or had something else happened?

Darke thought for a moment. He needed to recharge and take action – drastic action – if he was to be able to save the day before the day was gone.

Without bothering to undress, he laid himself out on his bed – now almost as if it was an altar – and adjusted his position to get the most from the dying blue light. He'd come to rely on this ritual almost to the point of addiction, for the relief it gave him not only physically, but for the mental release. He craved the vision – the insight he'd mastered – and needed now, more than ever, to be reassured.

The vision came, as it had been before, but this time it was sporadic. Broken would be a better word. Darke gripped the side of his trestle, unable to move or breakaway because there was something else happening. It interrupted the flow – the familiarity of it – and there was no colour. Darke didn't want to look, he didn't want to see, but he had no choice. Like being locked in a dream, there was no escape.

A face beneath a veil came and looked down at him. It was a grey veil – everything was grey – and as a wind blew so it flattened over the contours of the small face. Other similarly veiled faces joined in until there were dozens, all closing in on him. Darkness enveloped him and there was silence followed by a cacophony of manic, distorted laughter. He felt a knife being plunged into his chest and it was an agony he would never risk recalling.

The grey-veiled face returned and whispered as the veil was pulled aside. "I'm waiting…" tinkled Canatu and smiled sweetly as her words were drowned by a colossal wall of water that came from nowhere.

Darke snapped out of the vision, dripping with sweat. There was no knife, no blood, but his senses were confused. It was wrong. It was all wrong but that had to be due to his failing powers. It was imperative he acted now. Staggering to his feet, Darke called up the hologram covering the entire complex. He tapped in a code that required eye-recognition and two passwords. He undertook both without hesitation. "There, it is done."

A distant boom, followed by two further booms, announced the destruction of the dam. The clean, distilled water being pumped into the many aquifers and chambers hesitated then dwindled from a gush to a trickle. Operatives controlling the process didn't know what was happening and were powerless because nothing responded. The entire system was being overridden.

There was just one more thing he had to do to abort his entire operation – his last-ditch attempt to destroy the power of the Hourglass forever. He hesitated and felt almost wistful as his whole ambition flashed before him. If he took this action he would most certainly prevent the Hourglass being turned but he had to weigh this against another certainty – the certainty of the unknown – where, without the Hourglass, chaos would undoubtedly take precedence, leading chaos to beget chaos creating a world and potentially, a universe where never again would anything be orderly or predictable.

"I will fulfil the doctrines of the *Alternate Prophecies* and take my rightful place," he proclaimed and threw the switch. The sluice gates opened.

With all the grace and inevitability of a sinking ship, the corridors and passageways began to slowly fill with water. To begin with, the water didn't rush or bubble – except at source – and all appeared highly controlled. The powder-dry sandy floors that linked the connecting maze of roads, walkways and tunnels darkened and moistened until puddling began. There was a stealth not unlike the tide coming in. Soon it was ankle-deep and then knee-deep. The workforce – from cleaners to engineers, kitchen staff, drivers, guards and mercenaries – looked on in silent alarm and disbelief, not knowing which way to turn, trying to out-think the biggest killer of all. Panic. They'd done nothing wrong. They'd served, so where was the contingency, the instruction? The way out?

Hysteria built as the waters rose and became more violent. It was every man and woman for themselves. The disregard for their lives was both callous and calculated and the dawning of this – that they didn't matter – only added to a deep sense of injustice as survival became the only order of the day. Frantically they tried to recall the geography. There was only one way out and that was up but as the arteries filled it became impossible to remember – to choose. As one certainty failed so did another and another as the options became fewer. Those who did make it to the exits arrived only to find all exits locked. The precious space between the unyielding rock weighted above them and rising waters diminished inch by inch leaving no alternative to drowning. How many silent screams which echoed through those saturated walls did Darke hear? None. They were all expendable.

Darke stared blankly into his great wall of water as his masterpiece perished and drowned around him. The offices and the processing plant. The hospitality suites and service areas. Service vehicles and maintenance depots, staff accommodation and training areas. Catering and cleaning. It was amazing how, in such a short space of time, such a complete, self-contained hierarchy had established itself and how quickly it was now being destroyed as the water rose and filled and the lights went out.

Darke was safe within his womb-like capsule. He would rise to the surface – like a phoenix – and await the devastation that would herald the new world. His plant would be destroyed but it could be rebuilt. The *concept was sound in principle* and he'd already identified other strategically placed sites around the world. His objective was all but accomplished.

These thoughts cheered him as too did the knowledge that he would have been instrumental in hastening the demise of a world – a planet – that was already destined to die. That the balance would be tipped to rapidly induce flood, famine and ultimately drought. In short, all the predictions of the *Alternate Prophecies* would be fulfilled, and he would have played a crucial role.

For his own reassurance, Darke again identified himself with Noah and again recalled the scriptures of the Old Testament alongside the corresponding passages from the *Alternate*

Prophecies. He recited the words he knew off by heart as if they were a mantra.

"... and it came to pass Noah's three-decked ark represented a three-level Hebrew cosmos in miniature – the heavens, the earth and the waters beneath. He created the three-level world as space in the midst of the waters for humanity. As in Genesis 6–8, he fills the space with waters again, saving only himself, his family and the animals with him in the ark. The prophecies dictate the waters will again purge, taking over the earth, until only the heavens remain to take up the waters leaving dust to dust and the earth will be reborn...

"... except *no one* will be saved from this place," he added venomously and closed his cold black eyes.

81

Having met up with Motto and deciding that *being dead* wouldn't do much to help her sister in bringing Darke to justice, Anakee was charged with a new purpose. Although she had a family, it wasn't much of one to speak of, but after following an exhaustive episode in trying to locate them, she'd drawn a blank. It was if they'd never existed. Anakee had no recourse (and no other option) other than to return to Pythia. After all, Pythia had all but adopted her by becoming her *Guardian Angel* and even though it had always been more about Canatu than it had been about her, they still shared the same concern. She also wanted to clear the air and she could only do that if they met face to face.

Anakee found Pythia walking amongst the apple cordons in the garden of the Abbey. It was no coincidence because such a circumstance didn't exist, but the two women eyed each other cautiously, nevertheless.

"I'm sorry I left Raif…" was Anakee's opening gambit.

"And I'm sorry that I may have overreacted," replied Pythia. "We cannot fall out, too much has happened. I understand the pain is still raw and I sympathise, I really do, so let's walk awhile and see what can be done."

The two women walked side by side. It was approaching dusk and a huge blood moon was rising just above the hilltop. It was awe-inspiring and acutely unnerving.

"Where did you go when you left Raif with Gideon?"

"You mean where *didn't* I go! Gideon had arranged for Henry Mullet to bring me here but how do I put it... he isn't the best at astral navigation."

"Oh no! Not Henry! You must have..."

"Yes. I think we passed through dimensions not even you've been to, but we got here... in the end."

Both women laughed, which is all they could do at the sheer prospect of what *could* have happened with Henry at the helm. "But you're safe now and that's all that matters," said Pythia, then she hesitated. "Look... I'm sending in my army of Vitiators to destroy Darke once and for all. If you want to go along to bear witness, you have my blessing."

Anakee didn't answer; she just nodded her acknowledgement.

"Motto will make the arrangements."

Pythia didn't want Anakee to go. It was likely to be dangerous but she knew too that, left to her own devices, Anakee would do anything to seek Darke out on her own. Far better for her to be with Motto, and besides, how could she stop her?

"There's something else I must tell you too. This may come as a bit of a shock but I need you to know that Canatu isn't dead. She came to me in a vision, and as was unbeknown to us, she's trapped in Perpetuity, an eternity between this world and the next. She has reached out to us."

On her hearing this, Anakee's face became ashen. "You mean my little sister is still alive?"

"That's what I believe."

Pythia watched helplessly as Anakee struggled to comprehend what she'd just learned. "So... there is hope," she managed at last. It was evident from her expression that joy and panic were rising in her throat simultaneously. "But we can save her, can't we? You can save her!"

"No. I cannot. I cannot interfere, and you know that, but that's not to say it cannot happen. First, we must destroy Darke and at all cost retrieve the Hourglass, so go… go with my blessing… and find Raif. Tell Gideon and Dina and do what you must do but stay safe… Stay safe for Canatu."

82

Since the surface of the desert wasn't that far above the siting of the Mana Cave, Dina and her party were (as yet) unaware of the rising waters. On the contrary, the place felt dry and airy, emitting a sense of peace that could almost be described as dreamlike. To a large extent, the Hourglass appeared dormant with only small emissions of light dancing across the lower chamber as the few remaining grains of sand took their turn to fall slowly, one by one, from the top chamber into the bottom. Time within the Hourglass ran at its own pace. A second could become a minute, which could easily become an hour or a decade if it so wished, yet now as the hour approached, the Hourglass took on a mood of impatience – an acceptance that this not altogether satisfactory environment would have to be the place where the Turning would be performed.

Dina arranged the blue crystals to form a coiled three-tiered snake with the head facing due north. She knew how to do this having studied her ancient *Almanac* handed down to her over the ages and had rehearsed the procedure countless times. That she was actually doing it *for real* was a little daunting, but she kept a steady hand, nevertheless.

As the intricacies of the symbol began to take shape, so the Hourglass became more agitated. It became bigger as the light within shone more violently.

Dina paid no heed and continued. A flat, diamond-shaped crystal formed the centrepiece on which the Hourglass was placed with four similar-sized, five-pointed pentagrams representing earth, air, water, fire and spirit placed evenly around it. Dina made sure that the tip of each pentagram touched the inner coil of the snake.

With the four pentagrams in place, Dina created a circle around them – to contain them – then turned her attention to creating the Magical Triangle to the east of the circle above the snake's head. Still using the many hues of precious and semi-precious blue crystals, she created the triangle two feet away from the circle and made it three feet across. When she'd finished – and along each side of the triangle, she wrote, in the sand, the three names *TETRAGRAMMATON, ANAPHAXETON* and *PRIMEUMATON*, naming the deities (other than Pythia) who would protect them.

It was done. The hour was upon them and the preparations were complete. Gideon, Véronique and Fouad took a step back to leave Dina and Raif ready to step into the circle.

Being guided by the Hourglass, Raif and Dina took opposite sides, stepped into the circle and faced the Hourglass which now illuminated brightly. It shone from within, as the last eight… seven… six… five grains of sand fell. Trembling slightly, Dina placed her hands firmly around the bottom chamber while Raif – as instructed – placed his hands around the upper chamber. They looked at each other intently as in one single synchronised movement, they prepared to implement the Turning. But they couldn't.

Two remaining grains of sand remained unmoved, poised at the neck of the top chamber. They were ready to fall – they wanted to fall – but somehow, they were unable to do so.

Neither Raif nor Dina let go – they *couldn't* let go – and what happened next was beyond anyone's imagination or experience.

Dina was suddenly forcibly released and thrown backwards whereas Raif, who remained welded to the Hourglass, became charged with the same electrified current as it flamed blue – iridescent in its magnificence. More bewildered than terrified, he cried out for help but despite their best efforts, no one could reach him. The air was filled with the sounds of a rushing wind as celestial choirs competed with the desperate sounds of despair. It was so noisy!

Then suddenly, he too was thrown to the ground as the Hourglass doubled, trebled and quadrupled in size exponentially until it was huge and powerful yet still within the same – but now much larger – Magic Circle. Raif cowered; he felt so small but somehow knew the Hourglass was protecting him.

"We're in a Mana Cave!" shouted Gideon through the noise and the wind, which whipped around them throwing up dust and chaos. "It means anything could happen!"

"What should I do?" shouted Raif above the wind.

"There's nothing you can do!"

Raif shielded his eyes and was aghast looking up at the Hourglass now enormous in his vision, and he saw the last two grains of sand – now large and predominant – suspended. Waiting for whatever was to come next.

With the forces within the Mana Cave fluctuating equally, shifting the balance betwixt good versus evil, it would be anyone's guess which one would come first. It was the ravens. The ravens came first and that was a very bad sign. Screeching their hatred, they heralded evil. Attracted to the light and the shiny surface of the Hourglass, they landed untidily and chaotically as they jostled to be the first to peck, scavenge and damage. Black tongues protruded from large ugly beaks as sharp claws sought purchase in the sand while their bright inky eyes, alert and vigilant, scanned for opportunity.

"Go away from here!" shouted Raif as he ran in and amongst them, waving his arms wildly, causing them to flap and screech.

"Get down, Raif!" shouted Gideon as he took over battling the preying bird, "Stay close to the Hourglass."

Raif did what he was told, and it was a good job he did because, slinking out of the shadows, demons of every size and hideous description appeared silently and with menace.

Gideon's heart sank; he thought he'd dealt with all of these as in dismay he watched them patrol the circumference of the circle then enter as if nothing was there to prevent them. He waited for the attack to begin but the demons ignored him – they ignored all of them, as if they were invisible. The demons were only interested in the Hourglass.

Obscenely, they fondled it, running decaying hooked claws down and around the smooth rounded contours, hoping to scratch and disfigure. They rubbed up against the glass making vulgar gestures; licking, mocking and provoking. Then they became violent, throwing the full weight of their bodies up against it, breaking flesh and bone as they did so, but the Hourglass didn't resist or react. It just continued to glow stoically and, if anything, more brightly.

To everyone's enormous surprise, Fouad suddenly got to his feet and walked in amongst the flailing demons and spoke quietly in a monotone rhythm they could hardly hear let alone understand. But the demons did. At first, they took no notice of him then – one by one – they ceased what they were doing and listened as if spellbound. The sound that fell from Fouad's lips didn't belong to him. Rather, it was deep and terrifying.

"Hearken to me, O ye Heavens! O thou Spirit because thou art the disobedient one who is wicked and appearest not, speaking the secrets of truth according to the living breath; I, exalted in the power of God, the All-powerful, the centre of the circle, powerful God who liveth, whose end cannot be. Jehovah Tetragrammaton, the only creator of heaven, earth, and dwelling of darkness and, all that is in their palaces; who disposeth in secret wisdom of all things in darkness and light: Curse thee and cast thee down and destroy thy seat, joy and power, and I bind thee in the depths of Abaddon, to remain until the day of judgement whose end cannot be, I say, unto the seas of fire and Sulphur which I have prepared for the wicked spirits that obey not; the sons of iniquity.

"Let the company of heaven curse thee!

"Let the sun, moon, all the stars curse thee!

"Let the light and all the Holy Ones of Heaven curse thee unto the burning flame that liveth forever, and unto the torment unspeakable!"

As Fouad delivered these powerful words lifted from *The Seal of Solomon*, he produced from inside his tunic a small phial from which he sprayed the air with a bittersweet fragrance that even Dina failed to recognise. On coming into contact with the droplets, the demons disintegrated and fell to dust until nothing was left of them. The silence that followed was palpable as, through the stillness, a pair of white doves fluttered down and settled. Raif simply stared at Fouad in shock and admiration.

"What did I say?" Fouad asked sheepishly, unaware of the words he'd just spoken. He then looked curiously at the empty phial in his hand and pre-empted the question. "I dunno... I got it off a mate."

"Why didn't you tell me you were so... so mystical?" demanded Véronique, completely taken aback.

"You didn't ask," replied Fouad meekly and he shrugged his shoulders.

A sense of relief pervaded, although it wasn't over yet. In a gesture of affection (or maybe childish relief?) Raif lunged at the Hourglass and spontaneously hugged it. In doing so, he pressed himself harder and harder into the shiny convex surface as if to hold it safe.

Then it happened. Just as Dina could press herself through a dense laurel hedge, or Gideon could travel through countless dimensions, so too could Raif accomplish something quite extraordinary, and he found himself on the *inside* of the Hourglass looking out. He shouted and banged his hands on the glass, but no one could hear him. From the outside looking in, he looked pretty cramped, but from the inside, Raif experienced endless space and a landscape of everlasting sand.

All they could do was to watch in amazement. Never in the long history of the Hourglass had the *Scriptures* reported or predicted a Foundling *ever* being on the inside. But terrifying as it was, there was a familiarity. He'd had a vision – an experience – of this. He'd seen himself in his red pullover being swept along in the sand and he knew again not to be afraid.

83

This time there was no mistaking – or hiding – the profound shock Darke experienced at exactly the same moment Raif entered the Hourglass. It was as if the Hourglass was exerting its voodoo will – its dominance – and so strong was this seizure, he winced at the physical pain of it and doubled up. As he clutched the edge of the chair, his breathing was laboured and rasping, but this was nothing to the mental agony he experienced. He had to hold fast. It would only be a matter of time, minutes even, before the Hourglass would be engulfed, taking all accomplices with it. This gave him strength, and despite the hour being upon them, the blue crystals held their light and he turned his face towards them for strength.

That was a mistake. The light generated was no longer the issue of sunlight. Rather, it was the issue of moonlight – and whereas moonlight usually held the same healing properties, this was light from a very different moon that had risen dangerously full.

It was no ordinary moon – usually so cold and white in the night sky – it was a full *blood* moon, glowing deep red, emitting properties very different to those Darke normally encountered. This was a reflected light from the other end of the spectrum – the yang taking precedence over the yin – and a light that had penetrated then mingled with all the conflict being laid bare within the Mana Cave.

Darke turned his face towards this intensified light before he realised. Of course! The alchemy of the blue light affected by the blood moon had created the colour of nightshade! The colour associated with the repentance of sin! The colour as cursed by the *Alternate Prophecies*. The colour of good triumphant over evil. The colour of Order and Redemption.

Too late. Cold light can burn too, and as Darke put his hands to his face he could feel his skin blister.

84

All Gideon could do was watch helplessly as Raif pressed his face and hands to the convex curve of the Hourglass. The grains of sand above him hadn't moved – no grains had fallen – and it would seem that the Hourglass itself might soon explode such were the tremors and animation within it. A look of horror came on Raif's face as he pointed frantically. What was he trying to say?

It was Dina who turned first and saw the blue waters from the lagoon rise up and inflate as the huge weight of water was forced up from below. There was no escape; they were entombed in rock and crystal and in seconds they'd all be engulfed. Only Raif, inside the Hourglass, would have any chance of survival.

Gideon yelled and grabbed her, roughly throwing her forwards. "Stay in the circle! And hold on to the Hourglass!"

Véronique and Fouad did likewise and flung themselves against the glass. Dina shut her eyes tightly and took a deep breath, bracing herself for the deluge as the water hit like a cannon, like crashing waves on a shoreline, until all was still again with the contrasting quietness only being under tons of water can bring.

All Gideon could think was, why were they not all swept away? Why were they dry and still breathing? Without letting go of the Hourglass, he opened his eyes cautiously and saw that they were indeed engulfed in the blue water, but the water hadn't – and couldn't – penetrate the circle.

After a moment or two, the silence was disturbed by the appearance of two white doves that flew down and around as if unconcerned by either the circumstance or their amazement. They fluttered and circled around the Hourglass then took flight up towards the solid crystal blue ceiling, which now emitted shafts of blue, red and purple light. They circled as if trying to explain something.

Raif looked up and, in a moment of unprecedented clarity, knew exactly what to do. Just as he had coaxed the Hourglass off its pedestal when it was imprisoned in the vault, he now turned his attention to the two remaining grains of sand wedged in the neck of the Hourglass.

He heard a clock ticking. *Tick-tock, tick-tock, tick-tock.* Just like the longcase clock at the back of Mr Khan's Furniture Emporium, the gateway to this incredible adventure. It was quiet, to begin with, then the sound became all invasive. Did the Hourglass have a heartbeat? Why not? According to Dina, all things had a spirit.

Maybe it's an internal clock? he thought. *We've all got one, so why not the Hourglass too?*

He'd ask Dina when and if the opportunity ever presented itself, but for now, he needed to concentrate. "The hour cometh!" he said, just like Mr Khan always said when the great longcase clock in the back of his emporium was noisily preparing to strike.

Raif waited... He waited until the sounds aligned, until sure enough, a silence followed then the striking began.

One... two... three... four... five... six... seven... eight... nine... ten... eleven.

On the stroke of twelve, Raif put his hand in his pocket and took out the smooth moonstone Gideon had given him when they'd opened the silver box. He closed his eyes, opened them again and took aim as he willed the grains to fall. He threw the stone, pressed himself against the concave glass and waited.

It was a good shot. The shining grains of sand, now the size of rocky footballs, fell in super-slow motion as one followed the other, creating a blinding iridescent light. Becoming tiny grains of sand again, the grains landed and became lost amongst the millions of other tiny grains that made up this desert, after which there followed a mighty explosion.

Thrown sideways by the blast, Raif fell headlong and became engulfed by the sand as the Hourglass pivoted and turned. He shielded his eyes, but it wasn't the Hourglass that had shattered. It was the crystal ceiling of the Mana Cave.

Raif felt the first warm streaks of dawn alight on his face and heard the first call of a lone desert lark. The air was cool, cold even, as a light breeze fanned his hot, damp forehead. He didn't open his eyes because he didn't want to. He wanted not to know if he was dead – if they were all dead – or if the Hourglass was shattered *or if it was all his fault.*

He noted his breathing was shallow but regular – at least he was breathing – and he willed himself back to his home, to his mum and dad, to his bedroom with his collection of clocks and to the normality of his small, mainly insignificant life. But then he thought about all that had happened. His new-found friends. Gideon and Dina, lovely Véronique and crazy Motto. He thought about Fouad – now what a dark horse he was. He thought fondly about not-of-this-world Spiritas who'd shown him so much, not forgetting his blood brother Ganabek who'd taught him how to ride a camel. And what about Anakee? What had happened to her? Raif felt a quickening panic when he thought of her and it almost made him cry out, but somehow, he still couldn't move. He still didn't dare open his eyes for fear of what he might find.

And then he thought about the significance of the Hourglass, how he'd actually been *inside* it. He thought about where he'd been and what he'd done (his mum and dad would never believe any of it). It was too much to process – it would take a lifetime – but what he did understand was that this was only the beginning and he saw with blinding clarity that he did, and would, play a pivotal role. He didn't yet know what the future held but he knew that his life would never be the same.

The desert lark cried and swooped over him as one of the small white doves fluttered and settled on his chest just as the magnificent awakening of dawn flooded the barren landscape. Raif suddenly felt a powerful surge within him. He felt energised and empowered like he'd never felt before and he opened his eyes.

The first thing Raif saw was the Hourglass, now restored to its original size, propped up in the sand with his outstretched arm held protectively around it. It was upright, and he could just make out the tiny grains of sand – now in the top chamber – gently and uniformly falling into the now-empty bottom chamber.

He looked further and saw Gideon getting to his feet and taking stock of their surroundings. Véronique was attempting to tidy her hair, and in doing so, she glanced frequently at the diamonds (still there) that had inadvertently saved her life.

Fouad was in deep discussion with Dina – both absorbed most probably in some nuance of theology – and the day felt normal. Usual and every day, even though this couldn't be further from reality.

From what he could gather from the evidence strewn around him, they'd been spewed out of a massive crater. Rocks, boulders and shards of blue crystal lay everywhere. He surmised – rightly so – that the explosion had shattered the ceiling of the Mana Cave they were incarcerated in and had propelled them to relative safety. It was a miracle they were all unhurt.

"Are you okay?" asked Gideon, coming over.

"Did the Hourglass do this?" asked Raif in wonderment.

"It would seem so. I think the Hourglass just wanted us all to be out of there."

Dina found the latticed casing which thankfully had been spewed out like the rest of them. "I think we should return the Hourglass to the safety of its casing," she advised. "Véronique… would you help me?"

Raif smiled as he observed this offering of an olive branch. It was clearly a gesture of friendship rather than of need and he hoped Véronique would recognise it as such. "I would like that very much," she replied with due humility even as her diamonds flashed in the sunlight.

Replacing the Hourglass into the latticed, lantern-like casing was done with surprising ease, almost as if the Hourglass itself wanted the security. Véronique held it gently while Dina lifted the top half then secured the small window catch. The Hourglass was safely inside.

Within seconds of her doing this, the entire landscape changed as storm clouds gathered from out of the blue, ready to fall as if to wash away any evidence of what had just taken place.

"We need to get going," said Gideon, gathering things around him, pausing only to include a few handfuls of the blue crystals.

"I'll take the Hourglass," said Dina firmly and no one argued.

"But can I take turns in carrying it?" asked Véronique.

85

Not restricted by any conventional means of travel, Motto had returned to the Canning Factory. Having opted for Localeactic travel – a means of travel he didn't favour, but he did have Anakee to consider – he was relieved that his powers of concentration had been sufficiently in tune to deposit them at precisely the correct destination. For those not familiar with Localeactic travel, it involved the protagonist having a small modification to the left eye. Now as Motto's eyes were so complex, having two large eyes on either side of his head plus three 'ocelli' eyes on top, matters were further complicated as each eye was made up of lots of tiny lenses – a compound eye is how he explained it – so one had to be sure which lens to choose for focusing on the middle distance. He had no problem not blinking for the (required) full earth minute since he was devoid of eyelids. He had no problem either with reciting the prerequisite words '*ti evah seye eht*' but it was a long time since he'd used this method and as geography wasn't his best subject, a lot could go wrong. Fortunately, it didn't.

Having introduced Anakee as an envoy of the Collective, Motto listened intently as Askhat explained how they'd met up with Dina in the blue lagoon and naturally applied his own interpretation of the encounter. Of course, Askhat chose to omit any reference to how skilfully Dina had overpowered him.

"But she said she'd come back here?" Motto protested. "I couldn't go, so naturally I thought…"

Askhat shook his head. "I don't know. All I know is she met up with Gideon down in the caves and he sent us back here. He said we should wait but we can't just do that… not any longer, and now… seeing as you're here…"

"We could at least send out a scouting party," added Ganabek, finishing his sentence.

Motto wasn't sure if going out and looking for them would serve any purpose but if they *had* escaped – and regrettably he thought the chances of that having happened would be slim – they might be glad of help in getting back, especially if they had managed to find and rescue Raif. In fact, the more Motto thought about it, the more he became convinced, and besides, like Askhat and Ganabek, he couldn't just sit around and do nothing. He'd already consumed vast amounts of honey in preparation for any eventuality and couldn't face any more peaches in syrup.

"Alright, and we'll take two camels, we may need them. I'll scout from the air and if I see something… well…"

"And don't think you're leaving me behind!" piped up Anakee, which meant it was settled.

Askhat and his tribesmen had long since got used to Motto being a man one moment then a bumblebee the next, so it was no surprise to them when he again assumed his bumblebee persona.

"There's something happening out there," warned Askhat, looking up towards the dulled sun. "It could be a sandstorm building, so do we wait or go now and try to get ahead of it?"

"Get ahead of it!" The response was unanimous other than from Ganabek who'd already gone to prepare the camels.

With uncanny instincts of his own, Gideon led the way across the dunes, leaving Darke's rapidly flooding empire behind. After they'd picked their way through the barren rocky terrain for an hour or so, the weather really began to close in.

"We must take shelter," he called above the increasing shriek of the wind, and while shielding his eyes as he looked out from within his shemagh, which was tightly bound around his face, he could just make out the silhouette of a long-abandoned ship that projected almost comically out of the sand.

"It's like the airport, only it isn't," shouted Dina following his gaze.

"Can we just go there?" pleaded Véronique urgently. Although Dina had shared some of her desert clothing with Véronique, neither she nor Véronique would be able to withstand this sandblasting for very long. Raif wasn't properly dressed either in his red pullover, so huddled together with one helping the other they battled their way towards their timely sanctuary and all but fell into the welcome shelter of the rusted hull and its world of contrast.

"Before the storm takes hold I'll climb up and look to see if I can see the Canning Factory," said Gideon, already scaling the massive chain that held the now-defunct anchor half-buried in the sand.

Finding a viewpoint was easy as much of the panelling had rusted away leaving just an armature but seeing any distance was impossible. However, the sun still penetrated since – as yet – the storm was still localised, so taking out the largest of the blue crystals he'd salvaged from the crater, he held it up to where it caught the sun's rays. *If Askhat is out there...* he thought, knowing it was a long shot.

It was a long shot but Motto with his amazing more-than-incredible eyesight saw it. He saw a blue flash glint for less than a second and knew it would be Gideon. It *had* to be Gideon and he felt a rush of pleasure he normally only associated with honey.

But he was in trouble. The sandstorm had grown exponentially and now it was all around him, and being in a sandstorm was no place for a fragile bumblebee. He had a quick decision to make. Up or down? If he dived downwards and joined Askhat, Ganabek and Anakee with the camels, he could hope to make it into the calm of one of the saddlebags where he could concentrate sufficiently to effect his transformation. But what were the chances of him making it? None. Decision made. The only way was up.

As he spiralled upwards, the sand swirled and boiled around him creating a vortex and – like being in the eye of a storm – Motto found himself in the relative tranquillity of the epicentre. What he didn't expect was the sand to form a hand, attached to an arm, attached to a body, to a face (sort of) with an eye that glared at him, demanding an explanation. Could it be...?

Surely not? thought Motto. The Sandman was small enough to slip through a keyhole or trickle like a draught from an unopened window. He could be carried in a sandal after a visit to the park or lurk in the hem of a jacket. But now, here he was. Gargantuan.

"WHAT ARE YOU DOING HERE?" he roared.

"I could ask you the same question!" responded Motto, acknowledging his friend. It seemed like a lifetime since the Sandman had been called upon to help Motto soothe some restless child to sleep... perchance to dream. "I'm here to help find the Hourglass," he continued, hoping beyond hope he would still be in time.

"AND I'M HERE... O... ESTROY... ARKE. TO DO PY...S BID... AS PAR... F... HE ASK... FOR... CE..." volleyed the towering Sandman but such was the ferocity of the storm (the Sandman was either pretty fired up or, rather enjoying himself) Motto could only pick up one word in five. If that.

"You must wait! Gideon's out there, over to the east, and I hope – I just pray – he's got Raif and the Hourglass with him! Can you hear me...? Do you understand?!"

Motto was impressed that he'd found such a voice within himself. Such a loud resonance from one so small.

"THERE'S NO NEED TO SHOUT!" retorted the Sandman and, keeping Motto safe within his epicentre, he began to slowly veer eastwards (or so Motto hoped).

Motto saw Gideon sheltering in the rusted hull while they were still some way off and indicated to the Sandman to let him down and keep well back. Not only did he not want to alarm Gideon with the resurgence of yet another sandstorm, but he also needed a little time and space to resume his manform. Like a helicopter on standby, the Sandman's presence made it pretty blustery as the sharp sand continued to bite and swirl, but as Motto emerged from within it, there were no words to describe the relief on Gideon's face.

Now in man form, Motto ran towards him and there was no time for greetings. "We must get out of here – now!" he bellowed. "Pythia's sending in her Vitiators – her Armed Forces – to destroy everything!"

And then, for a moment, time stood still as much to his delight and unparalleled joy, Dina emerged clutching the Hourglass followed by Raif followed by a dishevelled but nevertheless rather attractive young woman whom he presumed must be Véronique. Finally, a gawky young man who squinted and rubbed his eyes brought up the rear and Motto had no idea who he might be.

"FOLLOW ME!" roared the Sandman, moving off towards the west where he proceeded to cut a swathe through the rocks, the sand and the salt. He cut a swathe so good – so clean – you could have landed a plane on it, yet it wasn't a plane Motto needed. All he wanted was to lead his friends back via the quickest way to the safety of the Canning Factory. There was no hesitation. No looking back. There was no time.

86

On encountering the sandstorm, Askhat, Ganabek and Anakee had been forced to return and could only hope that Motto with his exceptional talents had somehow escaped by rising above it. From the safety of the Canning Factory Anakee scoured the horizon looking for any signs of life. She was disgruntled, feeling she'd served no real purpose, when the supposed sandstorm shook the building as it passed over, depositing in its wake Gideon and his party at the blue iron gates.

Ganabek saw them first, and being mutually delighted to see one another, both boys rushed forwards. Anakee, unable to believe it was Raif running towards her, rushed forwards too, ready to scoop Raif into her arms, only for them all to falter as the ground shook.

"Quick! Get inside!" called Askhat and frantically ushered them in.

From the relative shelter of what was no shelter at all, Raif stood with his friends and witnessed a scene he would never again witness in his lifetime. The Sandman, now a huge ball of fury, swung around and passed a safe distance away, and as he headed back towards the horizon, the sand around them shifted and sank, leaving great sinkholes and craters. Then the ground trembled and rippled as it transformed into a live animation as the destruction began.

Firstly, previously camouflaged and now all too apparent, various snakes and vipers took over the landscape in a choreographed synchronised movement before disappearing beneath the surface to wreak destabilising havoc in the passages and caverns below.

Then the heavyweights whom Pythia had summoned rose up roaring. The Basilisks and Thorny Devils, the Amphisbaena with serpent heads snarling. The huge and unstoppable Mongolian Death Worm leading the way as all plunged down, deep into the sand, with the sole purpose of destroying whatever lay beneath. Pythia had summoned them, and they were there to do her bidding.

On the surface, the dunes remained calm, but beneath, the destruction was catastrophic as the aquifers crumbled and disgorged.

87

An aura of outward calm pervaded as Darke stared into the deep waters behind the glass wall. Usually so static, these waters now betrayed evidence of movement and were darker having lost much of their luminescence.

'*In the midst of movement and chaos, keep a stillness inside of you*', quoted Darke silently, recalling the mantra of Deepak Chopra as he contemplated the irony. He'd chosen to wait, only to find the alignment of the life-enhancing crystals completely annihilated.

What was happening out there?

He knew then – in that moment and with absolute certainty – that the Hourglass had been turned. He sighed heavily. He knew too that the Collective would have sent their forces to seek and destroy not only him but the concept he'd created. *So much for Noah*, he thought sagely and almost conceded his own vanity. Now it was only a matter of time, but hadn't it always been ever thus?

It was, therefore, no great surprise to him when the head of a colossal sea serpent loomed large behind the thick glass of the wall and stared at him unblinking as if to register and be absolutely sure that this was its intended quarry.

For Darke, the silence was comforting – like being in an aquarium where one could touch the cool glass and, at the same time, be only inches away from the jaws of death.

The sound of the glass cracking as the sea serpent lashed its tail against it would be a sound Darke would carry with him until his death and part of him was grateful in the knowledge that his death wouldn't be too long in coming. Again and again the gigantic tail lashed but still the glass held.

Darke didn't flinch until, with one final lash of its tail, the frenzied sea serpent smashed through the plate glass, releasing, within seconds, the millions of gallons of clear, clean water retained behind it.

Darke was simply swept away. Crushed by the weight of water and undoubtedly drowned. It was done; it was over.

And then there was peace on earth. The Hourglass glowed and as it did so it emitted a dazzling light that danced through the latticework of its casing. It shone a light so bright it was blinding, and with the light set free, it danced around Raif and all those assembled, blessing each one of them individually before shooting off into the wide-open sky to join the radiant sun just as it was setting, creating the most magnificent sunset.

Pythia, no longer needing her human form, appeared as her true self – a ghostly apparition of pure energy – and hovered above the Hourglass. As was her prerogative, she kept her address short.

"Our task is done. Dina will return the Hourglass to its place of safekeeping and we will each resume our normal lives, being mindful, however, that we must be ever vigilant… The

Hourglass was first turned some three thousand earth years ago and has since adhered to the symbiosis of Pi. It heralded the birth of Western civilisation, linking Classical Greece and Ancient Rome. It saw the world emerge from the Middle Ages to experience such transformative episodes as the Renaissance, the Reformation, the Enlightenment through to the Industrial and Scientific Revolutions and development of the liberal democracy we see today. Throughout these progressive centuries, a symbiotic balance between order and chaos has been maintained. For his own ends, Darke and his associates attempted to disrupt this balance by *preventing* the Hourglass from being turned. He failed. And now we can look to a new era where Order can continue to take precedence... On behalf of the Collective, I thank you and bless you all."

And she was gone.

The room remained silent as momentarily everyone became absorbed in his or her own thoughts. But there was so much to talk about! So much to ask, to exchange – to query – to examine, to try to understand. To learn.

This silent pondering was broken by Ganabek whose attention was taken by the braying of the camels. He went to investigate then burst back into the room shouting excitedly. "Quick, come and see!" he exclaimed. "You're not going to believe this!"

Raif was the first to follow him outside, curious as to his excitement, but soon understood why, as there before him the desert was transforming. First, it was puddles and just pockets of water that joined and multiplied to become larger areas of water. Then it became water with shallow depths that rippled and lapped as the Arrid Sea began its slow journey home.

Gideon looked out across the changing landscape and put his arm around Raif's shoulders. "We did it, Raif," he said quietly. "We all did."

Raif nodded and felt the sense of an ending as he stood and surveyed this changing foreign land. It didn't feel odd or strange or unusual or even incredible. He knew then – at that moment – that the future would never again hold any surprises for him because he knew anything could and would happen that would be far beyond any wild expectation. He was the Foundling and he had fulfilled his calling but knew his journey was only just beginning. He tried to recall the sequence of events. Uncle Frank's funeral and the wonderful clock. Would he ever see Spiritas again? His recurring vision about the boy and the football and the waterspouts. Motto the man-bee! Going a hundred miles an hour in Gideon's beaten-up old truck! Being in one place only to find himself in another. Flying in a paper aeroplane. Space travel. Giant scorpions. Lovely Véronique, and Darke…

Raif stopped himself there. So many friends – so many bonds – it would take a lifetime to examine and evaluate the extraordinary sequence of events. Darke had challenged the future well-being of mankind. He had failed and Raif was proud to have played his part. The Hourglass was turned. The future was safe, or as safe as it could be with the vagaries of mankind at its helm.

While Raif dared to glimpse the enormity of what had taken place, Anakee came and stood next to him as if to share his thoughts. She took his hand and squeezed to show her allegiance and support.

Still holding on tightly to Anakee's hand, he turned and spoke quietly to Gideon. "You do know that we have to rescue Canatu…"

"Yes," said Gideon then turned and went back inside.

88

It was a cold, eerie blue light that illuminated Darke's watery grave. Shards of glass drifted aimlessly, this way and that, along with other debris stirred by the deep underwater currents. There was nothing left. The underwater seascape was lifeless other than random columns of intermittent bubbles rising from the darkest reaches of the carnage. All that remained were shadows – ghosts.

It would have been so easy to miss him but on closer inspection, there was no mistaking. Darke hung there drifting with his black, dead eyes staring upwards as the last evidence of life escaped his nostrils. His blanched hands swayed – this way and that – as if in time to some tuneless melody but it was nothing, just the ebb and flow of the current… or was it?

The seemingly random movement betrayed structure… The flaccid hands slowly took on purpose until they became frantic and began grappling firstly at the collar that gripped his neck, then at the buttons of the smart shirt he'd been wearing – ripping and tearing – until finally, his chest was exposed. Pustulated and veined. White and bony.

But it was a chest that, on either side of his diaphragm, displayed two perfectly formed sets of gills, which pulsed into auxiliary life…

For exclusive discounts on Matador titles,
sign up to our occasional newsletter at
troubador.co.uk/bookshop